D1355928

IN THE GARDEN OF IDEN

IN THE GARDEN OF IDEN

Kage Baker

LONDON   NEW YORK   SYDNEY   TORONTO

This edition published 1997
by BCA
by arrangement with Hodder and Stoughton
a division of Hodder Headline PLC

CN 6222

Typeset by Hewer Text Composition Services, Edinburgh
Printed and bound in Great Britain by
Clays Ltd, St Ives plc

For my mother, Katherine Carmichael Baker,
and her mother, Kate Jeffreys Carmichael,
and for Athene Mihalakis,
a Gray-Eyed Goddess if ever there was one

Chapter One

I am a botanist. I will write down the story of my life as an exercise, to provide the illusion of conversation in this place where I am now alone. It will be a long story, because it was a long road that brought me here, and it led through blazing Spain and green, green England and ever so many centuries of Time. But you'll understand it best if I begin by telling you what I learned in school.

Once, there was a cabal of merchants and scientists whose purpose was to make money and improve the lot of mankind. They invented Time Travel and Immortality. Now, I was taught that they invented Time Travel first and developed Immortals so they could send people safely back through the years.

In reality it was the other way around. The process for Immortality was developed first. In order to test it, they had to invent Time Travel.

It worked like this: they would send a team of doctors into the past, into 1486 for example, and select some lucky native of that time and confer immortality on him. Then they'd go back to their own time and see if their test case was still around. Had he survived the intervening nine hundred years? He had? How wonderful. Were there any unpleasant side effects? There were? Oops. They'd go back to the drawing board and then back to 1486 to try the new, improved process on another native. Then they'd go home again, to see how this one turned out. Still not perfect? They'd try again. After all, they were only expending a few days of their own time. The flawed immortals couldn't sue them, and there was a certain satisfaction in finally discovering what made all those Dutchmen fly and Jews wander.

But the experiments didn't precisely pan out. Immortality is not for the general public. Oh, it works. God, how it works. But it *can* have several undesirable side effects, mental instability being one of them, and there are certain restrictions that make it impractical for general sale. For example, it only really works on little children with flexible minds and bodies. It does not work on middle-aged millionaires, which is a pity, because they are the only consumers who can afford the process.

So this cabal (they called themselves Dr. Zeus, Incorporated) came up with a limited version of the procedure and marketed it as truly superior geriatric medicine. As such it was fabulously profitable, and everyone commended Dr. Zeus.

Everyone, of course, except all those flawed immortals.

But about the Time Travel part.

Somehow, Dr. Zeus invented a time transcendence field. It, too, had its limitations. Time travel is only possible backward, for one thing. You can return to your own present once you've finished your business in the past, but you can't jump forward into your future. So much for finding out who's going to win in the fifth race at Santa Anita on April 1, 2375.

Still, Dr. Zeus played around with the field and discovered what could at first be taken as a comforting fact: History cannot be changed. You can't go back and save Lincoln, but neither can you erase your own present by accidentally killing one of your ancestors. To repeat, history cannot be changed.

However – and listen closely, this is the important part – *this law can only be observed to apply to recorded history.* See the implications?

You can't loot the future, but you can loot the past.

I'll spell it out for you. If history states that John Jones won a million dollars in the lottery on a certain day in the past, you can't go back there and win the lottery instead. But you can make sure that John Jones is an agent of yours, who will purchase the winning ticket on that day and dutifully invest the proceeds for you. From your vantage point in the future, you tell him which investments are sound and which financial institutions are stable. Result: the longest of long-term dividends for future you.

And suppose you have John Jones purchase property with his lottery winnings, and transfer title to a mysterious holding firm? Suppose you have an army of John Joneses all doing the same thing? If you started early enough, and kept at it long enough, you could pretty much own the world.

Dr. Zeus did.

Overnight they discovered assets they never knew they had, administered by long-lived law firms with ancient instructions to deliver interest accrued, on a certain day in 2335, to a 'descendant' of the original investor. And the money was nothing compared to the real estate. As long as they stayed within the frame of recorded history, they had the ability to prearrange things so that every event that ever happened fell out to the Company's advantage.

At about this point, the scientist members of the cabal protested that Dr. Zeus's focus seemed to have shifted to ruling the world, and hadn't the Mission Statement mentioned something about improving the lot of humanity too? The merchant members of the cabal smiled pleasantly and pointed out that history, after all, cannot be changed, so there was a limit to how much humanity's lot could be improved without running up against that immutable law.

But remember, Gentle Reader, that that law can only be seen to apply to *recorded* history. The test case was the famous Library of Alexandria, burned with all its books by a truculent invader. Technically, the library couldn't be saved, because history emphatically states that it was destroyed. However, Dr. Zeus sent a couple of clerks back to the library with a battery-powered copier disguised as a lap desk. Working nights over many years, they transferred every book in the place to film before the arsonist got to it, and took it all back to 2335.

Even though the books turned out to be mostly liberal arts stuff like poetry and philosophy that nobody could understand anymore, the point was made, the paradox solved: What had been dead could be made to live again. What had been lost could be found.

Over the next few months in 2335, previously unknown works of art by the great masters began turning up in strange places. Buried in lead caskets in cellars in Switzerland, hidden in vaults in the Vatican Library, concealed under hunting scenes by successful third-rate Victorian commercial painters: Da Vincis and Rodins and Van Goghs all over the place, undocumented, uncatalogued, but genuine articles nonetheless.

Take the case of *The Kale Eaters*, the unknown first version of Van Gogh's early *Potato Eaters*. It wasn't possible for the Company to go drug Van Gogh in his studio, take the newly finished painting, and leap home with it: nothing can be transported forward out of its own time. What they did was drug poor Vincent, take *The Kale Eaters* and seal it in a protective coat of great chemical complexity, paint it over in black and present it to a furniture maker in Wyoming (old USA), who used it to back a chair that later found its way into a folk arts-and-crafts museum, and later still into other museums, until some zealous restorer X-rayed the chair and got the shock of his life. Needless to say, the chair was at that time in a collection owned by Dr. Zeus.

As it happens, there are all sorts of chests and cupboards in lonely houses that don't get explored for years on end. There are buildings that survive bombings, fire, and flood, so that no one ever sees what's hidden in their walls or under their floorboards. The unlikely things that get buried in graves alone would astonish you. Get yourself a database to keep track of all such safe hiding places, and you too can go into the Miraculous Recovery business.

And why stop there? Art is all very well and can fetch a good price, but what the paying public really wants is dinosaurs.

Not dinosaurs literally, of course. Everyone knew what happened when you tried to revive dinosaurs. But the Romance of Extinction was big business in the twenty-fourth century. To sell merchandise, you had merely to slap a picture of something extinct on it. A tiger, for example. Or a gorilla. Or a whale. Crying over spilt milk was de rigueur by that time. What better way to cash in on ecological nostalgia than to revive supposedly extinct species?

In May of 2336, people turned on their newspapers and learned that a small colony of passenger pigeons had been discovered in Iceland, of all places. In Christmas of that same year, four blue whales were sighted off the coast of Chile. In March of 2337, a stand of Santa Lucia fir trees, a primitive conifer thought extinct for two centuries, was found growing in a corner of the Republic of California. Everyone applauded politely (people never get as excited over plants as they do over animals), but what didn't make the news was that this species of fir was the only known host of a species of lichen that had certain invaluable medical properties . . .

Miracles? Not at all. Dr. Zeus had collected breeding pairs of the pigeons in upstate New York in the year 1500. They were protected and bred in a Dr. Zeus station in Canada for over half a millennium and then released to the outside world again. Similar arrangements were made for the whales and the fir trees.

Anyway, when the public imagination was all aglow with these marvelous discoveries, Dr. Zeus let the truth be known. Not *all* the truth, naturally, and not *widely* known; business didn't work that way in the twenty-fourth century. But rumor and wild surmise worked as well as the plushiest advertising campaign, and the Company didn't have to pay a cent for it. It got to be known that if you knew the right people and could meet the price, you could have any treasure from the past; you could raise the lamented dead.

The orders began to come in.

Obsessive collectors of art and literature. Philanthropists sentimental about lost species. Pharmaceutical companies desperate for new biological sources. Stranger people, with stranger needs and plenty of ready cash. There were only two or three questions.

Who was running Dr. Zeus now? Even its founders weren't sure. Its most secretive inner circle couldn't have said positively. Suddenly they were surrounded by the prearranged fruits of somebody's labor on their behalf – but whose labor? Just how many people worked for the Company?

Also, were they now faced with the responsibility of making sure history happened at all? Quite a few species had been declared extinct, only to turn up alive and well in unexpected places. Were these Dr. Zeus projects they hadn't been aware of? Someone went digging in the Company archives and discovered that the coelacanth was a Dr. Zeus special. So was the tule elk. So was the dodo, the cheetah, Père David's deer. And the Company archives had an unsettling way of expanding when no one was looking.

Finally, where do you get the support personnel for an operation the size that this one had to be? Besides the cost of sending modern agents to and from the past, the agents themselves hated it. They said it was dangerous back there. It was dirty. People talked funny and the clothes were uncomfortable and the food was disgusting. Couldn't somebody be found who was better suited to deal with the past?

Well. Remember all those test-case immortals?

A team from the future was sent back to history's predawn, to build training centers in unpopulated places. They went out and got children from the local Neanderthals and Cro-Magnons, and shaved their diverse little skulls and worked the Immortality Process on their little brains and bodies. They brought them up with careful indoctrination and superior education. Then they went back to their own time, leaving the new agents there to expand the operation.

And what did Dr. Zeus have then? A permanent workforce that didn't have to be shipped back and forth through time, that didn't suffer culture shock, and that never, never needed medical benefits. Or, to put it in the corporate prose of the Official Company History: slowly these agents would labor through the centuries for Dr. Zeus, unshakable in their loyalty. They had been gifted with Immortality, after all. They knew they had a share in the glorious world of the future. They were provided with all the great literature and cinema of ages unborn. Their life work (their unending life work) was the noblest imaginable: the rescue of living things from extinction, the preservation of irreplaceable works of art.

Who could ask for anything more, you say?

Ah, but remember that Immortality has certain undesirable side effects. Consider, also, the mental discomfort of being part of a plan so vast that no single person knows the whole truth about it. Consider, finally, the problem in logistics: there are thousands of us already, and as the operation expands, more of us are made. None of us can die. So where are they going to put us all, when we finally make it to that glorious future world our creators inhabit?

Will they allow us in their houses? Will they finally pay us salaries? Will they really welcome us, will they really share with us the rewards we've worked millennia to provide them with?

If you're any student of history, you know the answer to *that* question.

So why don't we rise in rebellion, as in a nice testosterone-loaded science fiction novel, laser pistols blazing away in both fists? Because in the long run (and we have no other way of looking at anything) *we don't matter*. Nothing matters except our work.

Look. Look with eyes that can never close at what men do to themselves, and to their world, age after age. The monasteries burned. The forests cut down. Animals hunted to extinction; families of men, too. Live through even a few centuries of human greed and stupidity and you will learn that mortals never change, any more than we do.

We must go on with our work, because no one else will do it. The tide of death has to be held back. Nothing matters except our work.

Nothing matters.

Except our work.

Chapter Two

My name, my age, the village of my birth, I can't tell you with any certainty. I do know it was somewhere near the great city of Santiago de Compostela, where the Holy Apostle's body was supposed to have been found. During the Middle Ages pilgrims flocked there to see the holy relics (if they didn't get wrecked first off Cape Finisterre) and returned with cockle shells pinned to their hats (if they didn't get wrecked going back). There, in that city, the Holy Inquisition set up one of its offices.

Also there, in the enormous cathedral, the Infanta Katherine, daughter of Ferdinand and Isabella, is supposed to have stopped to hear Mass on her way to marry the Prince of England. Now, in this cathedral was a silver censer, big as a cauldron, that swung in stately arcs at the end of a chain; and during the Infanta's Mass the chain broke and this censer hurtled out of the church through a window and exploded like a bomb on the paving stones outside. Some people would have taken this as an omen, but not the Infanta. She went resolutely on to England and wound up marrying King Henry the Eighth. This shows that one ought to pay attention to omens.

Anyway, we lived near there. My parents were thin and desperately poor, but racially pure, as they constantly assured us; and that is about all I remember of them. Racially pure meant a lot in Spain in those days, you see. Presumably to extend the line of Old White Christians, my parents had half a dozen little children, which they soon regretted because our house only had one room.

This is where the story begins.

One day in 1541 (all dates approximate) my mother was sitting by the door, gloomily watching her little White Christians as they rolled in a screaming knot in the dust of the yard. Along the road came some people on horseback. They were very well dressed and looked as white as we did, nothing like Jews or Moriscos, though of course you could never tell nowadays. They reined in beside the gate and sat watching us for a moment.

'Good morning, gentle sirs and ladies,' said my mother.

'Good morning, goodwife,' said a tall lady with red hair. 'What pretty children you have.'

'Thank you, gentle lady,' said my mother.

'And so many of them,' said the lady.

'Yes, gentle lady,' said my mother ruefully. (At least, they said something like this, but in sixteenth-century Galician Spanish, all right?)

We children had meanwhile stopped fighting and were staring at the people openmouthed. They really did look wealthy. I recall the women had those things on their heads like the queens on playing cards wear. You know.

'Perhaps,' said the fine lady, 'you have more little ones here than you can provide for? You would perhaps entertain the idea of, say, hiring one out?'

Now my mother's eyes went narrow with suspicion. She didn't know who these people were. They could be Jews, and everybody knew that Jews bought and ate Christian children. Or they could be agents of the Church, sent to see if they could confiscate her property because she was the kind of woman who sold her children to Jews. They could be anybody.

'Gentle lady, please,' she said. 'Have consideration for a mother's feelings. How should I sell my own flesh and blood, which is very old Christian blood, you should know.'

'That is very obvious,' said the lady soothingly.

'In fact, we are descended from the Goths,' added my mother.

'Of course,' said the lady. 'Actually, this was an entirely honorable proposition I had in mind. You see, my husband, Don Miguel de Mendes y Mendoza, was wrecked on the rocks at La Coruña, and I am traveling around the country until I have performed one hundred acts of charity for the repose of his soul. I thought I'd take one of your children into my house as a servant. The child would have food and clothing, a virtuous Catholic up-bringing, and a suitable marriage portion arranged when she comes of age. What do you think of this idea?'

Boy, my mamacita was in a quandary. Just what every Poor but Honest Mother prayed would happen! One less mouth to feed without the expense of a funeral! Still . . . I can just see her racing mentally down the list of *One Hundred Ways to Recognize a Secret Jew*, posted by the Holy Inquisition in every village square.

'I would have to have some kind of surety,' she said slowly.

Beaming, the lady held out a purse, heavy and all clinquant, as the man says, with gold.

My mother swallowed hard and said: 'Please excuse me, gentle lady, but you will surely understand my hesitation.' She wasn't going to come right out and say, Would you care to stay for dinner, we're having pork?

The lady understood perfectly. Spaniards were as famed for paranoia as for courtesy in those days. She pulled out a little silver case that hung about her neck on a chain.

'I swear by the finger of Holy Saint Catherine of Alexandria that I am neither Judaizer nor Morisco,' she declared. She leaned over and put the purse into my mother's hands, and my mother opened it and looked inside. Then my mother looked at all of us, with our gaping little mouths, and she sighed and shrugged.

'Honest employment is a good thing for a child,' she said. 'So. Which one would you like to hire?'

The lady looked us over carefully, like a litter of small cats, and said: 'What about the one with the red hair?'

That was me. That was the first moment I can remember being aware of being *me*, myself alone. My mother came and got me and led me to the gate. The lady smiled down at me from the height of her horse.

'What about it, little girl?' she said. 'Would you like to come live in a fine house, and have fine clothes to wear, and plenty of food to eat?'

'Yes,' I said like a shot. 'And my own bed to sleep in, too?'

Whereupon my mother slapped me, but all the fine folk laughed. 'Yes,' said the lady, 'I'll take that one.' So I was taken indoors to have my face washed while the strangers waited, and my mother stripped off my filthy shift and pulled a clean one on over my head. Then she leaned close to give me her last piece of advice before sending me out into the world.

'If those people turn out to have been lying, hija, you go straight to the Holy Inquisition and inform on them.'

'Yes, Mama,' I said.

Then we went out and I was lifted up in front of one of the men: he smelled of leather and musk perfume. We waved goodbye and rode slowly away into the golden morning. Goodbye Mama, Papa, Babies, Little Stone House!

I didn't cry. I was only four or five, but I knew I was going off on a splendid adventure. Food and clothing and my very own bed! Though before we had ridden many miles, the lady carefully explained to me that what she had told my mother wasn't exactly true: I was not to be a servant.

'In fact, little girl, we are going to do you a very great honor,' she said. 'We are going to betrothe you to be married to a mighty lord. This will be much to your advantage, for then you will no longer be a little pauper: You will be a noblewoman.'

It sounded fine to me, except: 'I'm only a little girl. Big girls get married, not little ones,' I observed.

'Oh, gentlefolk marry off their little children all the time,' said the lady serenely. 'Little princes, little princesses, two and three years old they hitch them up. So you see there's no problem.'

We rode along for a while, past castles and crags, while I mulled this over.

'But I'm not a princess,' I said at last.

'You will be,' I was assured by the man who held me. He wore riding gauntlets with the cuffs embroidered in gold wire. I can see the pattern to this day. 'As soon as he marries you, you see.'

'Oh,' I said, seeing nothing at all. But they all smiled at one another. What a slender, elegant lot they were, with their smiles and secrets. I considered my cotton shift and my grubby sandals, and felt as strange as red wheat in a vase of lilies.

'Why is this lord going to marry me?' I wanted to know.

'I told you, I'm arranging it as an act of charity,' said the lady.

'But —'

'He loves little girls,' laughed one of them, a very young man, his face still downy over the lip. The others all glared at him, and the lady rode between us and said:

'He too is a very charitable man. And life will be splendid for you from now on! You'll wear gowns of fine velvet and shoes lined with lamb's fleece. You'll have a bed all to yourself with sheets of the whitest lawn, the counterpanes embroidered with ruby pomegranates and golden lilies. You'll have a servant to lift you into it each night. The pillow will be filled with whitest down from the wild geese that fly to England in the spring.'

I stared at her. 'What land is he lord of, this lord?' I asked finally.

'The summer land,' said the lady. 'Beyond Zaragoza.' I didn't know where that was. 'Shall I tell you about the palace where you'll live? The most beautiful palace of Argentoro, which is not least among the palaces of the world, being made of blocks of pure white marble veined with gold. The park around it is seven by seventy leagues to a side and filled with pleasant streams and walks; there are orange groves and pools where swim gold and silver fish. There are Indians and monkeys from the New World; there are rose gardens. Everything a little girl could want.'

'Oh,' I said again.

And again they all smiled at one another over my head.

Well, that had me floating on air. Except, in all the stories I'd ever heard, little princesses had big troubles. It was true that handsome princes usually came and rescued them, but the troubles came first and sometimes they lasted a hundred years.

Anyway, we rode on through green mountains, I asking questions and they laughing at me. By nightfall we reached a big old house set far back from the road, darkly shadowed by oak trees, and there wasn't a castle or an orange grove in sight.

They took me inside this dark house, and I must admit I had the biggest meal of bacon and onions I'd ever seen, all to myself. But when I asked them where the great lord was, they told me he'd be there soon; he was riding from a far country and it would take him days yet to arrive. Then they put me to bed alone in a room, all to myself – another promise kept – and for all my doubt I slept soundly.

I lived with those people in that house for maybe a week. I knew there was something odd about the household but, being a peasant child, didn't know that it was unusual for gentlefolk to live in a remote house with nearly no furniture, no servants, and no visible means of support – in that century, anyway. They had plenty of food of the finest quality (in my opinion), and their clothes were not threadbare. These weren't impoverished nobility; their purses were heavy with gold that never diminished.

They made no attempt to train me in any kind of work. In fact, I was left to myself to wander through the empty rooms of the house all day, while they came and went on mysterious errands. They were more and more evasive in answering my questions. Sometimes they gave conflicting answers, or fanciful ones a baby wouldn't have believed.

By sitting quietly where they didn't think I could hear, I gathered that the house was only a temporary place and we wouldn't be staying there long. The red-haired lady seemed to be their mistress; they all deferred to her. There was to be some kind of party soon, at a place called The Rocks, where other persons would be waiting for us.

The ring was turning my finger green, as the saying goes.

Then, one day, I was alone with the youngest man of the party. He was the only one who would play with me; he talked so much, the others were always cautioning him to silence. Watching from my cupboard window, I had seen the lady and her friends ride away that morning. I climbed out of bed and padded down the creaking stairs.

The young man was sitting on the empty kitchen floor. He had just opened a bottle of wine and raised it in a toast when he saw me peering around the doorway.

'Greetings, little one,' he said, and drank deep. I stared at him. His doublet had small white birds and red hearts embroidered all over it. The hearts were silk and looked shiny-wet, like candies.

'I'm hungry,' I told him.

'So eat.' He pushed a tray across the flagstones with his boot. It had bread and cheese and radishes on it. I picked up a loaf of bread.

'It's too big.' I pulled vainly at the crust.

He sent his dagger clattering across the floor toward me. I took it in surprise. Didn't he know that little children weren't supposed to play with knives? Suppose I planned to rob him? But I managed to slice some bread without taking off a finger as well and sat there chewing, staring at him thoughtfully. He kept on drinking the wine. By the time I had eaten most of the bread and cheese, his eyelids were drooping and his mouth was silly. I decided to try asking about my future one more time.

'What about this husband I'm supposed to have, señor?' I prodded.

He looked blank. Then he giggled and laid a finger beside his nose, which was the sixteenth-century body language equivalent of a broad wink.

'Well,' he said. 'Little lady, I'll tell you a great secret. He arrived here in the night.'

'He did?' Oh, how my heart leaped up. 'Where is he?'

'Ssh. Ssh. He's asleep. If you wake him, he'll be angry! He'll come down and strike you with a thunderbolt! Eh? So don't bother him. Anyway, you'll see him soon enough.'

'When?' I wanted to know.

'Tonight.' His smile got sillier. 'At moonrise.' And he took another long pull at his bottle. I sat there and fumed. Thunderbolts! Who did he think he was fooling?

He chuckled to himself for a while and finally took a long slow slide down the wall. When he arrived on the floor, he arranged his hat for a pillow and went unconcernedly to sleep. I headed for the staircase at once. I had to have a look at this great lord. Up the high bare creaking flight, narrow as a ladder, I went; round and round to the top of the house.

At the end of the passageway was a shut door. I ran and pulled it open.

No lord there, with riding boots and sword propped beside his bed; no fine aristocrat pale against the bed linen. No.

Only, leaning in the corner, the figure of a man all braided together out of sheaves of wheat. He was large as life and decked with colored ribbons, bright and frivolous as festival time.

Writing this down, I can still feel the howl of disappointment rising in me. I tiptoed into the room – God knows why I tiptoed, I could never wake him – and looked very closely to be sure.

A big straw dolly was all he was, like the play figures folk put up to decorate their houses at harvest time and burned later. I remembered seeing them. I remembered the priest scowling and telling us these were things of the Devil.

I had been crying quietly but clapped my hands over my mouth as Light Dawned on me.

Crash of cymbals for dramatic emphasis here. Actually, there had to have been quite a lot of crashing and other commotion going on downstairs at this point, but all I heard was my own heart pounding. These people were witches. The Devil gave them powers and that was where all the gold came from and of course all witches dressed in splendid clothes. No, wait, wasn't that secret Jews? Was it Jews who sacrificed little children to idols and witches who ate them, or the other way around? Whichever, I had to find the Holy Inquisition as fast as I could.

I turned and scurried down the stairs, arriving at the bottom landing to behold the hallway full of big men, booted and spurred. Two of them were dragging the young man out of the kitchen. He had puked all over his doublet in terror, and hung limp between them. A grim-looking fellow leaned down and said:

'Señor, the Holy Inquisition is waiting for you. It seems they wish to discuss a matter of faith.'

'Are you Inquisidors?' I inquired, peering through the stair railings. All their heads swung up in astonishment.

'Yes,' said the grim man.

With a cry of relief I ran down and hugged him around the legs. He stared at me in shock. I can't imagine he got that kind of reaction from people very often.

'Thank you, Holy Inquisidor!' I babbled. 'These people are witches and they were going to kill me and there's a big scary devil-thing upstairs, I saw it, and I didn't know how to find you but here you are! Please save me, señor!'

There was a moment's silence before he turned to his men and said:

'Seize this child also. And search the house.'

Well, I didn't think anything was wrong, even when they hauled me out and set me on a horse and bound my hands to the pommel. After all, everyone knew the Holy Office played a little rough. I was so grateful to be saved, I didn't mind in the least. All I had to do (I thought) was explain everything to the Inquisidors and they would understand the danger I had been in. All would be well. Of course.

They brought out the young man – he was crying now – and tied him to a horse too. They brought out a big bundle containing everything they had found in the house; I could see the trailing ribbons of the wheat man.

'See, señor?' I pointed as well as I could with my hands bound. 'There's the bad devil-thing. Are you going to burn this bad man, señor? Are you going to tell my mama and papa?'

But they wouldn't answer me. They all mounted; a man vaulted up behind me, and away we rode at a gallop. Just as before, my heart was bright and light. I was rescued! I was safe! Goodbye, dark house under the oak trees!

Well.

We came to the great city of Santiago in broad morning, by country lanes and by narrow city streets where not a soul moved, even in the light of day. I remember a city white with dust and blazing in all its stone ways: no people, I suppose because of the heat, but also because the Holy Office was secretive and came and went on near-deserted streets. The streets glared all the brighter for their emptiness. It hurt my eyes to look.

But soon enough we went under a big archway, the horses' hooves echoing back, and down steep stairs into darkness. And that was the last I had to worry about the sun hurting my eyes for a long time.

I was locked in a tiny dark room. There was a sort of wooden tray on the floor, filled with straw, to lie down in;

there was a crockery pot to do something else in. No other thing in that room at all; no windows. The only light came from the grated window in the door.

So there I was, in the dungeons of the Inquisition.

Chapter Three

It really wasn't so bad at first. I was full of optimism; I sat there in the straw rehearsing all the things I would say to the Inquisidors when they sent for me – any minute now, I was sure – with a particularly dramatic rendering of how I found the wheat man at the top of the stairs. And at least I still had a bed to myself, though this one had a moldy smell.

And it really didn't bother me (at first anyway) when hours and more hours went by and nobody brought me anything to eat. I was used to that, I could manage. Sometimes at my mama's and papa's we went a day or two without eating. But after I had slept and woken three or four times, I was very thirsty, so I went to the door and yelled up at the little window.

Eventually there came a clumping of boots, and a big nose poked through the grate. I could just see a scowl behind it.

'I'm hungry and I want some water,' I told the nose.

'You shut up,' it said, 'or I'll bring the gag in here.'

'But I want something to eat.' I backed away from the door a little.

'Got any money?'

'No.' I blinked. Was he serious? I'd never held so much as a maravedi in my hand in my whole life.

'Then you may ask San Fructuoso to bring you some,' he said, and clumped away. I sat down and cried. After a while I went back to sleep in the straw and was awakened by the sound of the cell door opening. A hand thrust through the blinding crack of light and set a pitcher of water on the floor; then it withdrew, and the door bumped shut. I scrambled to the water and drank greedily, until I got sick and spilled half of it on the floor.

After that I wasn't doing so well. I slept and woke and

still got no food; I was beginning to feel very strange, very bad. The next time I woke to see the hand putting water in, I cried at it:

'Please, I need to have some bread!'

It hesitated, and a voice replied: 'Your mother is supposed to pay for your food.'

'My mama!' I was so excited. 'Is she here?'

'Well, yes,' said the voice.

'Tell her to come get me! Right away!'

The voice laughed and the door shut.

I got through the next few sleeps in happy anticipation of my mama coming for me, until once again the truth began to insinuate itself, whispering nastily behind its hand like the Devil in the paintings. I don't know how long I was a prisoner there. I couldn't see the sun; time had altered its pace with me. The Holy Office, I was to discover, had a whole different perception of time from the rest of the world.

Time had a few more tricks to play on me, as will be seen. That old devil Chronos.

At some point my door crashed open and brilliant light streamed in. I rubbed my eyes and tried to sit up. The figure of a man appeared in the light and looked at me.

'Little girl? Get up and come with me.'

'You get me some food first,' I croaked, glaring at him. He took a step or two into the room and crouched down to look at me. And though I know he had to be speaking Galician, because of course I couldn't speak Cinema Standard yet, I swear to God I remember him saying:

'Wow. You're in bad shape, aren't you?'

'Nobody has given me anything to eat since I've been in here!' I tried to yell.

He looked at another man, who was standing just outside the door. 'Why is this?' he asked.

'Her mother, the woman Mendoza, has not made any provision for her keeping.'

'She's not my mama!' I exclaimed. 'She *bought* me from my mama! I don't have anything to do with her and she's a witch.'

'Well, she says she's your mother,' said the first man.

'She isn't either! She is Bad. I am Good. She's a witch and I told you all and you mean I've been stuck in here because nobody listened?' In my rage and frustration I beat my fist against the floor.

The man regarded me with interest. He was short, stocky, and dark, like a Biscayan, with a close neat beard. His clothes were good but rather sober and nondescript.

'Days and days down here without any food and you're pretty mad about that, huh?' he observed. I was so angry, I just stared at him in disbelief.

He gave a wry sort of smile and glanced over his shoulder at the other man. He gestured. The other man ostentatiously turned his back and stared at the opposite wall. From inside his doublet the Biscayan took a thing like a little book, and from its leaves he extracted something small. With great deftness he slapped it behind my ear before I could see what it was. I reached up to feel it, but he struck my hand away and said:

'Don't touch it. Maybe later you'll get some food, but right now the Holy Inquisition wants to talk to you.'

'Good,' I said sullenly as he picked me up.

'You think that's good?' He raised an eyebrow at me.

'Yes. I have a lot to tell them.'

He nodded thoughtfully and said nothing for a while as he carried me through endless stone passageways. Finally we came into a high room, very fine, with paneled walls and a distant ceiling. I felt swell and feared nothing.

There were three other men in this room, older than the Biscayan. One was a priest. One was dressed all in red. The other was mousy plain and I couldn't see much of him behind the lectern where his pen scratched. I was put down in a chair, and the others sat at a table to face me.

'So,' said the priest. 'You are the child Mendoza.'

'No, I'm not,' I said.

Raised eyebrows. 'May we ask who you are, then?' asked the man in red.

'I got kidnapped by that bad lady, and *her* name is Mendoza,' I said, 'She's a wicked, terrible, evil lady. And a witch.' The man in red looked interested. The other two exchanged glances. The priest leaned forward and said:

'Little girl, tell us the truth.' And, that first time, there was nothing terrible in the phrase, no ominous reverberation.

Well, I told them the truth, the whole story, just as I'd rehearsed it so often in the dark. I enjoyed the attention. They only interrupted me once or twice, to ask questions. I finished quite cheerfully and concluded:

'Can I go home now, señors?'

There was no reply. The man in red was flipping through some papers on the table in front of him. 'This seems very clear to me,' he said. 'Look here, at the inventory of goods taken from the house. A straw image of Satan. Various tools of witchcraft. Stars chalked on the floor.'

'But how many points on the stars?' asked the priest.

'Some had five and some had six,' conceded the man in red. The priest smiled tightly. The man in red went on, 'Therefore, in my opinion, this is genuine witchcraft. The woman and her confederates were courting the powers of the Prince of Darkness and intended to sacrifice this child at a Sabbat.'

'Yes,' I confirmed.

'I think otherwise,' said the priest, ignoring me. 'With respect to his Grace, the Holy Office does not concern itself with superstitions. These are modern times, señor. Peasants believe in witchcraft; the odd corrupt nobleman plays at it; but it is not a thing to be feared.'

'Surely you don't deny the evidence of the *Malleus Malificorum*?' demanded the man in red. His face was red too, and his eyes were bugging out a little.

'We disregard it entirely, señor,' said the priest. 'I mean, really. Women flying through the air on brooms. Toads that speak. What intelligent person credits such nonsense?'

'The Bishop, for one,' said the man in red hotly. The Biscayan's smile twisted deeper into his beard, and the priest sighed and rested his chin in his palm. The man in red went on: 'Do you deny that demons can be raised to give powers to those who worship Satan? The German, Paracelsus, was carried off by just such, as all men know. These things have been witnessed and proved, worthy Inquisidor.'

'You are treading on very shaky theological ground, señor.' The priest placed his hands flat on the table. 'I would not, if I were you, assert that the Devil has powers equal to God's.'

'I never said that.' Now the man in red went white.

'Good.' The priest nodded. 'So, to the matter in hand.'

'Nevertheless, we should remember that certain deluded souls do form cults to *attempt* to practice witchcraft,' said the Biscayan diplomatically. I lifted my head to stare at him. This time he had spoken in flawless, erudite Castilian, with just a little Biscayan accent. 'And the evidence found in the house resembles such things as these cults use.'

'That is possible, that they were cult objects,' admitted the priest. 'But there are other dark rites that involve, for example, stars.' He rounded on me. 'I believe this child is a secret Jew.'

Well, my hair stood on end. I couldn't get a word out, I was so terrified.

'Now, how have you arrived at such a conclusion, worthy señor?' the Biscayan was asking in an intrigued voice.

'I think that house was a nest of secret Jews,' said the priest. 'Look, in all this inventory you will find not one Christian object of worship. Those that dabble in sorcery keep inverted crucifixes, defiled hosts, and such trash. All their cult is based on Christian belief. But the secret enclaves of Judaism find such things abhorrent. Then, too, the woman Mendoza has consistently testified that this child *is* her child. I point out to you that they both have hair as red as Judas's beard. I think the child is lying, to disassociate herself from the others in hopes of escape. And you may depend upon it, she is our best hope of getting at the truth.'

I shook my head numbly. I didn't understand, they didn't understand, and what did all those big words mean? The man in red was looking considerably deflated, but he rallied enough to say (yes, I swear he did):

'She doesn't look Jewish.'

'None of them do anymore.' The priest pointed at me with a sneer. 'Insidiously they have married into our noblest families and polluted the most ancient racial stock of Spain. Even here in the north, where the Moors never conquered! She may well have fair skin; it's only the more likely there's polluted blood there. The Jews have no interest in honest Spanish yeomen. They want noble wives, with rich dowers.'

'No!' I yelled. 'I'm very poor! But pure, señor, my mama

says so, we're descended from the Goths!' Whatever they were, I certainly didn't know, but surely it was important.

'Tell us the truth,' said the priest.

'I am telling the truth!'

'Who is your mother, if not the woman Mendoza?' asked the Biscayan.

My downfall was coming, the consequence of spending my brief life as one of a swarming knot of children. 'She lives with my papa and the others. Our house is made of stones. It has tiles on the roof,' I stammered.

'But what are your parents' names?' pressed the Biscayan.

'Mama and Papa,' I said.

'What is your family name?'

I stared in confusion. The truth was, our house had been remote from the village and I had never heard anyone address my parents as Señor or Señora Anything. And my parents had been in the habit of addressing each other as Papacito or Mamacita or Mi Esposa. Very affectionate, I'm sure, but it sank me in deep waters. I sat there racking my brains.

The priest smote the table with his palm. 'What is your name?' he said slowly.

'Hija?' I said at last. I had a long sonorous baptismal name, I knew I had, but I couldn't remember what it was.

'What is the name of your village?' tried the man in red.

A memory floated by and desperately I grabbed at it. 'It's not Orense because Mama comes from there and she says it's better and she wishes she could go back.'

'But where do you live?'

'I told you, in a little house. With a fence. And we have a goat.'

Well, it went on like that for what seemed hours, with the dry quiet scratching of the pen taking it all down, establishing only that I was a little girl of unknown origin and apparently no Christian name. The priest seemed very excited, very happy. The man in red fumed. The Biscayan just looked fascinated by it all and kept pressing me for details, which of course I didn't have.

Then abruptly, in the middle of a question, he stopped and peered at me.

'Are you going to faint?'

'What?' I stared at him. But lights were dancing in front of my eyes.

'The child has had no food since the time of her arrest,' he explained to the others. 'It was assumed that she was the child of the woman Mendoza and her food would be paid for accordingly. However, no arrangements were made.' He looked encouragingly at the man in red. 'Which could be an argument for your point of view, señor. Surely, if the child was really her daughter, she'd have paid to send the child some food?'

'An oversight,' the priest objected. 'The woman has been in continuous interrogation since she was arrested. It could easily have slipped her mind.'

'On the other hand, if the child's story is true, then the Holy Tribunal has the responsibility of providing her meals, assuming that she is, as she says, a pauper.' The man in red tapped his finger on the documents in front of them.

The priest glared at him. 'We have not yet established that her story is true in any respect.'

'Worthy señors,' the Biscayan started to say, at which point I swayed forward and threw up bile all over the floor. So the man in red, acting as the Bishop's representative, was able to authorize a loan with the Tribunal that I might buy a supper of milk and broth. The Biscayan took me off to a little side room and watched me as I dined.

Before I drank, he took a flask of something from within his doublet and poured it into my milk. I grabbed it and gulped at it.

'That tastes funny,' I said suspiciously.

'What do you want, Rhenish wine?' he replied. 'Drink. It'll make you strong. And believe me, you're going to need to be strong.'

I shrugged. He leaned there, watching me. The intensity of his watching made me angry. There was no malice there, nor any sympathy, nor any human reaction at all that I could identify.

'You know, they put the woman Mendoza on the rack today,' he remarked. 'They're torturing her. To make her confess she's a secret Jew.'

Was he trying to make me cry? I'd show him. I shrugged.

He studied me. 'Doesn't upset you, eh?'

'She's a bad lady. She was going to kill me. I told you that.'

He just nodded. 'They're going to try to make you confess to being a Jew yourself, you know.'

'But I'm not a Jew. I told them that,' I said wearily. 'If they would only take me back to my mama, she'd tell them.'

'But they don't know where your mama is. You can't remember.'

He had me there. I blinked back tears.

'Come with me now,' he said, and held out his hand.

We went back into the other room, he sat me in my chair, and I glared at them all.

'Little girl, tell us the truth,' said the priest.

'I told you the truth already,' I said.

'If you do not tell us the truth,' he said, just as if I hadn't spoken, 'you will be severely punished.'

'I did tell the truth,' I squeaked.

'Are you a Jew, little girl?'

'No!'

'When were you first taught Jewish rites?'

'What?'

'Have you ever been inside a Christian church?'

'Yes.'

'That proves nothing.' The priest made a gesture of dismissal. 'The Jews go to Mass to mock the Sacrament. Many have confessed to it. What creed have you been taught, little girl?'

What was a creed? I sat mute.

'How often does your mother change her linen?'

'Oh, lots,' I said. 'She has to wash and wash, all the time.' I meant rows and rows of little diapers drying on the bushes, but that hadn't been what *he'd* meant.

'She washes, eh? And does she wash your food, also, before she prepares it?'

'Sometimes.'

The priest shot a triumphant look at the man in red. 'You see? Even considering the child's age and mendacity, certain things may be discovered.' Apparently he had scored a point of some kind. I looked from one to another of their faces, trying to guess what I'd done. The secretary got up to light a taper, because the room was filling with night. In this pause, the door opened and in came another Inquisidor.

'Excellence.' He bowed. 'The woman Mendoza has testified.'

'And?'

He looked cautiously at me, but the priest waved him on. 'She has confessed that she is a practitioner of sorcery and stole the child from her parents.'

'See!' I yelled, and the man in red positively grinned.

'She has also confessed, however,' the Inquisidor continued, 'to being a secret Jew, to being a Morisca, to being the concubine of Almanzor, and to being the Empress of Muscovy.' There fell a disgruntled silence.

'Continue the inquiry,' ordered the priest. 'Persuade her.'

The Inquisidor bowed and left. 'This always happens,' remarked the man in red.

The priest swung back to me. 'Do you see what happens to liars, little girl?'

'Yes,' I said.

'I don't think you do.' He stood up. 'We must show you.'

They got up, and the Biscayan took me firmly by the wrist, and we left that room with the secretary scurrying after us, fumbling his paper and pen. We went along some halls to a dark place that smelled bad. I could hear crying, loud crying. I remember a little window high in a wall. They opened it and lifted me up to look through. It was dark in there, but as my eyes got used to the darkness, I could see glowing coals . . . and other things I would prefer not to describe.

My eyes hurt. And I couldn't breathe. The priest put his face up very close and said:

'You can save your mother. All you have to do is tell us the truth.'

I remember trying to push his face away with my hand because his breath was very hot. I found myself staring at the Biscayan. He was leaning against the wall, watching me, his mouth set, his eyes blank.

I don't remember what I said, but I must have said

something to make them take me down from that terrible little window and let me look anywhere else. They didn't take me back to my cell. I was taken to a different room, a tiny place. One chair filled it entirely. Here I was put, and the door was closed. I was left alone in the dark.

But not for long. Briefly the door opened, and the man in red looked in at me. His eyes were full of compassion. 'Pray, my child,' he told me. 'Accept Jesus Christ as your Saviour. Take this comfort.' He hung something on the inside of the door and closed it again.

A little light slanted down from somewhere, and a figure swam toward me out of the darkness. It was Jesus on the Cross.

A word here about comparative styles in religious art. My little village church had been built in the Gothic style. Stone arches, no plaster, not much decoration. Its furnishings were similarly rude and rustic, for we were, after all, a very poor parish. A few rough saints chopped out of the local stone, smoky candles guttering on rock. The church's great crucifix was old and axe-hewn, stuck up in the shadows behind the altar, and what with the distance and the darkness, Jesus looked as if He were standing in a tree, watching us with alert if yellowed eyes.

But this crucifix, now, was a fine expensive modern thing, from Castile or maybe even Naples. This might have been the Bishop's very own crucifix. It was as real as they could make it. Someone had carved, someone had sanded and polished that poor gaunt body with such care that every bone and sinew shaped out perfect, anatomically precise. Someone had painted it with matte-smooth paint, the color of gray pearls or the skin of a dying man. And not to forget the details: the wounds pink and crusted with black at the edges for dried blood, just like the real thing. The wet yellow stain seeping down from the side wound. The artist who reproduced those thin red lines from the flagellum must have had a tiny brush, fine as an eyelash; yes, and he must have studied real welts, laid on live sweating backs, to show the bruising so well. The matted hair and vicious crown of thorns were reproduced with such veracity that you could see the dust caking the braids, you could see the bright blood drops.

But it was the face, of course, that was the masterwork.

An intelligent face, eyes wide and dark. You could imagine this Christ laughing, or angry, or asleep. Beyond all that, you could see the God shining through the man.

Having given you all this, this living Christ that your heart went out to, the artist put the knife in and twisted it. The mouth was opening in a gasp of pain, the teeth were bared in agony. Those live dark eyes looked out in desperation from that agony to plead, to ask a question I had no answer for. God was being murdered in front of my eyes.

So He hung before me in the gloom, illuminated by one weak beam of light. I was terrified. I couldn't get away, I couldn't.

'I'm sorry, Lord Jesus, I'm sorry, Lord Jesus, I'm sorry, Lord Jesus . . .'

'Why are you causing me such suffering?' cried my hallucination through bleeding lips.

'I don't know, Lord Jesus. I'm sorry, Lord Jesus. Couldn't we get you down from there and get you a barber-surgeon or something?'

'No.'

'Couldn't we put bandages on you to make you better?'

'No.'

'But why not?'

'Because my suffering is eternal. While men live, they must sin; and while they sin, I must bleed here. I am dying in torment for you. You are the one who pushes these thorns in my flesh by your sin.'

'But when did I sin?'

'In the Garden. Because you sinned there, God sent me to be crucified.'

'I'm sorry! I don't remember what I did in the garden, but I'm sorry! Can't you come down now?'

'Never.' The weary eyes closed for a moment. He was so beautiful, He was in such pain, and I'd have done anything to get those nails out of His hands and feet. But I was so afraid of Him.

'It's not my fault,' I wept. 'I wasn't even born then.'

'That doesn't matter,' He explained. 'As part of the human

race, you are born to Sin. You're one of the daughters of Eve. You can't avoid Sin even if you want to.'

'Then no matter what I do, I'll always hurt you?' I was appalled.

'Yes.'

'Who made things this way?'

'I did.' Sweat glittered on His brow. 'I took your state upon myself to redeem you from all Sin.'

'I don't think that's such a good idea,' I said. 'You should go back to heaven and live with the angels. How could I ever be happy again if I hurt you so much? I don't *want* you to suffer for me.'

'You will not be saved.'

I looked around at the darkened room, remembered my cell and the other room. 'But I'm already damned, aren't I? And at least you won't be up on that cross anymore.'

'You really mean this?' He looked intently at me.

I meant it with all my heart.

So He shrugged, and the nails came flying out of His hands and feet like bullets. The crown of thorns sprang away from His head like a lute string snapping. His stigmata closed, healed over, were gone. The weals of the scourge receded into His skin.

He stepped down from the Cross, pulled His red robe around Himself, and gave me a courteous nod before striding into the darkness and disappearing. I collapsed back into my chair, overwhelmed with relief. It was short-lived.

The door burst outward and light blinded me. My three Inquisitors stood there, dark against the light like mountains. The priest looked furious. He must have found out that I was talking to Jesus, I thought. 'Are you ready to tell us the truth?' he said.

'What?' I blinked at him. He reached in and pulled me out, twisting, by the wrist.

'We have been gentle with you to this hour. We will soon be driven to force if you do not repent.'

'I repent!'

'Then tell us the truth.'

'I did!'

'We do not believe you. We will go down, now, to show

you what will happen to you if you do not repent.' And then we went that bad way again, to the bad-smelling place. There the priest set me down and said:

'Now, tell us the truth. Are you a secret Jew?'

And for the first time I wondered: Could I possibly be a Jew and not even know it? Jews were liars, everybody said so. I told lies myself, now and then. Was it possible I'd fooled even myself? Was that why I felt so guilty about poor Jesus? Had I made up a story about Christian parents to conceal my crimes? I swallowed hard and said: 'I might be. I think. I don't know.'

'I see,' said the priest, all smooth now. 'And *we* see. *We* know the truth. You're a very wicked child, to have waited so long to tell us.' But I hadn't said positively. I stared at him in bewilderment.

'I'm sorry.'

'You can save your mother more pain if you tell us everything.'

I just stared. I couldn't think up things off the top of my head, I needed time. 'But we can continue later,' he said, as if reading my mind. 'At another time. Until then, you can think about the things you will tell me.'

How stupid I'd been, to try to hide anything from such a man.

The Biscayan led me away, back, I thought, to my cell; but halfway there he stopped and put his hand flat on a place in the wall beside us. There was no latch, no subtle engine that I could see, yet a little door clicked and swung inward. 'Come with me,' he said, and stepped through quickly and pulled me after him. The door closed behind us.

We went into a brilliantly lit room where there was another man. The man wore some manner of thin white surcoat over his clothes. He talked with the Biscayan in a language I did not know. He sounded nervous. When they had spoken together, the Biscayan left. I looked up at the man in the white surcoat.

He took away my rags and shaved my head. He had to put me in restraints to do that, and I thought the end had come. I screamed and screamed. I said I'd tell him everything. He never said a word in reply, but his face went very red.

He put needles in my skin. He drew out a tube of my blood. He spent a long time examining my bare skull with calipers.

Writing about this now, I still can't bring myself to laugh at it much.

In time he covered me with a blanket and went away. I was left there trembling under the glaring lights. Much later, the door opened, and the Biscayan came into the room. He pulled up a chair and sat down beside me where I lay. 'Well, little Mendoza,' he said. 'You're not doing so well, are you?'

'Are you going to burn me in the fire?' I asked him.

'No, Mendoza, not I. I am, in fact, your greatest friend in the world right now.'

I looked at him in deep distrust. His black eyes were kind, he was turning on the charm, but I had seen him looking on blank while the priest deviled me. 'I know who my friend is,' I said. 'The man in the red clothes. Not you.'

'Well, unfortunately he isn't here right now. He's been recalled to the Bishop for a reprimand. And you certainly know that Fray Valdeolitas isn't your friend. He thinks you're guilty. I, on the other hand, know you're innocent.'

'You mean I'm not a secret Jew?' I was dazed.

'No, of course not. You're only a little girl who has been treated badly for no reason at all. I think that's unfair. I'd like to help you, Mendoza.'

'Then why didn't you stop the priest?'

'I couldn't, then. His rank in the Holy Office is a lot higher than mine. But look, I've hidden you away here; and I am prepared to offer you even more safety.'

'How?' My heart beat fast.

'Let's talk a little first.' He pulled his chair closer. 'You know by now what happens to people when the Holy Office finds them guilty, don't you?'

'Yes,' I whispered. 'They burn in a big fire.'

'And you don't want that to happen to you.'

'Oh, no.'

'Right. But suppose I let you walk out of here right now. You've lost your mama and papa. Who will take care of you? Where will you sleep when night comes?' My eyes filled with tears, and the Biscayan patted my hand soothingly. 'It's scary, isn't it? But you know what's even more scary than that? Listen to me, Mendoza.

'You'd go out of here and maybe you'd starve to death in a week or two, because you haven't got any money, have you? Wouldn't that be awful? To escape from here and die anyway.'

'Yes.' I was glassy-eyed: New Horizons in Fear.

'But, suppose you didn't die so soon? Suppose you lived to be twenty years old. That's good, yes? Except that it's still very hard to stay alive. You'll have to do things you don't like, bad things maybe. And what if you get killed by the plague or soldiers? Terrible, terrible.

'Maybe you'd be lucky. Maybe you'd live to be thirty. Another ten years. That's not very long, is it? But do you know what happens when you live to be thirty?' He took my hand and held it up. 'Look here, look at your nice smooth skin. Some morning you'll wake up, and it won't be smooth anymore. It'll become cracked, crumpled. It won't get better. And see, can you see the blue veins here that run up the back of your hand? One day you'll think, Why are they sticking out so much? And why are my knuckles poking out so much?

'Only little things, but more of them will come with every year you cheat death. Your teeth will begin to break and hurt. You'll keep getting sick. Maybe you'll be beautiful when you grow up, but then you'll have to watch your looks slip away, year after year. Your flesh will hang and sag. One day you'll see your reflection somewhere and see the flesh has pulled back from your bones and you'll see ghosts: your mother's face, your father's, not *yours* anymore. You'll be very frightened.

'Do you know what happens then, if you live ten more years, or ten more? Such a short time, but do you know what you'll be then?' He leaned close. 'Did you ever see the old women with their black shawls who sit in the marketplace? Their mouths are loose and flappy because all their teeth are gone. They're all bent up like little birds, their fingers are twisted like claws. Some of them are blind. All their bones hurt, and they never have any fun. They're afraid to die, but the longer they live, the sicker and lonelier they become. But once, Mendoza, they were children like you. And some day, you'll be just like them.'

'No!' I burst into tears. He loosed the restraints and lifted me up against his shoulder consolingly.

'Yes, I'm afraid so,' he went on. 'If you don't die young, that's all you have to look forward to. But then the day comes when you die because your body is so old. Bad things happen to the dead. Have you seen dead men on the gibbet?' I had. I shuddered against him. 'And if you've been good, then you go to Purgatory, and devils torture you with fire until all the Sin is burned out of you. But if you've been bad, you go to Hell. You know what Hell is now, you've seen it. And it's so hard not to be bad.

'Now, there's a reason for my telling you this. I don't like to frighten little girls, I'm not like Fray Valdeolitas. But I had to show you what it is to be a mortal, to be trapped in the round of time. And you don't have to be trapped there, Mendoza. There is a way out, for you.'

I lifted my face and stared at him to see if he was lying. But he wasn't smiling at all. 'I would like to find the way out,' I said, conscious for the first time of what Understatement was.

'Who wouldn't?' He sat me up on the table and arranged the blanket around my shoulders. 'But you're one of the lucky ones. I'll tell you a secret, little Mendoza. I'm not really an Inquisitor. I'm a kind of spy. I go into the dungeons of the Inquisition and I rescue little children like you. Not just any little children; if they're stupid, or if their heads are the wrong shape, or if there's anything wrong with their bodies, then I can't save them. But the other ones I save, and I send them to my master, who is a very powerful magician . . .'

'Magician?'

'All right, so he's not a magician, he's a doctor. Such a learned doctor, he can cure you of old age and death. Mind you, you will grow up. You won't stay a little child forever.'

I nodded and wiped my nose. This was all right with me; I had no desire to stay small. Children lead a miserable life. 'What do I have to do, señor?'

His eyes warmed. 'You'll work for the doctor. It's the best

work in the world, Mendoza: you'll be saving things and people from time, just like me. What do you say?'

I swung my legs over the edge of the table and attempted to get down. 'Get me out of here and I'm all for this doctor, señor.'

He laughed and called in a guard. I looked at the guard fearfully, but the Biscayan said:

'This little girl unfortunately died under questioning. It will be some time before her body is discovered.' The guard just nodded. The Biscayan sat down and filled out a kind of tag, which he fastened to my blanket, and he stamped my hand with a device in red ink. 'It was nice meeting you, Mendoza,' he said. 'Now, go with this man and he'll take you to my doctor friend. See you in twenty years, eh?'

'Come on.' The guard nodded to me. We went into a tiny room that jerked and shuddered and dropped. Then a door opened on a corridor that seemed to stretch away for miles. For all I know, it did. The guard was carrying me by the time we got to the other end; we came out into a great cavern, big as a ballroom, the ceiling vast and distant.

How to turn my eyes back to the eyes of that little primitive and tell the thing I saw? A silver cannon. A gleaming fish. A tin bottle that somehow had rooms and windows in it, studded with rubies that blinked steadily.

Oh, I stared. There were people walking around in silver clothes, too. Over in a corner was some furniture: big, thickly cushioned chairs and a table. Huddled around it were three tiny children like me: blankets, tags, no hair. There were toys scattered on the table, but the little kids weren't playing with them. They clung to each other, silent and owl-eyed. Two of them had been crying. With them sat a lady as beautiful as an Infanta is supposed to be. She was watching them glumly.

My guard led me to them. Turning to us, the lady switched on a bright smile and stood. 'Here's the other one,' growled my guard.

'Welcome, little —' She tilted her head to read my tag. 'Mendoza!' she exclaimed in peculiarly accented Spanish. 'Are you ready to come meet some new friends and take a lovely trip?'

'Maybe.' I stared up at her. 'Where am I going?'

'Terra Australis.' Flash, flash went her smile. 'You'll like it there. It's lots of fun. Would you like to come sit with the other children now?' So I took her hand (she smelled like flowers) and went to sit down. The children cried and cringed away from me. I eyed them in disgust, looked at the cluttered table, and asked:

'Can anybody play with these toys?'

'Please.' She fairly leapt forward and swept them to me. 'See, here's a dear little donkey and a horse and here's a sailing ship and these books have pretty pictures on each page. Shall we play together?'

I looked at her, appalled. 'No, thank you, Señora,' I said. 'I'll just look at the pictures, all right?'

So I sat and paged through the bright improbable books. There were pictures of children watching other children play games. Children in gardens growing flowers. Children sitting at tables passing each other abundant food. Happy, healthy, laughing children. Not a skeleton or prophet anywhere in sight.

The others sat and stared at me. After a while, one of the boys reached out timidly for the horse. He held it up to his mouth and bit down on its head. I guess he was unnerved.

The people in silver clothes ran around and did things to the ship with silver ropes, feed lines they must have been, and there was shouting and now green lights began to blink with the red. I put down the book and watched, fascinated.

A man came and said something to the señora. She stood up briskly. 'Come on, niños y niñas! Time to go off on a wonderful adventure!' The two really little ones let themselves be scooped up like zombie babies, but the boy with the horse clung to the cushions and howled. The señora had her arms full of children and looked on helplessly.

'Shut up, you stupid piece of crap!' I hissed at him. 'You want them to give us back to the Inquisidors?'

'He can't understand you,' said the señora. 'He's a little Mixtec.'

A man came and picked up the boy and carried him with us. We all went into the ship, and we children were fastened into our seats with straps. I didn't care; at least, not until the cavern opened above our heads and we rose up through it into the night sky. Then I screamed like the rest of them. Goodbye, Spain. Goodbye, Jesus. Goodbye, human race.

Chapter Four

There were two ladies on the ship, the beautiful señora and a little woman with red skin, also beautiful. She wore a pendant with a feathered serpent on it. She went and talked soothingly to the little Mixtec in (I assume) Mixtec talk. He calmed down. Afterward she and the señora leaned back on a cabinet and talked wearily, in yet some other language. They sipped something from white cups. Then the señora crunched hers in one hand and flung it into a bin. She came toward me, turning on her smile again.

'How are we doing, uh, Mendoza?'

'Fine.' I looked up at her. 'Have you got any food?'

'Yes, we'll be serving lovely food in just a few minutes. Are you bored?'

Not me, no, I'd been waiting for the ship to fall out of the sky and kill us all. I shook my head, and she said: 'Would you like me to tell you a story?'

'Yes,' I said. So she settled into the cushions beside me and began:

'Once, long ago, when the world was very new, there was a queen and a wicked old king. This king's name was Time. Now, he had heard a prophecy that his children would be greater than he was. Do you know what a prophecy is?'

Of course I did. I nodded.

'And he didn't want this prophecy to come true, because he was very wicked and jealous. So, King Time did something very terrible. Do you know what he did?'

I could guess.

'Whenever the queen had a baby, the wicked king would steal it away. And then he'd eat it – whole – just like you'd swallow a grape.'

No way. He'd have to cut them up with a sword first. I folded my hands in my lap and waited to see what she'd say next.

'Yes, it's terrible, I know, but the story has a happy ending. Because, you see, at last the queen thought of a way to fool the wicked king. The next time she had a baby, she hid it, and wrapped a big stone in its swaddling clothes, so the king swallowed the stone instead. The little baby was hidden far away on a magical island and tended by beautiful nurses.

'He grew up into a hero whose name was Blue Sky Boy. He was king of all the thunderstorms. He had a spear made of lightning! But he thought, always, of his poor brothers and sisters who were trapped inside King Time. So, as soon as he could, he went and did battle with the wicked king.

'Oh, it was a dreadful battle! Against his son, King Time sent his years. They were giants, those years, and they fought hard with Blue Sky Boy. His handsome body became thick with muscles, his smooth face became rough with black curly beard. But in the end he defeated the years and hurled a big bolt of lightning right through the heart of Time. Time stopped dead. He fell helpless on the ground.

'And Blue Sky Boy cut open Time and, guess what? Out popped all his brothers and sisters. There they were, alive again. And even though Blue Sky Boy was the youngest of them all, he became the new king over them because he alone had conquered Time. And they were all so grateful to him, they became his faithful subjects.

'Now, this is a very important story for you to remember. Did you like it?'

'Yes,' I said. 'I know a story also. Want to hear it?'

So I told her the one about a man who kicks a skull out of his way as he goes along the road, and for a joke he invites it to come to his house for supper by way of apology, and that night it comes to his house and tears out his throat at the table. The señora didn't seem to care for it much.

The little red lady was telling the Mixtec boy a story too. Probably something involving a fratricide.

Chapter Five

I wouldn't have said Terra Australis was lots of fun. It was even hotter than Spain. But, oh, was everybody nice to us.

We crossed a lot of water and flew over a dry red land, remote and silent. We touched down within the high walls of Terra Australis Training Compound 32–1800. It had been there about fifteen hundred years when I was enrolled, and had had time to install all the little amenities: air conditioning, laser defense, a piano in the gymnasium. Within its towering walls were gardens and playgrounds and the domes of cool subterranean classrooms. And hospitals. And warehouses. In fact, most of the place was underground.

It wasn't all that different from any particularly demanding boarding school, except that of course nobody ever went home for the holidays and we had a lot of brain surgery.

That was the first thing they did to us, too, the Mixtec and I and a couple of other shaven-headed kids our size. They put us to bed though it was midday, stuck us all over with needles, and the next thing I knew, I was waking up with my head turbaned in bandages. Then everything was different, because they had installed the first of the high-tech stuff, had begun the Process that would transform us from mortal human children into something else entirely. I could now understand the excessively cheery nurses when they spoke to me. They brought me games to play with boxes full of winking lights. I made the right guesses: I touched the right pictures with the light pencil. A doctor pronounced me fit for further processing, and they sent me on down the line.

One day I was given fine clothes to wear, the uniform smock for the neophyte class, with the Company's device emblazoned on the front pocket, of course. The hat that went with it wouldn't fit over my bandaged head yet, so I

swaggered along after the nurse pretending I was Morisco.
She took me into a big room.

I stopped in my tracks. There were about twenty other
little children in the room, each one my size, each one
dressed just like me with a turban of bandage. There
all resemblance stopped. I saw blackamoor children and
yellow-skinned children and red and brown children. I saw
children pale as mushrooms. They were all lined up in rows
of identical desks, and I was ushered to one vacant one. I
sat there staring around. I saw the Mixtec boy not too far
away. He met my eyes and said:

'They cut open my head.'

'I know that,' I said.

'Did you get cake?'

'Yes.'

Then some grown-ups came into the room, and one of them
rapped on the wall and shouted, 'Children! Attention please!'
We all fell quiet as mice. Some of us cringed.

They were three big men who smiled at us. They were
really something to see. One was a white man, dressed like
all the men I had ever seen, in an ordinary doublet and hose.
One was a yellow man, in a beautiful silk robe. One was a
blackamoor man, who wore a long caftan. Worked into the
snowy cotton of the caftan, and into the embroidery of the
silk robe, and stamped on the doublet buttons was the same
device I had on my uniform pocket.

The men told us their names were Martin, Kwame, and
Mareo, and they were there to welcome us and tell us about
Dr. Zeus. In the splendid polycultural speech that followed,
I found out that the most amazing series of coincidences had
occurred! Not only I but *every single child in that room* had
been orphaned, or kidnapped, or abandoned. Every one of
us had been facing certain death when we met a nice man or
nice lady who promised us eternal life if we'd let ourselves be
rescued. I wasn't so sure my Biscayan had been a nice man,
but he'd certainly rescued me.

Anyway, here we were, all safe now, guests of a wonderful
hero named Dr. Zeus. This Doctor was very kind-hearted
and also very smart. He wanted to save the whole world. It
was a shame he hadn't been able to save our mommies and

daddies, but at least he'd saved us, and some day we'd all live with him in his magic kingdom, which was called the future. The future was a long way off, though, so until we got there, we were going to pass the time being the Doctor's helpers. We'd save all sorts of things for the Doctor, save them from the evil destructive mortal people like the ones who'd taken away our families: we'd save beautiful paintings and books, animals, flowers, even little children like ourselves. It would be easy for us to do all this, too, because we'd grow up stronger and smarter than poor defective mortals. And we had all the time in the world to do these things because we would never, ever die, and because Dr. Zeus was the Master of Time.

After they had explained all this to us, smiling with beautiful clean white smiles, other people came in and served us ice cream. If any of us hadn't yet been convinced, the ice cream won us over. We all decided we loved Dr. Zeus.

Later they ushered us out, two long lines of little ones, to the playground. It was in a cavern of white glass, open at the top to show a disk of blue sky, as though we moved under acreage of staring eye. There were trees in this cavern, and vast green playing fields. There were big kids playing ball. Boys and girls, they all wore their hair cropped close to the skull. We cowered together at the sight of them. But then our nurses led us to our own special playground, which made us feel safe because it had a nice high fence all around it. There were playbars and swings painted in brilliant colors, but we were told we couldn't play on them yet because our heads were still healing. So we moped around and stared at one another.

I wanted to look at the blackamoor children up close. I followed one little girl who had retreated behind some bright crawl-barrels to tear at her bandages.

'Did you get left in the bed by Almanzor?' I wanted to know.

She stared at me as though I was crazy. 'Who's he?'

'You know, he leaves black babies with people.'

She shrugged and went on pulling at the bandages. I studied her. She wasn't black like soot at all but brown, with copper lights under the brown. The palms of her hands were as pink as mine. Abruptly she said, 'We look awful in these hats. I hate them. We look like the Smoke Men.'

'Who?'

'*They* come in the night. They ride the animals that smell. My daddy went out with his spear and they cut his head off.'

'Oh.'

'This hat is hurting my hair.'

'Your hair is all gone now,' I pointed out. 'They shaved it off. They shaved everybody's hair off.'

She looked sullen. 'I know mine is under there. And I won't wear this ugly hat.'

'I thought Moriscos wore hats like this.'

'What is a Morisco?'

'You know.' I was confused. '*You* are.'

'No, I'm not,' she said firmly. 'I'm Spider People. What are you?'

Good question. 'I think I'm a Jew,' I said at last. 'But maybe not.'

'What's a Hue?' She put her head on one side to stare at me, tape trailing down.

'It's . . .' I had no idea, after all. She went on:

'You know how I got here? I'll tell you. The Smoke Men rode around and around, like big ghosts flapping, and set fire to all our houses. But I ran and climbed up in a tree. Dogs came and ate the dead people. Then it was night and I woke up in the tree and Spider was up in the tree with me. I could see Him, all black against the stars.

'Well, He said, You know who's down there? Dry Bone Dog. You don't want to go with him, do you? And I said NO.

'So then Spider said, I can steal you away from Dry Bone Dog if you want me to. I can turn you into a cane stick and carry you away.

'But *I* said, I hate You and all Your magic. You were supposed to look after my daddy and everybody. What's wrong with You anyway? Why did You let those Smoke Men come?

'He just went like *this* —' She shrugged again. 'And He said, I'll help you now anyway, if you want me to. And I could see Dry Bone Dog down there under the tree. I could see his eyes down there. So I said YES and we climbed up into the Sky Boat, I don't remember how. But He left me, now I'm here and He's gone. And I won't ever be His Spider People again! He's no good.' She clenched her tiny fists. 'And they put this ugly, *ugly* hat on my head.'

'No, no, no, dear!' A nurse found us. 'Leave the bandages alone. They're good for you.' She produced a roll of tape from nowhere and bound up the trailing ends again, while the little girl glared. 'Now, come over here with the other children. Nurse Uni will show you nice pictures and we'll have story time.'

So, sulking, we went, to hear all about the wonderful Oz Wizard and the magic body parts he gave people.

In this way our education began.

They didn't waste any time; they made us little geniuses right at the start. Languages, sciences, facts by the zillions, we got them as fast as they could spoon them to us. Speed reading, sleep teaching, hypnosis: when our cranial adjustments were far enough along, they could cram bytes straight into our heads. Encyclopedic knowledge and perfect recall by the age of six. Not bad, eh?

Making us immortal was more time-consuming. Our class had operations the way other students have midterm exams, thirty bandaged neophytes moaning in a ward at once. Always some new symbiote or nanobot or hardware to be put in, or some nasty defective mortal part to be excised. I don't recall anyone mentioning the ugly word *cyborg*, however.

We had years upon years upon interminable years of Phys. Ed. – not to get us into shape, for we were already perfect, but to train the new reflexes that enabled us to dodge bullets at point-blank range. Hypnotherapy to convince us it was impossible we should ever age or die, drugs to heighten our powers of unconscious observation, cellular tinkering I can't even begin to describe.

Do you have some mental image of a gymnasium full of us überkinder, flawless mechanized specimens training to smash the supervillains of the world with our bare hands? Well, you *would* imagine that, if you were a stupid mortal monkey. We knew better.

Smashing things is the violent way stupid mortal monkeys solve their problems. We were taught so many other ways of resolving difficult situations: negotiation, compromise, bribery, strategic falsehood, or simply running away at amazing speed. You see, being immortal just means you can't die. It doesn't mean you can't be hurt.

Besides, we weren't made to battle villains, because there weren't any. No nation, creed, or race was any better or worse than another; all were flawed, all were equally doomed to suffering, mostly because they couldn't see that they were all alike. Mortals might have been contemptible, true, but not evil entirely. They did enjoy killing one another and frequently came up with ingenious excuses for doing so on a large scale – religions, economic theories, ethnic pride – but we couldn't condemn them for it, as it was in their mortal natures and they were too stupid to know any better.

No, our job was to protect them from their own butchery, and (better still) to protect the other inhabitants of the Earth from the destruction wreaked by human nature.

Pretty lofty, isn't it? Imagine being told that it hadn't mattered whether the Christians or the Moors got Spain! I can still remember my shock. I got over it fairly quickly, though, because by that time I had learned enough history to know that in the long run it never mattered a damn where any particular race of people planted its collective ass. And, really, why should I care? I wasn't one of them anymore.

To be honest, I don't think I would have got on all that well with the human race anyway. The Company did not put that fundamental dislike there. Possibly the Inquisition did. Very likely my Biscayan saw that quality in me and knew it would make the estrangement from mortality easier.

In any case, my aptitude test scores determined that I should not be one of those immortals who works much with human beings. I was trained as a botanist instead. I became one of those cheerful and useful children out of our own books, trudging around my garden project with a watering can, growing big bright flowers.

It was a good decision, because I really loved the things I

grew. The leaf that spreads in the sunlight is the only holiness there is. I haven't found holiness in the faiths of mortals, nor in their music, nor in their dreams: it's out in the open field, with the green rows looking at the sky. I don't know what it is, this holiness: but it's there, and it looks at the sky.

Probably though this is some conditioning the Company installed to ensure I'd be a good Botanist. Well, I grew up into a good one. Damned good.

Chapter Six

Mr. Silanus paced across the front of the classroom. On the chalkboard at his back, a few names: MASADA. WARSAW. JONESTOWN. MARS TWO.

'So as we've seen, not one faith has ever lived up to its promises. The world has never become a paradise, quite the opposite, in fact: think of the millions upon millions slaughtered, tortured, imprisoned for this great idea, this good news, this revolution. The visionary who works against human nature to impose his – or her – sweeping vision on the world is inevitably its worst enemy.

'Now, who isn't? Consider the work of certain individual mortals who set themselves simple tasks. They saw no need to raise armies; they saw no need for revolution or bloodshed; they worked instead for realistic goals with the tools they had. And they succeeded, and *their* works have been of lasting benefit to humanity.' He erased the board with relish and chalked a new set of names: DICKENS, PASTEUR, LISTER, FLEMING, THERESA, MUIR, KOBIAR, LUONG.

'People like these have done more to relieve human misery than any prophet with a manifesto ever will. They number in the millions, these mortals, but they don't make it into the history books much. They don't do anything sweeping or controversial. They live their lives, contribute their bits of good work, and die quietly in their beds without recognition or reward. Usually. But they make a difference for the good that no true believer ever can.

'Before we meet again on Friday, access the biographies of these mortals and review their lives. Read the complete works of Charles Dickens and be able to explain them in their historical context. Accessing on your own, see if you can add more names to this list and be ready to explain your choices. All clear? Class dismissed.'

We drifted out of the classroom, we wonder children.

'Isn't he the most handsome man?' breathed Nancy, twisting at a lock of her wig. She'd never stopped trying to get her hair to grow. We'd both vowed to let it grow down to our ankles once the lab techs stopped tinkering with our brains.

'Double-plus wowie,' I agreed.

'I've heard he went to the Crusades to rescue Moslem babies. I'll bet he looked divine in armor.' She pressed the elevator button. The door opened, and we stepped in, our hoop skirts crowding the other passengers.

'You couldn't get me to work in the Holy Land for absolutely anything,' I stated.

She clicked her tongue derisively. 'As if you had a choice!'

'I do,' I said, smug. 'I'm fixing it. I'm making my specialty New World flora, so they'll have to send me there. Hardly any mortals out there at all. No bloodthirsty zealot fanatic murderers.'

'What about the Aztecs?'

'They're just in one part of the New World, aren't they? It's two big continents and there's miles and miles where mortals have never even set foot. You can keep your Europe.'

She rolled her eyes. 'You're fooling yourself. There are mortals everywhere. You'll have to work with them sometime, you know.'

'Not me. Not Mendoza. The only fieldwork I'm doing is in empty fields. No totally disgusting killer apes for me, thank you very much.'

'My, I can see why they didn't make you an anthropologist. You're headed for trouble with an attitude like that, you know.' She shook her finger at me. She was right, too. And far wiser than I: she became an art preservation specialist and didn't even have to set foot in the field until the seventeenth century. And then she got to pose as a wealthy art patron's Algerian mistress. In Italy. Some people have all the luck. I wouldn't mind lying around in a gondola in some nice civilized country but oh, no, I had it all figured out, hadn't I?

The elevator slowed to my floor.

'Oh, um, can I borrow your holo with the footage of Quin

Shi? Something happened to mine in the machine and I've got an assignment on him.'

'I'll leave it in your cube.' The doors clanked open. 'Bye, Mendy.'

'Bye, Nancy.'

Ah, the life of a teenage cyborg.

I have an old holostat online somewhere, more crackly and pointy with every passing year, of my graduation class at their Commencement Picnic and Swim Party.

There we are, a double row lined up on a beach in what will one day be Queensland, squinting happily into the imager. Our bathing costumes look particularly ugly and old-fashioned. We don't care, apparently: every one of us is smiling, even Akira who has just had his box lunch dive-bombed by a seagull. Why shouldn't we be happy? Twenty seventeen-year-olds and not one of us has acne.

And there I am, between Nancy and Roxtli. I have won the hair contest: mine waves down my back as far as my hips, while Nancy's only stands out around her head like a dark cloud. But she has grown into a petite beauty and I am plain, plain, plain. And freckled. And unbecomingly tall. Smile on, Mendoza, in the sun and sky and seaweed of that faraway day. If only you had a clue.

As soon as they brought us back and showered the sand off us and handed us our degrees, they gave us our individual appointments with the career guidance counselor.

Bright and early on the appointed day, I rode the elevator down to his office level and put my card in his wall. Moments later, I was bid enter.

The counselor was one of the older ones. He looked no more than twenty-five, like everybody else, but you could tell how long someone had been in the service by a certain facial expression. Moreover, his brow ridges were on the pronounced side. Other than that, his appearance was all up-to-date. His doublet and trunk hose were well cut, and he had on the newer, fuller ruff that was just coming into fashion then. He waved me to a chair and looked at my card.

'Mendoza, Botanist Level One. Well. How are you doing, Mendoza?' We shook hands.

'Great, thanks.'

'So.' He creaked into his chair. 'I've got your specs here, but why don't you tell me a little about yourself?'

'Well, I'm really, really interested in going to the New World,' I said at once. 'I've made a particular study of the native grain species and I think I could do a lot of good work there. And I wouldn't mind working in the remote areas at all, in fact I'd prefer it. I'd love to get in on the El Dorado operations or maybe even New World One. I've heard some interesting things about Florida, too . . .' He was punching buttons on his keyboard as I talked, which annoyed me. I shut up and pointedly waited for him to finish.

He stared at something on the screen for a moment. He reached for a pen, dipped it in ink, and began to write on a card.

'I wouldn't count on going to the New World just yet,' he said. 'Your profile has a recommendation here for Assigned Acclimatization Europe.'

'Oh, God.' Two years mandatory cover identity working among mortals?

'That's what it says. Nothing to be upset about, you know.' He kept writing.

'Why would they stick me with a job like that? I'm a botanist. I've prepared for the New World, not for growing turnips for maniac religious bigots.'

'They're not all like that, you know,' he said mildly. 'The mortal race has its points.'

'Tell me about it. I happen to have been recruited from the dungeons of the Inquisition,' I said nastily. My trump card. Top My Trauma time.

'Is that so?' he remarked. 'Ever hear of the Great Goat Cult?'

Of course I had. They were a Paleolithic religious movement whose principal activities were tattooing themselves and exterminating their neighbors who didn't. They were so good at genocide that they nearly wiped out what there was then of the human race, delaying the birth of civilization by ten thousand years. I looked at his gently prognathous face and felt hot blood rush into my own.

'Attitude problem. Don't mind me,' I muttered.

'It's possible to learn to live with mortals.' He took up the pen again. 'Trust me.'

I sat there mortified while he jotted a few sentences on the card.

'Besides, if Dr. Z says you have to, you have to,' he continued. 'Don't make trouble for yourself. Just be reasonable about it, go nicely where you're told to go, and in three years the AAE drops off your file. All you have to do is prove you can handle what's expected of any operative. Once they know that, they'll be more receptive to your requests for specific postings.'

He tapped up some more stuff on the computer. I watched his face as he stared at the screen. I could not see the data, of course. No operative ever sees detailed information on his or her particular future: even such information as the Company has is sometimes incomplete. Even kiddies as processed as we are aren't completely documented. Nevertheless I said resentfully:

'You've probably got it all there in front of you, where they send me and whether I get to go to Florida and what I'll be doing in ninety years.'

'That's right.' He nodded. 'Maybe.'

'Why do they bother to call you a counselor?'

'Because I can tell you things you need to know about where they're sending you,' he said, keeping his eyes on the screen.

'Well, where are they sending me?'

'England.'

'England!' I practically screamed.

England, home of grotesque old King Henry the Six-Wived. As children we'd followed his antics in Current Events with considerable amusement, but when he finally ate himself to death, he left a country as wrecked as his pantry. For years, assorted court cabals had circled each other warily, waiting for frail Prince Edward to reach manhood. We knew, of course, that he'd die in his teens and another era of civil unrest would result.

'What are they sending me to England for?' I cried. 'Isn't it, like, very unsafe there? Aren't there going to be all kinds of blood-baths soon?'

'Not where you're being posted,' he assured me. 'They want a botanist over there for a very specific project. You're the very one they need. Pretty soon we'll have the opportunity to send European personnel in. You'll be part of a Spanish team. You'll be perfectly safe.'

'Spanish?' I narrowed my eyes, doing a fast access. 'Now, wait a minute. Edward's sister Mary is going to get the throne when he dies. There's a Spanish connection there. Is that what we're talking about?'

'Yes. The place will be crawling with Spaniards. We can slip you in with no trouble at all.'

'It reads like a hazard to me.'

'Would we send you somewhere that wasn't safe?' he shuffled papers on his desk. 'Anyway. You'll go to Spain first to establish your cover identity, spend a year there, go over to England in' – he leaned over to peer at the screen – ' '54. You won't even be alone. You'll be part of a team, and you'll have a facilitator with you.'

I relaxed. 'That's better. As long as I don't have to interface personally with the killer monkeys.'

'Ah, come on.' He leaned back. 'This is England, after all. The land of, uh, Dickens.'

'He's Victorian Era.'

'It's green there. Beautiful countryside, I've seen it myself. Best beer in the world. Great cities, like York.'

'And London?' I perked up. 'Will I get to go to London?'

'Maybe.' He smiled. 'You might even get to meet Shakespeare.'

Dates whirred behind my eyes. 'He won't be born for a dozen years.'

'Well, you never know; you might get to like England. I've known plenty of operatives who opted to stay on somewhere after their assignment was served, even if they hated it there at first. And England's heading into a Golden Age, uh' – his eyes flicked to my file – 'Mendoza. You could be in on it from the beginning.'

I thought about it. London was supposed to be the flower

of cities all, as Chaucer said, an incredible cosmopolis in an otherwise primitive country. Really fashionable clothing, maybe, for a change. New dances. New music. 'It might not be so bad,' I conceded.

'You'll see.' He smiled. He handed me a stack of printouts. 'Now, here's a recommended holo list and an events graph. You can study them privately. The starred entries are mandatory, the highlighted entries are strongly recommended. You'll be issued a field kit sometime in the next two weeks. Your departure is scheduled for July twentieth. Nice to meet you, Mendoza.'

I went wandering back to my room. In this present moment I'd fling myself down on my bed to think; in that era of corsets and bumrolls one did no such thing. I perched on a wooden settle instead and looked at the recommended (actually mandatory) holo list.

Might as well start with the history review, I thought. It was starred. I scanned its access pattern, and suddenly I remembered, I had known all along, and I let the information fill up around me like a nice hot bath. Here was the score card, here were the players:

England was a cold, backward, rebellious little kingdom. Its king: Henry the Eighth, remembered principally for his six wives and the chicken legs clutched in his fat fists. Oh yes: and for booting the Roman Catholic Church out of England, though he'd started out as a Catholic, married to our old friend Katherine, Infanta of Aragon. But years of marriage to her produced no son and heir for Henry: only a daughter, Princess Mary. Henry was tired of Katherine anyway, so he divorced her (against the express wishes of the Holy Father) and married Wife Number Two, a court tart with pretensions to trendy radical religious opinions, named Anne Boleyn. Jumping on her Lutheran bandwagon as well as on the rest of her, Henry imported the Protestant Reformation into England.

Next round: Anne Boleyn couldn't produce a male heir either, only a baby, Princess Elizabeth, so Henry had Anne beheaded and took Wife Number Three: the devout little Jane Seymour, who, like many of his subjects, was still sympathetic to the Catholics. Before her death there even were rumors that

England might go Catholic again. She did die, however, right after giving birth to the long-awaited Prince Edward, and any chance of an early Counter-Reformation died with her.

Endgame: Henry married, in quick succession, three more wives, which sure as hell made rapprochement with the Pope unlikely. By the time Henry died, the Protestant faction was in firm control of the country, especially with the council of regents who ruled for the frail little King Edward.

New game card: the Royal heirs, in order of their respective rights to the throne. Three stiff children with the coldest eyes in Christendom.

Protestant Edward, the boy king, soon to die, his prim face closed and folded shut.

Catholic Mary, sad old maid, with her bulldog face. She'd done a slow burn for years as she watched her father abuse her mother and her Church. She was shortly to get revenge in a big way.

Noncommittal Elizabeth, somber and alert, despised by the Catholics and Protestants alike for her mother's disgrace. Cunning and cautious, she was destined to survive her siblings and inherit the throne. She was famous in our classrooms as one of the Exemplary Mortals, right up there with Charles Dickens. She hated war and wastefulness, and didn't really give a damn what prayers people said as long as the economy thrived and nobody tried to dethrone *her*.

Yay, Elizabeth. I scanned for the current events I'd be concerned with.

1553, June. Edward is dying, lingering on in the last stages of heavy-metal poisoning administered by Mary's adherents. He finally, horribly, dies, and then —

Oh, dear. After a messy interlude involving an abortive Protestant coup, Mary Tudor (a.k.a. Bloody Mary) would be crowned queen. She would make the mistake of assuming that her loyal subjects were all still true Catholics in their hearts, eager to forget the distasteful heretical interlude That Bitch had seduced her father into ordering. But, surprise: a whole generation had grown up sincerely Protestant, and wanted none of the old faith. Riots and rebellion would break out, and here I caught the names Wyatt and Dudley. In desperation, she'd begin burning her disobedient subjects at the stake, earning her nation's everlasting hatred before she died.

But before she died, she'd marry a Catholic monarch in the hope that he'd (1) love her and (2) help her bludgeon the True Faith back into people's hearts. Grimly she yearned for love. She was never to have any love out of him: but in the matter of religion he'd assist her ably.

For she was to marry Philip, most Catholic heir apparent to the throne of Spain, and when he came to England, he'd bring all his pet Inquisidors to share with her. A great respecter of the Holy Office, Philip. Very eager to discuss matters of faith with the English Protestants. They must have run out of secret Jews to burn.

I sat blinking, taking all this in. They were going to send me with Philip's entourage. With all those Inquisidors. The Spanish were going to be as popular as smallpox with their English hosts, and I would be one of their number.

Chapter Seven

It was July 21, 1553. Clutching my wicker suitcase to my bosom, I made my way to the transit lounge.

Behind me, the ship blinked and hummed. People in flight-tech coveralls ran around with service hoses. There was no evidence there that time had passed: nothing had changed but me. Now I, too, was beyond change.

I dropped my luggage on a settle and collapsed beside it, pushing my hat to the back of my head so the long comb wouldn't bore into my skull. I leaned back carefully. I was frightened.

This was sunny Spain, land of my birth. A concrete floor, stretching to the other side of the cavern. Three green couches set around a coffee table. A row of beverage dispensing machines. I thought longingly of coffee and wondered why there were no cups on the stand. Then blared a voice from the steel box directly over my head.

'Botanist Mendoza, please report to the arrivals desk.'

I blundered to my feet and looked around. Not ten feet away, the clerk was putting down her microphone, looking straight at me. I glared at her and dragged my suitcase over.

'Reporting.'

'Please sign in. Your transport shuttle has arrived.'

I signed in. I put down the stylus and looked at her. She was buffing her nails. After a moment she glanced at me, as if surprised to see me there, and said:

'Up those stairs.'

I looked around. The stairs were steep, narrow, concrete, and rose into darkness. There was no hand rail. Cursing, I hitched up my skirts and struggled upward. The first few steps were littered with the debris of any transit area: snack wrappers, crushed paper cups. The treads had been painted green once. Traffic had worn a path through the paint, polished the cement to a greasy luster. Cement is one of the few things that look worse polished.

The light at the top of the stairs was out. I found the VIA panel by groping and flattened my palm against it for identification, hoping the panel wasn't broken too. It whirred and clicked, but no door appeared. I turned to shout down that chimney of a stairwell but heard a gentle whoosh. The door swung open behind me. I stepped through.

I was standing on a rock terrace on a mountainside. Big tumbled boulders and cliffs of red stone sat there in utter silence. It was seven o'clock on a warm summer evening, and the sun was low in the sky. Air warm and heavy as milk, but clear: I could see range upon range of mountains stretching out before me to the horizon. Where the late sun slanted on them, they were red and gold. Where it did not, they were violet. A few stark trees, pines mostly, were aromatic in that calm air. I was shaking badly. It wasn't supposed to be beautiful.

When I got my nerves together, I picked my way down from there. On a curve of road below me waited a coach. There were two horses standing patiently in harness. There was a small man talking to the horses.

He was the first mortal I'd seen in years. My transport shuttle had a mortal driver. I would have to put my life in mortal hands. He looked up and saw me. His eyes widened.

'Señorita!' He swept down low in a bow. 'A thousand apologies! You are Doña Rosa Anzolabejar, whom I have been sent to meet?' That was my cover name. How nice that my one travel outfit was elegantly cut.

'I am even she,' I said in my snootiest Castilian, starting down the hill. 'Pray fetch my luggage, if you will be so kind.'

'Immediately, Señorita.'

While he bustled after my suitcase, I hastily scanned the coach. Mid-sixteenth-century model, built like a Conestoga wagon without appreciable springs. No structural defects, though, no weaknesses nor excessive wear in the wheels. I scanned the horses: all eight shoes on tight, no flaws in the harness, placid healthy animals unlikely to bolt or fall over dead. Carefully the mortal brought my belongings down. He opened the wagon door and bowed again, extending a hand to help me in.

'Allow me, Señorita.'

I took his hand gingerly. He was young, there were no traces of alcohol or toxic chemicals in his sweat, his vision was normal, heartbeat and pulse rate normal, muscular coordination above average. He did have an incipient abscessed tooth, but he wasn't aware of it yet, so it wasn't going to distract him from his task. He helped me in.

'Have we far to go, or shall we arrive before nightfall?' I inquired.

'It is not far to your father's house, gracious Mistress. I will bring you there before moonrise.'

'I thank you, Señor.'

He sprang up into the driver's seat, and we rattled away. Dust billowed. We snaked along the road down out of the mountains. I tracked the landscape fearfully for bandits or other lower life forms but I found none, which was good. Nor had my mortal flown into any chest-pounding homicidal rages yet, nor was he being reckless and driving too fast. So far, okay.

Down, then, to a plain of wheatfields, spreading away empty. A single windmill stood black against the yellow sunset. Where were the dark and crooked streets? The gibbets? The bonfire smoke full of human ashes? This was mortal land, wasn't it?

The sunset deepened to red, and another house appeared on the horizon. As we drew near, I saw people assembled by the front door. Some of them were mortal servants, peering in excitement at the coach. Four of them were my own kind, a man and two women standing together and one man who waited by the gate. He came forward smiling as the coach shook to a stop and I was handed down.

'My most beloved daughter, I am overwhelmed with joy to behold you again!' he cried, opening paternal arms. I made my deepest curtsey and began:

'Dearest and most reverend father, it is with the utmost delight—' Our eyes met, and I froze. It was the Biscayan. He blinked. His smile twisted up into his beard, just as it used to. '— that I return again to your loving care,' I concluded, and we embraced with seemly affection. I was as tall as he was. He took my arm, and we turned toward the house.

'And how did you find the convent of the Sisters of Perpetual Study, my child?'

'Truly, Father, a right holy place, and the good sisters taught me so well that I am *everlastingly* in their debt. And in yours.' I shot him an arch glance. He just laughed, patting my arm. The servants were nodding and smiling and trying to make eye contact. I wondered if I was supposed to tip them or something.

The Biscayan waved at them. 'Well, here she is, my daughter the most chaste Doña Rosa. You have seen her. Perhaps you will go home now?' They edged out of the yard, still smiling. 'Anything for some excitement in their lives,' he told me sotto voce. 'And here, my child, are the others of my household. This is your duenna, Doña Marguerita Figueroa. This is my housekeeper, Señora Isabella Sanchez. This is my secretary, Señor Diego Lopez.'

They had been cast well. The duenna looked swarthily formidable, the housekeeper meek, and the secretary nearsighted. In reality they were a zoologist grade seven, a cultural anthropologist, and a systems technician first class.

'Doña Rosa, we welcome you,' said the secretary. We all turned to stare at the servants, who got the hint and took off at last down the road into the evening.

'You know, I never connected the name?' said the Biscayan. 'Little Mendoza, all grown up! So welcome back to Spain. How the hell are you?'

'Immortal,' I said. 'Glad to see you again. What happened, though, that you had to send a mortal with the transport? That startled me a bit. Regular driver busy?'

'Oh, Juan's all right. He *is* the regular driver, you see. We hire a lot of mortals, it's cheaper. Hey, everybody, I recruited this kid! Must have been, what, fifteen years ago? Small world, isn't it?'

'Right now, anyway,' said my duenna. 'Come on in, honey, and we'll celebrate. Three whole chickens have been killed in your honor.'

'Plus there's lots to brief you on,' said the housekeeper as we went in out of the night. 'You'd heard the poor king of England died?'

'Yes, I heard that.'

'So Bloody Mary's got the throne now, and there was the most awful debacle for the Protestants. Half the regents' council is in prison already.' She led us into a room dark-lit by candles, where a table was nicely laid for five.

'Has she killed Lady Jane Payne yet?'

'Grey. Lady Jane Grey, the little Protestant claimant. No, but that's coming.'

'Golly.' This was surreal. I was so nervous, I was tracking a radius of two miles, but the house was warm and the chicken tasted wonderful. We did it justice, postponing my briefing until the second bottle of Canary had been opened. My new father lounged back from the table and lifted his glass.

'To your first assignment, Mendoza. All the best.'

Everybody drank. Clearing my throat, I said:

'Thanks. You know, I never learned your real name.'

'I guess you didn't, did you?' He looked amused. 'My character's name is Don Ruy Anzolabejar, but I've used Joseph as my real name for a long time now. Ms. Figueroa is known among us as Nefer, Ms. Sanchez uses Eva, and Mr. Lopez has been Flavius for almost as long as I've been Joseph.' He pointed to each with his wine-glass. 'Good servants to a good master. You, of course, are my only child from an early marriage, and I am a humble physician who's been knighted for certain discreet services to the Court. I inherited my fortune from an uncle who worked for the Holy Office a few years back.'

'Convenient.' I held out my glass, and Flavius topped up my wine.

'About the stuff you're supposed to be growing in the back area?' he said. 'I have my matrices set up there, but I can move them in a couple of days.'

'Am I growing things?' I looked at Joseph.

'You are, as a matter of fact,' he said. 'This time' – he popped open his chronophase and peered at it – 'next year, we'll be in England on our various little missions. We have twelve months to get ready. You're supposed to come up with an exotic plant as a gift for an Englishman.'

'What's our objective over there, anyway?' I said, sipping my wine nonchalantly and trying to sound like all the spy novels I'd ever accessed.

'Black-faced sheep!' said Nefer with enthusiasm. She was the zoologist. 'We're going after genetic material for the original breeds that won't be around much longer. Well, *I'm* going after them. You're going some place called, what was it, Joseph? Iden City?'

'Iden's Garden,' he explained. 'Country estate in Kent. Kind of a private botanical garden and zoo. This guy Iden is a retired gentleman who's nuts for collecting rarities. He's got some that are even rarer than he thinks. That's *your* game. We're bribing him to let us come in and take specimens. It would be a nice gesture if you came up with a nice gift for the man. A showy new plant for his collection, maybe. Something splashy, exotic, impressive.'

'Like?' I had another swallow of the wine. It was heady stuff.

'How should I know? You're the botanist.'

'Oh.' Light dawned. 'Right. Improvise. Okay, I'll get going on it tomorrow.'

'Good. You've got a year.'

'But, really, is this Englishman just going to let a bunch of Spaniards come in and ransack his private garden in exchange for a new plant? Is that enough of a bribe? Won't the English hate us, because of all the burnings?'

'Relax.' Joseph spread out his fingertips. 'We're offering him a lot more than one potted palm, believe me. All will be goodwill and brotherly love where we are, you'll see. The fix is in, Mendoza. That's what a facilitator does. Our traveling arrangements are already made, I'll have you know.'

'That was neat.' Eva put down her glass in surprise. 'The marriage negotiations haven't even started yet.'

'Nah. The Court has seen this coming for years. You want to know something? When the couriers rode in with the news of Edward's death, back on the eighth? Within forty-eight hours, no less than three noblemen I personally know sold their estates: land, dogs, and all. The reason? They figure they'll be able to pick up much better places in England, cheap.'

'No wonder the English will be sore.' Flavius shook his head. 'They don't like invaders, let me tell you.'

'Ah, the lure of barbarian lands for the civilized entrepreneur.' Joseph reached for a toothpick. 'When Philip the passionate pilgrim sails, there'll be one hundred and one Spanish ships crossing the channel, kind of a marital Armada, with (get this) *eight thousand* predatory hidalgos on board, to say nothing of their cooks, confessors, catamites, and' – he placed a theatrical hand on his heart – 'personal physicians. Of which I shall be one. Don Alvarado has asked me already if I'll accompany him on the great adventure. He's the one I fixed up with penicillin, remember? I said I'd be happy to go if I could take my household. He said, Why not? He's bringing his confectioner and Señora Moreno. The emperor is making noises about no women being allowed on the voyage, but nobody's taking him seriously.'

'I hope you're bringing more penicillin,' snickered Flavius.

'Hey, this isn't the Armada that gets wrecked, is it?' asked Nefer in sudden alarm.

'They call me El Señorito Milagro,' mused Joseph.

'No, no,' Eva assured Nefer. 'That's about thirty years down the line. You remember, *Fire over England*, Dame May Robson as Elizabeth?'

'Raymond Massey as Philip. With Laurence Oliver and Vivian Leigh.' Nefer relaxed. 'Okay.'

'Isn't that the holo where they burn Atlanta?' Flavius grinned at her. He looked over at me. 'I'll clean out that back area tomorrow,' he promised. 'Next week at the latest.'

Actually it took him a month, and Joseph was obliged to throw a tantrum about it first. I needed the time to adapt, though, I really did.

It was fortunate I was portraying a shy girl from a convent, because I hid upstairs the first day while our mortal servants came in to work. I could smell them through the floorboards. They were actually in the same building with us, in reach of fire and sharp objects and, and, and . . . Nefer finally hitched up her skirts and stomped upstairs after me, muttering under her breath.

'Will you come down, for hell's sake!' She swung open my door. 'It's only the damn laundress and groom, anyway.'

'He has an abscessed tooth, and it could start hurting at any time and send him into a killing frenzy,' I informed her, looking up from my work. 'And the female's in a highly volatile emotional state. Possibly premenstrual. She's also sustained several contusions and is in pain, which could prompt a psychotic episode.'

'Her husband beat her up last night, that's all.' Nefer came into the room. 'Believe me, she's used to pain. Does her work just fine anyway.'

'She might suddenly snap.'

'And do what? Chase us around with wet laundry? Mendoza, I know this is your first time out, but you can't let the monkeys get to you this way. They're just mortals. In fact, these are our very own hired mortals, security cleared and all. If you can't cope with them, you are surely going to have trouble when we go to Mass this evening.'

'When we what?'

'Go to Mass.' Nefer grinned. 'Every day, rain or shine. Three miles' walk each way. Rainy days we get to use the coach. Don't tell me you weren't briefed on this. We're Spaniards, remember? And you really were one. You of all people ought to know the drill.'

'Shit.' I put my face in my hands. 'They'll be all around us at Mass.'

'That's right.' She sat down on my bed. 'Look, Mendoza. In the entire time I've been in the service, you know how many homicidal maniacs I've encountered? One. And he weighed seventy pounds. Mortals may prey on one another, but they're not all that much of a threat to us. Believe me, sooner than you think, you'll get used to being around them, and you'll find you can actually eat with them, have conversations with them, uh, sleep with them even —'

'You're kidding!' I sat bolt upright. Nefer may have blushed, but with her somewhat Moorish complexion it was hard to tell.

'I didn't mean like that. But ... well, you know ... that happens too, actually. Quite a bit, if you want the truth.'

'You aren't serious! We were always told, Never Engage in Sexual Recreation Except with Another Operative!'

Nefer looked at the floor, looked at the ceiling, looked out the window. 'Sexual recreation with other operatives,' she said finally, to the wall, 'is . . . sort of dull. And uncomfortable. Say, what are you working on?'

'My assignment. Uncomfortable how?'

'Just, you know, embarrassing. Is that the genetic code for some kind of plant?'

'It's maize. American maize.' I displayed the screen proudly. 'See? We're playing Spaniards, so we'd have access to strange-looking stuff from the New World, right? And the coloration and viral streaking on this variety are really spectacular. It'll knock that Englishman's eyes out. I can have the seeds ready by January.'

'That's great.'

'And it can't mess up the biosystem over there at all, because it doesn't grow well in England and it'll never catch on there as a major food source. It's not nourishing enough, for one thing.'

'Is that right?'

'Yes. Maize is the biggest of the domesticated grains, but as a food source it's a dud because it's got this incomplete protein, see.'

'You don't say.'

I was going to tell her about amino acids, but her eyes were glazing over. I looked down at my calculations and sighed.

'I know everything there is to know about New World flora. God, I wish they'd sent me there.'

'Oh, well, you'll go one of these days,' Nefer reassured me. 'I wouldn't mind a good look at a llama myself.'

Specialists. One-track minds.

On that long, long daily walk to Mass, Nefer and I had quite a lot of conversations about sheep, as I recall. We became pretty good friends, but her interest in life was hoofed quadrupeds, and to hear her tell it, you could forget about the pyramids: the height of Egyptian achievement had been the domestication of the wild ass. In our endless trudges together I learned things about water buffalo I have since labored in vain to forget. I did my best to introduce her to the exciting world of four-lobed grains, but she kept getting that glassy look in her eyes.

Still, the walks had to be taken, because there was no question of our missing Mass. We made solid identities for ourselves in the neighborhood. We did not become well known, of course; that was not the Company way. Not one of his neighbors could have told you much about Don Ruy Anzolabejar, other than that his uncle had been connected somehow with the Inquisition, and certainly that magic word put a damper on gossip. It was known that Don Ruy traveled frequently to Court. But there were no stories about strange devices or supernatural lights in our windows at night, no indeed. No heretical talk about tolerance or enlightenment or sanitation. We made sure we were an utterly unremarkable Spanish family.

I spent more time on my knees that year than in the rest of my life to date.

I did get used to the presence of mortals. I could sit there at Mass among them, though bombarded by the smells of their humanity: dissatisfactions, diseases, passions, hormonal tides, digestive upsets, religious raptures. I learned to ignore the pathetic beauty of their children and the horror of their old age. And, once, there was a young man, a student by the cut and shabbiness of his clothes, who sat and stared at me with smoldering eyes. I stared back at him, wondering what on earth was the matter, until he mouthed a request at me across the church.

My shock and amusement reverberated loud enough to alert Nefer, who came out of her reverie on bison long enough to look around at the boy and glare at him in a proper duenna way. He averted his eyes at once and slunk out right after Communion. Too silly to be disgusting, but the incident stuck in my mind somehow.

I remember that the weather was hell. The clear and windless night I arrived had been a rare one: most days the wind came roaring across the miles of wheat fields and filled the sky with dust. White haze hid the mountains and hung like a mirror in the air. I developed a permanent squint, which has done nothing for my looks, to keep that furnace glare out of my skull. When summer was over, the wind did not lessen; it only turned cold.

Sometimes, though ... I remember the sound that wind made, coming over those fields of wheat. It was like the sea. I used to walk far, far across the open land, till the house was almost out of sight behind me, and stand there in the high wheat only listening. The wind would begin in one place and come across to me, sighing like voices, silvering the tops of the grain.

Then harvest came and men with scythes came and cut it all down. There was sweet-smelling stubble for a while, but the wind did not sing coming across it, and the autumn fogs were thick with dust.

The news that winter was that things were already beginning to sour for Mary in England. She had announced her betrothal to Philip, our prince; the English, as everyone had predicted, were furious. Rebellion was working all through the country, and popular sentiment lay not with poor little Lady Jane, the previous Protestant candidate, but with Elizabeth.

Unlikely Elizabeth. For years she'd been a zero politically; no ambitious nobles tried to use her to further their careers, since it was rumored she was a tawdry sexpot like her mother the Great Whore. Suddenly nobody remembered those nasty innuendoes: the same people who used to call her the Little Whore now saw her as a virtuous Protestant princess, the Reformation's only hope in England. Elizabeth smiled her cold smile and demurred graciously – she knew what was likely to happen to people who rocked the throne. All the same, Mary didn't trust her not to become the focus of a coup attempt. Just before Christmas she had Elizabeth sent away to a remote country estate where, it was said, the princess was beginning to show signs of heavy metal poisoning ...

After Christmas came interminable rains that turned the roads to clay. No excuse for us to stay home from Mass; we took the wagon, and still had to slop back and forth from the door, holding our skirts up out of the mud. Only Joseph went out anywhere else, tending his little plots and plans at Court. The rest of us mostly huddled around the fire in the kitchen, accessing novels or holos or staring out the windows at the landscape.

A day came when a man led a horse to the edge of the nearest field. He hitched it to the traces of a plough. Man and horse began to move, and the earth crested and broke dark beneath them like a wave. Away down the plain they went, cutting a long stripe on the land, turned at some point and came back, and at length doubled back again, and so down once more.

All day I watched. By nightfall the field had a weave on it, like the fabric of my overskirt. The next day, men came and walked the long lines, casting seed into the furrows. The next day, the field was alive with birds, and the next day, it rained. That was the day I set out my maize seedlings in the earth I'd prepared for them, closed around by the garden wall. There was no more chance of frost now, anyone could have told from the feel and the smell of the air. The earth was black and wet. Bright green as flames were the little blades of corn.

Late in February, Joseph came back from Madrid with the news: open rebellion had finally broken out in England and been promptly squashed. As a further punitive measure, Mary had Lady Jane Grey (still on ice from the previous coup) summarily executed.

'Well, there,' I remarked, from where I shivered by the fire, trying to make sense of *Tirant lo Blanc*. 'I knew she died sometime.'

Eva flashed an access code at me. '*Lady Jane*, Helena Bonham-Carter, Cary Elwes, Patrick Stewart.'

'Real pointless business, too.' Joseph poured himself a sherry. 'Mary'd much rather have disposed of her sister, but Elizabeth's too popular with the people. She's got her locked up in London now, letting the poisoners have another shot at her. When that doesn't work, she'll try sending her to the Tower, to see if the English will stand for it.'

'Will they?' Nefer moved a pawn, and Flavius leaned forward to study the chessboard.

'No. Mary has no idea how unpopular she really is. She's sure this rebellion problem is confined to Kent.'

'Kent?' I registered alarm. 'The rebellion's in Kent? Kent where I'm being posted?'

'It *was* in Kent. Was. Past tense,' Joseph soothed. 'By the time you're there, everything will be dullsville. Would we ever send you anywhere dangerous?'

'You don't think this sounds dangerous?' retorted Flavius. 'I'd like to see sometime what you consider dangerous. Every single time I've been shipped over there, they've told me —'

'Take it easy, friends.' Joseph held up his hands. 'We can but trust Dr. Z., after all. We may catch a rotten egg or two but no sticks or stones, I positively guarantee it. Trust me.'

'I don't think I'm happy about going to Kent, Joseph,' I said, with considerable restraint I thought.

He surveyed us all with a sympathetic expression.

'What we have here is a morale problem, that's all,' he told us. 'Poor kids, cooped up with nowhere to go. But I just happened to have stopped in at the transport warehouse on my way back . . .' He hauled his rain-soaked saddlebag up on the table and rummaged through it. '. . . where they just happened to have got in a new shipment.' Beaming, he pulled out the silver-wrapped bars and tossed one to each of us.

'Theobromos!' cried Eva. I tore open mine and inhaled the fragrance hungrily. Almost at once the buzz set in. This was powerful stuff, nearly Toblerone quality.

'Highest grade Guatemalan,' Joseph informed us. He struck the same pose as the little togaed Greek on the label, waving cheerily.

The fields changed again. There had been a mist, pale and close along the ground; then one day the blades of new wheat stood up green in the sun. Greener. Deeper. A solid carpet of green, going out to the edge of the sky. There was no more rain now, and the green went to silver as the wheat began to come into the ear.

My maize was standing high, setting big ears like clubs, showing bright tassels. I would drag a settle out into the garden and sit for hours, just watching the wind sway the corn. Our mortal servants would come to stare at it in silence; they'd notice me there apparently reading my missal, and edge away with a bow or curtsey.

Another exciting day: I was issued two new gowns for the

trip to England. They arrived via courier from the transport station and, once unwrapped, proved to be not exactly the height of current fashion, which was a disappointment. One was a brown broad-cloth thing for working in that looked like a servant's livery. Still, it gave me something to wear besides my peach wool, which looked smashing on me but was fast wearing out.

Was I ever really that bored girl, pining for new gowns? Time, time, time.

Joseph held up his knife, eyed the chunk of potato skewered there.

'I love potatoes,' he remarked. 'How I used to wait in longing for 1492. Before then you could only get them if you were stationed in the New World. Or occasionally at the transport station commissaries, but then of course they were instant mashed. Little whipped peaks of starch and gray gravy.'

We all sat staring at him. The wind howled relentlessly outside. It was June, 1554. He took a little bite of potato and chewed slowly, staring back at us.

'Now, before the Crusades,' he continued with his mouth full, 'food was even more limited. Bland, bland, bland. Not even cinnamon, except in the bread pudding at the transport station commissaries —'

'When are we leaving?' demanded Flavius.

'Next week. By coach overland to La Coruña, where we have a berth on the *Virgin Mary*. It isn't exactly a stateroom – hell, it isn't exactly a cabin – but I've pulled some rank and greased some palms, so we should be reasonably comfortable.'

'England at last!' cried Eva. She was all afire; she'd been to the British Isles before and actually liked the climate. I gathered from Flavius that that was fairly unusual for our operatives. I went to the window and looked out miserably.

'Next week, eh?' Flavius shook his head. 'The diant units won't be ready by then. I have to grow the matrices.'

'You what?' Joseph stopped eating. 'You've had months!'

'Grow them too long before you're going to use them, and they dry out.' Flavius shrugged. 'They have to be fresh.'

'Dear friend. Old colleague. You get me four working credenzas for England, or I'll personally see to it that you get posted to Greenland for a couple of generations.'

'I can try. I can't promise.'

'Remember when we used to get stork all the time?' intervened Eva tactfully. 'And swan? Nobody ever serves swan anymore.'

'You'd *better* promise. You'd better do a green invoice if you have to, understand?' Joseph slammed his fist on the table, but Flavius went right on eating. Joseph growled and clenched both hands in his hair, as if to tear out handfuls. The others ignored him. Eva sighed and reaccessed *Tirant*. She was getting lots more out of it than I had.

'Down on my knees at Court every day kissing the hems of cassocks, and are they grateful? Riding over every rock in the road between here and Madrid, and does anyone care?' ranted Joseph. He didn't give a rat's ass really about the credenza parts, he was just being theatrical. He did that a lot. Isometric exercises to maintain human emotions, I think. I didn't understand then, but I've since learned.

After banging his head against the table a few times, he picked up his knife and continued: 'Anyway, I've sent letters to our Paid Friends about housing. Nef, I'm sorry, but there's going to be a delay in your posting. You'll go on standby with us in Kent.'

'Hell!'

'They won't be ready for you in Northumberland until next year. I'm sure you'll find something to do in Kent during your layover. That's life in the service, kid.'

There were clouds boiling up into the sky beyond the thick little panes of glass. A storm was coming, and I wanted to go see.

'What about me?' Flavius wanted to know. 'I suppose I'm getting sent to London. Again.'

I put a shawl around my shoulders and went out the kitchen door.

God, the wind, how it scoured and lay flat the little green herbs of the garden: they cowered. The maize tottered and staggered. Beyond the low wall the wheat danced with the wind, all song and combat. It moved and moved like the sea, with the rustle and scream of stiff silk.

I pushed the gate open and walked out into it, finding the rows with my feet, meaning at first just to leave the sounds of the house behind me. Oh, but the clouds that massed in the East were beautiful. They were domed cities and explosions, such meteorological violence touched with the tenderest colors, pink and lavender and fathomless blue. So soft-looking a home for howling angels with flaming swords.

I could never get any nearer that place, though I kept walking, though it moved endlessly toward me out of the sky. In the sough and boom and murmur of the wind it came, and each stalk of wheat circled through its endless arc among the millions of stalks that nodded all around me. The colors in the clouds glowed brighter. Something was about to happen. I wanted to see it happen.

The wind was hot and smelled of orange trees, distant. It smelled of green-cut hay. It smelled of rain and fever. What was going to happen?

Suddenly the wind fell. Click, on cue the summer crickets started up. Then I heard a hoarse cry from far away:

'Mendoza! What in hell are you doing?'

I turned to scowl at them. They were crowded together at the door, staring out at me in consternation. I had left the house farther behind than I'd thought. Joseph opened his mouth to shout again; but the blue flash came and with it the thunder, like barrels rolling downstairs. Rain began to fall, a few big hot drops. There came another blue flash.

I covered that half mile in seconds and stood beside them, trembling, and they pulled me in through the door and slammed it. I stood there in the storm gloom, and they stared at me, their faces shut like books. Joseph was the only one who spoke.

'How about a little talk, Mendoza?' he said. 'Upstairs, in the rec room. Now.'

God, how embarrassing. I had to follow him up the stairs and sit still while he ran a diagnostic. He said nothing to me while it was running, and I noted the blankness in his eyes. He'd looked just like that when he worked for the Inquisition.

But I tested out normal. He leaned back and looked at me, and let a little human irritation show in his face.

'So, were you trying to get yourself fried? No problem with your evaluation of hazard data, and you knew damn well what those meteorological changes meant. So what's your excuse for generating a Crome field out there, hm?'

'I wasn't!'

'Yes, you were, kiddo, in about a five-meter radius. And if you think this is a way to get yourself sent back to base for repairs so you can get out of going to England, forget it.'

'I swear I wasn't!' I was stung. Also intrigued. Was it possible to duck duty that way? Joseph read in my face what I was thinking (one picks up that knack working for the Holy Office) and shook his head grimly.

'Don't even think about it. We're not supposed to malfunction. Dr. Z. will excuse you for crying wolf once or twice, but you'll be disciplined. You won't like that. If you're really in need of repairs this early in your career, that's a bigger problem. You won't like the solution to that either.'

'Look, I just wanted to look at the storm. It was neat. I didn't do anything wrong. I got out of there the second it got really dangerous, didn't I? So I throw a little Crome when I'm excited. How was I to know that? It's not in my specs. It must have developed since I was posted. I'm only eighteen.'

He nodded. 'It happens, every now and then. The Company doesn't like it, but it does happen.'

'Well, if I'm glitched, it's not my fault, is it? They made me. And what can they do to me if I'm not all up to standard anyway? I'm immortal.'

He wasn't smiling. 'They'll find a way to use your talents. The Company never wastes anything. But let's just say it's not a career choice you'd ever want to make.'

This was distinctly scary. There were stories I'd heard about flawed agents.

'Look, I tested out normal!' I said in a panic. 'I'm sure I'm all right.'

'Don't let me down, Mendoza,' he said. 'I recruited you,

remember? If it wasn't for me, you'd be out there in the zoo with the rest of them.'

'What do you want me to do?' I could feel sweat starting. There was a creepy sense of déjà vu to this conversation.

'Watch yourself. Don't do anything dumb. Be the best little agent you can be, and you'll probably do fine.' He decided to lighten up. 'To let you in on a secret, nearly every operative I've known has had one or two little kinks. Most can function well enough so there's no trouble. Most.'

'What about yourself? Are you flawed?'

'Me?' He smiled. 'Hell no. I'm perfection itself.'

Chapter Eight

On the appointed day we closed up the house, sent away the servants, and rode in the coach, miles and miles and horrific bumping miles through Spain. Days it took us. There were problems with axles and horses. The windows were too small to see much of the passing scenery, which was a comfort to me when we passed into Galicia, because I feared I might feel a pulling, a home-sickness or something, and I was now determined to be the most dependable operative the Company ever had. But what little I could see of Galicia looked pretty much like everywhere else. Mostly it just jolted and danced beyond the wooden frame of the window.

And we came to La Coruña on the seacoast, and it stank.

It stank of the lives of mortal men, but also of the deaths of fish, and of rotting, leaking little ships. The crowded stone town was filled, it was true, with sunlight and air, and a brisk breeze snapped the banners in the rigging of the ships, and there were big joyful clouds white as snow in the blue sky. But the town still reeked.

I crawled out of the coach, took one look at the little ships, and yelled in horror.

'We have to go all the way to England in one of *those*?' I gasped. Joseph put his face close to mine.

'Daughter,' he said quietly. 'Dear. When we board our particular ship, you will notice immediately a number of alarming structural flaws. Do not, I implore you, broadcast this fact to your fellow passengers, the ship's crew, or anyone else you can think of, because if you do, you will be sent directly to the Convent of No Return. Your affectionate father is quite serious. For your spiritual comfort, I can tell you that it is a matter of historical record that the good ship *Virgin Mary* will not sink until the year of Our Lord fifteen hundred and fifty-nine, when neither you nor any of our party will be aboard. Therefore, my child, a silent and discreet botanist has the best chance of not being throttled on her way to the lamentably heretic island of England.'

'Okay, okay,' I muttered.

'I came over in a galley my first time,' remarked Flavius. 'What a panic.'

'Cheer up,' Eva told me. 'Look at all the courtiers! Look at all the clothes!'

Look at all the clothes indeed. The cream of the Prince's court was walking all around us, and it was as if all the cloth merchants of Cathay, Antwerp, and Italy were having a trade war in the streets. All the jewelers, too. Such gold tissue, such brocade and velvet, trimmed silk, figured satin! Such colors! Orange-tawney and sangyn. Primrose. Willow. Peach. Gingerline. Popinjay. Slashes, sashes, and dashes. Peasecods and pansied slops. Picardiles and epaulets. Shoe roses. These were the bright young things, the new generation, not the gloomy old intriguers of the emperor's court.

There were courtiers walking their little dogs. Courtiers gossiping and sniffing at pomanders. Courtiers in tight silk hose showing off their calves to very attentive sailors. Courtiers directing the loading of their baggage, with screams of alarm for their sweet wines, their sugared comfits, their gold plate. A pair of them, male and female, paraded by in complimenting shades of emerald sewn with pearls.

'I want their clothes,' I moaned under my breath.

'I do too,' Eva moaned back.

'You don't really. Can you imagine the body lice?' observed Nefer. We glared at her.

Joseph ignored us all and scanned the harbor for our ship. Given the absolute forest of masts and rigging, and the fact that *Virgin Mary* turned out to be a popular name for ships that year, he was not having an easy time of it. We stood there, clustered protectively around our crates of disguised field gear, and the absurd mortal carnival flowed by on all sides. Just as Joseph thought he had located our particular *Virgin Mary* among the rest, there was a blare of trumpets. All heads turned.

Shouting. People scrambling back.

Make way! Make way for his Royal Highness, the elect of Princes in the whole of Christendom, the most Catholic Philip, Infante of Aragon, Castile, and Brabant, King of Jerusalem, Archduke of Austria, Duke of Milan and Burgundy, Count of Hapsburg, Flanders, and the Tyrol, Defender of the Faith!

Boom. Everyone went down on their knees.

And I think a cloud must have crossed the face of the sun, for there was a sudden darkness and coldness. It could hardly have come from the man riding there among his pikemen and priests. He was not even wearing black. Yet we all looked involuntarily to see what was casting the chilly shadow that he was.

But really, now. How could I or anyone else have seen anything that day but a handsome young prince riding to meet his intended bride? Handsome, that is, if you found the barracuda Hapsburg looks appealing. And it is true that the bride he was riding to was nearly forty and no beauty. So maybe he did look a little gloomy. But evil? Did we really see mortal evil somehow incarnate there?

Of our journey, the less said the better. It took us over a week. I will tell you, though, that I would rather spend a month in the dungeons of the Inquisition than a day under hatches. Any time.

Not soon enough, we crossed the channel.

England was gray curtains of rain. When the salvo came booming across the water, all the women below decks and some of the men shrieked and wept. Joseph looked up from the detective novel he was reading.

'We must be in Southhampton Water,' he remarked. 'That's probably the English warning us to lower our flags.'

'Good old Britain,' grunted Flavius.

'I want to see!' Eva leaped to her feet. 'Anybody else want to come?'

I was only too glad to get some air, so we found our way above decks and peered out from under an overhang.

Mist and drizzle. Lots of ships. Some Flemish vessels. Men shouting across the water. It began to rain harder.

'There's England!' Eva was all excited. 'The Groves of

Amadis!' I peered out but could see nothing distinctly. Rain pocked the surface of the sea, streamed from the ropes and rigging. Sailors shouldered past us, giving us to understand that we had picked the most inconvenient spot on the ship to watch the rain.

'Let's go inside,' I shouted in Eva's ear. 'It's too wet.' She nodded, and we went back below, lifting our skirts well clear of the pools of vomited wines and sugared comfits. So much for England.

We made landing as darkness fell with more rain, but remained on board that night because the English wouldn't let us come ashore. As we understood it, no Spaniard was allowed to set foot on English soil until Philip himself was officially granted permission; and his serene shadowy Highness was prostrate seasick in his own cabin on the *Holy Ghost*. It was the first inkling a lot of those grandees had that they were in another world entirely. Here was Mary, longing to see her royal intended, and these sons of merchants were telling her whom she could and couldn't have setting foot on the soil of her own country!

The following day, the prince had recovered himself enough to meet the great golden barge of state when it arrived. We all crowded up on deck to watch the distant scene. Eva quoted ecstatically to herself about burnished poops. Through windy sheets of sunlight and rain we saw the green-and-white figures of the bargemen bring the barge up alongside the *Holy Ghost*. Stiff little gesturing figures in scarlet: those must have been the English lords. Someone descended into the barge from the *Holy Ghost*; shade and dimness, an abrupt fog. Yes, Philip must have boarded. Guns boomed in salute. We all ducked involuntarily.

The golden barge was rowed to shore, and for a while nothing happened, so a lot of people on deck got bored and went below. Eva and I, thus able to see better, were the only witnesses when the wedding party disembarked and took horses on shore. I made out Philip, on a mare with red trappings. Then they all rode off into the countryside, and I swear there was darkness spreading behind them like exhaust smoke.

That was the last I saw of Philip of Spain but not, I regret, of his shadow.

We still weren't allowed to go ashore until the following day, by which time we'd have killed for solid ground under our feet. After hours of jockeying around, we got somebody to row us in with our baggage, under a freezing mist.

'It's July, for crying out loud,' I murmured, watching the quay draw nearer. 'Doesn't it ever stop raining in this country?'

Flavius just laughed sadly, but Eva said:

'July fifteenth was St. Swithin's Day. The English have a traditional belief that if it rains then, it'll rain for the next forty days.'

'I guess it rained then, huh?' said Nefer, wringing out a corner of her shawl.

'What ho!' boomed a voice in English as we bumped up to the landing. 'Two fine magnificoes and their ladies with trains of Spain, all wet. How like you our English weather, Grandees?'

There was a chorus of nasty English laughter, and we looked up defensively, but the speaker was one of our own. A big blond man in a leather hood, he was standing at the front of the crowd with arms akimbo.

Welcome to goddam Sherwood to you too, transmitted Joseph sourly.

Careful. These people are ready to lynch you, they're so frightened. Let's play this scene as a comedy, shall we?

Comedy? All right. One order of broad slapstick served hot. Joseph stood up in the boat and stretched out his arms.

'Por favor, good Señor Englishman, will you not offer us some assistance in conveying our baggage to shore? We have much gold and will pay you well.'

'Aye, that thou wilt, I doubt it not.' Our representative grinned broadly around at the English, wink wink, who were watching us like vultures. 'We'll convey thy Spanish gold any day of the year, will we not, my hearts?' They all laughed appreciatively, and Joseph climbed up the creaking ladder. Our man put out a hand to help him up.

'Ay, Señor, muchas gracias, muchas —' Joseph broke off as

they did the stunt: the operative, appearing to assist Joseph, tripped him, and Joseph went rolling neatly into a mud puddle with loud Hispanic cries of distress. Nefer and Eva stood on cue, screaming shrilly, and the assembled mob howled with mirth. Several dropped the stones they'd had ready to pitch at us. We weren't dangerous: we were only comic foreigners, after all.

'Oh, sir, you have rolled in horse dung.' The operative went to raise Joseph with a great show of concern. 'I am most heartily sorry for it. Let me take you to a fine clean inn I know of where belike you'll have a fine sea-coal fire for drying your fleece, I mean your cloak. Rates very reasonable, sir.' The word *fleece* had its subliminal effect on the crowd, and they went off to range along the quay, where other wretched Spaniards were attempting to come ashore.

Nice tumble. You okay? The operative leaned down to Joseph, shaking his hand. *Xenophon, facilitator seventh class. Welcome to England.* Between them, he and Flavius got our baggage loaded into an oxcart, while the rest of us stood shivering and looking around.

I can remember being astonished at how green everything was. Electric green, glowing emerald-green, green growing out of the cracks between the stones, and green crowding in the gardens. Looming tunnels of green trees and green meadows rolling away that pulsed against the eye, they were so green. In Spain and Australia what passed for spring was a sedate olive season compared to this, and it made the green of the tropics look dried out. No wonder the English had a reputation for rowdiness. They must have been drunk on pure oxygen their whole lives.

The other thing that impressed me was the persons of the English themselves. They were the tallest people I'd ever seen and uniformly, man, woman, and child, had skin like rose petals. I saw a grandmother holding up a toddler to curse at us: the old woman's face was no less white under pink than the baby's, and her cheek only a little less smooth. I felt swarthy, with my freckles and Spanish sunburn.

We clambered into the oxcart, and Xenophon drove away with us, chatting subvocally the while. We learned he was taking us to a Company safe house disguised as an English country inn. I could have cried when we pulled up in front of the Jove His Levin Bolt, with the Company insignia carved into its beam ends, and were shown upstairs to private quarters. I saw my first flush toilets in over a year. I leave it to you, whoever you are, to imagine the bliss of a hot shower after so many unspeakable days in the hold of a ship.

When we assembled in the briefing lounge, steamy and as clean as we were going to be for a long while, Xenophon was sitting with a big tray of food and drinks and our assignment dockets. We found seats while he poured out tankards of room-temperature beer and passed them to us.

'Welcome, everyone. Here's a classic English ploughman's lunch for each of you along with our local beer. We brew our own, by the way. We think it's pretty good. Please feel free to eat while we talk; this is all informal. Well, now.' He cleared his throat. 'I guess you heard some of the things people were shouting at you as we drove along.'

'I did get the impression they weren't exactly happy to see us,' Nefer said and blew her nose.

'Yes, that's pretty close to it. The thing to remember is, they're just as frightened of you as you are of them. And the law is technically on your side, if one of them attacks you without reason, though of course I imagine you're all too good at keeping low profiles for that kind of situation to develop. If you're from Spain, you may be expecting the same muscle from the local law enforcement you'd have at home. Not the case here. Robin Hood stories notwithstanding, you'll have a fairly hard time getting hold of any sheriff to help you in this shire if you get robbed. So *don't* get robbed. Exercise caution. Any of you operatives who've been here before – you, I think?' He nodded at Flavius, who nodded back. 'Yes, well, you're familiar with the crime in urban London. Don't make the mistake of thinking you'll be safer in the country. You're much more visible here, particularly those of you with darker skins. People are frightened, ignorant, and superstitious, so you might as well have targets painted on your backs. Travel fast and keep your heads down. London in fact is pretty cosmopolitan these days, so you're less likely to have your throat cut for racial reasons, though of course you still run the risk of having it cut for your purse.

'So. Enough of the safety lecture. Try some of the cheese, it's the famous Cheshire cheese. Now if you'll all open your dockets . . .'

Rustle rustle crackle crackle. There was a silence as we all dutifully accessed and integrated. Then one by one we handed the sheets to Xenophon, who tossed them on the fire. 'Nice and tidy. Are there any questions?'

'Why can't I stay at the HQ in Eastcheape?' Flavius wanted to know.

'It was decommissioned fifty years ago. History decrees other use of the site.'

'Damn.'

'You mean you won't be going where we are?' I stared at Flavius. It wasn't that I was going to miss him, particularly, but I'd got used to him.

He shook his head, and Xenophon laughed. 'Too much work for him in London. We need systems techs desperately over here right now.'

Eva had been sitting with this special little glow on her face ever since she'd accessed her codes. She was feeling such giddy delight, it was coming through on the ether. We turned one by one to stare at her, and Xenophon leaned forward across the table with a grin.

'I see we have a Shakespeare fan here.'

'Stratford!' she burst out. 'Yes! When do I go?'

'You've got a little identity work here, and then we're sending you off to meet your Arden "cousins" next month.'

So she was going away too, and to live among mortals. This was the first time I had any inkling of how alone we really are. I had been thinking of my team as a family, getting used to everyone's little quirks. But we weren't a family. Well, I was new then, and hadn't learned yet that that's life in the service.

'I'll be with you the first year, you and Joseph,' Nefer told me. Thank you, Nefer. More livestock discussions.

The briefing went on from there to a discussion of the local currency, to national politics and gossip, to the weather (bad), to the latest field technologies available to us (inadequate, everyone felt), to the merits of British beer over German beer. When the meeting broke up we stayed by the cozy little coal fire and learned English card games, because the rain resolutely kept raining. As I fell asleep that night, I was thinking that I would have to see if I could spot any cowslips or osiers while I was here. And weirs, I'd read about them in English novels too.

Chapter Nine

July 22, 1554. I'd been in the field a year and a day. It was a space of time that figured in old songs and poetry.

We said farewell to Flavius and Eva in the dark of morning before we rode off. I never saw him again, and her I saw only once, a long time after, in a transport lounge in another country. We were going in opposite directions and had no time to talk.

And into darkness we descended, Joseph and Nefer and I, to ride the famous Company underground. It linked all parts of that island in a series of arrow-straight lines, and the operatives on duty in England were terribly proud of it. I thought it was awful, but there was no other way to get from Hampton to Kent on schedule, and it did cut down on our chances of getting lynched.

So we shuttled through shadows on a track in a tiny closet box going twenty-three kilometers an hour. The box thudded to a halt at last in a gloomy alcove, and we groped our way up uneven steps, flight after flight of them, hoisting our baggage well clear of the puddles, until we emerged at the back of a cave.

'This is a cave,' I said accusingly. My voice echoed back, and Joseph and Nefer just looked at me. Somewhere ahead a horse whinnied uneasily, and we followed the sound to daylight.

In fact there were three horses in the mouth of the cave, all saddled and bridled, and a little dark man who sat watching the rain. He jumped up when he saw us emerge from the depths and backed off a pace or two.

'*Akai, chavo.*' Joseph tossed him a bag of coins. The man took it and slipped away out into the rain. 'Three transport shuttles at the ready, ladies.' Joseph smirked.

We rode into Kent therefore on good horses, with our

baggage bound around us, in our Company cloaks issued specially against the rain that rained every minute. Most of the journey was a blur of leaves and water for me, so I can't tell you if there were cowslips by the wayside or not.

Still, as the day wore on, we came into an open landscape. Hop fields wide to the horizon, dotted here and there with toy towns, each with its steeple and cluster of trees. Low rolling hills and rivers. At some point we clattered across a little bridge, and Joseph reined in his mount and said, 'I guess it's around here somewhere.'

Actually he knew exactly where it was, he had directionals fixed and homing, but he never could resist the temptation to pretend he was real.

'Some ride, huh, ladies?' he remarked brightly. 'All ready to make a good impression? Are we in character? Mendoza, have you got the whatsit all ready for presentation?'

'The Indian maize,' I told him. 'It's right here. In a fancy case and everything.'

'Great. Nef, your veil is crooked.'

'Thanks a lot. Aren't they going to be a little surprised to see us so soon?'

'No. How are they to know just when the ships put in? Xenophon has been sending letters quote from me unquote to our hosts, so they know we're coming, but they don't know when to expect us. Turn right here, I think.'

We set off down a green aisle, with green willows looming across our view of the gray sky. Before we had gone a mile, we picked them up, scanning: three mortal males in a highly excitable frame of mind. A quarter mile farther on, they appeared, just sort of stepped out from between the hedges and stood staring at us. They completely blocked the lane. They were bare-legged, blue with cold, and carried great sharp pitchforks caked with manure. They stared hard at us, and Nefer and I shrank back in our hoods.

Get your thinking caps on, girls, transmitted Joseph. Then in flawless South London English he said, 'Good day to ye, goodmen.'

'Be ye Spaniards?' said one of them. He had very white teeth. So did the other two. I noticed this, because they were baring them threateningly.

'Nay, I thank our Lord Jesus Christ,' said Joseph with an easy smile.

'But there be Spaniards come among us now,' persisted the man. 'We heard tell from Sir Thomas. And monks come to burn us all.' His friends were staring at our trappings and baggage.

'For very fear of that, good lads, I and mine are removing to Flanders. *That* for the Pope!' and Joseph spat elegantly, though he had to wrooch around a little to avoid hitting anyone, because we were so crowded there in the lane.

'Aye,' said the man.

They just stood there.

'Well, we must on. Jesu keep you, good lads, and keep England, and God save the Princess Elizabeth!' cried Joseph, urging his horse forward. They let us through.

'You have a ready wit, my father,' I said, digging my nails out of my palms.

'Smooth, that's what I am,' he replied. 'Good navigator, too. Here we are.'

The way opened out in front of us. I don't know what I had expected to see, but it certainly wasn't wrought-iron gates four meters tall, fantastically gilded and ornamented, little pennants fluttering, little weathercocks spinning, and above our heads foot-high letters set with bright enamel that spelled out:

Iden His Garden

And underneath, only slightly smaller, was the legend:

Here Ye May See Where the Desperate CADE Was Taken, With Divers Other Curious Marvels Whereat Ye May Wonder

'Holy Cow,' said Nefer.

Down by the entrance was a small porter's lodge, almost a booth you might say, and on its window a placard reading:

Penny to See the Great Garden of Wonders

Through the gate we could make out some brick walls, an avenue of hedges clipped into geometric shapes, and what must have been the manor house at the far end of it, looking not all that big really.

But here came a man in blue livery, wearing a crucifix the size of a shovel around his neck, advancing on us with hands outstretched.

'Your worships! Welcome, welcome in the name of the Pope! Oh, Jesu bless your worships!'

Is this guy one of ours? I inquired of Joseph.

No. Just a sycophant. 'Buenos dias, good fellow! This is then the residence of that worthy friend of Spain, Señor Walter Iden?'

'It is even so. The blessed saints be thanked that you met with no heretics on the way!' He seized our horses' bridles and led us in. 'I am Francis Ffrawney and I serve Sir Walter and I pray your worships remember me as a constant friend and a true believer. If you should lack for aught the whiles you stay here —'

'Truly you are a courteous gentleman and doubtless faithful.' Joseph grinned at us over his head. 'The Pope shall hear good things of you.'

The man went pasty white. 'H-huzzah!' he got out. 'And is it true, then, that you have come to spy out foul heretics in Kent, and intelligence the Pope thereof?'

'Peace, friend. I am but a physician come to gather simples in the garden of good Sir Walter. Though I would be served,' and Joseph leaned down and looked very Spanish indeed, you could almost see the auto-da-fé smoke in his beard, 'by those with discreet tongues in their heads.'

'Oh!' said Master Ffrawney; he went a whiter shade still, an ugly color in all that greenery. By this time we had come up before the house, and there were grooms running to help us. Faces peered from all the leaded windows and over one or two of the clipped hedges, and all those rosy English faces looked terrified. Two men were descending the steps of the manor house. The more elaborately dressed of the two stepped forward to meet us.

'I have the joy of beholding my great friend Doctor Ruy Anzolabejar,' he said carefully, putting a not quite audible question in the statement.

'My beloved friend!' cried Joseph. 'How many years has it been since we lay at the Seven Ducks?' That was the code response, and Sir Walter relaxed visibly.

He was not a tall man at all, for an Englishman, but his presence expressed itself in at least three contrasting hues in his brilliant doublet. His hose were vivid yellow, the heels of his shoes were built up, and there was a great deal of gold-colored ornamentation sewn all over his clothes. The rather ordinary face that commanded all this fashion looked intelligent enough. He must have been about sixty, quite old for a mortal in that era.

We all dismounted, and Joseph went forward and embraced him. 'Mi amigo viejo! It has been so long since our youth in the days of the late and sanctified Queen Katherine. Ah, what joyful times they were, when England and España were one in amity. What high hopes we have for the present union. It quite brings tears to mine eyes.' He actually dabbed at them with a large lace handkerchief.

'And to mine also,' stammered Sir Walter. 'You look most, uh, youthful.'

We'd told Joseph he should have grayed his hair more.

'That, my dear friend, you may lay to a certain Greek physick that you wot well of.' Joseph looked at him meaningfully. 'Of which, more anon. But now, let me present to you Doña Marguerita Figueroa, a woman whose chastity is renowned throughout Valladolid.'

Nefer curtseyed, looking regal.

'And allow me further to present to you my daughter, Doña Rosa.' Joseph put out his hand to me, and I curtseyed low. 'The comfort of my middle age and a scholarly child. Are you not, daughter? She will assist me in my study of your most justly famous garden. Hija, present to our worthy host the most unworthy trifle we have brought him for his collection.'

Sir Walter looked scared and greedy at once. This was fun. Demure and theatrical as could be, I brought out the fancy case I had carried so far. With a flourish I opened it and displayed the contents. Sir Walter caught his breath. Ha, I thought.

It really had turned out especially well, my Indian maize. One whole ear rested on a bed of harvested kernels. The kernels were big as marbles and all colors: white like pearls, yellow like gold, red like garnets, blue like bruises. Sir Walter reached with a trembling hand, greed winning out completely in his face. He was desperate to grab it, I could see. This mortal was a serious collector; he would give anything to have this exotica in his garden, to show it off as it grew tall and bore strange flowers. The man could not have cared less what services were said in his chapel. Perfect for use. The Company was so good at finding these people.

But it wouldn't be mannerly to snatch it out of my hands. He got control of himself.

'How rare! Here is true magnificence! Pray, what call you this thing?'

'It is called maize, gentle sir, out of the New World,' I said.

'The New World! I have a vine of potato of the Indies, but it bears no such fruit. Nicholas, you shall tell the guests who pay at the gate that that the savages of Ind do feed on very jewels, and so show forth this maize! And belike we shall have Master Sampson paint upon a board a map of the New World, in some several colors, or yet some figures of men all naked to signify that they be savages —' He controlled himself again.

'Fair Lady Rose, you are most welcome to Iden's Garden. And you, good lady . . . Lady . . .'

'Marguerita,' supplied Joseph.

'Even so she is. I bid ye welcome to my poor house, though I may say my garden is a pleasance for kings to command. Nicholas – ah. My friend, this gentleman is my secretary. Master Harpole. Nicholas, hither now.'

The other man stepped forward. We craned back our necks to look. He was tall even for an Englishman, and in his black scholar's gown positively towering. He peered down at us sternly.

He was long and lanky but solid through the body, this young man; he had good legs on him. His face was nice too, with high wide cheekbones and a wide mobile mouth, though the mouth was presently pulled down at the corners in an expression of mulish disapproval. He had a long nose with a slight break to the left; his eyes were pale blue and frankly rather small, or at least looked that way glaring at us in icy Protestant dignity.

How interesting, I thought to myself.

'Master Harpole,' repeated Sir Walter, with a rising inflection. Master Harpole bowed stiffly.

Oh, how well he moved. And what fresh color in his smooth English skin.

'It is pleasant to meet you, young man,' said Joseph brightly. 'Sir Walter, shall we see this garden, which is of renown even to the limits of Muscovy?'

I was still holding out the maize in its open box. I shut it and my mouth but did not look away from Master Harpole. I thrust the box at Sir Walter, who grabbed it eagerly and mustered his good breeding to reply:

'Even to Muscovy? Surely not so. Yet, I promise you, you shall marvel at it! Nicholas, pray walk forth and show it them, as you are accustomed.'

Nicholas Harpole extended his long black-draped arm and said: 'Gentles, will you walk hence?' And though he was being as unpleasant as he knew how, his smooth rich tenor hung on the air like a violin.

So as the grooms hustled out baggage within, I followed Master Harpole into a green confusion of pleaching and pruning and apricocks and yew. The rest of our party came along too, of course, but it should be obvious to you by now that they might have been invisible for all I knew or cared.

The first place we came to was surrounded by a high wall of brick. The area therein enclosed was planted with sorrel, herbs, and a few vegetables. Over in one corner was a dungheap. 'The garden, proper, of Alexander Iden, Esquire. A kinsman of our present Sir Walter,' intoned Master Harpole. 'The very garden where the recreant Jack Cade was taken, in the reign of our late King Henry, sixth of that name. It fell out —'

'But, Nicholas, this is the crown and glory of the walk, the chiefest primature of our attractions! Were it not well considered to hold it forth to the last, being as it were the cake and comfits of our discourse?' cried Sir Walter.

Calmly, Nicholas drew himself upright and folded his arms. 'I cry you mercy, Sir Walter. I have but followed the customary walk as presented to our penny-paid guests. What shall it please you I present for the, as it were, bread and broth of our discourse?'

Sir Walter looked at him peevishly. 'See you, Doctor Ruy, how it was. This Jack Cade, whom you must know was a most vicious and murdering caitiff, of common low birth, he here being pursued by all loyal Englishmen for his bloodthirsty crimes against our sainted King Henry (who, I would have you know, was a true son of the Church and a faithful friend of the Pope) – the said Jack Cade, hunted all through Kent, in desperate wise scaled this very wall.' He ran outside the enclosure, put his leg over the bricks, and slid back in rather awkwardly, as his slops were thickly padded out. 'Thus, and went to gather him salad herbs which were here growing, he being in sore need of food. So was the villain engaged when my, uh, kinsman, that famous Alexander Iden, then but an humble esquire of Kent, happed upon him here.'

'Verdad?' said Joseph pleasantly. 'And what then occurred?'

'Why, they fought, sir. At first the good esquire offered Jack Cade no violence, and would have shown charity to a poor starving fellow, but that the man boasted of his crimes, crimes too hideous to relate here. Wherefore my kinsman took his pruning bill like *this*, and the said Cade drew his sword like *this* – Nicholas, what say you, would it not be better told if we had two mannequins here, in the very posturing of battle, one to figure forth Iden and the other Cade? The better to make it all plain?'

'I will inquire the cost of Master Sampson,' said Nicholas gravely.

'Or belike statuary. More expense, but a lasting monument. Well, sir, the fight being over and my kinsman having valiantly slain the accursed Cade, he smote off the head and threw the ignoble body on a dungheap, and bore that same head to blessed Henry where he lay at London. And there, for his great deed of loyalty to his king, Iden was that same day made a knight and given a thousand marks to boot. Such was the king's gratitude! And though the fortunes of the house of Iden have not run constant since that time, mine own success in the wool trade – no valiant work but honest, I assure you – hath furnished me with the means to make suitable commemoration of the Iden valor.'

'I am overwhelmed with astonishment,' said Joseph. 'And this, then, is the very dungheap where Cade's body lies buried?'

'Why, as to that —' Sir Walter grew a little red and looked in appeal to Nicholas, 'as to that, family fortunes being what they were —'

'The history Sir Walter hath related here is very old, some hundred years or more,' explained Nicholas, smooth as music. 'In the natural course of time, the original garden vanished, as all things will under Time's crushing heel. Nor could the descendants of Sir Alexander, less favored by fortune than their sire, hold title to the ancient family seat. But when Sir Walter came into this county, having a mind to restore the family greatness, he was assured by sundry persons of good character that this was that same garden, or the place where it had been. All that you see is restored. This dungheap, therefore, hath been placed here solely for your edification.' He made a slight bow.

'As well as many another marvel unknown in Sir Alexander's day,' piped up Sir Walter. 'Whereas he grew but salad herbs and such things as befit a poor esquire, I with my fortune have made such a collection of wonders, both animal and vegetable, as ye may well exclaim over! Of course, nothing looks its best just now,' he added parenthetically. 'The rain, you know.'

'What would you have them see next, sir?' inquired Nicholas.

'Oh, my roses. The nonpareils of the world, my roses.'

Nicholas led us deeper into the garden, and we saw a whole arbor where there actually did grow just about every variety of rose that existed at that time, with a couple of variegated petal mutations that were probably unique. I made a mental note to get genetic material from them.

But it was as we were going to see something Sir Walter grew in a hothouse called The Great Engiber Pea Out of

Africke that my gaze was distracted from contemplation
of Master Harpole's long back. My head snapped around
as I turned to stare, and I nearly collided with Nefer. Ilex
tormentosum! I transmitted frantically to Joseph. *My God,
he's got a whole hedge of* Ilex tormentosum *over here!*

Is that good? Joseph queried. I responded with excited
profanity.

What's going on? Nefer wanted to know.

'This hedge here, it is a form of holly, is it not?' Joseph
inquired casually of Sir Walter.

'This? Indeed, sir. Not our English holly, but one I have
heard tell was brought with Julius Caesar from Rome for
some properties it hath, though what they may be I confess
I know not. It is not so common as once it was, I think. In
faith, I have not seen it but here this many a year now.'

Oh, what a score. Pharmacologists of the twenty-second
century had three miserable endangered specimens of this
plant, source of a specific for liver cancer, and here was a
whole hedge. If Sir Walter had this kind of botanical loot,
what else might he be growing? I looked more closely and
began to spot them everywhere: *Cynoglossum nigra, Oxalis
quinquefolia, Calendula albus, Carophyllata montena, Genista
purpurea ascendens* . . . Meanwhile Nicholas was solemnly
holding forth on Sir Walter's prized Portingale orange and
Cathay coriander and even a sad-looking palmetto plant. I
had months of work, fabulous work to do here!

But when the sky suddenly opened and sent black buckets
of rain down on us, we had to turn and run for the house.
Only Nicholas seemed to know his way through the maze,
which would have been difficult to traverse quickly even
without the rain, the darkness, the flight between our legs
of a despairing peacock, and the disappointed wails of Sir
Walter.

'So much of my collection yet unseen!' he lamented. 'None
of my zoological wonders touched on at all. But 'tis no matter.
There'll be clement weather yet. You must see my unicorn
of Hind.'

I wondered what that was, but not much. My head was
spinning. Who'd have thought England was such a delightful
country?

We made it to the house, and the drafty wooden floors boomed under our shoes, but there was a roaring fire laid out in what passed for the great hall. This was indeed a fairly modest little manor, but the Iden arms were blazoned on every surface.

Everyone crowded to the warmth of the fire, gasping after the run. I sidled up to Nicholas Harpole. The heat of the room had brought high color into his face. I must ask you to believe that I had no idea what had befallen me, there in that garden. My God, that the heart can be so stupid.

I said to him, in my very best Latin: 'What manner of thing is this unicorn, youth?'

He straightened up from the fire and raised an eyebrow at me. Then he replied, in better Latin: 'It is no more than a beast, as other beasts are. And how appropriate it is you speak the tongue of Rome.'

'Master Harpole,' said Sir Walter sharply. 'Go thou and see the baggage has been placed in the chamber I gave orders for.'

'I go, sir.' He bowed again. 'Lady.' He inclined perfunctorily to me, then strode from the room. I watched him go. I couldn't fathom it. He smelled good.

Chapter Ten

Master Harpole did not dine with us, which was disappointing, but since it was our first meal prepared by a non-Company cook without sanitary preparation training, it was just as well: I needed all my attention for the food. The bread was safe to eat, and the chicken with a sauce of oranges and lemons; but there was a venison pasty that was practically crawling, the meat was so far gone, and a custard dish ridden with bacteria of an extremely undesirable kind. I watched disbelieving as Sir Walter tucked it in happily. His system must have been used to such things.

'My friend, what a bountiful repast!' Joseph pushed his plate away, pushed his chair back from the table, loosened his doublet, and otherwise obscured the fact that he'd eaten nothing more than one chicken leg and a slice of bread. 'I am stuffed like a sausage! We have not such fare in Spain.'

'It is our custom to dine heartily in England,' said Sir Walter smugly. Then he looked uncomfortable. 'Though I am sure they do have most excellent feasting in Spain too. And the, um, the vintners of Spain do make a most wondrous Sack, I have heard.'

'Ah, yes, the sweet wines of Spain. How I wish I had brought some with me.' Joseph looked around to note the absence of servants from the room. He leaned closer to Sir Walter. 'And now, old friend, I will be plain with you. Have no fears for your house or your people: I have come into this land, as was told you, only to take simples from your garden and for no other purpose. We will work quietly here and give no offense to any man. Ye may all worship as ye list, or think or speak as ye list; it is all one to me. Only have a care that you be discreet when speaking to other men of who dwelleth here, and we shall all be well pleased alike, you, I, and my masters. Understand my meaning, friend.'

Sir Walter leaned forward until his beard was in the custard.

'Oh, sir, mine are loyal folk – loyal to *me* – and no great talkers but one or two, who love Spain well. For the rest, why, they are young folk and cannot remember Queen Katherine that was, rest her soul, nor the wrongs done her. They fear Spain, aye; but it is a fear that will pass upon greater acquaintance, God willing.'

'Your secretary loves us not, I think,' Joseph looked sideways at me.

'A young man, a young man! In truth, he is something stubborn in his ... um ... Gospel reading, but he will do as I bid him, I assure you.'

'That is all my masters desire. Come, we shall all be friends. My daughter shall have leave of days to walk your garden and gather what I require. I by night shall distill such liquors as will purge cold heavy melancholy and dry up all unwholesome humors that make a man old.'

'The Greek physick,' whispered the old knight.

'Even as my masters promised.' Joseph held Sir Walter's gaze with his own.

A silence fell. Master Ffrawney came in, with many a soulful glance at Joseph, and oversaw the removal of the dishes. I scanned Sir Walter, wondering what Joseph was going to do with him. Hypertension, arteriosclerosis, gout, caries, cholelithiasis. Plenty to keep a physician busy.

'I require some part of each day cloistered with you privily.' Joseph reached for a pear and examined it. Taking out his dagger, he began to peel the fruit in a long spiral. 'Perhaps your secretary will assist my daughter in her labors.'

I turned my head to stare at him.

'Doubtless they will find many botanical subjects to discuss.' He smiled at me and popped a slice of pear into his mouth.

Pleading exhaustion from the journey, we retired early and were shown to our two rooms on the second floor, nice paneled rooms with a connecting door. Our baggage had been left in the middle of the floor and appeared undisturbed; no danger if it had been, because everything issued to a field agent is disguised to look like something else. Even Joseph's book of holo codes for *Great Cinema of the Twentieth Century* was bound in calfskin with a printer's date of 1547.

'Some bed, huh?' Nefer sank down on the big tapestried four-poster. 'I get the window side, Mendoza. Oh, do we have to do that now?' she protested as she saw Joseph pulling out his tool case and setting up the credenzas.

'Yes, we do. Look around for a cabinet or something we can integrate this with. I'd like everything to be installed and invisible before the servants feel confident enough to venture back in here. Especially our friend the very tall Protestant. Speaking of whom . . .' He turned to give me a meaningful look.

'What?' I demanded.

'Oh, nothing. I just thought it might be a nice idea if you took it upon yourself to keep him busy. Change his outlook on evil Spaniards. Show him we're really a bunch of nice guys. And dolls. Get it?'

I didn't know what to say. I stared at the credenza rapidly taking shape in his hands. The drift of our conversation finally sank in for Nefer, who had been hanging upside down trying to read a motto stitched in the canopy.

'Hey!' she cried, sitting up abruptly. 'Joseph, really!'

'Really what? He's a hazard to the mission. He obviously disapproves of our being here already. You want the guy walking in on me when I've got his employer opened up like an oyster, installing funny-looking little glowing things? No, no. I want Mister Reformation kept distracted, preferably out in the garden with a little Spanish popsy. And Mendoza did seem rather struck by his personal qualities, if you'll pardon my saying so, kid.' He turned to me. 'And you're young and healthy and just chock-full of hormones.'

Nefer lay back on the counterpane in disgust and resumed her attempts to decipher the motto. I watched as Joseph fitted in the last panel and lifted the unit in his hands, where it glowed a transparent blue. Finding a likely clothes chest, he swung the unit through the side, and it gave a soft beep to let us know integration had occurred. He nodded his satisfaction and went off to his room, whistling the first few notes of 'Forty-Second Street.'

There was a soft knock on the door.

'Enter, por favor.' Nef jumped to her feet. The door opened, and a maidservant edged her way in, carrying a basin and a tall can of steaming water.

'Your washing water, my ladies,' she gasped, and set them down on the credenza. From a recess in the expanse of her apron she drew forth a ball of soap – marjoram-scented, what a luxury – and set it beside the water. 'There will be a man brings water to his lordship the doctor,' she informed us, 'but I am to serve you in all things, for clean linen and what else ye require. Have ye aught to be sent to the laundress?'

Boy, had we ever, after that voyage. 'Many thanks, good woman,' I chirped, as Nef and I pulled open our respective bags and began to fling out a veritable snowstorm of shifts, stockings, and other garments both muddy and malodorous. 'What shall we call thee, pray?'

'Joan, my lady,' she replied, watching without interest as the stuff piled up. Our clothes looked pretty much like anyone else's, so there was nothing worth her attention, until I, in my enthusiasm, inadvertently snatched up with a bilge-stained underskirt my calfbound copy of the latest issue of *Immortal Lifestyles Monthly* and flung them both on the laundry heap. The magazine bounced once and clattered to the floor, landing open at the new holo releases page.

There in large blackletter was trumpeted the rerelease of *Metropolis* (the silent version, not the 2015 Spielberg remake) with a full-page photo of Maria the Robot in all her brassy glory. I raised horrified eyes to the chambermaid, who was staring fixedly at the picture of the villainous she-mechanism. *Omigod!*

Nef cleared her throat. 'Do not be afraid, good Joan. It is what we call in Spain an iron maiden. You have such things here, have you not, to punish the wicked? In this book it doth depict the torments awaiting sinners,' she said firmly, scooping up the magazine and snapping it shut. 'For shame, thou, Rosa. Holy monks labored a year to paint this missal for thee, and wilt thou carelessly drop it?'

'I pray you excuse me, Doña Marguerita,' I stammered. 'For, to be sure, those holy monks paint like the angels.'

Don't overdo it. 'Look you, good Joan, this gown of

mine hath been sadly stained by mud.' Nef thrust it at her. 'I would not for all the world see it ruined. Bid the laundress take some pains with it.' And she put sixpence in the chambermaid's palm.

Now the chambermaid's gaze did a fast shuttle between the money and the gown, and in the thought balloon over her head Robot Maria was fading, being replaced with an image of all the nice things Joan might buy if she kept the money for herself. Having distracted Joan with this moral dilemma, Nef tucked the magazine out of sight in the depths of her bag.

'That will be all, Joan,' she prompted. With a half curtsey Joan stooped to gather up our clothes and backed out of the room, muttering her thanks.

'What're we going to do?' I collapsed onto a chest, wringing my hands. 'Do you think she'll tell anybody? I can't believe I did that!'

'Oh, it happens.' Nef, eyeing the water, stripped down to her shift.

'But they told us in school —'

'It'd be the end of the world if the monkeys saw anything anachronistic, right? Uh-uh.' She poured out water, grabbed up the soap, and began to lather vigorously. 'I mean – you *know* history can't be changed. So does it matter if an illiterate chambermaid sees something she can't understand? What's she going to do, write to the newspapers? As long as you can explain something away with a good story, you're covered.'

'You don't think I'll get in trouble?'

'Nah.' Nef groped in her trunk and found a linen hand towel. 'Because, you know what? Even when our little mistakes make it into the history books – and it happens, every once in a while – nobody notices. Well, sometimes people do, but if they try to talk about it, everyone thinks they're crazy. In this century, anyway. So don't worry.'

I watched doubtfully as she bathed. 'But shouldn't we make a report to Joseph about it?'

'I wouldn't.' Having finished, she opened the window and tipped the basin out. 'Unless you want him to fuss at you unnecessarily.'

'Not really,' I admitted. I sat there irresolute a moment,

grateful for the advice of an older and more experienced operative, until it occurred to me to wonder whether she'd left any hot water for me.

That first night I lay awake in the darkness for hours, listening. There was the beat of rain on thousands of green leaves, outside in the wet night. The breathing of nine mortal souls, slowed and trapped in dreams. A mouse busy in the walls of the kitchen. A clock. The horses in their animal dreams, out in the stable. Distant, chaotic animal thoughts, from farther out.

But *he* did not dream. Four walls away and a floor above me, I could hear the creak of a wooden chair as he shifted his weight from moment to moment. I could hear pages turning, exactly one minute apart, page after page, perfect as a machine. I could hear his breathing and the pulse of his angry heart.

Chapter Eleven

Next morning I packed my field kit, though rain still sheeted down the leaded windows. We had all accepted the fact that it wasn't ever going to stop, but I hadn't let myself think about having to work in it.

Sir Walter was seated at the long table in the great hall when we came down; he was breaking his fast on buttered eggs and fried beefsteak. Nicholas sat opposite him, though he was not eating: they seemed to be having an argument. Nicholas's fists were clenched, making the knuckles white. Sir Walter's face was red, and his eyes protruded slightly. They fell silent as we entered the room.

'Good morrow, good friends!' cried Joseph easily. 'And is this the morning meal in England? The famous English beef?' His gaze took in the eggs, fatty beef, and butter, and Nefer and I could hear him ticking as he evaluated what the cholesterol was doing to Sir Walter's arteries.

'It is even so.' Sir Walter turned glaring from Nicholas. 'Shall I order another mess of eggs fried, Doctor Ruy? Or there is excellent venison pasty, cold —'

'I think not.' Joseph smiled. 'Our Spanish stomachs are not yet accustomed to English abundance. We eat but sparingly before the midday. Perhaps a little of your English small beer and plain barley bread? What say you, ladies?'

I was dismayed. No coffee? Of course not. Not even any tea, yet. Orange juice?

'There were excellent oranges in your garden,' I ventured, curtseying. 'I would be most honored, gentle sir, and most grateful, kind sir, to taste of one.'

'Fair lady, what you will! You shall have a paste or conserve of orange, or perhaps a dish of cloves and marchpane kneaded up with peel of orange, or a dish made up with oranges boiled with parsnips —'

Joseph was shaking his head at me. 'Even a plain orange, simple of itself, please you,' I stammered.

'*Raw?*' Sir Walter looked incredulous.

'At some better time, daughter, when good Sir Walter need not send his poor servants out into the rain for such a trifle,' reproved Joseph.

'To be sure, my father. Sir Walter, I pray you excuse my inconsideration.' Bright pink with mortification, I curtseyed again and sat down. When I raised my eyes, I found myself looking straight into the cold stare of Nicholas Harpole. I lowered my eyes hastily.

'No, no, we will have a new custom now, a dish of fruit to the table,' Sir Walter said gallantly. 'There are orange groves in Seville, as I hear tell. Are there oranges in the New World?'

'No, my friend, the fruit there is of a different sort from our accustomed fruit,' Joseph told him. 'There is, for example, the *aboccado*, which doth resemble your English pear, save that . . .' Blah blah blah. I sat there burning with embarrassment. After a while I sneaked a look at Master Harpole. He was still looking at me.

Servants brought in our bread and beer, and I picked at mine, still preoccupied with being a self-conscious teenager. Joseph talked on and on, too boring for words; then, suddenly, there was light in the room, as though God had opened an eye and looked in the window. It took us all a moment to realize that it was the sun.

'Why, look you, the rain hath ended,' remarked Sir Walter. 'Lady Rose shall have her orange at last, shall she not? And see my garden at its best to boot! Pray you, Nicholas, bear her company and show her what oranges there are.'

Nicholas rose to obey, and so did I, groping for my field kit. And so did Nefer, like the good duenna she was supposed to be. 'Doña Marguerita!' – Joseph spoke up. 'By your leave, remain with me. I would discourse with you privily concerning certain things.'

She gave him a narrow look and sat down.

'Lady.' Nicholas gestured toward the doorway. In silence he led me from the house and out into the garden.

There were still clouds breaking up and rolling back,

but most of the sky was blue. The difference was breath-taking. England seemed three times bigger. The garden was, impossibly, more green; the beech trunks shone like bronze. Somewhere near us a river rushed and chattered. Birds cried out. England was aggressively alive, to the point of being intimidating.

By the time we reached the orange tree, the wet grass had soaked our shoes. Nicholas squelched up to the tree and assumed his tour-guide stance.

'The orange, Lady,' he told me. I looked for a ripe one.

'Truly I did not think to put you to trouble,' I murmured. 'I minded not where I was. In Spain it is our custom to have fruit at breakfast.'

'Your Spain is not our England,' said Nicholas.

'That's true too. I pray you excuse me.'

'What needs your excuse? Sir Walter has bid you make free with his oranges. Take his oranges therefore and so make an end of it, Madam.'

Green leaves dripped on me. He stood so perfectly still, with such composure, and his voice was so beautiful saying such cold things. I pulled an orange down and showered us both with late rain. He did not even flinch, but watched distantly as I dug my thumbs into the peel and tore the orange into sections. It did not want to be peeled. Juice dripped on my palm, ran stickily down my wrist. 'Will you have any?' I held out a piece, vain social gambit.

Without thinking he reached to take the fruit from my hand; then halted and jerked away, with an odd expression in his eyes. He took a full pace backward from me.

I gaped at him. Then I understood. Christian mythology, right? Adam and Eve in the Garden, primal woman as tempter to sin. What *subtle* symbolism. Now I hated him.

'Thou ill-mannered and arrogant man!' I exploded. 'Thinkest I have read no Scripture and will not see the insult in thy refusal?' I switched to Greek. 'And have you read the Gospels in Greek, as I have, uncivil one?' I switched to Aramaic. 'Let me tell you, young lord, this is not Eden and you are not Adam but rather Lucifer himself, you are so full of pride, so do not compare *me* to Eve!' And to Hebrew: 'Shame on you! I am a stranger come into your country and have done you no wrong.' And to Italian: 'If you hate the Pope, you may write him an insulting letter for all I care, but I assure you he is not hiding in my skirts!' And to German: 'Now I wish earnestly I were again in Spain, for though God knows it is a land of monstrous cruelty, yet folk there have good manners!'

Of course I had to spoil the effect by flinging the orange at him too. He sidestepped it neatly without appearing to notice. The orange sailed out of sight and landed with a soft thump somewhere in the grass.

'I'm sorry,' I said at once, in English again. He stared at me a second longer before he recovered himself, setting his scholar's biretta straight on his lank hair.

'Well, I am cast down. The point is taken, Lady. You speak eight languages.'

'More,' I said resentfully.

'Is it even so? Well, well, there's a marvel. And canst quote Scripture too!' He said it snidely enough, but he came a step closer.

'Folk have tongues to proclaim truth in Spain as well as elsewhere,' I said. 'But they dare not. Nor would you, Señor, if you were there, lest the Inquisidors come for *you*. And if once you learned a lesson of silence from them, you would not soon forget it.'

I was pale and shaking. The adrenaline rush, of course, but it was effective. He came close and peered into my eyes. 'Now, I truly crave your pardon,' he said abruptly. 'But if you do not love your Inquisition in Spain, you may imagine how much the less we wish to see it here in England.'

'Pray to God, Master Harpole, that you never have such cause to hate it as I do,' I said. There. Would the old trump card work?

It did. His hostility was deflected. He took my hand in his own and squeezed it. His hand was warm.

'Well, what a fool I am,' he said. 'Come you, Lady. Another orange, and shall we walk this garden whiles the sun doth shine? What would you see here?'

I swallowed hard. 'I would see Julius Caesar's holly bush again,' I told him.

*   *   *

He led me straight to the miracle hedge. I set down my field kit (designed to look like a quaint wicker basket) and drew out my holo camera (designed to look like a pair of horn-rimmed spectacles). I held them up to my eyes and paced slowly along the hedge, shooting the images, grateful for the work to calm my nerves. Nicholas leaned against a tree, watching me.

'Had you your learning from your father?' he inquired at last.

'I had.' I broke off a leaf and held it up to the lens, turning it slowly. 'He is a doctor, as you know, and a very learned man. I am his only child, wherefore he hath taught me much.'

'Ah.' Harpole nodded. I groped for my knife (designed to look like a knife) and cut a whole sprig to display for the imager.

'He hath many books, on divers dangerous subjects, which, were they found, he would be burned for a heretic at least,' I ventured. Well, it was true. 'And, sorrow to tell, he was for some while in the dungeons of the Inquisition.' Also true.

'I am sorry to hear it.'

'They did not murder him, praise God; but he came from that place a ruined man,' I improvised.

'He hath healed himself well, then. He looketh not old,' remarked Nicholas.

'That is thanks to a certain Greek physick he hath learned of. I promise you, sir, were it not for that, he'd be in his grave now this many a year.' Certainly true again. 'There was great learning in Spain once, sir, though none would know now.'

He just nodded.

'You have read your Galen and Averroës, then,' he said. Was he setting me a trap?

'Yea, and my Avicenna too, howbeit the Moors are not so well regarded as formerly.' Under guise of examining the hedge's roots I thrust a soil corer in for a sample. I wrapped it with the holly branch and folded it into the basket. Not two feet away I spied a beautiful little specimen of *Calendula albans* and pounced on it, holo camera at the ready. Nicholas observed me closely.

'You see this for what it is, then,' he remarked with gloomy satisfaction. 'A rarer thing than ever the old knight's

Portingale orange, but because it is no more than a little pale flower, he regards it but scant.'

'For the light shineth in the darkness, and darkness comprehendeth it not,' I quoted smugly. 'John, chapter one, verse five. Tell me,' and I slipped into Latin for clarity, 'where does Sir Walter find these unusual plants?'

'He collected some of them himself, when he was a young man.' Nicholas matched me verb for verb easily. 'And now he has a standing offer out in this part of the country for anything rare or strange. The result is that men come continually to his gate with two-headed calves, or with common plants that have been altered to make them look rare. One man brought a cherry tree with tin bells fastened to its branches with wire and tried to make us believe they were the natural fruit of the tree. Sometimes Sir Walter has been deceived and paid money to a charlatan. Still, sometimes one will come bearing a true wonder for sale: and then the silly old man buys it out of habit, without true understanding of what he has bought. So he bought this flower.'

'Do you make a study of botany too?' My heart beat faster.

'No. But I know enough to discern that a white marigold is a marvel, whereas a unicorn is a lie.'

'What is this unicorn? I have heard it spoken of three times now. I would pay money myself to see it.'

He smiled contemptuously, but on him it looked good, and at least the contempt wasn't directed at me now. 'Why, you may see it for yourself.' He extended his right hand and took mine. 'Come, Lady, and do not fear. He is a tame beast.'

Only slowly I let go of his hand. We walked on through that garden, past banks of flowers lifting their unbelieving heads to the sun, past beds laid out in patterns intricate as Morisco tiles. Down a lane between clipped privet hedges we caught a glimpse of little white flanks. Nicholas flung out his arms and announced: 'The unicorn of Hind!'

The tail end backed out of the marjoram knot the animal was destroying, and a little head appeared, to look at us inquiringly.

'Ay!' I exclaimed, and bent down to stare. It thought I had a treat for it and came trotting up to see.

'Don't tremble, Lady. It will do you no harm,' said Nicholas with a straight face.

'He's a goat.' I examined him. He was as white as milk, his tiny hooves had been gilded, and some cruel surgery had been done to his horn buds before they had sprouted, and some crueler binding had fused them into one stubby twisting spike. But he was a sweet and trusting little goat all the same.

'A goat!' Nicholas held up his hands. 'Can this be true?'

'Señor.' I looked up at him. 'I was born in Spain. I know a goat when I see one.'

He just folded his hands.

'Go, goat.' I swatted the unicorn's flank, and he ran off to do further damage to the herbs. 'And yet, strange to tell, there is such a thing as a unicorn.'

'Surely not!'

'Truly, but it looks nothing like this. A big creature, rude and ugly. It is called in the Greek, *rhinoceros*.'

He nodded, sounding it out. 'Unfortunate. Sir Walter would not be pleased to discover that he paid twenty pounds eightpence for a goat.'

'Why tell him? The worthy Erasmus says, in his *Praise of Folly*, that no man is so happy as he who lives under an illusion.'

'Very true.' Nicholas's eyes lit up. 'You have read Erasmus? What do you think of his *Ichtuophagia*?'

Thank God, thank God I'd accessed that Strongly Suggested column. 'I think it is outrageous. All the same, I agree with what he says,' I replied with perfect composure.

'So you admit that it is unnecessary to salvation to eat fish on fast days?'

'Oh, señor, really, what nonsense.'

'Even if the Pope commands it?' he pressed.

'Particularly so. Do you imagine God cares what we have for dinner? How can one worship when religion is so ridiculous?'

He opened his mouth to speak, then paused. 'You have no faith, then,' he said after a moment. There was a silence while we considered each other. 'I have an excellent book I would like you to read,' he said at last.

'Ah! He is going to convert me to the Church of England!'
I exclaimed.

But that darkened his mood. He took a step closer and
loomed over me.

'The Church of England?' he growled. 'The one whose
leaders even now recant like the hypocrites they are?'

He must have been close to seven feet tall with his
biretta on.

'The crawling Council have sold this land to Spain, for
the right to keep their miserable lives. Our Northumberland
– you know who he was?'

'The Protestant faction leader,' I stammered. 'He made
Lady Jane Grey Queen.'

'Poor maid. Yes, he did. And when he fell, he turned ranting
Catholic at once, in the hope it would save his head. *She* died
with more bravery. What man was that to lead us? But the
ones who remain at Court have been more subtle in changing
their coats. They remain on the Council, they conform. By
the collusion of the men who should most defend them, the
laws of our late king are set aside. How should I counsel
you to join the Church of England, Lady, when it is made
up of such rogues?'

'What has become of all those Bible-reading heretics we
hear so much of in Spain?' I asked, startled by his vehemence.
'All those learned merchants disputing doctrines?'

'Fled to live among the Germans,' he said bitterly, 'for
safety. Yet had they had the courage to stay here and fight
for the Faith, we would all be safe enough.' *Except for the
ones who died fighting for your faith*, I thought.

'All the same, I would be interested in reading this book
of yours,' I said at last. 'Even if there is no true faith in
England.'

He took hold of my arm. He was very physical for such a
godly man.

'Lady, the Faith is here,' he stated. 'But we must build
churches in our hearts, for surely those built in the world
have all betrayed us.'

Now this was such a remarkable observation – for a
sixteenth-century man mired in the perceptions and prejudices
of mortals, I mean – that I was really impressed.

'Worldly institutions fail because they require power and gold to operate.' I explained, graciously, I felt. 'Power and gold attract wicked and greedy people. Wicked and greedy people are corrupters and betrayers. Therefore, worldly institutions become corrupt and betrayed. Churches, being in the world, are worldly institutions. Thus it is demonstrated.'

He raised an eyebrow at me. 'Very good. And very true, for all that you rattled it off like a parrot.'

Parrot! I tried to flounce away, but he still had hold of my arm. 'And where have you ever seen a parrot, I'd like to know?' I said scornfully.

'We have several in the aviary. Yes, he collects birds, too. Come, tell me, where did you learn such a nice little piece of sophistry? Never in Spain.'

Sophistry! 'We have not always lived in Spain,' I extemporized. 'We fled to France for a while. After my father got out of the dungeons of the Inquisition.'

'How old were you at that time?'

'Four. It was not either a sophistry! If philosophers had ever thought about this for two minutes, humanity would stop building stupid worldly institutions like churches.'

'Not necessarily. Anyone can see the disease, but what is the remedy? Tell me, doctor's child. Demonstrate for me the solution to the problem you have propounded.' His eyes were blazing, intense, *interested in me.*

'You are asking me for a solution for human evil? Don't give your heart to any church, any leader, any idea. Collect rare plants like Sir Walter, or study them like me, but leave the damned world and its struggles alone.'

'No! A hermit may do as much, or an animal, and never lessen human misery one particle. One *must* work for a better world.' He had me by both arms now. 'Listen to me. Shall we not struggle over ages to burn away what is evil in ourselves, until at some far day the angel with the flaming sword will relent and grant that we reenter Paradise?'

I hung there, gazing into his face, which shone with a radiance of belief so glorious, I didn't think to point out to him that his own Bible specifically says people are going to get worse, not better, until his God finally ends the whole mess in a shower of blood and flames.

No, all I could feel was admiration. Somehow he had figured out the truth. For what he spoke of really would happen, of course: except for the part about the angel. The human race, sick of its own mortality, was going to develop the technology to produce Us. And We, obviously, were the next step, We were the perfected ones, the immortal and infinitely wise and intelligent beings he believed men would become.

I did not heed his racing pulse, nor mine. I loved the sound of his beating heart.

'Now, truly I think you could move mountains with your speech,' I gasped. 'You almost do persuade me to such a faith as yours.'

His eyes held mine.

'I *will* persuade you,' he said. I ought to have heard warning sirens then, my heart ought to have run for a shelter.

But he was warm and solid as palpable sunlight, and I thought hazily: He wants to save my soul. How quixotic, how extravagant, how romantic.

He smoothed my coif. 'Forgive me,' he said. 'I am too forward with my hands, when once I begin to speak.'

'No, no.' I blinked and shook my head.

'I have been beaten for it ere now, and belike shall hang for it yet. Come, art thou well?' He lifted my chin in his hand and looked down into my eyes.

'Yes! Yes! Very well!'

'Come, Lady Rose. Let us go about our tasks as we were bid. Now I will show you a cabbage said to be like none other in the world.'

It turned out to be nothing more than a bok choy plant, though how it had got there was anybody's guess. But there were real strawberries, growing from jars set cunningly in a wall; Nicholas could only find four ripe ones, but he picked them for me. And he dutifully pulled down a branch of *Eucalyptus cordata* that I could not reach, and he waited with patience while I took careful samples of what must have looked to him like the dullest of weeds. He led me to the aviary and, yes, by golly, there were parrots there: several African Grays, half-a-dozen assorted Amazons, and even a big blue-and-gold Macaw ceaselessly chewing its way up and down a bar. It cocked an eye at me.

'Buenos dias,' it said.

'Buenos dias,' I replied.

'Why, here at last is one who will welcome a Spanish lady to England,' jeered Nicholas pleasantly, just before the Macaw said something so pungent, explicit, and imaginative that I blinked. Nicholas's face went red. Evidently his Spanish too was pretty good.

'You must have had him from a sailor, yes?' I guessed.

Nicholas, recovering himself, looked at me a long moment; then we began to laugh. He had a nice laugh. I hadn't thought godly people laughed.

So we were good friends, you see, by the time we came wandering back to the house that afternoon. But when we entered the great hall to find Joseph sitting placidly at the head of the long table, Nicholas stiffened. The mood dropped away, like a curtain or fine frost falling.

'Buenos dias, daughter, young man.' Joseph looked up from his book. He had a glass of perry and a dish of wafers at his elbow. The fire, all cheerful, set lights dancing in the perry.

'Good day, sir. Where is my master? This is his accustomed place at this hour of the day,' said Nicholas.

'I administered him a purge.' Joseph smiled at him. 'He is in his private chamber. You may seek him there.' I wished he wasn't looking so damned comfortable, after I'd gone to such trouble to depict him as a tormented scholar.

Nicholas turned to me, bowed slightly, and withdrew. I heard his footsteps receding into the depths of the house.

'Wafer?' offered Joseph. 'Well. Did my weary eyes deceive me, or were you two young things smiling at each other as you came in?'

'I could punch you sometimes.' I slammed my basket down on the table.

'You could try,' he informed me mildly. 'I'd duck. So, did you have a nice day?'

'Actually, yes.' I sat down across from him. 'I got some beautiful examples of the ilex and an obscure periwinkle and a white calendula, can you imagine?'

'Remarkable.' Joseph turned a page. 'Striking fellow, your Master Harpole. Big. Seems to share some of your interests, too.'

'Don't beat it to death. He *is* nice. Okay? How did your day go with Sir Walter? He's really a mess, isn't he?'

Joseph nodded. 'Comparatively. He's made of stern stuff, or he wouldn't have survived this long. I did a little tinkering. Can't take things too far too soon, but the old man will certainly get his new lease on life. Ha ha. It's the young man I'm worried about.'

'Haven't you got a one-track mind!' I rose to make an affronted exit.

'Now, now. Just my little way of looking after our best interests. By the way, I've left a list of the drugs I need synthesized on your credenza console. It's two pages long, so you might want to get an early start on it.'

I made my affronted exit anyway.

Sir Walter reappeared at supper looking pale and shaky, and took only some toast and a cup of watered Rhenish; but Joseph told a series of anecdotes concerning the king of France and a Spanish mule driver. Joseph was so adept at telling a funny story that Sir Walter was red with laughter soon, making high shrill barks of mirth like a terrier, with his mustache points spiking the air. Even the servants were giggling.

Nicholas came to supper with us for the first time, very reserved and correctly courteous. He smiled at the anecdotes, though everyone else at table was crying from laughing so hard. But when I struggled to shell a handful of filberts, he leaned over and took them in his fist and cracked them, so, and cast them on the table between us where they rolled like dice. I looked up into his eyes. Was it quite right for a godly man to show off his strength like that? But then, there'd been no reason for me to act helpless with the nuts, since I could crush them to powder if I had to.

'. . . so the mule driver saith, "But, Your Majesty, that was why I married her!" ' finished Joseph. Sir Walter beat his hand on the table and whooped his appreciation. Joseph leaned back in his chair, beaming, watching us.

'Nefer?' I turned the Rami lens slowly, fixing on a cell wall.

'Uhuh.' She did not look up from my magazine.

'What do you think of Master Harpole?'

'Who? Oh, the tall guy. Gee, wasn't Joseph being a stinker about that this morning? Sending you off into the garden alone with him like that. Especially with you so nervous around mortals.'

'Well, it went okay. Really. In fact, he's not so bad at all, for what he is. Have you scanned him?'

'Not closely.' Her attention was drifting back to the magazine.

'He's so . . . healthy. And perfect. He's a lot like one of us.'

'Head's the wrong shape.' Some article was deeply interesting her. I cranked back the slide and processed it for transmission.

'Do you remember what you told me about having recreational sex with mortals?'

'Hm?' she said, and then played it back and lifted her head to stare at me. 'Oops. No, I never said any such thing. Whatever it was you think I said. Listen, don't let Joseph pressure you into doing anything you really don't want to do. It's perfectly understandable if the idea of, uh, you know, makes you sick. I may have said something kind of dumb about acquired tastes, but if I did, it was only to show you how comfortable some of us can feel around mortals. Okay?'

'Well, okay, do you think you'd feel comfortable around a mortal like Nicholas Harpole?'

Her brow furrowed. 'I guess so. He looks clean.'

'He's *intelligent*. I never met a mortal with a real working brain before.'

'Big surprise, isn't it?' She focused in on the magazine. 'Well, congratulations. At the rate you're going, you'll have that AAE off your file in no time.'

'How did you know I had an AAE?' I was stung. 'Those things are supposed to be confidential!'

She just looked at me bleakly. 'Sorry,' she said. 'They're not. Another big surprise.'

'Boy!' I flung another slide into the credenza, so hard it beeped in protest. Nefer sighed.

'You work for the Company, Mendoza. This is what it's like.'

'I saw a unicorn today,' I told her maliciously.

'Sir Walter has a rhinoceros out there, huh?' She lost herself in the magazine again. 'Wow. They're releasing the complete series of Jason Barrymore films on Ring Holo next month.'

So who cared.

Chapter Twelve

I know nothing of your life, Master Harpole, do you know that?' I said coquettishly. It was difficult to be a coquette while trying to keep artichoke leaves out of one's mouth. We were busy wrestling a very determined taproot up out of the mud.

'Hm?' he said, and then 'Ha!' as the nasty thing sagged over, defeated in the grass. I bent to cut the parts I needed for processing.

'Your artichoke is not your phoenix among herbs,' panted Nicholas, wiping his hands.

'Pardon?'

'This is not a rare plant, you know,' he pointed out, switching to Latin.

'No, not rare, but very good for gross humors of the blood.' I sliced off spines. 'Or so my father says. Sir Walter is troubled with them, I am told.'

'And is your father troubled with them also?'

'Sometimes.' I squinted up at him. 'There, behold. I have told you more, and you have told me nothing. You have drawn volumes of information out of me. You'd make a good spy.' Coquettishness in Latin. I felt pretty proud of myself. He gave me a look.

'Why, Lady, for all I know some friar is hiding close by, writing down every word we say.'

'He'd be more likely to be spying on me than on you, I fear. But, since I am a woman and therefore given to curiosity, I must know all about you. Where were you born?'

'Hampstead.'

'Where were you educated?'

'Balliol.'

'What are you doing here?'

'Using my wits to earn my bread.'

'This rush of personal confidence is making me dizzy,' I told the artichoke. 'So you were at Balliol? At Oxford? And you didn't enter the Church?'

'No. I lack personal discipline. But a good friend recommended me to Sir Walter, and so I keep his accounts and dine at his table, and no man has cause to complain of me.' He folded his hands in a manner that suggested the story was at an end.

'Did you get all that, Fray Diego?' I called over the hedge. 'Well, you must excuse me. You know how we women are. Once we think something's hidden from us, we die to discover what it is.'

'Now you're quoting from our Chaucer,' he said. 'Aren't you?'

'*Wife of Bath*,' I admitted. 'But Aristotle too.'

'Yes.' He watched me, smiling. I folded the parts of the artichoke I needed in a clean napkin and considered the remaining mess. I wondered if I should leave it for the gardener to clean up. Nicholas said, 'You surely aren't saying you accept Aristotle's views on the female sex.'

'What, that we're evil? Really, señor, would you believe something like that about yourself simply because some old pagan said it? And a Greek too.'

'Our Lord had several female friends,' observed Nicholas. 'And women lived among His disciples. Without sin, we must assume.' My turn to give him a look.

'I suppose so,' I said. 'The issue is whether carnal intercourse is sinful. Do you imagine Jesus Himself was a virgin at the age of thirty-three?'

He gaped.

'Did you often say things like that in Spain?' he asked finally.

'No, of course not. It wasn't safe.'

'Nor is it any safer here, especially with your prince in our land. Please, think before you speak.'

'I do. Am I not safe from betrayal with you?'

He leaned closer and switched from Latin to Greek. 'And if you are, it is because we are alone in this place, and I see no danger in striving with you in the little intellectual contests you propose. But I would not speak so recklessly in front of anyone else, and neither must you.'

'Why? Would Master Ffrawney run off to tell the nearest bishop?'

He snorted. 'Without doubt. And then your father would have much to explain! The last thing anyone expected to see in England was a Spanish heretic.'

'Oh, well.' I got up from the grass and brushed off my skirt. 'And I was so hoping we might have a discussion of the nature of *agape*. When the term is defined as a "love-feast," do you suppose they mean —'

'Hush! Hush! Hush!' He scrambled to his feet and put his hand over my mouth. I looked at him over the edge of his hand. He looked away. 'I think I would like to have your father beaten,' he said finally. I pulled away.

'You'd have to catch him first,' I said.

'Yes, and I have a feeling that that would be difficult. He seems to be an able little twister in the nets of the law. By your leave. But he had no business bringing up a daughter so.'

'What do you mean? Should he have denied me an education?' I was actually insulted.

'By no means. But he ought to have taught you discretion as well as Greek and Aramaic, Lady, lest you come to harm.'

'Am I not discreet? Only with you would I say such rash things, because I know *you* would never do me harm,' I said, flirt, flirt, wishing I had a fan to flutter.

'And you are correct! I hope I know better than to meddle with the daughter of a man who administers purges.' He folded his arms and smiled.

'He's an able swordsman, I'll have you know,' I told him when I had stopped laughing.

'No doubt.'

'Renowned throughout Madrid, Valladolid, and the Alhambra.'

'In truth.'

'Deadly with a blade of Toledo steel.'

'Deadlier with a good dose of laxative. No, if ever I wronged you, I'd keep close to my chamberpot, lest calamity befall. You need not fear me. But in God's name, Lady, have a care what you say.'

I was in high spirits at my credenza that night, let me tell you; my fingers just flew over the keys. I synthesized four vials of antihypertensive in the time it took Nefer to repair her mantilla, which had met with an unfortunate accident in the trailing canopy of the bed. She was going crazy with boredom in England but not me, boy. I liked it here.

It happened that a remedy for Nefer's ennui arrived only the next morning, much to her surprise.

The day dawned dark, pouring black rain, so we were all gathered in the great hall watching Sir Walter eat his healthful, low-cholesterol breakfast. Joseph was watching him, anyway, and maybe Nefer; I was too busy making eye contact with Master Harpole to pay attention. But here came Francis Ffrawney, bowing and scraping, to announce:

'Sir Walter, there is a common sort of man at the gate saying he hath property of Doctor Ruy's and would speak to him thereof.' All eyes turned to Joseph.

'What sort of man?' Joseph inquired.

'A poor sort, sir, a very rascal in a leather hood, that swears great oaths and will not move from the gate without he be granted your ear. I must warn your worship, he may well be some heretic malcontent.'

'Why, that honest fellow!' Joseph leaped to his feet in feigned surprise. 'This should be that same innkeeper that brought my baggage ashore. He must have found the chest I so unwittingly left behind.'

This was news to me, but I piped up: 'Truly, Father, the men of England are as honest as they are tall.' More flirting and wished-for fan in Master Harpole's direction.

So Xenophon was admitted, all muddy and horsey, with a lot of stamping and swearing. He clumped up to Joseph and went down on one knee, holding out a plain wooden chest. It was not one we had brought from Spain.

'My good signior!' he said. 'You had scarce been gone an hour when our lad Wat, him that carries away the chamber-lye in the jordans, he comes a-running down the stairs. Quoth he, "That there Spanish grandee hath left a thing like a box in his room!" "That's a wonder to be sure," quoth I, and I went and looked, and to be sure you had left this. And since meseemeth this must be a very important casket, doubtless filled with what ye shall sore need in England' – wide take to be sure we got the point – 'I thought it were best to bring it straight here myself.'

'May God and the good Saint James bless thee for thy care,' effused Joseph. 'Let me give thee something for thy troubles.' He groped in his purse and handed out what looked like a doubloon but was actually a mint Theobromos patty in silver paper.

'Such munificence!' exclaimed Xenophon. 'I'm a-going to go out and buy me a cow with this, see if I don't.' He prostrated himself at Joseph's feet. 'I could kiss thy shoe of Cordovan leather, sir, that I could.'

'Away, worthy peasant.' Joseph waved at him. I was wondering how long they were going to carry on like this when Master Ffrawney sniffed:

'Will you not open the box, sir, and satisfy yourself that all your goods are safe within?'

There was an awkward pause. Joseph and Xenophon exchanged glances. Xenophon shrugged imperceptibly. 'An excellent thought,' conceded Joseph. Coding the unseen lock, he lifted the lid.

The chest contained things that appeared to be books but weren't, a couple of things that appeared to be surgeon's tools but weren't, and what appeared to be three jars of medicinal herbs. All these must have been the electronic tools and chemicals Joseph would need for his work on Sir Walter. Packed carefully apart from the rest was a little ornamented box with a couple of gold birds, or something, on the lid. Joseph held it up to the firelight, and his smiling face did not betray that he had no idea what the hell it was for.

But Nicholas leaned forward, frowning in astonishment. 'That is a model of the Ark of the Covenant of the Israelites!' he stated.

'Yes, of course,' Joseph agreed. 'It's a, uh, reliquary. Enshrined within is a fragment of the pelvis of Saint Mary Magdalene. I never travel without it.'

Nicholas sat back, his face a mask of disgust. Xenophon stepped forward and said: 'Pardon me, sir, but an angel appeareth to be loose.' He reached out and gave one of the lid ornaments a little twist.

Click.

– KZUS, continuing your round-the-clock coverage of the royal wedding. And it looks like the rain's letting up here, so we may be able to go down into the street in a minute or two and see if we can interview somebody. I've certainly got an impressive view of Winchester Cathedral from where I'm stationed. I can see the floral decorations that the town council put up and believe me, folks, they certainly had a lot of work last night in the rain. And, say, those flowers are just beautiful. What kind are they, Justinian?

Well, Decius, it says here those are pansies and heliotropes and of course the famous red-and-white Tudor roses. Folks, it's nine-hundred hours and counting on this day of the royal wedding. We'll be back to you on KZUS with the latest developments after this musical interlude. The strains of a basse-dance filled the room.

And Sir Walter went right on spooning down his oat porridge, and Nicholas still sat with his arms folded, staring sullenly into the fire. Master Ffrawney was still gazing on the reliquary with a suitable expression of reverent awe. They couldn't hear a thing, of course. It was being broadcast in a frequency out of mortal range.

'I desire to offer fervent prayers of thanksgiving.' Nefer got up and took the radio out of Joseph's hands. 'Give me leave, señor, to commune with the blessed saints for a while.'

It would have been dangerous to get in her way. He bowed her out of the room, and she swept up the stairs, music trailing after her. Joseph pulled at his beard thoughtfully. He extended a hand to Xenophon.

'I shall see thee to thy horse, good fellow. By your leave, Sir Walter?'

Sir Walter waved his spoon at them in a dismissive way. They exited together. I got up and went to sit beside Nicholas. We looked at each other: he was still fuming. Yet he moved his thigh just a little closer to mine on the settle.

'What a joyous occasion this is!' exclaimed Master

Ffrawney, when he realized that nobody else was going to make conversation. 'Now good fortune and the blessing of the saint will surely attend the faithful in this house!'

'Even so.' Sir Walter did not look up from his porringer.

'Amen!' Master Ffrawney looked pointedly at Nicholas. Nicholas did not move, but his eyes swiveled to look at Master Ffrawney.

'Now I wonder,' Nicholas drawled, 'what miraculous cures we shall owe to the holy pelvis of the Magdalene?'

Oh, what a smell of testosterone. Bright red and flashing, the readout appeared in midair, showing me the changing blood chemistry of all three men, with figures on the statistical probability of violence erupting. My body was already moving of its own accord, but as I got up to leave, I touched Nicholas's shoulder.

'Master Harpole,' I quavered. 'There is a thing I saw from the window, that I would know more of. Will it please you to come see it with me?'

With a last contemptuous stare at Master Ffrawney, Nicholas got to his feet and followed me out of the room. I led the way to a gallery on the second floor, well away from the monkey smell, and looked out a window at the rainy landscape. I found a gilded cupola to point at.

'There! What is that, please?' I asked. He looked briefly.

'That is the roof of the aviary,' he said.

'Oh. We went there, didn't we? How different it all looks from up here.'

He didn't say anything. I looked down at the floor. 'I would not have had you come to blows with Master Ffrawney,' I explained.

'Small matter if we had.' He smiled bitterly. 'Belike I'd have cracked his hypocrite's crown for him.'

'Wrath is a sin, is it not? Wherefore be glad you have not sinned.'

He nodded, calming down a little, watching the storm.

'I am sorry about the box,' I said at last.

'What, the Ark of the Covenant?' He lounged against the wall, turning to face me. 'Sweet Jesu, Lady, what a piece of arrant popery! And your father a learned man too. Truly the more I know of him, the less I know what manner of thing he is.'

'Master Harpole, there are no religious relics in that box.'

'No!' He flung up his hands in mock amazement.

'But my father did not feel himself amongst folk he could trust, and he had to say something. The box is —' I thought fast. 'The box is connected with his studies. His more arcane studies.'

Nicholas gave a slow incredulous grin. 'What? A wizard?' Damn it, didn't *anybody* believe in witchcraft anymore?

'Rather, I should say —' I looked up and down the corridor. I switched to Greek. 'My father has made some study of what you might call alchemy. Also mathematics and the properties of physical bodies.'

'Ah.' Suddenly Nicholas was interested. 'You mean he is an hermetic philosopher? He has studied Vitruvius?' What was I getting myself into? I did a fast access and discovered that he was talking about early, early science and technology, which only secret societies and clandestine brotherhoods were concerned with right now.

'Yes,' I said cautiously.

'Then I understand you.' His face brightened with speculation. 'Why, all the several parts of your story now become a whole. His Greek physick, his sufferings at the hands of the Inquisition – and it's evident he hath been at the Emperor's court – and this careful model of the Ark of the —' His mouth dropped open. He closed it.

'Your father is a Jew,' he said quietly.

I remember thinking calmly, 'How silly,' just before the shock wave hit. I saw the men and the glowing coals in the little room. I saw the bullying face of the priest. I saw, I saw, *I saw* —

Babbling frantic denials, I began tearing at my sleeve, I guess to show the blue veins that would prove I wasn't a *chueta*. Wouldn't you think a sophisticated creature like me would be able to handle a few bad memories? Except that this was the central trauma that Dr. Zeus had used to fix my indoctrination, to remind me always why I worked for them. They'd never meant to cure me of it. They'd tucked it deep down inside, the battery that powered my machine heart.

'Look, look —' With a great ripping of brocade my bare

arm emerged. Nicholas seized it and held me still. His face was horrified. 'Look!' I sobbed.

'Rose!'

'Look . . .' A yellow light stopped flashing, and a noise died away. Far off, Joseph was running back toward the house in a panic. He saw us at the window. He stopped. He watched us.

Nicholas had put both arms around me and embraced me, lifting me clear off the floor. He was so warm, and the gallery was freezing cold. I stopped shaking. Systems normalizing. 'Your father was not alone in prison,' he guessed in a whisper, setting me down carefully. 'They had you, also, and —' Something in my face must have told him to stop there. But I had control of myself now. Yes. I could speak.

'Have you any idea,' I enunciated, 'what such a base and unfounded accusation means in Spain?'

He nodded slowly, not taking his eyes from my face.

'You could be as pure of blood as the Emperor himself, but if you were ever even so much as accused,' I began to gasp again, '*just accused* —'

There were footsteps approaching the bottom of the stairs. Nicholas glanced down and drew me away with him, swiftly up the corridor to a smaller stair. It ascended steep as a ladder. We climbed it in haste, I hitching up my skirts so I wouldn't trip.

Through a little cut-corner door at the top was his room. It was Spartan and small, its slanting ceiling high and sharply angled.

The bed had been extended for his great length by having a chest put at the foot of it. There were books piled and tumbled on every flat surface. There was a chair by the window. There was a candle, upright amid drips of cold tallow from hours of reading.

He led me to the bed and sat me down on it, then wrapped my torn sleeve back about my arm. He put his blanket over my shoulders for good measure, then looked around his room in a helpless way. 'Wait,' he said at last. 'I'll come anon.'

He hastened down the stairs again. Clunk, clunk, clunk, I heard his footsteps descending.

I sat there on his bed. I could pick him up descending

through the house in great agitation, with bursts of interference when someone else spoke to him. Nefer's radio was
broadcasting a pavane now; nothing much must be happening
with the royal wedding. Joseph had moved about thirty meters
from his previous position and was reading me.

Mendoza?

Go to hell.

No, seriously. Are you —

I'm just embarrassed. Horribly embarrassed. Now get out.

He politely withdrew. How could I face Nicholas again?

It was calming to try to read his books' titles, all scattered
as they were. Let's see, this one was the *Enchiridion Militis
Christiani*. Predictable. *De Servo Arbitrario*, also predictable.
The Wicked Mammon, this one was supposed to be out of
print, wonder how he'd got a copy? *The Prologue to the
Romans*, in English. *A Preservative against the Poison of
Pelagius*, wow. I had begun to cry, little snively tears. I
wiped them away angrily.

Clunk clunk clunk, there was Nicholas shouldering through
the doorway. He was carrying a pint of something that
steamed, and a ball of thread with a needle stuck in it.

'I must go,' I said, mustering all the Hispanic dignity I
had available. 'This is not seemly, señor.'

'Your sleeve must be mended first, lest it be remarked upon,'
he said. 'And I think you will not want your duenna to do it,
involved as she is in her devotions.'

'She is a good woman and greatly stupid,' I covered. 'She
truly believes that thing is a holy relic, and my father hath
not seen fit to enlighten her. Nor doth she know of his private
studies. I trust, sir, you will not tell her.'

'Not I.' He sat down beside me and put the pint pot in
my hand. 'Now, drink that off straight. It will calm thee.'
Awkwardly he threaded the needle.

'What is this?' I peered into the drink.

'Burnt sack and eggs.'

Oh, no. But scanning revealed no pathogens, and it smelled
all right, so I tasted it cautiously. Not so bad; something like
egg nog. I sipped at it and watched him mend my sleeve with
big clumsy stitches.

'Now, God He knows I am no tailor, Rose, but this will

hold thee until thou canst better mend it thyself. Thou hast learned to use a needle?' he asked dryly.

'Yes.'

'It is well. I am glad that thou, knowing so much Greek, hast a plain skill or two.'

'You are too kind,' I said, cold.

'Kindness is the duty of any Christian, Lady, is it not so?' He switched to Greek. 'Hear me. What I have been told today, I will tell to no one. But, having said this, I must caution you again to hide your past. Better you had let me think your father a papist knave than to tell me such secrets. I believe you are innocent and pity your sufferings, yet there are those who would gladly see you burn even here in England. Though, God willing, this shall not become so fearful a place as Spain.'

'Spain.' I laughed and took a gulp of my drink. 'I'll tell you what the trouble with Spain is, señor. We *read* our Scripture. We discovered therein, long before the rest of you, that this God we all serve is cruel and irrational. We are made in His image, are we not? In Spain, we derive grim pleasure from dragging ourselves across the coals of His will.'

'No!' He took my hand. 'Never believe such a thing! You must understand that God is Love.'

'Must I?' I had another drink. 'That same God who sent bears to kill the little children that mocked His prophet's baldness? That same God that slaughtered His own worshipers for trying to prevent the defilement of His carrying box? Love, you said?'

Wind buffeted the eaves, and a fresh torrent of rain streamed down the window. We sat looking at it.

Nicholas's voice was quiet. 'This is truly the Devil's work: not women rolling on the floor and spitting toads, but this, the despair that you wake and sleep with.'

I shrugged.

'*How shall I save you?*' But there, look, he actually had tears in his eyes. I felt a sudden rush of affection and wished I could console him. I wished I could tell him the truth. He didn't have to worry: I was saved, I was one of the lucky few who really would inherit the World to Come, in that wonderful faraway future where every toilet shall flush

and there are cinema palaces on the moon. I was immortal,
enlightened, and perfect, wasn't I? But not Jewish. No, no,
absolutely not, never, not me.

'Don't fear for me,' I told him. 'If your God is truly what
you say He is, He must forgive me. I came alive out of the
Inquisition's hand; have I not spent my time in Hell?'

'I cannot judge you, certainly,' he replied, folding his arms.
'I have never suffered as you have. I hope my soul should fare
no worse, if God so chose to test me. And who can see what
is to come?'

How cold it was, the storm beating at the window.

Nicholas went down the stairs first to make sure that no one
would see me leaving his room, beckoning me down when
he saw the coast was clear. He bowed to me, I curtseyed to
him, and we parted.

When I entered our room, Nefer was staring intently at the
radio, which was broadcasting liturgical music. 'You missed
it,' she told me. 'They just got married.'

'Who?'

'Philip and Mary.'

'Some duenna you are.' I reached around to unlace my
bodice.

'Huh?'

'Here I've been alone with a man in his room, and you
didn't even notice,' I giggled, just a bit shrilly. 'Help me out
of this, will you? My sleeve got torn and I —'

'Torn?' She sat upright. 'Did you — I thought I heard —'

'Boy, who writes your dialogue?' My Shrill went up a notch
toward Hysterical. 'Yes! See? Mad with passion, he rent my
sleeve. Turns out he's an elbow man.'

'Oh, shut up.' She came and helped me with the laces.
'Here I am, bored out of my mind for three days, and the
minute I have something interesting to listen to . . .'

'Knock, knock,' said a voice outside our door. 'Whisk
those frilly underthings out of sight, girls, I'm coming in.'

Enter Joseph, smiling and shaking rain out of the crown
of his hat.

'Quite a little tempest we had there.' He looked me in the
eye. The sound of the choir stopped, and a voice announced,

That was the Agnus Dei as performed by the choir of Winchester Cathedral. Things look pretty quiet down there by the altar right now; Their Majesties have received the Sacrament and appear to be praying. You'll recall there was quite a stir earlier when the prince's new titles were announced. Supposedly they're a wedding gift from the Emperor, though it's popularly speculated that they are in fact a bribe to get the prince to go through with the wedding.

'Yes, sir, quite a little electrical disturbance,' continued Joseph. Nefer yanked off my bodice and handed it to me. I clutched it to myself in dismay.

'I'm *trying* to listen to the broadcast!' she hissed at him. He raised his eyebrows at her and opened the door to his room.

'Mendoza?' He gestured. I followed him in, hastily shrugging back into the bodice.

'Have a seat. Have a glass of muscadel. On second thought, don't have a glass of muscadel; you've been drinking burnt sack. *I'll* have the glass of muscadel, and you can tell me why you're metabolizing burnt sack in a torn bodice.' He went to a sideboard and poured from a decanter.

'Where'd you get the muscadel?' I asked very calmly, sitting down and folding my hands. Yes, I was completely in control.

'Master Ffrawney found it. He's been bringing me all kinds of useful stuff to prove he's a good Catholic. Wine. Sweetmeats. Gossip. On the subject of gossip, you want to tell Papa all about it?' He settled across from me, tasted his wine, and set it down.

'You're really good in this role, aren't you?' I said, not without admiration. 'You've really become the Spanish Intriguer. But what possible use could you have for local gossip in a place like this?'

'Oh, you'd be surprised.' He stroked his beard. 'Lots of strange stuff goes on, and it's all interconnected, and you never know when you'll discover something that may be useful later. Works for Miss Marple every time. Mostly, though, I get into the habit of being nosy about everything because the character I'm playing is supposed to be nosy. If I'm true to all Doctor Ruy's mannerisms, I *believe* in him, and all the

mortals I encounter believe in him too. Characterization is
very important in the field. I don't think you've exactly got
a handle on that, yet.'

'I have too,' I said hotly. 'I think I'm portraying a late
medieval Spanish adolescent very well.'

'No. You *are* a late medieval Spanish adolescent. It's not
a role for you, not yet. You need to develop that little bit
of emotional distance between yourself and the person you
want mortals to see. That person is your mask; that person is
the one who reacts to the things you encounter. You, yourself,
don't get emotionally involved; you let your character do all
the reacting so that you, personally, never lose control. As
so lamentably happened just now.'

I fumed. He had another sip of wine.

'So. Just what happened up there in the gallery with Master
Harpole?'

'It was your stupid explanation of the radio. Why'd you
have to say it had a holy relic in it? You know how Protestants
feel about stuff like that! So I was explaining how it was really
something connected with your scientific research and, you
know what, Mr. Smart Guy? He leaped to the conclusion
that you're a secret J-J-Jew.'

Silence, but for some distant bishop droning out a blessing
on Philip and Mary.

'Tsk, tsk, tsk,' said Joseph at last. 'This was obviously where
little Mendoza got excited. Dear me. And what a clever guy
this Harpole is, isn't he? Awfully good at noticing all kinds
of little unusual things about people and keeping them on
file in his head. So he's built a theory around us, has he? He
added two and two and came up with five, but nobody else
in the house was aware there was anything to count. This is
just the sort of mortal that puts a mission in jeopardy. What
can we do about Master Harpole, Mendoza?'

'I don't know!' I snarled. 'Is the Spanish Intriguer going
to put poison in his ale?'

'Nothing so crude. Speaking of drinks, who gave you the
burnt sack?'

'*He* got it for me,' I muttered. 'And he mended my
sleeve.'

'All right, this is a good sign. And did he recoil in horror at your supposed ethnic origin? No, he obviously didn't. What does this tell us, Mendoza? Think.'

'He's brilliant and tolerant and humane and ahead of his time. He's like one of us.'

'Well, now we know how you feel about him. And he feels —?'

'He's interested in me,' I guessed. 'Sympathetic.'

'Bingo. Vulnerability can be very appealing. So, what do we do about Master Harpole, Mendoza? I've been saying all along, in my jolly avuncular way with just a hint of the pander, that you two would make the cutest couple.'

'You have got to be crazy! I just embarrassed myself to death in front of that man.'

'Oh. I see. All right. Forget I ever mentioned it. Say, I've always meant to ask you: Did you ever remember what your mortal name was?'

'What?' I started.

'Your name, when you were a mortal. At Santiago? We couldn't figure out if you were so little you didn't really know, or if you knew your name but were afraid to tell us.'

'I really didn't know.' Sweat broke out on my forehead.

Joseph sipped his wine.

'Remembering something?' he inquired.

'No!'

'Well. I guess we needn't worry too much about Master Harpole. Now that I know I'm supposed to be a Rosicrucian alchemist-kabbalist, I'll drop a few corroborating remarks here and there. Doubtless that will satisfy his curiosity. Okay? And I'm sure things will work themselves out.'

I stayed in my room the next four days all the same. It rained steadily, so I had an excuse, but meals were awkward. Nefer brought me bread and cheese a couple of times; I could hear her downstairs, graciously informing them that Doña Rosa was indisposed, with that monolithic dignity she could summon at will. She had a good grasp of cover identity. Joseph was right: I had to work at my character more.

But I sat on my bed and watched the rain falling forever, and I entered requisition codes at my credenza, and I ignored Joan when she came in to clean, and I listened to the radio. There was steady music all day, some of it live. There was an evening news broadcast, and a great talk show in the afternoon: one of the station staff had a mortal cover identity as a lawyer, and he'd invite his clients to talk about their lives and problems in a room rigged with microphones. Occasionally the results were hilarious. Sometimes, lying awake at night, I heard strange little electronic noises coming from Sir Walter's room – Joseph in there with his pocketful of cryptotools, performing some secret rearrangement of Sir Walter's insides.

I listened for Nicholas, too. His long stride came sometimes down the hall and paused outside our door before moving slowly on. He sat up each evening late, before his bed creaked with the weight of his length settling on it. He read a lot. I wondered what he was reading now.

The fifth morning dawned bright and clear. No help for it: this would be a great day for collecting rare specimens of variegated shepherd's purse or green fumitory. I crept down the stairs behind Nefer, trying to look as inconspicuous as possible, and so naturally everyone was assembled in the great hall and all heads turned to stare at me as I entered.

'Why, well met, Lady Rose!' Sir Walter rose and bowed. 'Are you with us again? I trust our English air hath not given you the tisick?'

'No, I thank you, sir. I am recovered now,' I murmured.

'Excellent well! You shall dine on oranges in the Spanish fashion.'

Oh, God, there was a bowl of ten oranges set at my place at table. I smiled feebly.

'Master Harpole himself hath brought them in this morning. I thought we should never get more than three together ripe at one time, but it seems the weather likes them well,' Sir Walter babbled on. I glanced up at Nicholas. I glanced away.

Hey, Nefer transmitted sternly. *These people are trying to be kind to you. Behave yourself.*

Taking your role as duenna a little seriously, aren't you? I shot back. But she was right. 'Truly I am unworthy of such care from so gracious a host, Sir Walter, but I pray you accept my wholly inadequate thanks for this abundance of orangery.' I curtseyed.

So with my bodice dagger I peeled one and set to, and

as the others sat there with eggs and oatmeal, I ate oranges until the corners of my mouth stung. Nicholas kept looking at me, but I avoided his gaze.

Just as the meal was concluding, Master Ffrawney hurried into the room.

'Sir Walter, there is a great party come on horseback, express to see the garden. John hath collected their pence, and they wait but for a guide – *thy* duty, man,' he nodded peremptorily at Nicholas, who stood up and glowered at him. 'And they have been at Penshurst Place and seem to be persons of gentle birth and consequence, and – *wilt* thou not go, Nicholas? – and one gentleman, being a Master Darrell of Colehill, particularly wisheth to speak to you, sir, wherefore I judged it best to advise you directly.'

'Thou didst well.' Sir Walter rose in excitement, his mustache points quivering. He practically ran for the door, then halted, conscious of the fact that he had Spaniards sitting in his dining room. 'Er, Doctor Ruy, for appearances' sake —'

'Say not a word, my dearest friend.' Joseph rose majestically. 'You shall see that Spanish discretion is as great as Spanish love of fruit. Doña Marguerita? Daughter? Let us retire. I feel an urgent need to pray.'

'A thousand thanks,' breathed Sir Walter, and hastened away with Nicholas stalking after him. As they departed, something strange drew my eye.

Sir Walter was taller.

High heels on his shoes? No. No, he actually was taller, coming farther up to Nicholas's shoulder than he had, and his movements were nimbler. I watched their retreating backs with some wonder. Joseph's clandestine retooling was beginning to show. How about that?

'Yes, a day of retreat and meditation will serve me well.' Joseph selected an orange from the few still in the bowl. 'Master Ffrawney.' He inclined in his direction and swept from the room. Nefer rose and hurried ahead of him, doubtless hoping to catch the morning news program. I got up to follow them, but Master Ffrawney stepped before me hesitantly and bowed low.

'Good Lady Rose,' he said. 'A word in your ear, with my

most profound apologies for making such familiarity, but I must speak.'

I felt the bridge of my nose arch just a little higher. 'What meanest thou, good man?' I said with condescending grace.

'By your leave, Lady, it is Sir Walter's man Nicholas. In him Sir Walter is much abused, I tell you, Lady, though he harbors him out of kindness. The knave is a pernicious heretic and an obdurate Gospel reader.'

'Something of this I had heard before,' I informed him solemnly, 'and I pray hourly for his poor soul. But thou needst not concern thyself, señor. We are well aware that many in England are subject to such vice.'

'Yea, but it is no common viciousness that is in this man, Lady.' Master Ffrawney looked over his shoulder uneasily. I stepped closer to him, suddenly interested in his story. Having satisfied himself that Nicholas was not lurking nearby, Master Ffrawney stuck out his neck and spoke just above a whisper.

'You must know, Lady, that of late there hath been much apostasy and such like wickedness practiced here in Kent. Not only the new heresies of the German distemperature, but certain ancient ones too.' He dropped his voice still lower. 'More I may not tell a virtuous maid, but there was a community of such lewd persons in these parts, young persons given to idleness and heresy, and such a one, Lady,' he looked around again, 'was *Nicholas Harpole!*'

Wow! 'I am shocked and horrified,' I said.

'Yea, Lady, you shall find it is so, and though he came near to being hanged for his brawling and lasciviousness, he had friends at the University who excused and huddled it up, and set him here like a viper to be nourished at Sir Walter's bosom.' He leaned back with pursed lips, nodding.

I was ready to die with laughter there on the spot, but I clutched my rosary and said, in most grave tones: 'Now by Saint Mary and Saint James, can this be true? Was he verily given to the lusts of the flesh? Thou must understand that I am only an innocent and hath been among the blessed sisters all my days, and know nothing of the twisted sexual practices of Anabaptists.'

Master Ffrawney drew back at the very word, and we both made the sign of the Cross.

'The more reason, gentle Lady, that I must warn you, for you go into the garden alone with this man and there is rumor (saving your grace) you were seen abovestairs with him, though no honest man believes it. But pray, beware this Harpole!'

How very, very amusing. 'Fear not, good man, I will heed thy timely warning. Who would have thought he was one of those vile freewillers?'

'Aye, forsooth! I could tell you such things; but you see the sort of creature this Harpole is, do you not? You will not be deceived by his smooth speech or his politic looks. He is a very Satan in persuasion, I say.'

'I go forth fortified by thy counsel,' I promised him. 'And now, I join my dear father in prayer. Buenos dias, señor.'

I skipped up the stairs and fell through our doorway giggling. Nef was sitting hunched up on our bed with a strained expression. The radio was on, as usual.

'You will never, never guess what I just found out!' I whooped.

'Mendoza, this is an interview with a mortal who raises Red Alderney cows, and if you talk through it, I'll make your life miserable for weeks.'

'Well, pardon me.' I started to flounce out of the room, but paused. Somehow I didn't feel like telling Joseph. I wandered over to the window instead and looked out at the bright day.

All in the garden green, there were the mortals moving. The top of Nicholas's biretta appeared above a hedge and traveled slowly along it until he emerged, so tall in his black robe that the visitors scurrying after him looked like dolls. Two little ladies in claret-colored velvet, four little gentlemen in their flat caps with swirling feathers. One of the little gentlemen was in heated conversation with Sir Walter. Nicholas pointed at a particularly fine old elm tree and said something about it, and everyone stared at it intently, except Sir Walter and the fourth little gentleman. I looked down on them like a goddess leaning out from Olympus.

What a snotty child she was, the little botanist Mendoza.

Also gleeful, gratified, newly self-confident, and intrigued. She'd known there was more to Nicholas than met the eye. A wimpy Bible apologist is one thing, but a dark secret anarchist with a tortured soul, participating in religious orgies – well!

As I observed the mortals with a cool and distant smile, Nicholas suddenly lifted his head and stared straight at me. I caught my breath and backed away from the window, into the middle of the room.

Nay, good sir, they's good milkers, my cows be. My Silver, now she do give place to none in filling of the can. Why, I could tell — The transmission dissolved in a burst of static as my hardware disturbed the frequency. Nefer jumped like she'd been shot and glared at me.

'Sit down, dammit!'

Meekly I sat at the credenza and took out my sample analysis reports to work on. At least *they* did not give me unaccountable sensations in the pelvic region.

Chapter Thirteen

I t was the middle of August and the first warm day since we arrived. Little rare plants were consenting to bloom, which meant I had much to do.

So I found myself in the garden again, threading my way through the green maze with Master Harpole and wondering what to say besides: 'Pray, where do the best specimens of *Cochlearia officinalis* grow?'

I think he must have felt a certain shyness also, for he finally ventured to remark:

'The season grows hot at last, methinks.'

It must have been all of twenty-one degrees Celsius outside.

'I think you have but one season in your England,' I said. 'Nothing but rainy spring all year round. Your King Arthur poet saith of the Isle of Avalon that it is a summer country, but I find it not so.'

Nicholas smiled absently. 'You misunderstand, lady. This same Isle of Avalon is not England but some country to the west, beyond the sea.'

'Ireland?'

'Not so, neither; for I understand the wild men there themselves believe in a western island where the flowers never fade.'

'Think you they mean the New World?'

He shook his head. 'Ships have been to the New World,' he said in Latin. 'That is an earthly place too, like Ireland, except that it is bigger and its savages wear feathers, not wool.' Latin had become our favored language for straightforward conversation, because one didn't have to keep coming up with flowers of speech.

'What a disappointment. Surely, this Blessed Isle, it must be somewhere,' I maintained. 'Perhaps it lies to the west of the New World?'

Nicholas looked at me sideways. 'It's a poetic device,' he informed me. 'A fantasy, a metaphor for the heart's desire that can never be found here on Earth.'

'You think there is no place on Earth where flowers always bloom and it is always warm?' I found a nice little example of rupturewort and bent to examine it.

'Certainly you may find such a place, if you go to the equator. The Blessed Isle of the poet is a land without human grief or sin.'

'Ah, well, that is a fantasy, certainly.' I took a quick holo shot.

'Let us hope not.' His voice was quiet.

I snipped a few sprigs and put them away in my basket. 'But I remember now. You believe men will defeat human nature and become perfect here on Earth. Tell me, how do you hope to accomplish that? What will you do about old age? Or death?'

I was smug, because I thought I had the answers myself. But he sat down on the grass beside me, put his fingertips together, and said, quite seriously:

'It's obvious. If men no longer sin, there will be no old age or death.'

'What?' I stared, laying down my trowel.

'Have you read a book by Miles Coverdale on the old faith? Just a moment.' He fished a dog-eared quarto from an inner pocket and thumbed through it. 'He says – this is in reference to the Fall of Adam and Eve – he says, to paraphrase the English, that the Lord God made man with both an immortal soul *and* an immortal body, and that when Adam sinned, his flesh became mortal and only his soul remained everlasting. Here, he says it. Now, since we know that enough sin can kill even the everlasting soul, would it not therefore follow that *freedom* from sin might preserve even the earthly body so it endures forever? Read this page, here.'

But I stared unseeing at the black-letter text. He had it right again! Men could defeat death, just as he believed, though technology, not grace, would be the weapon.

Though, come to think of it, we had done away with sin too, hadn't we? And not only by abandoning the concept: we eternal ones worked tirelessly for the good of man. His hideous wars, his politics, his greed and ignorance and wastefulness were abhorrent to us. We were perfect. Well, no, not *perfect*, exactly, but . . . Then again, define perfect.

'Nor is this idea without precedence in Scripture.' Nicholas tucked the book away. 'For example, the prophet Elijah was taken into Heaven in his mortal flesh, alive.'

But I too had been taken to Heaven in a chariot of fire. What a depressing thought, somehow. Nothing to do with a soul or a spirit: a mechanical conjuring trick, a deus ex machina. And so what was I? The machine's child?

It's frightening, that moment when the ground first washes out from under your feet.

I wasn't even a human being. And this warm mortal man, with his broken nose and unshaven chin, speaking so confidently of such crazy ideas, seemed to stand in a lamplit room. I stood without in freezing darkness, by a sealed window. But I touched his hand and he took mine without even noticing. He folded it between his hands and kept on talking.

'The end of sin, therefore, is the end of death.'

'Is there no way out of all this sin?' I cried in agony. Must I be trapped in this conversation my whole life?

'None for me. I have sinned, and I will surely die; but I have been closer to the true faith than my father was, and the child born tomorrow shall come closer yet than I. So long as each generation works tirelessly for the perfection of the soul, His Kingdom cannot fail to come on Earth.'

Shut up, shut up, I thought. It was my own creed he was outlining, and it terrified me. There *was* no hope for him, he *would* surely die, but he didn't matter beside the greater good. I didn't want to think of my eternal labor through generations of men yet unborn, when Nicholas would be so much forgotten dust. I wanted to breathe in the scent of his mortal body and listen to the rhythms of his voice, without understanding.

'What madness this is, this idea,' I said. 'Living forever on Earth. Where will we all go, tell me, if no one ever dies? Next you'll be telling me that men will travel to the moon and stars.' If he started to prophesy about space travel, I really was going to scream. But he only shrugged and smiled.

'As easily as traveling to the Isle of Avalon,' he said. 'For men must be without sin before they can do either.'

Well, he was wrong about *that*, at least. 'Enough of this talk of sin, in God's name,' I begged him. 'We are here, now, in this beautiful place. Isn't this enough? This garden, and the sun, and you and I here, and the poor little unicorn?'

'But the sun will set tonight, Rosa,' he said. 'And our lives will be over in a moment. And we know the truth, you and I, about that unicorn. What will sustain us but working for the eternal realm?'

Eternal work. My God, couldn't the man talk about anything else? What business did he have being so holy, with that big body of his so well made? With a sob of exasperation I caught hold of him, rock-steady as he was, and kissed him to make him quiet.

His first reaction was to kiss back. He did it very well, he took the initiative at once, and his hands set to work busily doing all the right things. He kissed like an angel of God. It figured.

He lifted his mouth, though, before even one lace had come unfastened, and set me at arm's length. 'We must not,' he said.

I looked at him, speechless. He could not snatch it away, whatever this was. I had stopped shaking and begun to grow warm inside, warm right through, even to that secret cupboard full of shattered glass and broken dishes. Yet it wouldn't do, would it, for Master Ffrawney or poor Sir Walter or even unexpected penny-paying tourists to come upon us sprawling in the long grass? Nicholas must have learned to dread scandal, if what was said of him was true. I looked down sullenly and said, 'So love is a sin too.'

'No!' He caught up my hand. 'Before God, I tell you, flesh is innocent enough. But you are yet young and I . . .' I looked longingly at his big fine hands. He drew them back. 'Would to God I had never sinned,' he said.

We went on through the garden then, as we were supposed to do, and through all that long day I filled my basket with rarities, each priceless sacrifice saving its kind from extinction. The finest work in the world, as per my contract.

He didn't look happy either.

*   *   *

I bid Nicholas adieu at the top of the stairs that evening, and went into my room and worked at my credenza, like the good little operative I was supposed to be. I worked until late hours without a break, though Nefer brought me a plate of some kind of supper. I made immortal seven different varieties of cinquefoil, root, leaf and blossom, for the benefit of the unborn generations who would thank me someday.

Wouldn't they? Wouldn't they appreciate the miraculous survival of seven rare subspecies of a common wildflower? Surely in the glorious future we were all headed for, such things would matter to everyone.

I was only a little distracted by Nefer pacing the floor, though I thought it very unusual for her to be disturbed about anything. Joseph came in to retire, cheery and relaxed, chuckling at some private joke. It must be nice, to find life so funny.

At eleven o'clock Nef came and tapped me on the shoulder.

'Lights out,' she said flatly. I shut off the ultravey, and we were left in the wobbling candlelight to undo each other's back lacing.

'What's wrong with you?' I inquired.

'I'm doing nothing here,' she sighed.

'Oh. Yes, I'd noticed that.' I pulled her lacing free at the bottom, handed it to her, and turned my own back. Her fingers dug at the knots she'd tied that morning.

'It's not fair. There's so much work I could be doing. I hate these dead shifts, where you get stationed in the middle of nowhere for six months at a time with no assignment. At least in Spain there were cattle. I haven't seen anything but two oxen and three horses since I got here. Just wait, they'll pull this on you sometime.'

'I don't see how. Domestic animals may be scarce in some places, but plants grow everywhere,' I pointed out.

'Ha!' She jerked out a lace. 'Ever been in the Sahara? Ever seen pictures of New York Terminus 2100? Or Luna? Not even a cactus. Wait'll you do a ten-month layover in metropolitan Bikkung.'

Nonsense. She was exaggerating, surely. Though I recalled

holos of urban canyons of the time to come, monoliths of millions of tiny windows, and now that I thought about it, I couldn't recall seeing a blade of grass anywhere there. But if that's what the future held —

'Nef,' I said, 'did you ever have second thoughts?'

'About what?' She stepped out of her skirts, and her hoops fell to the floor with a gentle whoosh. The candle flame danced.

'Just . . . everything.'

'You mean Doctor Zeus?' She stared at me as if I were crazy.

'Well, no,' I lied.

'I mean, yes, I'm fed up at the moment, and some of my assignments have been in some awful places, but the job is, well, the job, isn't it? How could anybody have second thoughts? I mean, who'd rather be *dead?*'

'Yeah, right,' I said.

The candle was out, and the house was quiet. And all the talk, all the hours of good work were done. I was alone in the dark, sweating sick with the terror of eternal years.

Nicholas Harpole was sitting in his room, reading. He shone like his own candle through the walls. I could hear his breathing. He was aroused. That was what it was, the change in his scent. He closed the book. *Snap*. He put out his candle. *Ssst*. He rustled out of his clothes and into his creaking bed.

As he was poking his feet down into the bed to get them warm, my feet were touching the icy floor. No one made a move to stop me. I drifted from the room and up the long dark corridor, up through the house, with shades pressing close around me on all sides. I didn't run. I found my way to the top of the house, and I opened up the door of that high narrow room where he lay.

He sat up in his shirt, staring at me. I stood there in my nightgown. Oh, the floor was cold. What could I possibly say to him?

'I'm lost,' I said. Ha ha; but it was true.

'Think, Lady,' Nicholas whispered. 'Consider your honor. Consider what you do.' But he was already moving over and making room for me beside him, folding back the sheet with those superb hands.

'It is very frightening, being lost.' I came closer. 'Also I am cold, señor.'

'You would be warm in bed,' he conceded.

'Can you remedy my being lost, too?' I sat down on the edge. He put out his arm in the darkness and folded me to him.

'Why, Lady, I have found you. How then are you lost?'

He swept me in close, jumping a little at the touch of my icy toes on his shins, and leaned down for a kiss. Oh God he was warm, and his mouth tasted good, and his bed smelled of books and maleness and late nights. He was bare under his shirt, as I was bare under my shift.

'Well met!' He came up from the kiss laughing. 'Hadst thou not come here, I swear I'd have lived thy constant friend in chastity, but my poor Friar John would scarce have left me alone.'

'Friar John?' I was incredulous.

'Why, to be sure. The upright monk with his hood, who ever entreats me to seek out holy places.' We were both giggling now. 'Who would ever live in contemplation in some close dark cell, who, um, weeps great tears of remorse at my sins ... Who ... who ... oh, the devil with the metaphor.' We kissed greedily; but my fear had not gone yet.

'Everything I was ever told was a lie.' I clung to him. 'And I have gone too far on a road with no turning, but there must be a way back. There must. I can't take that road, though it lead to Paradise.' Not many men would have taken thought for my spiritual state just then, but Nicholas lifted his head and said seriously:

'Sweet love, we shall go to Paradise. Here, now, in this idle pleasant way with our flesh; but also through grace. I will make you love God again.'

'You're after my *soul*,' I murmured, looking up at him. This was more wickedly exciting even than our nakedness. I could tell it was working that way with him, too: his nostrils flared, and he lowered himself to kiss me, but slow this time, and we settled down for serious work. I wonder if the careful reader has figured out what was bound to happen next. If you have, are you laughing? Are you really?

Our bodies are designed as indestructible sanctuaries. We are trained to flee every assault on their integrity; and if we cannot flee, then to fight. It's hardwired, we can't help it.

But even now I grit my teeth. He leaned back on his elbow to look at me, gingerly touching his cheek where I'd hit him. I had to turn away and cry.

'Thou art of two minds, it seems,' he remarked, in such outrageous understatement that I nearly had hysterics then and there. He put his arms around me (brave man) and tucked me up into his shoulder.

'Hush, then, thou. Is this all? Why, love, it is no shame to be afeared so early in the dance. We'll have no leaping yet, shall we, no bouncing galliards? No. No. A slow pavane is more to the taste of a lady, I think. An easy dance, that may be learned by any little maid. We'll not spoil with haste.'

'My body is frightened,' I tried to explain. 'Not me.'

Patiently Nicholas held me until my sobs had gone quiet. Then he leaned up to look me in the eye and said:

'Now, why didst thou play the wanton with me? I would not have hurt thee for the world, Rose.'

'I came to you because I love you,' I said, as a defense; but I realized, with a certain gleeful horror, that it was true. 'I have never loved anyone before in all my life, and I am so frightened.'

'Flesh is a comfort to flesh,' he said. 'Though not, I think, the remedy for thy fear.'

'My fear is not of you,' I protested.

'What then?' he said. I took too long to come up with an answer, because thoughts began to turn behind his eyes and they grew small and suspicious.

'Did thy father bid thee come here?' That was so close to the mark that I had to catch my breath, which he interpreted correctly. His scowl deepened. I knew I must make the best of it, so I said:

'He hath counseled me to make much of you, señor, I will admit.'

'What manner of man sends his virgin child —' Nicholas began in thunder.

I rushed on: 'But in an honorable manner, señor, as any maid might do. He wisheth me to be married well and, having some care to my happiness, bade me look to wed with an Englishman.'

'For safety,' Nicholas muttered.

'It may be so.'

'What storm is it he runs before? He hath some black business, thy father, hath he not? And this it is that maketh thee pale and sick.'

I clung to him. Let him think what he wanted, I was in over my head. 'It's true,' I whispered in his ear. 'I want no part of his life. Let me stay here with thee. Keep me, love.'

He gave a long sigh, a brooding angry sound, but his hands began to move again on my skin. 'Tell me the truth, Rose,' he said. 'What dost thou fear?'

'So many things, I have forgot them all,' I said wearily. 'But I struck you because I thought you would tear me and make me to bleed.'

He gave a rueful laugh. 'I hope I may couch a lance with more skill than that. Will you prove me, love?' I kissed him where I had hit him. With great care and gentleness he began the game again.

'Some order ought to be taken for the better education of virgins, that they read no old romances,' he grumbled pleasantly. 'For there they will read of this maiden come near to dying when her lover beds her first, or that maiden staining seventeen ells of linen by her defloration, swooning for love, and I assure you it is not so. Look you, Friar John shall preach you a sermon on it.' He began to speak in a little squeaky voice for his penis:

'*Now you must know, child, that what passeth between a man and a maid is no ordeal but a delightful measure, as many happy country girls witnesseth, who are never the worse for making familiar with a plain and well-intentioned prick. Nay, further, our Lord that loveth us surpassing well hath ordained this matter to be pleasing to the partakers thereof, as we may read in Holy Scripture, where it saith: O that thy mouth would give us a kiss, for thy breasts are more pleasant than wine, and —*'

So as I rocked in his arms, helpless with laughter, he pressed his advantage; with such courtesy that my castle, as they say, fell without further defense.

And as the apple tree among the trees of the wood, so was my beloved among the sons. Et cetera. What would I give, to have that night back, out of all my nights? No treasure fleet could hold it, what I'd give; no caravan of mules could carry it away.

Chapter Fourteen

In the black morning he guided me down the stairs, though on the bottom step we clenched and melted, and had to run right back up to bed again.

When I finally crept back into my room, the eastern sky was starting to get light. Our windows faced east, so everything stood in black outline against them: very distinct, the posts and the drapes of the bed, and Nef's Egyptian profile where she sat upright watching the dawn. She turned to look at me.

'You all right?' she inquired.

I just smiled, the way you do when you're newly nineteen on a summer morning in England and you've just discovered Paradise on Earth. Were there stars in my eyes? I suppose there were. I came and settled gingerly on the foot of the bed.

'You know something?' I said. 'All my life I've been fed this line of utter garbage about mortals. They're just the same as we are, and some of them' – meaningful pause here – 'are *better*.'

The pity in her face was a thousand years old. I didn't understand it, so I ignored it.

'I just spent the night with a mortal man who's got God's own intellect,' I swept on. 'And the body to match. He's enlightened, he's fearless, he's seven hundred years ahead of his time. The only thing that makes him different from me or you is the hardware.'

She just nodded and said, 'Well . . .'

'The thing is, I've been operating all this time with an incredible sense of superiority over this race that produced Caligula and Hitler and the other monsters, and all the while ignoring the fact that this same race is capable of turning out Da Vincis and Shakespeares. How can we all be so arrogant?'

She shrugged a little and said, 'Sometimes . . .'

'I mean, there's a whole world here I've never even thought about. There must be millions of these sane, intelligent individuals whose lives are every bit as meaningful as our own, and if it weren't for a few aberrant types screwing it up for everyone else, they'd probably be well on the way to the perfect civilization. This is tragic. We have to help these people. I mean, they made us, didn't they? We came from them. In a sense, we *are* them. Aren't we?'

How infinitely wry was Nef's smile, on that two millionth morning of her life.

'Yes and no,' she said.

'What do you mean?' I bounced impatiently on the bed.

'You'll find out.'

'Oh, baloney.' I jumped up and crawled in on my side of the bed. 'Don't go all metaphysical on me. And anyway – anyway! Why didn't anyone ever tell me what happens when you – you know – for the first time? I went into automatic defense mode and nearly hurt him!'

At least she winced. 'Sorry about that,' she said. 'I thought you knew.'

'Well, I didn't, and it nearly ruined everything,' I said crossly, yanking most of the blankets over on my side.

'The man has to be careful, and you have to relax a lot,' she explained.

'Thank you, we figured that out.' I burrowed down into the pillows. 'And now I'm going to sleep for hours and hours. I won't be down for breakfast. You can tell them whatever you want.' To her everlasting credit, Nef did not pick up the candlestick and club me over the head. She only sighed and climbed out of bed to begin her two millionth day.

When I woke, I was as happy as if it were my birthday, and someone had crept into my room and left a rose by my pillow.

Well, who cared about work after that? Not I, and not Nicholas Harpole, except that it gave us an excuse to get out alone together in the garden. His God even favored us with a miracle, for it stopped raining; and this is always a marvel in that damned green land, but more so in that particular summer when the Cloud Prince was in residence.

Now that I come to write of what we did together, I have a peculiar reluctance to put pen to paper. Yes, this is definitely pain I feel. There is a locked door, you see, hinges red as blood with rust: it screams upon being opened and tries to close again, but through its narrow space I see the color green.

Long grass where we lay, in the heart of the maze, and the little white flowers of the hedge had a sweet smell, like semen. I had filled my overskirt with damson plums, and we took turns eating them and reading to one another from *De Immensa Misericordia Dei*. I can still see the explosion of green at his window, the summer leaves crowding thick as though they would burst in on us where we sat naked on his bed. We had a dish of strawberries and a flagon of Rhenish wine, and he cradled a mandolin on his lap, for decency's sake, he said; his big hands closed on the frets and plucked the strings. Sweat formed on his fair skin. He taught me songs.

This truly hurts. But I need to record that green filtered sunlight streaming in through the great hall, where we made eye contact over breakfast. His foot sought mine under the table. He peeled oranges for me in long curls of gold. I ate them for him in suggestive ways, eloquent with lips and tongue. God knows what the servants thought.

So you may laugh at my heart's nakedness, but I'll tell you this much: all my nasty expectations fell away like stone birds that summer. With each sexual act and variation, layers of fear came away to reveal a commonplace, comfortable pastime.

It wasn't that the obsession died – Christ, we couldn't keep our hands off each other. What clutchings in the maze, what passionate and explicit notes in Greek we left for each other! But it became *innocent*. Maybe wholesome is a better word. Pleasant and unremarkable as eating. No sense of sin. What a revelation for me, eh?

We played mental games with each other, too, he still asking oblique questions about alchemists and I poking with casual remarks about weird Anabaptist sects. Stimulating discourses, as it were, to counterpoint our play.

Enough of the idyllic sex scenes. What we did, we did, and now you know.

*   *   *

Nef was very accommodating about it, because now she had the bed to herself and could play the radio as late as she wanted. Mind you, all there was usually to hear was a weather broadcast and a nightly program of madrigals by a popular group of castrati; but those things would comfort you too if you were trapped in a back country manor house and the only other woman around was younger than you and having a torrid love affair besides. Joseph made a few cheerful remarks about how great one's first little mortal fling was. Beyond that he didn't comment much, being very busy himself at that time.

In August, Mary the Queen and Philip her consort went on up to London, where it promptly rained buckets on all the Londoners who nonetheless staged elaborate pageants for his Gloomy Grace. I remember where I was when I heard the broadcast floating out of Nef's open window: in the center of a privet hedge with Nicholas. We were having a fierce post-coital discussion of Savonarola. Nicholas defended, I attacked.

In September there were news reports every day on how badly our quondam countrymen were getting on in England. Somewhere there was a plaintive hidalgo with gonorrhea who wondered what had become of the private physician whose passage he had paid for. Joseph could disappear in transit like a check, as he found it convenient.

There were rumors of revolts, of barricades and Imperial treachery; but nothing came of them, and the sun kept shining down. No, it was in our own bright Garden that the trouble began.

People had noticed when the color began to come back into Sir Walter's hair and beard, but even the servants assumed it was only a dye job, if a subtle one. When he got to handling and pinching the kitchen girls, his household chalked it up to male menopause. Dotage, they used to call it. But the day he fell down at the breakfast table in a fit, no one knew quite what to say.

Myself, Nicholas and Master Ffrawney, Nef and Joseph and the steward and two scullery boys, all looked down at him in horror. He kicked. He foamed. He grunted. *Oops*, transmitted Joseph. Out loud, he said:

"Why, he hath the falling sickness. How unusual that he never told me of it."

What do you mean, Oops? I questioned, and Nef echoed me. He ignored us as he and Nicholas hastened down to their knees beside Sir Walter. With some struggle they edged him away from the table so he wouldn't brain himself, and did all the helpful things one is supposed to do for an epileptic. While Nicholas was busy unhooking fastenings, Joseph discreetly broke a little capsule over the throbbing vein in Sir Walter's temple.

'He hath never been so taken,' gasped Nicholas, dodging a flailing shoe.

'Well, perhaps he had a surfeit of something that drew the sanguine humors up into the brain.' Joseph pretended to take his pulse. 'Eels, or oysters, or venison pie, perchance. Hmm?' But he struck a false note then, because his tone was too light and careless. I guess he was badly rattled, or he wouldn't have slipped up like that. And he only slipped a little; but Nicholas caught it, though the rest of the company were oblivious. He threw Joseph a quick, wondering look.

Watch out, I transmitted.

Slight miscalculation of dosage, Joseph returned. *The little guy must have been at the beefsteak again. I warned him about that.* Sir Walter gave a final thrash and went limp, apparently unconscious. Joseph called for a cushion and placed it under his head with great solicitude. 'There is no cause to be alarmed, good people,' he said loudly. 'Doubtless this unfortunate incident was only the result of intemperate diet.'

Sir Walter shot out his arms and legs and crowed like a rooster.

'Jesu bless us!' shrieked Master Ffrawney. 'He hath a devil in him!' He and the scullery boys all made the sign of the Cross. So did Nefer and I, belatedly. Joseph was too busy trying to catch Sir Walter's flapping arms.

'I have it now!' he shouted. 'It is, uh, an effusion of melancholic bile in the liver. The Count of Alcobiella was afflicted with the very same. Please, my young friend, let us get your master to his bed.' Between them, he and Nicholas hoisted Sir Walter, who was grinning idiotically, and struggled with him up the stairs. Near the top, the old man began to howl:

'Dookies! Dookies! Dookies!'

I was too frightened to laugh. Nefer looked around at our terrified faces and pulled out her rosary. 'Let us pray,' she said firmly. 'Entreat the Blessed Virgin in our efforts on Don Walter's behalf. *Ave Maria, Gratia plena . . .*'

We mumbled with her, occasionally glancing up as thumps and crashes came from the room above. At last there was silence. Three quarters of the way around the rosary, Nicholas came slowly down the stairs. His face was set and closed. I ran to him. 'How does the good man?' I cried. He turned to stare at me; then he looked at the others and said:

'By the grace of God, Sir Walter is sleeping now and his fit hath passed. The doctor says he will be well.' And as Nef and the others resumed prayer, he took me by the arm and led me outside.

'What is it, in God's name?' I said, peering up at him. He led me a little way from the house and looked at me.

'I have just seen a thing I cannot understand,' he said.

'Before God, I don't doubt it!'

He glanced around before he replied in Greek. 'I mean, above the extraordinary sight of a gentleman of reverend years crying cuckoo before his whole house. Men have lost their wits before. No, my love, when we carried my master up to his room, we stripped away his doublet and shirt so that your father could bleed him.

'Now, when Sir Walter was a young man, he saw some service with our late king in France, and took a wound from it. (Or it may be that as he sat in a tavern one night, he was set upon by thieves; I've heard him tell both stories.) However he came by it, he certainly had a great scar across his ribs.'

'Had,' I said uneasily.

'Yes. Past tense. Now he has but a little red line there, like a track of scarlet ink. How should this be, Rose?'

I took a deep breath. 'Well, did you think it was sorcery? It's the physick, no question. Every hedgerow charlatan has a potion to take away wrinkles and scars. My father's remedy works, that's all.'

Nicholas relaxed a little. 'Certainly it's a great remover of scars. So long as it doesn't take Sir Walter's life away with the scar, all may be well. Pray that your father knows what he's doing, Rose, or people will swear there's been murder done. And witchcraft, very likely, or whatever else comes into their heads.'

Mendoza!

I'm busy! I transmitted.

So am I, and I need somebody to hand me things. Now. On the double!

'Your advice is well taken.' I squeezed Nicholas's arm. 'I will go warn my father at once.' He stared after me as I hitched up my skirts and ran back into the house.

Up the stairs and up the stairs and *up* the damned stairs, clattering, past staring servants. *All right, where are you?*

In here. I heard a bolt slide back at a near door, and the door opened just wide enough to admit me. It was a narrow room, like a cell. Once inside, I gasped and fell back at what I saw in it, as though physically pushed against the wall.

Sir Walter was laid out on a baize-covered table, smiling and stone dead. Had to be dead: his skin was gray, his stare was glassy as a doll's, and his chest had been opened out and folded back to expose its contents. Joseph was leaning down into the bloody cavity, working frantically with little tools. Organs were draped everywhere.

'Oh, my God, you've killed him,' I said.

'Shut up and hand me that box,' Joseph hissed. Too stunned to argue, I handed it to him: a red bakelite component about the size of a matchbox, with a couple of tiny wires trailing from it. He snatched it from me, and it disappeared into the mortal mess.

'Pliers,' he demanded. 'Goddamn faulty regulator!'

'You really think you can revive him?' I edged closer to peer into the gaping hole as Joseph rummaged around in it frantically. Oh, gross.

'Yes. Grab that hemostim and stick it up his nose!'

I began to giggle in spite of my horror. Somehow I found the slender pointed tool and inserted it just above Sir Walter's mustache. Joseph growled, 'Farther!'

Suddenly festoons of tiny colored lights were blinking inside Sir Walter, all over his lungs and heart and liver, as though his organs were throwing a block party. It was pretty, in a ghastly sort of way. One of Sir Walter's thumbs began to waggle back and forth.

'Good. Great.' Joseph twisted the pliers and leaned with all his strength. Something gave a little click, and the blinking stopped, the lights shone with a steady soft glow. 'Now take the hemostim out of his nose.'

I obeyed gingerly and dropped the tool into a sterilizing pail. The lights continued to shine. Joseph exhaled loudly and began to close up Sir Walter.

'If you don't need me for anything more . . .' I moved toward the door.

'No, stick around. Your boyfriend noticed some stuff he couldn't account for, didn't he?'

'You mean, like scars vanishing? He's not an idiot. Don't worry, though, I explained it all away.' I leaned against the wall and folded my arms, grinning. 'I did *my* job. Your little mistake won't leave any lasting suspicions in his mind.'

'It wasn't *my* little mistake after all, wiseass. See this?' Joseph slam-dunked something into the sterilizer. I peered at it. A little bakelite box, twin to the first but obscured by a film of blood and tissue. 'Defective. If I ever get my hands on Flavius again —'

'Wow. What was it supposed to do?'

'Regulate the release of pineal tribrantine 3, not dump a week's worth into his system.' Joseph reached for the skin plasterer.

'No!' I whooped with laughter. 'No wonder he went tilt! You're lucky you didn't have to get him down out of a tree!' Joseph just glared at me and troweled new flesh into Sir Walter's wounds while my snickering subsided. After a moment a thought sobered me.

'How come you're giving him tribrantine anyway? I thought only we got that.'

'Special case.' Joseph put away the plasterer and grabbed up the retoucher. 'It can be given to mortals, and it'll do for them what it does for us; it's just that their systems can't learn to produce it like ours can. Costs a fortune to keep pumping it into 'em, too.'

'But it wouldn't make them immortal, would it?'

'Nah. But they'd be good-looking corpses when they finally

died, believe me.' Joseph looked up at me. 'Thinking of the boyfriend, huh?'

Sir Walter twitched and groaned. His eyes had closed. I stared at him, watching the color return to his face. 'No, actually,' I lied.

Joseph appeared at supper grave and solemn as a church elder, close at Sir Walter's elbow. 'Nay, I thank ye, I am very well now.' Sir Walter waved easily at everyone. 'It was but the falling sickness, brought on by immoderate diet. Doctor Ruy hath explained it all.'

There were some dark looks in Joseph's direction from the household staff, but the truth was that Sir Walter did look perky as a cricket again. He reached out now and dragged a bowl of watercress across the table to his place.

'What's this? Cresses? You, Dick, this wants oil and salt! Alexander the Great was much given to the falling sickness, did you know that, madam?' He turned to Nef abruptly.

She blinked. He had scarcely ever spoken to her before. 'Why – no, señor, I knew it not.'

'Verily, lady. Julius Caesar, too. And Pompey, so I believe.' He stroked his beard complacently as one of the scullions fussed with the salad. 'The ancients, being deluded heathen, held it to be a sign that Jupiter, who as you know was their principal idol, had marked a man for greatness. God's marrow bones, fool, I said *salt!*' he shouted, glaring at the boy. It was a loud and deep shout, a resonant sound, very striking on the ear, as it came from old, dry lungs. The boy cowered. Everyone at table stared.

'Perhaps it would be wise to take but little salt,' reminded Joseph.

'Well, well.' Sir Walter dredged up some cress between his thumb and forefinger and stuffed it in his mouth. He wiped his hand on a piece of bread and turned back to Nef, chewing busily. 'Where was I? Aye, aye, that great ones were ofttimes marked. Or so the Romans held. I myself was born with a mark like a cobbler's awl upon mine elbow.'

'Doubtless a prophecy of your piercing wit,' smiled Joseph.

'Ha, ha, ha! Though I may tell you, Doctor Ruy, that I

have made good fellows to laugh in my day, forsooth! I was once sought after for my good conversation.' He coughed modestly.

Well, he was boring enough now. Not my Nicholas, though. I gave him a sultry smile, but he was watching Sir Walter, frowning a little. A moment later he noticed and smiled at me, and gave me a compensatory nudge under the table. Then his gaze wandered away again.

'Lewd fellows, those Romans,' Sir Walter went on, digging out another handful of cress and wolfing it down. 'They cut an image of Hercules in one of our chalk hills and – well – hum.' He glanced over at me and then back at Nef. 'I shall tell you of it another time, lady. Take some of the cress, I pray you, it is very good. Now, Master Ffrawney, did I not call for a capon to table?' Hurriedly the serving boy presented a whole roast chicken from the sideboard. 'Aah,' cried Sir Walter; and as he leaned forward to pull off a drumstick, we all heard a distinct tearing sound. He froze.

'Your doublet is broke open behind, sir,' observed Nicholas.

'Is it so?' Sir Walter scrabbled at the front buttons with greasy fingers. 'Well, out upon it, it was an old thing and shabby besides. I shall have a new one! Nicholas, bid Master Fish the tailor to call upon me. I must have six doublets cut in the new fashion. See that it is done.'

He got his six new doublets, and new shirts and hose as well; and the tailor went away shaking his head, because everything had to be made bigger in the neck and the shoulders. There was talk in the servants' hall, let me tell you.

There was more talk when Sir Walter began to sleep with the laundress. She was a well-mannered person remarkable chiefly for her cleanness – she must have taken her line of work seriously – and for her breasts, which were like river rocks. Pretty soon she was making regular calls at Sir Walter's creaking ancestral bed with the Iden arms on its hangings. I think the servants felt an obscure pride that somebody their master's age should have a backstairs squeeze at all. But they really did not approve of his flirting with Nef too.

Chapter Fifteen

One fair bright morning, I was running along an aisle of the privet maze, ever so picturesque: my hair down, cheeks flushed, eyes sparkling, et cetera. Just like the beginning of a historical romance. Never mind what I'd been doing. I found a green alleyway and ducked inside. My breathless giggling and the whining of the gnats sounded loud in my ears. There was a rustling from the hedge, and I poised to shriek: but it was Nef's long profile that came around the corner.

Pop went the ambiance. 'What the hell are you doing here?' I snarled.

'Hiding,' she said gloomily.

'Well, go hide somewhere else!'

'Ssh.' She put out her hand. We listened for a few seconds but heard nothing.

'Who are you hiding from, anyway?' I resumed in a stage whisper.

'Sir Walter.'

'You're kidding!' I began to giggle again. She favored me with a look that would have frozen anybody older and less stupid.

'He keeps trying to get me to ride down to Dorset with him to look at this Hercules thing. From the way he leers, I get the impression it's something improper.'

'It sure is! It's a Neolithic nude with a twelve-foot penis.'

She rolled her eyes. 'Why me?'

'Because he figures you're a gentlewoman, what do you want to bet? And with all the improvements Joseph's making, the old man's fancy must be heavily turning to thoughts o.' love. I bet he feels like a million bucks. I bet he's beginning to regret that he never married and furthered the heroic Iden line. And you're the only available female of his social status, right? *Quod erat demonstrandum!'*

She took a swing at me with her rosary, which was solid silver and would have done me injury had it connected, though of course it only whirred harmlessly through the space where I'd been a nanosecond earlier. 'Mendoza, you're a rotten kid.'

'Don't you feel honored? How many years do you think it's been since the old boy thought of anything but his garden?'

She slumped down to a sitting position on the grass. 'This is too embarrassing.'

'Seriously, though, would you mind being embarrassed somewhere else? Nicholas and I were —'

That was when the unicorn appeared. Tiny and demure, he came around the corner nibbling daisies from the grass. He halted when he saw us. Nef sat bolt upright, staring.

'What —' she said, and I started to explain; but she put out her hand, and the little creature ran to her at once. It nuzzled her, and she swept it up into her arms. 'Little baby, what's the matter?' Her hands found the twisted stumpy horn, and she gave a cry.

'It's the unicorn,' I said uncomfortably. 'The one I keep telling you about. Sir Walter's pride and joy. You know.'

'Oh, the poor little thing!' There were actually tears in her eyes.

'See, somebody took a baby goat, and they did some sort of primitive surgery on its head —'

'I can see what they did, damn it!' She was examining its little feet. 'And somebody gilded its hooves once, too, look at this, that's why they've grown out this way. What kind of bastard would do a thing like this?'

'Somebody who wanted to make some money.' I shrugged. 'Look, if it makes you feel any better, remember that at least he's running around in a nice green garden this way. If he were still a goat, he'd probably have ended up as somebody's barbecue by now. And it's not as though he's in any pain.'

'How the hell would you know?' She gave me a truly savage look. 'How would you like to have a pair of your wisdom teeth bound so they grew into each other?'

How graphic. I backed off a pace. 'Okay, okay, so it's cruel. What can we do about it, though?'

'You'll see.' Grimly, she rose, the unicorn docile under her arm, and swept away with him.

'But you can't —'

Crash. Nicholas burst through the hedge, breeches already at half-mast. His whoop of triumph was strangled as Nef turned to glare at us. 'God save you, madam,' he choked, sweeping off his biretta.

'Buenos dias, señor,' she replied icily. The unicorn bleated. She turned away and marched on. We stared after her.

'What ails the lady?' he inquired at last.

'She hath discovered Sir Walter's unicorn, and the truth of it hath moved her to a great passion of rage,' I explained.

'Charity to dumb beasts?' His eyes began to spark again. 'Why, perhaps she should have been a shepherdess. God knows she's no duenna.' And with that we changed the subject and had great joy of each other, there and then. Still, in the back of my mind a small beacon flashed red, red. I'd never seen Nef angry before.

It was a week before anybody found out what she meant to do, exactly a week to the day, and in that seven-day span summer left us: overnight. Nicholas and I went to sleep sprawled on top of his blankets and in the morning woke huddled under them.

I sat up in astonishment, in the dry cold air. The green leaves at the window stared in at me with a shocked look. What was wrong with them? I slipped out of bed to stare back. Yellow edges like fire beginning all around, chlorophyll breaking down, sugars blooming. I turned away. Nicholas lay watching me, an odd expression on his face.

'It's so cold,' I said. 'And the air has a smell.'

He nodded. 'Autumn,' he said. 'Time to put the pavilion about the Portingale orange, lest it die of cold. Come back into the bed, love, lest thou do likewise.' I scrambled back in beside him gladly enough. He pulled me close to his body.

'It is very deciduous in this country, is it not?' I remarked. I could feel him bemusedly sorting out the meaning of the word, and then his heartbeat quickened. He burrowed down to face me and said in Greek:

'Leaves fall in England, yes. But do they not also fall in Spain?'

I answered warily. 'Yes, we have autumn in Spain. But not so much. There were not many trees where we lived. Pines there were. So, you see, I have never seen such a season.'

'I thought you said you also lived in France. And there are many trees in that country.'

'We were in the south of France,' I countered. 'In the spring and summer.'

'Aah.' He narrowed his eyes.

'And perhaps I went to Egypt once,' I added.

'Egypt.' One corner of his mouth lifted. Sneer or smile?

'Yes. Or somewhere in the Holy Land. I remember seeing great seas of sand when I was small. There is no autumn in the desert, you know.'

'Truly?'

'Yea, truly.' I kissed him, and wriggled upward to the pillow and the safety of English. It was a great language to be evasive in. 'But we have no time to debate these things, señor. The season changeth! Winter is at hand! The acorn shall drop for the rooting swine, and each little herb of the field shall bear seed according to its kind, señor! The holly berry waxeth red, doth it not? And I must gather fruiting body and example of them all. Quickly, señor, quickly!'

'I'll show thee seed enough.' He reared up like a dolphin cresting a wave.

When we waltzed down to breakfast, very pleased with ourselves, the whole house was bustling. A brisk fire roared and snapped on the hearth. Sir Walter finished his oat porridge and poached egg in a gulp and lounged back in his chair, eyeing Nef.

'I think me this would be good weather for hunting,' he remarked. 'Have you never seen one of our English hunts, Lady Margaret?' I rolled my eyes at Nicholas.

'Never, señor.' Nef did not look up from her dish of eggs and bacon.

'I think they have no such hunts in Spain. Our English

hound is the only beast for the chase, I may say, and our English red deer the prince of quarries.'

'I know little of these things, señor,' she said calmly, buttering a slice of bread.

'Of course, I never kept a deer park.' Sir Walter looked out of his window with a sigh. 'The Idens of old, though valiant, were but modest gentlemen and had no such means.'

'Come, sir, think of your ancestor! Old Sir Alexander hunted traitors, did he not? What need to take a deer when he had taken the monster Cade, eh?' cheered Nicholas, biting into an apple. It spat wine.

Sir Walter did not brighten much, though. 'Tis true. A valorous man. Still, I could wish . . .'

I don't know what he wished, because even as I sat there savoring their mortal grace and silliness, there came a terrible outcry from the garden.

Before it was sound, there was a great blast of smell: two adult males in extremes of fear and dismay. I caught my breath. Nef lifted her eyes to mine. Sir Walter maundered on, Nicholas's fine teeth champed away at his apple, the serving boy with quiet pride lifted the cover from a dish of pudding. Then the shouting became audible to them.

'Sir! Sir! You are robbed, you are robbed outright, you are plundered!' yelled Master Ffrawney, bursting into the great hall. He had one of the servants by the collar, a little old wreck of a male. Nicholas had pointed him out to me as the animal keeper. The man staggered forward weeping and collapsed on his face.

Sir Walter leaped up, reeking with alarm. 'Speak, man! What say you?' he demanded. But the keeper was incoherent, and Master Ffrawney spurned him impatiently.

'It appeareth, Sir Walter, that through the negligence of this lying knave one of your chiefest treasures hath been mutilated. Someone hath stolen the horn of your unicorn!'

A chorus of gasps from the assembled company. Eyes met horrified eyes, except for Nef's eyes, which were staring straight ahead. Another horrified gasp, this one of realization, from me, and quite drowned out by Sir Walter's roar:

'Let me see it! Is he butchered?' He did not wait for a reply but ran for the door, closely followed by the keeper, who was

wailing out that it weren't his fault; and so followed the rest
of the household, nearly, streaming down the manor steps
through the sweet crisp air.

The unicorn was tied near the aviary, kicking and bleating.
Sir Walter dropped to his knees beside it and raised profound
ululation when he saw what the vandal had done to his heart's
zoological darling. I pushed close to see. Dear, dear. The horn
had been removed neatly, all the way down to the skull.
Cleanly, with surgical clipping of the fur. And a tidy smooth
bandage of, as I live and breathe, Graft-O-Plast.

'My unicorn of Hind!' screamed Sir Walter. 'My thirty
pounds!'

'Twenty pounds eightpence,' said Nicholas faintly.

'Chide me not, master, for sweet Saint Mary's sake!' The
keeper groveled. 'Devils roast me forever if I ever slacked at
my post. I put him in his pen last night, and shut the door
fast, and when I comes in this morning, he were like that!
God smite me with blindness if it weren't just so!'

'Thou liest, whoreson knave!' Master Ffrawney kicked at
him again, but the keeper dodged. 'Well we know thou hast
taken the horn for thyself!'

'By Jesu and the heavenly host, master, I never did!' The
keeper grabbed Sir Walter's ankles. 'What should I do with
the thing if I stole it?'

'Why, rogue, sell it for gold! All the world knoweth the
horn of the unicorn hath great virtue for healing. Any
learned doctor —' Master Ffrawney almost bit his tongue
off, he stopped so fast.

Too late. The implication went off like a psychic bomb. The
air before my eyes danced with red numbers, red readouts for
eight mortals' mounting blood pressure all trying to claim my
attention at once. I could scarcely breathe for the smell. And
of course here came Joseph at the run, aware something had
happened but only just beginning to get an idea of what. He
paused. Every head turned to fix on him. Sir Walter's eyes
were like a furious dog's.

The reading went off the scale. Killer apes. '*Spaniard*,'
someone muttered.

I edged a little backward; in another few seconds I'd be
unable to resist the urge to wink out of there and reappear

in a safer place, and the mortals would startle away from where I'd stood. Too bad, but I couldn't help it. Oh, the smell. A hand closed on mine, and I jerked and looked up into Nicholas' eyes, cold and sane.

'Doctor Ruy,' said Sir Walter. 'Hast thou meddled here?' What a thick, barbarous tongue English could be.

Joseph took a step backward. He could read them all, he took in the bandaged skull of the goat in a glance, he met my eyes and knew. He turned his head to Nef, who stood still and quite composed beside me. There was an impact. I staggered. Nicholas's arm went around me.

Joseph strode forward and went down on one knee beside the goat. 'Never, sir. Why, this is German wax,' he said.

What?

Sir Walter blinked a few times. 'How now?'

'This.' Joseph tapped the bandage. 'I have seen it in the Low Countries. Ferriers use it, and cattle thieves. It cannot be found in England. Some villain of a Fleming hath been here, as God is my salvation.'

'A Fleming?' The keeper was bewildered.

'My friend, it is well known what price the horn of a unicorn brings in Flanders, and for what terrible purpose. Sir Walter, my heart is sick with grief at your loss. We must be grateful that the miscreant did not slaughter your little beast outright, though you may be sure he refrained only so that another horn might grow back, when peradventure the cunning thief may return, hoping to work yet another outrage! Precautions must be taken, my friend!'

They all shook their heads, trying to make out what he was saying. The violence index was dropping. Joseph turned to John, the gatekeeper. 'Hath there been any come to see the garden in recent days who spake like one from Flanders?' Joseph inquired sternly. 'Or ragged men, who might be soldiers back from foreign wars?'

'Uh —' John's mouth opened. An idea was put into his head. 'Aye! Aye, they was two such.'

'Two.' Joseph nodded. 'You see, he had an accomplice.'

'Damned Flemings!' Sir Walter clenched his fists.

'German wax?' said the keeper.

I closed my eyes with relief. The little screen of numbers

trickled down, out of imminent hazard. The mortals were only confused and angry now. Someone muttered that he had seen a soldier drinking in the village, and someone else was telling a third what his old father used to say about Flemings. Sir Walter was shouting orders to search the grounds.

Joseph walked through them to Nef. They looked at each other. Impact again. The whole garden skewed and slid over sideways, with its tiny creatures gesticulating and running about all flat and far away. Standing through that ephemeral reality were two towering clouds with edges sharp as razors, in terrible conversation: Joseph and Nef. Their words were sound below sound, unspeakable violent silence, a quarrel to break the inner ear. Off in a corner, a little squiggle of smoke, wailing and scrabbling: me. Surely Heaven was going to crack right open with that percussive wrath. Then the garden was back in real time, and I was standing, clutching my ears. Joseph and Nefer had not moved. He still looked at her, and at last she looked aside, diffidently, and arranged a fold of her skirt.

They were not any kind of human creature at all.

'Rose.' Nicholas touched my shoulder. I swung around to him and wrapped my arms tight about his neck. Without even a word or a question he carried me away, good man, away to the long walk under the rose arbor. I lay there with my head in his lap, crying like a fool. How I wished, how I wished I were a mortal girl.

'Ah. There she is.' Joseph, at the end of the walkway. Hurriedly I sat up. He strolled in and knelt on the grass beside us. Nicholas sat straight and squared his shoulders.

'My poor child. This nasty business hath unsettled thee quite, I see. Please do not be frightened, daughter. All, I promise thee, shall be well.'

'So we trust, sir,' Nicholas said. Joseph just smiled at him.

'It is an act of loving charity to comfort my child that is so distraught. I must offer my profound thanks, young man.'

'Why, sir, I accept them with a good will,' said Nicholas coolly. 'And must express my admiration, in good sooth:

there were hounds on your track just now, and you faced them down as boldly as any fox God ever made.'

Joseph's smile quirked up into his beard. His gaze, though, was flat and assessing.

'Come, come, young man, your metaphor! Any fox that faced down his enemies would be torn to pieces where he stood. The fox hath more discretion: he hath speed, he dodges and feints, he hath a thousand places to hide himself.'

'And leaves a stink wherewith he may be tracked, alas; and so is slain,' added Nicholas.

'It seems thy young man is hostile, daughter.' Joseph cocked an eyebrow at me.

'By no means, sir.' Nicholas took my hand in his. 'But I do grieve for the kits of the fox, who are slain with him though they have stolen no hens. Nor unicorn's horns.'

'My young friend, what should a fox want with such a thing?'

'What indeed, since surely such a fox hath the wit to see that the creature was only a goat!'

Joseph blinked. 'Aye.'

'What a comedy! And I would have laughed, but that you were nearly murdered before your daughter's eyes.'

There was a long silence. 'You are a clever boy.' I didn't like Joseph's smile at all. He settled into a more comfortable position, and his voice took on an edge like cutting glass. 'Loquere mihi, puere.'

'Facio libens.' Nicholas matched his Latin without a second's hesitation. 'Senex.'

'You have a bright and questing mind. Why have you turned its light on my personal affairs?'

'I did so at first because I perceived you to be a threat to my master, my faith, and my nation. Having satisfied myself that you were not such, or at least not directly, I continued in the second place because I fell in love with your daughter, whose unlikely talents, remarkable opinions, and charming lies present an enigma I feel compelled to understand. Not merely to know the truth about her, but also better to comprehend the strange events taking place under Sir Walter's roof.' Nicholas leaned forward to emphasize the last point.

Joseph looked very calm. He stroked his beard a moment before inquiring:

'What conclusions have you drawn, may I ask?'

'None that I think you would care very much to have spoken aloud. I will not judge your life; but I will say that it has not agreed much with your daughter. Accordingly, I had determined to ask you for her hand.'

Oh dear. Oh dear. How sweet, but oh dear. Joseph looked vastly amused.

'In light of your present sleeping arrangements, this is a generous offer indeed, but I am afraid you have overlooked the fact that I am not the only man in this rose arbor whose past does not bear close examination.'

Nicholas went pale.

'Oh, yes, my young friend, you have enemies. Talkative ones. And you and I have something else in common, you see: I too am fascinated by mysteries. I suspect my sources have told me a great deal more about you than my daughter has told you about me.'

'Rose . . .' Nicholas glanced at me. He ran his tongue over his lips.

'Now, my child, as you pointed out, is of remarkable opinions and doubtless would not be very shocked if I told her of your intimate connection with a group that interpreted Holy Scripture in a highly . . . original way. In fact, I think she would find the allegations of your personal stamina and appetites quite amusing. And, having experienced it herself, she would well understand that your considerable personal charm drew not a few converts to a fairly disreputable sect.'

Nicholas winced deeply. He turned and took me by the shoulders. 'Rose. What he is saying is the truth. But I . . .'

'I know.' I glared at Joseph. 'I don't care.' I turned and put my arms around Nicholas' neck and kissed him. He returned my kiss in confusion. Joseph leaned back, watching us.

'There, my friend, you see? She has a forgiving nature.'

Shut up, I transmitted.

'But I am somewhat more cautious. Call it the point of view of an old fox, perhaps, watching from the safety of his den as a young fox makes a stand before an oncoming pack of hounds. This is a valiant young fox, surely, but he is soon to be a dead fox as well.

'I will not grant my daughter's hand to such a fool. However, I trust that we may still remain good friends. Good day, young man. Daughter, when you are sufficiently composed, you may wish to speak to me privately, but there is no immediate need to do so.' He made his exit.

Nicholas was distraught, and I was furious, but please note what Joseph had just accomplished: my panic horror, brought on by the vision of the inhuman force he really was, had vanished. I now wanted to kill the smug little son of a bitch, but I wasn't afraid of him. Further, he had just spared me the ordeal of explaining to Nicholas why I couldn't marry him. I could no more marry him than I could believe in his God, could I? I was no more human than Joseph was.

As soon as Joseph's back was out of sight, Nicholas cleared his throat. 'Rose.'

'What?' I turned to him, almost irritable. He was watching me closely.

'Shall I plead my case?'

'It matters not.' I jumped up and shook rose petals out of my skirt. It had become cold in the garden. 'All his talk was lies and ill will.'

'Ill will, yes, but not lies.' He got up to follow me. 'I must confess I did such things.'

'I knew it before. Master Ffrawney came to me with just such a story,' I announced.

There was a silence. Nicholas smacked his fist into his palm a few times, meditatively, quite hard. 'And didst thou believe it, love?' he inquired.

'I hardly know.' I stopped to look him in the eye, which of course I had to tilt back my head to do. 'What should I believe?'

'That I was only a boy. That I came among folk who were hypocrites, though they spake the Word of God, and I believed them.' His mouth set at the memory.

'These people did no more than preach the Word of God?' I adjusted my comb, ever so casual.

He looked away. He shrugged. 'No,' he said.

The silence fell between us again. I could have stamped

my heels and shrieked. 'Such dreadful things are told of, for example, Anabaptists, I am certain my imaginings are far worse than the truth,' I nudged hopefully.

'I doubt it.' He looked glum. 'Now, I wonder how long I shall pay for having been seventeen.'

I wondered what he looked like at seventeen. 'Speak, dearest love.'

He took my hands and led me to a bench. He drew a deep breath, not meeting my eyes. 'Know, sweetheart, that my birth was . . . obscure. And my father would do little for me but this: he provided me with a tutor and sent me to school, that by having some education I might earn mine own bread, and he should hear no more of me.

'I revered my tutor as a father, for his learning was great, but also for this: he spoke like an apostle with Christ's words still ringing in his ears. He taught me to read the Holy Scriptures for myself in the original, and showed me by many examples how far the Church had gone from what was written there.

'So far as this went, he was a light unto my soul.

'I called him Father, he called me Son; and he had besides some several other sons in this kind, and not a few daughters, for he was tutor to many well-born children.'

Yes, I could see it coming. I leaned forward sympathetically.

'We came together in secret places to hear him preach the Word of God truly, and to discuss its meaning with him. We lived like disciples.'

Secret meetings, drinking parties, and hanging on their master's every word.

'Or as Adam lived before the Fall, in perfect charity and communion.' He took a deep breath again. 'The serpent in our Eden became manifest, even so; and it is a lasting confusion to me, and a bitterness, that God could so gift a man with the Holy Spirit and leave him so open for the Devil to meddle with.'

'Go on.'

'Better to show us what divine love was, he concerned himself with lifting from our eyes that veil which makes us perceive gluttony, drunkenness, and lechery as vices.' His lip curled back in a sneer. My God, he was handsome. 'Mark me, love, in Eden they are no sins, but we are not in that place. Such a subtle distinction cannot be easily understood by a boy, look you, but even I began to see his folly. Others saw it before me. They left our community, and there was scandal.'

I could imagine.

'And I despaired in my heart, seeing that our master had deceived us. Even I, by my example, had led folk to idle, filthy pastime. But I saw further, that as my master had done, all the leaders of the Church had done, by a thousand twistings of the plain truth.'

'Then the truth is not so plain, is it?' I pointed out gently. But his face was grim; he was living his memory.

'It is as plain as the blazing sun!' he cried.

'And as hard to look at,' I said. 'My love, this sun in the sky, we live by its grace; but it does well enough where it is, and we do well enough minding our own business down here. Seek to stare at it, and thou wilt burn out thine eyes.'

'Better to go blind bringing the light to those who have never seen it,' he answered. 'And so I determined. I went forth into the lanes, and I began to preach the Word of God. I called upon the righteous to live as we had lived, without sin in a Paradise of love, where flesh is no enemy to the soul.'

'Oh, my love.'

'And I was taken and beaten,' said Nicholas composedly, 'a drunken boy spewing and blaspheming before the horrified multitudes. I was put in irons, but privately, for I was a gentleman's son. And I was conveyed to prison in another town by night, lest the neighbors come and burn me where I lay. Some months I sat in prison, while good men came and reasoned with me, making so evident the peril I stood in that I recanted all my former words, so great was my terror.

'Well, my father had done some service to the king. Clothes were found for me, and I was sent from England awhile, until folk had forgot my disgrace. And so back into Kent, where I have lived these several years a blameless man.'

'Thanking God that thou still breathest,' I finished in awe. He had come just as close to death as I had.

'Aye,' he said, and then, 'No!'

I looked at him. His eyes had gone small and angry. 'No,' he repeated. 'I have suffocated, breathing this air. I lied so that I might go on living in this world, I who had lived in Eden! To creep into this little hole and never bear witness to the truth again, that was the price of my life. My soul.'

This kind of talk made me very uneasy. 'But if thou hadst been hanged, I'd never have known thee.' I gave a little laugh.

His gaze came back to me. He put out his big hands and drew me close. 'That much good has come from it, at least. And God knows, this is the first honest work I've done this seven year.'

On which note, we melted into a kiss, but I thought: Work?

Before I could voice my question, there was a trampling of feet, and we jumped apart guiltily. Sir Walter came into sight around a hedge, accompanied by two servants bearing pitchforks. 'Nicholas!'

'Sir.' Nicholas stood and bowed. I curtseyed, and Sir Walter acknowledged me with a brisk nod.

'Nicholas, I have sought thee. We must carry the search into the surrounding fields.'

'Aye, sir. Shall I muster the household?'

'No. I have done that. Go thou with Tom and Peter out into the way toward Sevenoaks, and hunt there. And think how we may remedy this, when thou shalt speak with Master Sampson. A new horn, of wax or bone, for appearance's sake?'

'Very good, sir.' Nicholas bowed again.

I walked slowly back to the manor. There were servants scurrying everywhere, poking into hedges and peering up trees. A few gave me surly looks, but said not a word to me.

The house was virtually empty. I could hear the radio blaring from Nef's room, so I went up there. Nef, however, was not in sight. Joseph was stretched out on the bed, reading one of her magazines. I froze in the doorway; but he looked up with a charming smile.

'Mendoza. Baby. Do come in.' I stepped inside and shut the door. 'Sorry I had to beat up on your boyfriend, your very tall boyfriend, but I figured it wouldn't hurt to deflect his line of questioning. Bright guy, isn't he? Beautiful command of Latin.' He turned a page.

'Where's Nef?' I stared around sullenly.

'In there.' He pointed with the magazine. 'Dictating her report to the disciplinary board. Be a good kid and don't bother her, okay? She's going to be at it awhile.'

I looked at the silent door. I couldn't hear anything but the radio, which was playing dance music. I went over and turned the volume down.

'Look, I, uh, wanted to apologize.' Joseph laid the magazine aside. 'Nef and I really blew up at each other, and I'm afraid the shock waves kind of got to you. Didn't they? And I know that can be unsettling to a young op, especially in the field. We let ourselves go, and we shouldn't have. I'm sorry. She's sorry too.'

'I bet she's really sorry.' I looked at the door again.

'Not as sorry as she could be.' His mouth became hard for a moment. 'But she's a good operative, she's done good work for a long time; they'll let her off with a slap on the wrist. I was the one who had to deal with the consequences. I thought I saved us from getting lynched rather neatly, don't you? Are they still down there searching for dastardly Flemings?'

'As a matter of fact, yes.'

'I guess we'll have to provide them with one.' He got up and went to the window. 'Is that your guy down there in the search party?' I went to the window to look but couldn't make out anyone amidst the leaves. Joseph put a hand on my shoulder.

'You're sore about this, I can tell.'

I didn't know what to say. 'You were awful to Nicholas.'

'That's true. Yes, you're right. I'm truly sorry. I got the impression, though, that he was going out of his way to be awful to me.'

'He doesn't like you.'

'Gee. And I cut such a dashing figure as a freethinking victim of the Inquisition. Well, you can't please everybody. You appeared pretty agitated when he asked me for your hand, by the way. Did he just spring that on you?'

'Yes.' I grew hot with embarrassment. Why didn't he leave me alone?

'Yeah. Poor kid. It's a good thing I was there to field that one for you. Marriage with a mortal! It's been done from time to time, actually. On a limited basis. Of course, you always have to desert them later, or pretend to die, or something like that. But, yeah. Naturally, it was out of the question this time, so I'm glad I was there for you, but with your next one —'

I felt dazed. 'You mean I could have said yes?'

'Well, in principle, sure. Not to this guy, though. I've been married myself, you know, quite a few times. It's occasionally useful, and once in a while you just can't avoid it. But, believe me, it's the easiest thing in the world to get out of.'

'But – but how can you do it? What if you really love one of them?'

'Is that a problem? I've loved my mortals, too. But, honey, the bottom line is – they're mortal. They're going to die. Nicholas is going to die. Now, do you want to stick around and watch it happen, or do you want to skip out and keep a beautiful memory? Of course you want the beautiful memory. Mendoza, it's painful to watch mortals get old. You have no idea yet.'

'I've been thinking, actually.' Although I hadn't been; I was desperately inventing this on the spur of the moment. 'I had this thought. Nicholas is very unusual, you said so yourself, he's almost like one of us. He's absolutely physically perfect, and you wouldn't believe the things he says sometimes. His whole interpretation of the Christian cosmology is so close to the truth, it's scary. I'll bet he could adjust really well if he were told about us.'

'No. I see where you're headed, but no.'

'But just listen a minute! I know he can't be fixed like one of us, I know you're not supposed to do the Process on an adult, but look at the stuff you're doing for Sir Walter. And we have paid mortals who know about us, who work for us. So why couldn't you do the same for Nicholas, and we could take him away with us when we leave here, as a sort of — sort of . . .'

'A pet?' Joseph snorted. 'Mendoza, we may be very

attached to Fido, but sooner or later he's going to dog heaven, all right?'

'You bastard.'

'No.' He took my arms. 'Sweetheart. Please understand. It wouldn't change anything and would only hurt you worse in the end. Trust me, I've been there. I feel very responsible for you, you know. I spotted you in that dungeon in Santiago. And I've watched you grow up into a damn good operative. Seriously, I think you've got what it takes to be the best in your field. I know I kind of encouraged this, it seemed like a good way to deal with the guy, and I thought the experience would be good for you. But I'd hate to see you get burned out this early by a bad relationship.'

I pulled away and sat down, not looking at him.

'Besides,' Joseph added, 'his skull's the wrong shape.' He came and sat down beside me. 'And another thing,' he went on. 'I'd think you'd find the fact that he's a religious bigot kind of wearing at times.'

'He's not a religious bigot!'

'Oh no? Remember his remarks about me being a secret you-know-what? And all that Jesus, Jesus, Jesus stuff. It must drive you crazy.'

No, of course that wasn't true. Much.

'Yeah, they're funny that way.' Joseph leaned back with a rueful chuckle. 'I remember one of mine once. Golly. She was a sweet thing, you know, and I was just nuts about her, but she had this devotion to Ishtar and you simply could not argue with her. I had to become an initiate, go the whole route. When she finally died, I was heartbroken, really, I just moped around for weeks, but on the other hand – it was so great not to have to paint my ass blue and go whack the heads off doves at the temple every night. Always date atheists, that's my advice.

'By the way,' he went on, 'how's the work coming?'

'Oh.' Slight uncomfortable pause from me, and a close examination of the brocade pattern on my sleeve. 'It's – I had kind of taken this week off, because I've pretty much got the range of specimens in their summer growth phase. Now that autumn's here, I'll have to get busy again.'

'Hmm. Any chance you can give me a preliminary completion date?'

'Well.' I cleared my throat. 'Well, I'll want to do a full scan on the plants that live through the winter, of course, and then we missed the spring because we didn't get here until July, so – er – I think we're looking at April or May.'

That was the Eastcheape Waits performing Vous Avez Tout Ce Qui Est Mein. *A crisp voice from the radio spoke over a burst of static. We break now for an update on the Newsmaker of the Hour, Edward Bonner, that hard-line Catholic Bishop of London. Minor riots followed in the wake of his announcement yesterday that he is initiating an inquiry into the conduct and opinions of Protestant clergy. Results are in from our citizen correspondent's survey of Londoners: eight percent declined to state, fifty-two percent were opposed, forty percent said they favored the inquiry. Of the opposed percentage interviewed, most felt that this was the first move in a conspiracy to bring the Spanish Inquisition to England and deprive Englishmen of their civil liberties. The Council is expected to call a special meeting this evening to discuss the civil unrest. We've received no word yet from our correspondent on the Council, but as soon as we have the minutes of the meeting, they'll be broadcast live. Meanwhile, all operatives with Spanish identities are advised to avoid the following municipal areas —*

'Now, that's interesting.' Joseph leaned over and switched it off. 'I didn't think there were that many Spanish-cover ops out here. I wonder who else came over with us?'

'My God, aren't you the least bit alarmed?' I cried.

'No. Look, this will all blow over. The Council will reprimand this bishop, and he'll lay off for now. I'll bet they won't even hear about it in Kent for another week. Trust me.' Joseph got up and stretched. 'We have more pressing concerns right now.'

'Such as?'

'Such as getting hold of a three-inch piece of deformed goat horn,' he said.

Chapter Sixteen

Amazingly enough, just such an object was found two days later, in the purse of a man floating facedown in a nearby river. He had been bludgeoned about the head and shoulders, making identification difficult, and his clothes were in rags, except for a fairly new buff soldier's jerkin.

Francis Ffrawney was quick to point out that this must be the thief, for Doctor Ruy had described just such a man as the probable culprit; doubtless the scoundrel had fallen out with his villainous Flemish accomplices. This theory was accepted by everyone except Nicholas, who gave me some very troubled and searching looks.

However, I was able to look right back at him with wide-eyed innocence, because I knew perfectly well that Joseph hadn't killed anybody; the Company would never permit such a thing. He'd just found a convenient corpse that was *already* dead and used it as a decoy, that was all.

At least, I thought that was what must have happened . . . but when I questioned Nef about it, she glowered and refused to tell me anything. She made herself pleasant enough to Sir Walter, however; became quite attentive. She coaxed him to let her tend to the poor little mutilated unicorn during its recovery, and the result was, it ended up sleeping in a wicker basket beside her bed. Joseph had a fit. Joan the chambermaid took to muttering darkly about how she was a *house* servant, not a stable girl, and I was doubly glad I wasn't rooming there anymore.

The wet weather began again. For about a week the hills were golden, the forests were rustling clouds of gold. Then the rain took it all away. There was suddenly a great deal of blue sky in England; a chilly wide sky, pale blue, like Nicholas's eyes.

The first morning there was a break in the rain, we went

out for a bit of a frisk in the garden, but we had to take some care in our merry chase, with the mud and piles of wet slick leaves. As we neared the end of the path, we saw a traveler out by the gate, peering vainly in. He could see us perfectly well, too, so we slowed to a dignified walk and pretended we had been coming to meet him.

'The porter is not at his post, sir,' called Nicholas.

'I can see that!' shouted the man in exasperation.

'I mean, sir, that there be no penny-paying guests after the rains begin,' explained Nicholas as we drew nearer. 'I fear most of our marvels are lacking their proper foliage. You may see the Great Aviary, or the Walk Historical. But the roses are a dead loss.'

'I have come expressly to see Sir Walter Iden,' grated the man.

'Oh,' said Nicholas, and since we were at the gate by this time, he produced his ring of keys and let the traveler in. This gentleman shoved through and stood shaking the rain out of his hat, for the branches had been dripping on him where he stood. He glared at us. I had seen him before. Yes, he had come one day back in summer, with a party of other folk.

'Master Darrell.' Nicholas bowed slightly, having placed him too.

'I am he.' Master Darrell jammed his hat back on his head. 'Pray announce me to your master.'

'At once, sir. There is hot wine and a good fire in the hall,' Nicholas placated. Master Darrell brightened considerably at the prospect as we walked back to the house.

'You have come on some business, sir? Or for the pleasure of Sir Walter's company?'

'A little of both, I think,' the traveler replied, puffing out his breath in a frost cloud. 'And I hope to sweeten your master's inclination to business by pleasant discourse with him. Heard you the news about Her Grace the queen?'

'I think not,' said Nicholas cautiously. I put my arm through his as we walked. I knew what was coming.

'Why, she is with child.'

Nicholas came to a full stop, gaping at him. Master Darrell eyed him wryly.

'Ah, that was how London did receive the news; then the

folk all tore their caps off and cried huzzah, and blessed her name. As I think you will too, sir, being a prudent man.'

'But . . .' said Nicholas.

At this moment Sir Walter emerged from the house and came springing nimbly down the steps, ready for his midmorning trot around the garden (per Joseph's orders). Master Darrell peered at him, and it was his turn to gape.

'Sweet Jesu, man, thy beard is red! How hast thou grown young?'

'It is a restorative physick, recommended by my personal physician,' said Sir Walter airily. 'Run along with me, for I may not stop, and I shall tell thee more.' Master Darrell clutched his hat and panted off after him. I tugged at Nicholas's hand.

'My love, be of good cheer. The queen is old. A child is impossible.'

Horror was slowly dawning in his eyes. 'But if she brings forth an heir to the Spanish prince, then farewell England's liberty.'

'She won't,' I said, treading on thin ice. 'She can't. I know it, love. She'll die.'

'And what if she doth not die? Or what if she should die, and the child live?' Nicholas clenched my hand. 'An infant crowned and the Inquisition to stand as regent over us all? This must not be.' His grip was painful. I wanted to tell him about Mary's ovarian tumor and the hysterical symptoms, but all I could say was:

'Your God would not desert England so. Consider well, love, the late Queen Katherine bore but the one live child and that was Mary. All the rest died babies. Have faith. Pray.'

'I cannot pray for the death of a child,' said Nicholas wildly.

I racked my brains. 'Hear me, love. My father has tended gentlemen of the Emperor's court and heard them tell tales current there, from the very spies come from England. And the saying is, that the queen is so troubled in her monthly courses, and so subject to swollen distemperatures of her womb, that they doubt she could have borne a babe even when she was young.'

'If the Emperor believed that, why did he send his son to marry the old cow?'

Well, that was a good question. 'It's only dropsy,' I said. 'I'll stake my life on it.'

'So thou mayest, and so may we all,' growled Nicholas.

Later we heard rumors he liked better: that beaten Spaniards were leaving the country in droves, having failed to make their fortunes in this unpleasant country, and that their prince wished bitterly he could go with them. All true, according to our radio commentator.

We poor Spaniards, though, were stuck in an English *winter*. The bare fields like a gray sea frozen. The sky all lowering slate. Lead, steel, silver weather. The smell was oppressive. I don't mean that it stank, though there was a lot of death in the smell, and it wasn't the normal mortal reek of men and beasts. It was a cold, black kind of smell. It urgently needed jolly wood smoke to cover it, and piercing sweet winds off the sea to carry it away.

Visually winter was beautiful, especially if seen from behind thick windows and with a good fire at your back. The bleaker it got, the more the mortals in the household seemed to want to go out and rush around in it, especially after the snow started. No wonder the damned things died.

Yes, snow utterly failed to charm me. On the day I first saw snow, the *Ilex tormentosum* was fruiting at last, and I had crunched through frozen puddles to get at it, had wrapped myself in very garment I possessed plus a cloak of Nef's, smelling of goat though it did. For those sharp branches with their distinctive oblong berries I braved frostbite and an increasing atmospheric disturbance niggling at the edges of my sensory array. Nicholas, holding the basket beside me, looked perfectly comfortable in his ordinary clothes.

'This same holly we cut in the summer, I well recall,' he observed. 'Why do you take it again? Is there a particular virtue in the berry?'

'Oh, yes.' I thought of diseases yet unnamed, in lands yet unknown. How to explain to him about Taxol, or *vinca rosea*? 'Blessed virtue. Their quality distilled will do more than garland thy house at Christmas, I'll tell thee. It's said the common kind keeps witches out; these will keep out Death himself.'

'A likely story.' He shifted the basket to his other arm.

'Well, it's true,' I grumped at him. 'Would I be out here in this filthy cold to get them, if it were otherwise?'

'It maketh thee look a spirit.' He peered at me dreamily. 'The leaves so green and the berries so red, and thy little blue hands and blue wrists and little angry blue face. I think if I tumbled thee under this green bush now, thou'd vanish like an ice cloud.'

'Then should Friar John find himself out in the cold.' I backed away a pace, just in case he intended to try it. Though he did look so handsome, with the frost bringing up the color of the good hot blood under his skin. He leaned down and lifted my chin in his own warm hand.

'Well, one must be prudent,' he said, and kissed me. He radiated such heat it was delicious, and I leaned in to him and we could have kissed and kissed like that forever. I could have, anyway. I suppose his back would have gotten tired. As we came apart to breathe, something drifted between us. It was followed by several other somethings, white and falling swiftly. It looked exactly like the excelsior we used to kick around in heaps near the transport pad at Terra Australis, from the supply crates that were unloaded there. Of course, this was impossible. I frowned at the things, which were dropping everywhere now, and said:

'Where are all the feathers coming from?'

Of course I knew my mistake as soon as one of them touched my bare skin, and a second later I blurted, 'It's snowing!' in dismay. I made a grab for my basket. But Nicholas had it, and he was staring at me in a mixture of alarm and delight.

'Thou knewest not what it was,' he said. 'Thou hadst never seen it before.'

'Of course I have,' I lied, getting the basket away from him. I had seen it in movies and paperweights and holos, and I had even done a five-thousand-piece jigsaw puzzle of a winter landscape once, but it hadn't prepared me for the reality. 'I spake in jest. Come away now, quick. We must to the house.'

'Thou'rt frightened.' He paced along beside me, leaning down to look at me. 'Sweetheart, it is but snow.'

'So it is; and even in England folk must have enough sense to come in out of it, must they not?' I came to the end of the hedge and could see no garden anymore; only outlines rapidly obscured by the flying white. I panicked. 'Where is the house?' I wailed; then my infrared cut in, and of course the house was the flare of light seventy meters northwest. Nicholas at my side blazed like an angel. He reached out for me.

'Peace, love, peace!' he called. 'Follow my hand.' But it was his light I followed, all the way back to Iden Hall. Contrary to the expectations fostered by literature and art, 1) snow does not fall in beautiful crystal kaleidoscopic flakes, and 2) it does not fall silently. It sounds like rain, only stealthy.

'Still blue,' Nicholas marveled, helping me out of layers of cloak by the fire in the great hall. 'They tell no lies that call thy Spanish gentry bluebloods.'

Actually in my case it was antifreeze, but I looked haughtily at him. 'Well, I shall not so chill my blood again until the spring returneth. This snow is a horrible marvel.'

'Oh, but snow is a merry thing in England.' Nicholas spread out his hands to the fire. 'Many jolly country pastimes may be had, at the year's dark end. You may sled upon snow, or walk through snow to your neck deep, or make some defense and fight battles with snow. You may go skating on frozen millponds and with good fortune not drown.'

'You go skating on frozen millponds.' I told him firmly, and we kissed, right there in front of a servant that was bringing big logs into the hall, and parted then. I had risked my fingers for *Ilex tormentosum*, and it had to be preserved for the ages.

Nef's room smelled like Nef's cloak, only more so.

'And how is our patient today?' I inquired, holding my nose as I went in.

'He's the sweetest, cleanest little baby in the world,' Nef said. 'And he's much better, thank you.'

He looked better, sitting there nibbling on a corner of the brocade coverlet. The Graft-O-Plast had come away from the wound, and fur was growing back; the horn buds were obdurately two, as nature intended, and not one, as the fantasy of man demanded. 'How nice,' I said without enthusiasm. 'Say, do you mind if I open a window while I work?'

'Yes.' She didn't look up from the magazine she was reading. 'It's snowing, in case you hadn't noticed.'

At least it was warm in there. She hated the cold even more than I did and had built up a roaring fire on the hearth. I opened my credenza and resolutely set out my specimen prep slides. 'So, what are we listening to?' I nodded at the radio.

'Pierre Attaignant memorial concert,' Nef answered. 'It's been going on for hours.'

'Then I haven't missed the news.'

'Nope.'

'I've never seen it snow before.' I switched on the ultravey.

'Lousy, isn't it?'

That was yet another set of bransles, a voice announced, sounding slightly desperate. *And with that we conclude this afternoon's segment of our tribute to the most prolific publisher of dance music of his time. Our thanks to studio musicians Dorin, Mark, Lucan, and Aristaeus of Thebes. Now for the news.*

News story of the hour: the first snowfall of the season has begun over southern England. Those of you stationed up north, of course, have already been experiencing nippy weather, and more of the same is expected over the next two weeks, as the cold pattern settles in over northern Europe. If you're having difficulties picking up our signal, we recommend you tune in at 9 PM for our special program on how to construct amplifying antennas out of common household items.

BZZZT! A burst of interference drowned Newsradio Renaissance.

'Sounds like you need to tune in to that one,' I remarked. The signal screeched and then came back:

Newsmaker of the hour: Number one topic with the man in the street appears to be the unexpected return to England of Reginald, Cardinal Pole, after more than a quarter century in exile. A former humanist, this rabid Catholic has been petitioning the queen since the start of her reign for absolute restoration to the Catholic Church of all monastic properties confiscated during the reign of Henry the Eighth. Since most of these are now in the hands of the private sector, Pole's return is expected to galvanize resistance among members of the council.

News from the Continent: the Emperor Charles's health continues to worsen, and the prince consort has expressed concern, but any return to Spain has been ruled out at this time due to the queen's pregnancy, supposedly now in its third month. This isn't stopping his countrymen, of course, and the official count of Spaniards leaving England this week was . . .

'Those lucky, lucky guys,' Nef shook her head.

'You're not serious. You want to go back to Spain?' I looked over at her, incredulous.

'Anywhere but here.'

'I thought you were all hot to get up to Northumberland.'

'If I could actually get out of here and *go* there, I'd be happy. It's the waiting that I hate. I hope at least I'll have some Blue Albions to work with, after all this.'

'Blue Albions? Is that a kind of beer?'

'No, dummy, it's a cow,' she said in disgust.

'Aren't you a little worried by the news?' I flipped a slide. 'I mean, with this religious fanatic descending on England.'

'No. Who cares what the monkeys do? We know how it all comes out in the end, anyway.'

'But not how it's going to happen. Don't you find it interesting to follow the politics? Here's Mary with this council dead set against her. How's she going to push through her pro-Catholic legislation? We know it's going to happen, but at the moment I can't see any way. Aren't you curious?'

'Hell, no. If I want to find out something that badly, I'll access a tape.'

'Well, I think it's fascinating.'

'You sound like a cultural anthropologist.' She tossed her magazine aside.

'Gosh, excuse me.'

'How's my little pal?' Nef leaned over and picked up the unicorn. 'How are we feeling? It's almost time for our favorite show!'

'You were the one who said I had to learn to cope with mortals.'

'I didn't mean you had to take them up as a hobby.' She

dandled the unicorn. 'I remember when you couldn't stand the idea of coming to England. The New World, that was all you talked about, morning, noon, and night. Changed your mind, haven't you?'

'Maybe,' I admitted. 'England does have its charms.'

'Get a load of her! We know the charm she's talking about, don't we?' she told the unicorn. 'It's big, and it has a busted nose, and it looks like a horse.'

'Oh, he does not.' I jammed a slide in the wrong way and had to pop it out. 'So where would you go if you had the chance? If you could make the Doctor station you anywhere you wanted?'

'India,' she said right away, looking wistful. 'No question. Anywhere in India. Or, maybe, Greece; Greece is swell.' She kissed the unicorn's nose. 'You'd like it there, wouldn't you, sugar face?'

'Pleeeease!'

'Ssh. Ssh.' She jumped up and turned up the volume. 'It's time for the livestock report!'

But another crackling roar of interference rose, only slightly louder than her wail of protest.

Snow fell. And fell. Cardinal Pole came back to England and was welcomed with great ceremony by the queen and our prince. Things started happening quickly, and it was worth braving the smell in Nef's room to catch the news broadcast every day.

Poor Mary. Our prince was not such a great actor, and she must have been increasingly aware that the honeymoon was over. But Cardinal Pole was sympathetic and attentive, and had big plans for a Counter-Reformation in her kingdom.

'This is crazy.' I went into Joseph's room, having left Nef pounding on the sputtering radio and screaming at it. 'They can't turn the clock back thirty years. They'll never bring it off.'

'You wait.' Joseph shook his head. He had taken to listening to the radio broadcasts with me, snow static and all, as the big soap opera got moving. 'You'll see. They'll get help.'

'From whom? The Emperor's going to die soon and so's the Pope.'

'You'll see,' he repeated. 'Do a fast scan if you don't believe me.'

I didn't want to do that. It was riveting, spell-binding to watch history as it unfolded. Why spoil it by fast-forwarding to the end? Besides, there were other stories to follow. A snowbound manor house is its own many-layered play, full of intrigues, confrontations, and twists.

It had gradually dawned on just about every inhabitant of the hall, thanks to Joan's intelligence reports, that Nicholas and I were sleeping together. Master Ffrawney averted his eyes from me any time we were in the same room, but all the others seemed rather relieved. Angry young men are uncomfortable to have around, and apparently getting laid regularly did wonders for Nicholas's temper. And what better way to quench a young firebrand than to have him fall in love with a nice Catholic girl? There were a few raised eyebrows over Joseph's apparent complaisance, but he was a foreigner, after all, and anyway people were too busy watching the other scandals to question it much.

The laundress continued steadfast in Sir Walter's bed, but somewhat less securely as his regeneration advanced. Indeed, she began casting slit-eyed glances of hate at Nef when their paths crossed, though that was seldom, and Nef barely noticed anyway. Now that I come to think of it, maybe the laundress's animosity didn't stem from a jealous heart after all. I certainly wouldn't have wanted to have washed Nef's linen, full of essence of unicorn as it was.

Nef, meanwhile, continued to respond to Sir Walter's efforts just warmly enough to get to keep the unicorn in her room. They flirted ponderously at table, and I believe things got physical once or twice. She was interested in his livestock, he in her noble lineage. Joseph and I had to invent a long string of Castilian ancestors for her and write it down so she could memorize it, because she was no good at making things up on the spur of the moment herself. Though she was good enough at home electronics . . .

Bloodcurdling screams in the night!!

I sat bolt upright in bed, scanning in a two-kilometer-wide radius. Nicholas was up and on his feet, staring. When another volley of shrieking sounded in the dead winter night, he strode to the door and opened it, and leaned out looking downstairs into blackness.

'What, help, ho! Is it fire?' someone on the second floor was shouting.

'What's the matter? Be there thieves again?' yelled somebody else, from belowstairs. There was no reply, but the screams died to hysterical sobbing, and a second voice from the same location was now heard making soothing noises.

'My master!' One of the servants came pounding up to the second story landing. 'Are you murdered? Is it the Spanish doctor?'

'Stay thou, Rose,' Nicholas told me. He made a hasty descent, and in a second I could hear him beating on Sir Walter's door. 'Sir Walter! Open, sir, if you can!'

I shivered and pulled the covers up around me. The weepy voice was moaning incoherently:

'It were on the chimney! O Jesu and St. Mary save us, I saw it!' To which the other voice – why, it was Sir Walter – replied in a hissed undertone:

'Peace, now, Alison, peace! Thou hast had no more than a dream! Hush! Thou hast roused the house, silly wench!'

'But I tell you it was the Devil! I saw his black wing!' the laundress (for it was she) shrilled.

'Sir Walter!' Nicholas couldn't hear the old man's frantic attempts to shut her up. 'In God's name, sir, do you live?'

'Aye! Aye!' Sir Walter shouted in annoyance.

Mendoza! There was a dark shape pressed to our tiny window. I nearly screamed myself.

'But what's amiss, sir?'

Let me in, for God's sake, it's freezing out here!

'There is naught amiss! I merely . . . er, merely . . .'

I jumped up and opened the window. Nef's face, inexplicably upside down, stared in at me.

'Sir, are you held to hostage?' demanded one of the servants who had gathered in a small throng with Nicholas.

'Oh, God, I'll never get in through this,' whimpered Nef through clenched teeth. 'Can you break out the frame?'

'Nothing of the sort!' Sir Walter snarled. 'Now go back to bed! Nicholas, bid them go!'

'I can't break out the frame, how'll I explain it?' I stammered. 'What are you doing out there, anyway?'

'Sir, I must be assured that all is well with you,' Nicholas explained patiently.

'Well —'

'No! There's a curse upon this house!' wailed the laundress. 'I saw the Devil with mine own eyes, a-hanging from the chimney-pots —' Her voice broke off in a muffled bleat, as though someone were forcing her to eat her pillow.

'Nef!' I gaped at her in dawning and horrified comprehension.

'I assure you, all is well!' Sir Walter could be heard scurrying across the floor. There was a creak as he pulled the door open an inch and (presumably) stuck his nose out.

'It was the best placement for the signal,' Nef explained through chattering teeth. 'I made one of those radio antennas out of a broomstick and copper wire off the grip of that old sword of Joseph's – oh, shit, my fingers are completely numb —'

'There! Ye see I am unmurthered. Now, get ye back to bed!' grated Sir Walter.

'And, you know, it was dark up there, and I slipped a little, but of course I didn't fall, except —'

An indecisive muttering as people began to obey Sir Walter. Nicholas, the alarm in his voice replaced by a certain masked amusement: 'It was no more than this? The woman had bad dreams?'

A thump as a window flew open one floor down and around the corner. *GET IN HERE!* thundered Joseph.

'Foolish fantasies,' Sir Walter whispered. 'The silly slut gets her up to piss and frights herself with supposed shadows. This is all!'

Don't you shout at me, Nef transmitted sullenly, but she went. She moved slowly past my window and disappeared. I stuck my head out into the night and glimpsed her crawling downward on a diagonal, until she reached the corner of the house and maneuvered around it and out of sight.

'Then I bid you good night, sir.' The door slammed, and I could hear Nicholas returning. I shut the window and was back in bed in one bound. When he climbed in beside me, he was beautifully warm, even after standing around in a drafty hallway.

There was plenty of talk in the servants' hall the next morning, let me tell you, and plenty of venturings outside to peer and point at the chimney where His Satanic Majesty may or may not have been doing midnight gymnastics. Somehow nobody noticed the radio antenna wired unobtrusively into the leads.

There was plenty of dark speculation about the probable connection between Satan and Spaniards (perhaps he had just been looking in on us to see if there was anything we needed?), and there were plenty of molten glares between Joseph and Nef. Still, the English are rather fond of haunts and horrors in the season of ice and snow, so the denizens of Iden Hall let us go unlynched a while longer.

And our radio reception *was* much improved.

So the world turned, and so turned the small wheel of Iden Hall within the great wheel that was England, and the year rolled on toward the solstice.

Chapter Seventeen

W e must keep Christmas well this year, what think you, Nicholas?' said Sir Walter at the dinner table. All eyes turned to him at this announcement. We beheld, one and all, a robust fellow no more than forty years of age. He resembled a fox now more than a terrier; his hair and beard were red with just a little graying, or more correctly a yellowing, such as red-haired men get. He was bigger, he was bulkier, and his new clothes had been cut in better taste and of subtler colors. Altogether a different man.

'As you will, sir,' said Nicholas. 'Your revenues shall support it.'

'Excellent well. I would have feasting, methinks, and dance. Take some care to find a consort for music. A fine consort, wanting nothing; there must be cornets and sackbuts, crumhorns and regals, and a great bass rackett – aye, and dulcians, too. I want this dull quiet hall to resound upon itself like a beating heart! Look to it, Nicholas.'

Nicholas pulled out a little octavo book and a pencil and began making notes. I looked up from my dish of sops in milk. Dancing?

'I want . . .' Sir Walter leaned an elbow on the table and stroked his beard. '*Young* folk about me. Send word to the Elliseys and the Brockles and Master Syssing and his daughters, bid them all come. Tell them there shall be a great dance this Christmastide at Iden Hall.'

I hadn't danced since I left Terra Australis. I looked hopefully across the table at Nicholas as he jotted down instructions.

'And I would have Christmas masquings and guisings, too, all fantastical, such as the king used to have,' Sir Walter remembered fondly. He meant Old Henry, of course. As far as most men's memories were concerned now, poor little Edward had disappeared right back up his dead mother's womb.

'Master Sampson hath gilding and forms for masks.' Nicholas wrote steadily.

'Why, lad, there must be more to it than that! God's death, these country folk have never seen the like. The whole matter of masques is that they must be some play or pageant, some spectacle. Doctor Ruy!' He looked over at Joseph. 'You have been at Court. You know whereof I speak, surely.'

'Yea, I assure you,' Joseph agreed. 'There are many spectacles at the Emperor's Court, some of them greatly astonishing.'

'Just so!' Sir Walter smote the table. 'I would astonish these folk! Now, you are a doctor and a learned man. Could you not then, as a friend, devise some dramatical interlude for the masquers?'

'Ah.' Joseph blinked and then smiled. 'My very dear friend, you do me too much honor. I would be delighted to do as you ask, but my skills are paltry —'

'Oh, but we must have a play, a diversion such as the Emperor hath, and what man better to know that than yourself? No, it shall be a splendid thing, I have no doubt. Now, may we not also have some subtlety at table, or some gorgeous marchpane semblance of a thing, as . . . a ship at full sail, or a wood with deer and little men . . . ?'

'Now where shall I find a pastry cockatrice a yard long, bearing the Iden arms upon its bosom?' said Nicholas in exasperation. He put out the candle and scrambled hastily in beside me.

'Can the cook make such a thing?' I burrowed up close to his chest. He put his arms about me, and we settled down. He replied:

'No. She cuts pastry leaves to deck baked apples: that is the whole of her craft. He wisheth a fantasy from the queen's own table, and belike I'll have to go begging to the same.'

We lay looking at the square of moonlight cast on the wall. 'Why should he stop with a cockatrice?' I said. 'If he would make folk stare, what about the Great Whore of Babylon riding on the Beast?'

There was silence for a moment, and then he began to giggle. 'Painted in scarlet and purple, with seven wires stuck up the necks of the Beast to hold them still,' he said. 'That'd set tongues wagging!'

'Yet I would see this English Christmas.' I wriggled around to look at him. 'England is famous among all nations for celebration of this season.' Though of course Dickens hadn't been born yet.

'Is it so?' He looked amused. 'Have they no mummery, no masques and spiced ale in Europe?'

'Last year in Spain I prayed at High Mass until midnight, and then came home in falling sleet,' I remembered.

'Bid thy heart be of good cheer, then, for we have no Romish Mass in this land,' he said.

This made me acutely uncomfortable, because Parliament had already met to restore the Mass, and it would go through by a landslide. It had been on the radio this morning. Well, what he didn't know wouldn't hurt him.

'Though, to be sure, prayer is more fitting for celebrating the birth of Christ than drunkenness and revels,' he continued thoughtfully.

'But thou must not put an end to Christmas revels!' I protested, and added, 'When first I heard we should come into this land, I thought, At last I shall dance! Which I have not done yet, save only the shaking of the sheets with thee.'

He grinned. 'There shall be dances and sweet cakes to spare, my heart. As in sooth there must have been in France when thou wast a child. Is it not so? Or was it in Egypt thou toldest me last time?'

'Very likely,' I said. 'Or far Cathay.'

'And do they hold Christmas revels in far Cathay?' He put his nose to mine. I thought about my childhood at the base. We celebrated a holiday loosely fashioned after the old Roman solstice festivals, and at Terra Australis it was in the summer anyway. I remembered hot dry horizons, sports matches, swimming parties.

'Be assured they do,' I said. 'And small apes climb palm trees at midnight to ring Christmastide bells.'

'Sweet liar.' He rolled over, and then we did something else.

*   *   *

'Whatever you do, don't touch the peacock,' said Joseph, entering the room. 'They've got it killed and hanging up already, and the party's over a week away.' He looked at me, busy at my credenza, and at Nef, who was combing the unicorn's fur. 'Not that the smell will bother you much,' he went on. 'But it'll be bacillus under glass by the time it's served.'

'The Lollard statutes were voted in today,' I told him angrily.

'The what?' he said, and did a fast scan. 'Oh. The anti-Protestant laws, huh? Say, have either of you had any ideas about a Christmas masque I can write?'

'They aren't just anti-Protestant laws,' I fumed. 'They're special statutes that put the bishops above the law. They can arrest people, judge them, condemn them, *and* execute them – and the civil courts can't interfere! The Parliament just voted them in!'

'Did you think it couldn't happen here?' Joseph grinned briefly.

'For God's sake, it's crazy! These people are giving up their civil rights! It's a step back into the Middle Ages!'

'Funny thing about those Middle Ages,' said Joseph. 'They just keep coming back. Mortals keep thinking they're in Modern Times, you know, they get all this neat technology and pass all these humanitarian laws, and then something happens: there's an economic crisis, or science makes some discovery people can't deal with. And boom, people go right back to burning Jews and selling pieces of the true Cross. Don't you ever make the mistake of thinking that mortals want to live in a golden age. They hate thinking.'

'But this doesn't have anything to do with intellect!' I protested. 'It's a question of survival! Don't they realize they've just voted absolute power to their enemies? My God, where's their common sense?'

Joseph and Nef just laughed, such a hollow sound that I wanted to run from the room. Joseph flung his hat up to the near bedpost, where it caught neatly and swung. 'You think this is bad? You should have seen the stuff the English stood for under Henry the Eighth. Screw the monkeys anyway.

Can't either of you come up with some jolly Yuletide high jinks for the old man?'

'Why don't you adapt something from Dickens?' Nef suggested. 'Who's to know, anyway?'

I reached for my cloak. 'I think I'll go out for a while.'

The snow packed us in and insulated us from any news by word of mouth; so the mortals got busy with their Christmas in the merriest of moods, and tacked up big swags of holly in the great hall, all blissful ignorance.

I had expected that we, as Spaniards, would be asked to stay in the background through most of the festivities. I got a big surprise: far from being an embarrassment, we were suddenly considered social assets. Sir Walter planned Spanish dances and Spanish refreshments and was confidently expecting some theatrical extravaganza from Joseph. Every time he asked about it, Joseph smiled wider and with increasing desperation. Nef and I gave him all sorts of helpful ideas, the best of which, as I recall, had the Man of La Mancha meeting the Ghosts of Christmas Past, Present, and Future, but Joseph finally came up with something on his own that required large amounts of pasteboard and secrecy.

He had lots of time, at least. In the sixteenth century, Christmas was celebrated from Christmas Day to January 6. In future times, of course, it would shift forward until it began in November and ended abruptly on Christmas Eve, which was how it was calendared at Company bases. I observed the Solstice by climbing from bed to watch the red sun rise out of black cloud, and marked his flaming early death that evening through black leafless branches. So the mystery passed, and the mortals hadn't even begun their celebration yet.

The first thing I saw on Christmas Day was, appropriately enough, the New Testament. Nicholas had it open on his chest and was reading in silence from the first chapter of the Gospel of Saint Luke. I yawned and stretched, and leaned up on my elbow to peer at the staggering black letters. It was a beautiful little story he was reading, and a perfectly simple one. How all those bishops and grand inquisitors drew what they did from it is beyond me.

I lay back and watched Nicholas's profile as he read. He was always pale when he first awoke, as though it took a little time for the blood to rise into his face. So at this hour he looked severe and autocratic, carved from ivory, and his light eyes flickered restlessly over the Word of God, or their pupils dilated in the crystal when a particular verse moved him.

He closed the book and blinked back tears. What was it like to believe in something that much?

The rooms smelled of spice, smoke, cut green branches, and mortals. They began arriving before noon, in wagons drawn by great stamping horses that had Nef running to the windows with cries of delight. Little mortal males in furred robes, the older ones clean-shaven, the younger ones with styled and pointed beards. Little mortal females in the latest fashions. I realized with a pang that my green gown, which I had planned to wear that day, was now hopelessly out of style. I spent a frantic hour sewing glass aglets on my peach outfit to cover the moth holes.

But my fussing was minimal compared to the scenes that were going on in the kitchen, and as for the great hall – *caramba*. A cartload of consort drove up, unloading musicians and their instruments, and for a desperate half hour no one could figure out how to let them into the minstrel's gallery, which hadn't been opened in thirty years. A makeshift bandstand was being hammered together in a corner when somebody finally located the key, in a tin box at the back of a shelf. Most of this business Nicholas had to supervise, as well as a host of minor things forgotten until the last minute. Sir Walter was too far gone in hand-kissing and back-slapping among his guests to be reminded he had not made a final decision on whether he wanted the consort playing before, during, or after the feast. So they started about ten o'clock and just tootled away, growing ever louder as the level in their ale barrel dropped.

The entrance of the Evil Spaniards was delayed, thanks to me.

'I can't wear this!' I wailed. 'I stuck on every shiny doodad I own, and there's three big moth holes I didn't even see on the sleeve!'

'So take the sleeves off.' Joseph examined his beard in the reflective surface of the credenza.

'Are you nuts? Every single one of those ladies downstairs has an outfit with matching sleeves,' I said. 'I can't look like a frump in front of Englishwomen!'

'So start a new fashion.'

'If you'd put in the requisition for field dress like I'd asked you to —'

'Oh, here.' Nef dove into her wardrobe and found a big pink ribbon, which she tied hastily around my arm. 'Look, they'll never know.'

'The color doesn't match,' I fretted.

'Think of it as an accent.'

'And it's cutting off my circulation.'

'You want to see some circulation cut off?' Joseph started across the room menacingly. 'It's going to be hard enough making an entrance in front of all those monkeys without being late, too.'

'Will you both please shut up?' Nef demanded. Easy for her to say: she had a gorgeous plum-colored gown that was practically new. She grabbed my hand, hooked one arm through Joseph's, and dragged us out into the corridor. 'Anybody would think you'd never been to a mortal party before,' she scolded Joseph.

'Artist's nerves. I never wrote an entertainment before,' Joseph muttered. We started unobtrusively down the stairs. People were milling all about.

'Well, you didn't really write this one, did you?' said Nef. 'You copied it from —'

'Good gentles all, give greeting to the most renowned Doctor Ruy of Ansolebar, most learned physician to the Court of the Most Gracious, Serene, and Catholic Emperor Charles!' yelled Master Ffrawney, popping out unexpectedly from the foot of the stairs. We froze in midstep. All those mortal folk turned to look at us.

Only Nef's grip on my arm kept me from backing rapidly up the stairs. A great suffocating wave of smell came up to me. It was mortal fear, and a good quantity of mortal hatred, too. Riper than the holiday food. More pungent than the evergreen boughs. So bright in their Christmas finery, the little mortals regarded us out of animal eyes. Then, unnervingly, they all smiled. The males bowed; the females curtsied.

'Oh, Master Ffrawney, you flatter me,' said Joseph, with no trace of a Spanish accent at all. 'To be sure, good people, I am only Sir Walter's old friend. Why, were we not boys together?'

'Certes, so we were.' Sir Walter picked up his cue (for all I know, he believed it by this time) and emerged from the throng. 'Come, Doctor Ruy, there is excellent muscadel here, none better may be had at the Emperor's table. And we shall have a Spanish viand later,' he announced to his guests.

This did not help the smell. Yet we edged out way down with tiny frightened steps, and the mortal guests drew away from us as though Joseph had a cloven hoof.

'How festive it all looks,' he remarked gamely.

And here came Nicholas in his severe Protestant black, towering head and shoulders above the guests. He met my eyes. People stared at him now, and the fear smell sharpened to anticipation. They were expecting a clash, but he took both my hands and kissed them.

'Well met here, Lady Rose. Doctor Ruy, I will be so bold as to carry your daughter away for a cup of hippocras.' And he pulled me after him. The crowd registered astonishment. The tension broke.

'Ha ha ha,' rattled Joseph. 'Yes, go on. These young folk *will* be kissing in corners,' he explained to the crowd.

It was all right now. Mortals love lovers, especially young ones. Everyone made way for Nicholas and me as we went in search of a punch bowl. 'Thy hands are ice-cold,' said Nicholas under his breath.

'And so should thine be, facing so many English,' I replied. 'If gazes were cannonballs, they'd have blasted us off the stairs.'

'Oh, fear not.' He located a steaming flagon of wine and filled a goblet for me. 'These folk are the best small gentry of Kent! They'd no more harm thy father than wear a doublet that was out of fashion, which is to say they durst do neither.'

'Good.' I gulped at the wine. He watched me drink.

'Aye, sup that down. Thy face is pale as milk.'

'If you think of anything else to build up my confidence, please tell me,' I snapped in Greek.

He considered. 'I like the aglets,' he offered.

The operative words for this phase of the merriment seemed to be drink and mingle, as the scullery boys set up the long trestle tables in the hall. All we lacked was a cocktail waitress with a tray of little sandwiches. I took Nicholas's arm, and we moved cautiously around the edges, looking for a quiet place to talk. This soon proved impossible, however, because no less than four mortals came up to wave their crucifixes at me and tell me how their parents had been gardeners, or ladies-in-waiting, or household-account keepers to poor old Queen Katherine.

'God's my life, is it Nicholas Harpole?'

Nicholas turned abruptly, carrying me with him. We beheld a stout young male with a full beard, very steel-and-leather military in his bearing. Nicholas regarded him with narrowed eyes. 'And he knoweth me not,' added the speaker. 'But I'd have known thee, Nick. Jesu, man, it's Tom!'

And he put out his hand, but Nicholas drew back as though he were a snake, and radiated such anger I was nearly knocked down. The other only laughed.

'What, art afeared still? I can tell thee, I've well washed away the stink of our tutor's blasphemies. I see thou hast done the same.'

'Why are you here?' asked Nicholas, very quietly.

'I am a wooer.' Tom jerked his thumb at a crowd of girls around Sir Walter. 'Sweet Anne yonder. Not any goddess Venus, as you see, but I'll warm myself with her dower lands. Time to turn one's thoughts to such things, eh? I wot well we are not boys anymore.' His eyes glinted wickedly. 'How does it go? ''When I was a child, I spoke as a child'' —'

Oh, Nicholas was going to hit him. There went the arm muscles contracting! I braced myself, but his back molars clashed together like boulders, and he said:

'In Christ's name, be silent.'

'Tush, man, no one will mark me. And who'll mark thee? Though hast found thyself the warmest bed in the house, and a Spanish bed to boot.' He swept my knuckles to his lips. 'Lady, buenos dias. Nicholas, thou wast ever a lad of excellent common sense. With any luck, wilt wear a cardinal's hat before thou'rt forty.'

That really did it. Nicholas grabbed the front of Tom's doublet and yanked him up to eye level. I said, 'Nicholas!' and Tom said, 'Peace, man, remember!' and one or two people turned to stare. Nicholas put him down.

'If I insulted thy lady, Nick, I'm sorry on't.' Tom shrugged his doublet back together. 'And Christ be my witness, I meant no harm. But what I said in jest, my heart meant.' With a sincerity that was worse than his bantering he put a hand on Nicholas's arm. 'Thou wert ever the best scholar among us. There's new men at Court, Nick, the old papists die and make room for young ones. There's benefices, Nick, there's gold, there's Dame Fortune with her knees wide apart! Get thee to Court and try her, Nick, and shalt rise higher than poor Tom with his plain wife and two farms in Kent.' He looked across the room at his girlfriend and sighed. 'God grants each man his gifts. I have only a prick; thou hast both a prick and a brain. Get thee to Court, I say.' And with a final melancholy smack on Nicholas's arm he wandered away, and so just missed having his head ripped off. My turn then to drag Nicholas to a sideboard and pour him a drink. Some Christmas so far, eh?

By this time the tables were all set up and ready, so we were seated in order of our status, and the first of the dishes were brought in with great ceremony.

'A dish of small birds!' announced Master Ffrawney from his post by the hall door. In came the small birds, pigeons probably, all roasted and set on end with little pasteboard heads and wings. 'A dish of pike in gallantine!' cried Master Ffrawney next, and in it came: phew, week-old fish in a sauce that smelled of cinnamon candy. 'A dish of pie caneline!' ushered in one of the aforementioned industrial-strength pies, borne by a gasping server who just barely made it to the table.

And after that we were brought a dish of olives of veal, and a dish of boar Porpentine, and the very boar's head itself: splendid as on a Gordon's gin bottle, with big bulging eyes of half lemons stuck in its blind sockets. I'd have given a lot for a gin and tonic as the sweet cavalcade of indigestion rolled on.

They brought in the peacock: the whole skin had been flayed off, then tucked back, feathers and all, on the roasted bird to make it look lifelike. Only, they hadn't been able to unclench the little sphincter or whatever kept the tail folded up, and the plumes moreover had become sadly draggled on the ride from the poulterer's, so they had taken the tail apart and stuck the remaining feathers on a big pasteboard fan, and painted in the missing ones.

Ducks by the dozen, chickens by the tens, packed like sardines into dreadnought pies or propped up in little mounds of golden dead bodies. Peculiar combinations of fish and flowers. Clods of roast beef colored blue with heliotrope juice to make them look like venison. Wonderful eggy pancakes, dusted with cinnamon and sugar. Cinnamon and sugar were in nearly everything, actually.

They brought in a trumpet to fanfare the arrival of the Spanish viand, a nice digestible recipe they'd coaxed out of Joseph, and when it hit the table, everyone really stared: it looked great, a sort of sweet rice pilaf, a big mound of rice and nuts and raisins, but all around the edge of the dish were perched big insects sculpted out of almond paste. 'Rice after the fashion of Saint John the Baptist!' screamed Master Ffrawney triumphantly. 'A pudding of Biscay!' There was polite silence as everyone tried to figure out what the bugs were there for.

'I do not recall that I specified such a curious subtlety as this,' said Joseph at last.

'Please you, signior, but you said that we must have syrup of locusts to pour about the top, signior, and we had it not, wherefore Mistress Alison made locusts out of marchpane,' explained the serving boy. 'It were the best we could do, signior.'

'The locust I meant is an evergreen tree bearing sweet beans,' Joseph informed him.

'Oh,' said the boy.

It was a great success anyway. The guests had drunk so much hippocras by this time that they thought the bugs were funny, and walked them up and down the table until their little toothpick legs fell off, or set them on ladies' headdresses or bosoms.

Nicholas was not amused by anything. He sat beside me looking dangerous, with the corners of his mouth pulled down from bad temper and a bright flush on his cheekbones from wine. I smiled at him timidly, but he sat staring unblinking into the fire.

When the first lull fell in the eating and drinking, Sir Walter lurched to his feet, rubbing his hands together. 'Now, my neighbors, my friends, we shall have some diversion, shall we not?'

There were shouts of 'Aye!' and general jolly laughter, and Sir Walter peered down the table at Nicholas. 'Nicholas, my boy, what have we?'

'A cockfight, sir.' Nicholas stood and signaled to men who waited at the door. Then he sat down beside me and folded his arms. In came two men, each bearing a gallant little bird with a bright cockade tail. They were held up for the guests to view, and what howls, what wagers, what quantities of coins were flung down on the banquet table!

I looked at Joseph. He was gazing into space with a vague smile, but his eyes were utterly blank. Nef was staring fixedly into her goblet and would not lift her head. The men put the cockerels down and backed away fast. The shouting in the hall grew deafening, and what happened next was as bad as you can imagine. Blood spattered everywhere, feathers flew. The little birds cut each other to ribbons, and one was blinded before the fight was done.

I leaned back shaking and found Nicholas's arm about me. 'Take heart, Rose, and play the Spaniard. Whatever shalt thou do at a bull baiting?' he muttered. I burst into tears, but it least it got him out of his rage; he was contrite and kissed me, while the hall rang with bloodthirsty laughter.

A lamprey pie and maumany were served up next, as the blood was hastily mopped away. Then we were treated to an exhibition of fencing by two Frenchmen, very exciting, especially since they had no buttons on their foils. At least they didn't blind each other.

Then we had hasletts and troycream and date justles, just in case we hadn't had enough sweets to suit us, and the Four Tumbling Brothers of Billingsgate came in and vaulted all over one another for a while. People applauded greatly and threw them pennies. I saw a few spoons disappearing into the brothers' sleeves and hats as well.

By this time the tables were long highways of gnawed bones and fragments of piecrust, so Master Ffrawney entreated us all to decamp to the other corner of the great hall. There, arrangements had been made for card games in various nooks and crannies for those inclined to sit sensibly quiet after such a meal. For those not so inclined, the consort began to play dance tunes. At last!

But nobody began. People stood milling about as a good old-fashioned morisque opened; heads were lifted uncertainly, but not a foot moved, not a hip swayed.

I couldn't bear it. I seized Nicholas's arm. 'Is this the way you dance in England?' I cried.

He looked around. 'It is the custom for the master of the house to dance first,' he explained, as his eye lit upon Sir Walter just sitting down to a nice game of primero with Nef and some other lady. 'Sir Walter! Would you dance, sir?'

'What?' The little knight glanced around and became conscious of the gaffe. 'Oh.' He looked longingly at the cards in his hand but then brightened. 'Nicholas, thou shalt lead for me. Hark ye, gentles, this tall fellow shall be lord for a little while in my place! Do you all take your steps from him!'

The master of the consort, who had been watching for a cue all this while, stopped the music abruptly. Nicholas stood aghast as all eyes turned to him. I took his hand. 'Come, love.'

The music began again, and I drew him into the dance. In those days dancers saluted each other first, as fencers do, very stately. A little stylized kissing of hands, the fellow bowing and the lady making a curtsey, then into the patterned intricate steps.

It was slow for a morisque, which was good because Nicholas hadn't danced in – how long? But the music caught us up, and the grace of his body came back to him. What bliss.

It disturbs me to remember how happy I was, how my blood moved in that hour. Music at that time was still brazen with colors picked up in the East during the Crusades, harsh with rhythms in a way it would not be again until the classical rock of the twentieth century. Dancing was erotic, formal, and feverish together. Nothing much more than hands touched, but what tension can crackle in fingertips. I forgot all about the terrible Christmas and the stinking food: there was only the music and my lover, who might as well have been naked there beside me, so fine he looked. Other couples had moved out beside us and were following in the steps. The music shook the very house; the bass rackett vibrated in the walls. Unreal at the corners, all kinds of little dramas were being acted out. Over there by the window at primero, Nef was beating the trunk hose off Sir Walter. Her face perfectly impassive, she accepted a card from him.

Over there by the carved panels, Joseph was surrounded by four or five anxious old males who had got enough of a look at Sir Walter to know that whatever physick he had, they had to have it too. Joseph's face was bland and slightly apologetic. I heard cracked elderly voices offering him many things, strange things, some of them.

And over there by the fire, nasty Tom was talking to someone, grinning and pointing at Nicholas. A bad man. Dangerous. His face went pale suddenly, and he clutched at his throat, and the concerned friend had to thump him on the back. We kept on dancing.

A basse-dance, a tourdion, a saltarello; bransles in sets of threes, and allemandes. Night fell early and black beyond the windows. Cressets were brought in, to flare and smoke. They made the dance more sensual, with complications of moving lights and shadow.

Pavanes we danced. A pavane is an ideal dance for lovers, because it's so slow, you can flirt or talk without losing your step. My very favorite pavane was 'Belle Qui Tient Ma Vie' (the one from *The Private Life of Henry VIII, Romeo and Juliet*, the Leslie Howard version, and *Orlando*: both the 1993 version with Tilda Swinton and the 2150 remake with Zoë Barrymore), and it had just begun when Nicholas said: 'Thy father will not give consent for me to wed thee.'

'I know.' What on earth did it matter? I took his hand, turned, swayed. He shifted the conversation into Greek.

'What do you think,' he turned and bowed, 'of an elopement?'

I stared but did not miss a step. Yes, a good dance for this kind of talk.

'Run away?' I said at last. 'But where would we run, love?'

He took my hand and we turned. 'To a safe place.'

'Do you know of any?'

He was silent down the whole passage of the room, but when we turned again, he said:

'Some place where we are not known. Neither you nor I. We would have to leave Kent.'

He had to switch into Latin for that, calling it the Place of the Cantii. It sounded very strange. I had a momentary vision of him blue and howling in a chariot, making life miserable for Flavius. 'But how would we live?' I began a slow curtsey.

'I could teach boys. I could keep another man's accounts.' He looked a little desperate. 'There must be some way for a husband to feed his wife. And children.' He glanced at me to see how I reacted to that.

'If God grants that I have children,' I said primly, avoiding his gaze. 'It is not the fate of all women.' Certainly it was not my fate, since the installation of my contraceptive symbiote. Up until this time I'd been saying I took one of Doctor Ruy's secret potions to prevent a baby, but if we got married, Nicholas would see no reason . . .

If we got married . . .

Threading through the dance, I thought about it seriously. It wasn't unheard of. Joseph had admitted that. What if we really did run off together, elope, and wed?

I would have years and years, happy years with Nicholas. Someday he'd die, and my heart would break; but later was better than soon, and the good times would come first.

In the end, I could return contrite to Dr. Zeus. I was sure I knew enough about Company methods to avoid being caught until then. I'd accept the disciplinary actions there'd undoubtedly be, but it would have been worthwhile. Then I'd go on with my life. I could do that, couldn't I? I mean, if you're an immortal, they have to let you get away with peccadilloes like that, because what are they going to do? Kill you?

Instantly I had a plan. 'I know what we can do,' I told him. 'We can get away to the Continent. England is not safe anymore. Europe, love, that's the place to go! We could go to Geneva! Many English are living there in exile now, and you'd find work easily. Translating. Teaching. Something!'

But he had been thinking about it too, as he measured his steps to mine. When I mentioned Geneva, something went dark in his face. 'Running,' he said. 'Hiding. Just like your father, living by his wits. We would be paupers, and year by year your eyes would grow more frightened. No, sweetheart, it would not be a good life. I must think of something better.'

Slowly we turned. He bowed. I bent to him. *Mendoza*, said an urgent voice. *Don't do it. Don't even think about it.*

I looked around, startled, to meet Joseph's dark gaze. *How dare you listen in on my signal?* I raged at him.

What signal? he retorted. *You're talking as loud as the music.*

I turned my back on him, but lowered my voice as I said:

'Nicholas, we'd be safe in Switzerland.' Which was true; Dr. Zeus practically ran the place. Well, perhaps we wouldn't be so safe there. 'Or Italy. Or France. Nicholas, a black storm is breaking over England. Any dumb animal knows enough to get in out of the rain. We must go to Europe, love.'

'Your metaphor is badly chosen.' He rose to his full height. 'It is no storm that comes, but a war. No man seeks shelter in a war. He fights.' He looked over at Tom in contempt. 'Or he surrenders.'

'If we were safe in Geneva,' I ventured to Nicholas, 'among so many righteous people, surely I might learn to trust your God.'

He looked at me bleakly. 'Or you might learn to hate me for a coward. I must save your soul and mine own too, and flight is not the way. Give me time, love, to think what we can do.'

'All my time I give you,' I promised. And the dance came to an end, in slow final steps. Now I can never listen to that music without feeling sad, though it was my very favorite pavane. I have never danced to it since.

I realize now that I must have talked him out of elopement, without meaning to. His idea must not have seemed stupid until he heard someone else agree with it.

It wouldn't have worked, of course.

After so many dances, people began to flag, and by this time the tables had been spread with clean cloths; so everyone trooped back in and found places for round two. The mortal guests were stupefied with all the eating and dancing, too sleepy to be quarrelsome. The musicians were tired too: they were doing mostly lute pieces now, very quiet, very soothing.

Only Joseph and Sir Walter were agitated. I looked over at them curiously. They were whispering together just as if they really were old friends. Nicholas got up and went over to them and leaned down. Sir Walter spoke rapidly in his ear. Nicholas listened, his face impassive; he nodded once, and then rose to exit the room. I leaned, trying to catch his eye; he gave me a peculiar smile and disappeared into the servants' hall.

How disappointing. I was hoping we might dance again, if the musicians woke up a little. I rested my chin on my palm and watched the mortals gossip, or doze, or stuff themselves.

Then they began to go out, the mortals. Not to leave the room, you understand, but to go *out* – like lamps. They were flickering out all around me and becoming transparent; one and then another vanished into the silence of the torchlight. Pop, here went a little lady in a great starched ruff, in the very act of talking behind her hand to her neighbor. Pop, there went a rakish fellow with mustaches, even as he poured wine in a long red stream from a high-held pitcher into his cup. Pop, there went both Master and Mistress Preeves, between one snore and the next. Before long there were no people at all, only tables, and then they too were gone. The fire burned down dim and cold, and the room itself changed, grew small and dark, the timbers blackening and warping. All the gilding and bright decoration went away.

Whoosh, the fire went out. I was alone in a cold blue light that streamed in through the windows. I looked at the windows, and they were distorted, for the leading had sagged and thrown the bright diamond panes out of true. But they faded and were gone, lingering for a moment as thin gray lines crossing the face of the moon. I looked back into the room, but it had gone too; I was alone in an expanse of snow mounded over ruins, and there was no house, no garden, only moonlight and dark trees in the distance . . .

I jerked upright in the midst of chattering mortal folk having their Christmas. I grabbed for a cup of wine. My teeth chattered against the rim. Sir Walter was standing, raising his hands for silence; he beamed around at all the guests.

'My neighbors all! Ye have supped this night on many a rare dish, and sported even as folk do at Court. Yea, I am assured that they keep Christmas no better even at the Emperor's very Court —' The door at the far side of the hall slammed open, and one of the serving boys ran in.

'My master!' he shouted. 'Such portents, such signs and wonders! A great stag has been sighted, afar off, and he hath fire all along his horns!'

There was startled silence. Then the buzz of comments started up, and Sir Walter cried above it:

'Now what could this mean?'

We heard pounding footsteps, and another servant burst into the hall. 'Oh, sir!' he cried. 'Such strange things are abroad this night! There has been a great cloud hanging over the wood, and it shouted with the voice of a man!'

Before anyone could react to this, a third servant appeared. 'Now Christ save us all! I have just seen, with mine own eyes, a tree that burned and yet was green! Surely this prefigures some fearful thing!'

It did, too, because there came a tremendous crash, and both the great hall doors flew open. At the same time the blazing fire dimmed and went out, just as in my vision, and though I had seen Joseph throw something into it, I still scanned nervously, involuntarily. Something was approaching, each step a thunder that shook the house. There was a flare of light from somewhere beyond; it threw a vast shadow that rippled across the wall, moved closer with each heartbeat.

Then it was in the doorway, silhouetted against the spectral glow: the figure of a knight, immensely tall, bearing in his hands a great double-headed axe. Several people screamed. Another flare of light, from a ball of green fire that hissed upon the floor. By its flickering light we could see the knight as he moved stiffly into the room.

His armor was wound about with ivy and stuck with holly branches here and there. His helmet was monstrously high, higher for the branching antlers at the crest; the visor was down, and no face could be seen. More green lights popped and rolled before him as he proceeded down the length of the hall. The faces of the guests shone out like masks as the light passed them: frozen in astonishment, terror, or laughter. He came to a stop just before Sir Walter's place at table. The candles burned high there, outlining Sir Walter in a golden halo.

'WHO IS LORD IN THIS PLACE?' cried a great hollow voice from within the helmet.

'I am he,' said Sir Walter, trying to sound dignified but coming across smug. 'What art thou, apparition, that troubles our festivities? Whither hast thou come, and wherefore?'

'I AM A SPIRIT THAT DOES NOT REST,' boomed the voice. 'AGE AFTER AGE I COME AGAIN, TO TEST MEN'S HEARTS: FROM OUT OF THE DEEP HILL I COME, UNDER THE STARING MOON.'

'Come, spirit, tell us thy purpose!' demanded Sir Walter. The knight took a step backward and swung his axe up high. The lights came up slightly; the blade winked as it rose.

'I CRY A CHALLENGE TO THIS MORTAL COMPANY! WHO SHALL TRY ODDS WITH ME? WHO HATH A FEARLESS HEART?'

Sir Walter slapped his hand on his sword hilt. 'Why, who shall match thee but this hall's very master? I take thy challenge, phantom!'

'NAY, LORD, THIS CANNOT BE,' replied the knight. 'BY LAW MORE ANCIENT THAN THE STANDING OAKS, I AM BID CHOOSE MINE OWN CHAMPION FROM YOUR GUESTS. WHO IN THIS PLACE SHALL STAND A CAST WITH ME?'

He began to stalk along the tables, turning his helmet this way and that.

'WHO HATH A VALIANT HEART?' he called. 'WHO

DURST HAZARD A CHANCE?' Nobody spoke up, though somebody was crying hysterically. Goodness, hadn't these people read their own literature?

Finally he stopped and again lifted the axe high. Slowly he brought it down, down, down, and pointed at a very small boy, who sat wedged between his parents. Relieved laughter from all the adults as the tension broke.

'THIS SHALL BE MINE OPPONENT,' declared the knight. The little boy shrank back, his eyes huge in his white face.

'Why, Edward, it seems thou must play the hero now,' his father joked.

Edward shook his head mutely and made himself even smaller; but rowdy grown-ups all over the room were shouting for him now.

'I can't, Dad,' he said in a tiny voice.

'What, sirrah, wilt thou not?' His mother reached down and pinched him, hard, which brought him yelping to his feet; and his father hauled him up onto the table, telling him:

'If thou'rt a coward, thou'rt no boy of mine!'

I am always so sorry for mortal children.

Well, the knight put down his axe and lifted Edward to the floor, where he stood shaking in his little holiday clothes.

'NOW, EDWARD,' admonished the knight. 'THOU SHALT TAKE MINE AXE' – he lifted the weapon and put it in the child's hands – 'AND I SHALL BEND MY NECK TO THE BLOW. THOU SHALT PLAY THE HEADSMAN, AND TRY WHETHER MY HEAD COME OFF OR NO.'

'I dursn't!' gasped Edward, and there were jeers and catcalls from all around the room.

'NAY, EDWARD, TAKE THOU HEART.' The knight turned to sweep the room with his gaze. 'WHAT THOU MUST DO, ALL THESE FEAR TO DO THEMSELVES.' The noise subsided a little. The knight turned back.

'STRIKE ONLY ONCE,' he said. 'CLEANLY, AND QUICK.' Then, ever so slowly, he bent down, and the broad antlers raked the air in their descent. Edward made a little terrified sound; but he dragged the great axe aloft, tottering with effort, and let it come crashing down.

A crack, a smash, and a shower of sparks. All the lights burned high at once, and the knight's head came off and shattered on the floor, spilling out sweets and trinkets and little sugared cakes. Nicholas rose up smiling and tousled.

'A Merry Christmas, neighbors, to you all!' he shouted.

I laughed so hard, there were tears in my eyes. All around me mortals whooped and applauded. Joseph closed his eyes in relief that all his special effects had worked. Little Edward blinked at Nicholas. After a careful survey of the grown folk, none of whom were watching him, he knelt and began methodically scooping loot into his doublet.

Now I remember the detail of the boy, but then I saw only Nicholas in his pasteboard armor. Nicholas looked charming and silly and very sexy too, in a kinky sort of way. Somehow it all recedes from me as I write it down, like a fade-out in an old film. I remember that Nicholas came clumping back to his place at table, and that amid all the clamor we slipped off upstairs. There I played the squire, or maybe page is the better word, and helped my knight get naked in the darkness. Jolly Christmas pastimes then, I can assure you, as peach wool and green carapace scattered together on the floor.

Yet the first memory that comes when I think of that night is the wary face of the child. I wonder who he was, and what became of him.

Chapter Eighteen

The big surprise the next morning was that most of the guests were still there.

Waking slowly in Nicholas's arms, my first drowsy scan of the house told me it was pullulating like a beehive. When we crept down cautiously in the first winter light, we saw rows of makeshift beds all along the gallery, most of which were still occupied by sleeping mortals.

'What are they doing here?' I whispered. Nicholas shook his head in amazement. As we came to the stair landing, we met Master Ffrawney coming up with a tray, followed by Joan, whose expression was even more martyred than usual. Ffrawney smiled at us maliciously. Nicholas ignored his ill will and pointed in the direction of the gallery.

'What means this?' he said. 'Have these folk no homes?'

'Oh, to be sure they do.' Master Ffrawney leaned the tray on a corner post. 'But snow is deep and bitter cold, or so Sir Walter wisely said last night, when he was far gone in wine. Further, he assured his many friends that the hour was late, and all those present solemnly agreed with him. Lastly, he said he was not such a starveling beggar as to bid his guests depart when his splendid house could accommodate them all. Whereupon beds were made, and those folk who could still walk went off to sleep in them. I am bound for His Grace's chamber now, to tell him that the folk who remained at table clamor for breakfast.'

'Doth he think this is Whitehall Palace?' Nicholas was aghast. 'His revenues will not feed all these folk the whole Christmastide, he cannot afford it.'

'Well, no doubt *thou* hadst told him so, hadst thou been there. But *thou* wast abed early, if I recall me.' And he gave me an arch glance.

'I must speak with him privily.' Nicholas started back up the stairs.

'Then thou must ask the youngest Ashford girl to get out of his bed.'

'Oh, sweet Christ!' Nicholas halted. He turned back and took the tray. 'I'll bear him this.'

'As thou wilt.' Master Ffrawney shrugged and turned to descend. 'I'll go and see what manner of fare we have remaining.'

This was grim. With an apologetic look Nicholas left me. I picked my way through the bodies to Nef's door and slipped inside.

They were sitting there listening to the radio, Joseph, Nef, and the unicorn.

. . . the consequences of the Act of Supremacy were tremendous, and its proposed repeal is viewed as a token measure only by the Council. Of course, they have no idea yet of the extent to which Pole will implement the repeal. Roderick, can you give us the story from Court?

Well, Decius, the cardinal appears to be having a temporary eclipse of his power over the queen right now, because of course with the Christmas festivities the queen and the prince consort are publicly together quite a bit, so the growing rift between them isn't as apparent as it was. The cardinal's doing most of his damage in the Parliament, though, and a few of the Council members are beginning to get an inkling of just how far to the religious right things are going to swing. Sir William Cecil, in fact . . .

'Smart man. Cake?' Joseph held out a small plate. I inspected it gingerly and took a slice.

'None of those awful people went home!' I announced. 'Couldn't you have done something? They're going to eat us out of house and headquarters!'

'What will be, will be. The little guy was in what you'd call an expansive mood last night. I guess he'll just have to send out for a few more sides of beef.'

'I won thirty-seven pounds last night,' remarked Nef.

'So, what did you think of my diversion?' Joseph leaned back and sipped wine. 'What about those pyrotechnics, huh? What about that sleight of hand?'

'Not bad. The piñata I liked particularly. Nicholas was a surprise too.'

'He's tall and real loud. Perfect for the part,' said Joseph. I bristled, but Nef said thoughtfully:

'Sir Walter will need more entertainment if all these people stay until Twelfth Night. I'll bet I could make a fortune at cards.'

How could millennia-old superbeings be so boring? I wandered over to the window and watched the snow fall. Spreading my fingertips against the glass, I tuned in and scanned.

Many voices, inquiring about breakfast and sanitary arrangements. Dark voices belowstairs, complaining of the extra work. Master Ffrawney saying something high-pitched about the snow. And there, there it was, Nicholas's voice in earnest entreaty.

'Sir, I tell you plainly that you waste your substance. What will you do? Where will you get more money?'

'Why, with any luck I shall better my fortune.' There was a faint defiance in Sir Walter's voice.

'In God's name, sir, how?'

'I have my plans.' Now there was desperation. 'I am revolving in my mind some several stratagems, any of which may bring me fortune enough.'

Nicholas radiated bewilderment.

'By feeding peacocks to the Syssings and the Preeves the whole Christmastide?'

'Um, no. But, Nicholas, I must think of myself! Gold I have had for many years, and the good name of my fathers; but mine own name is unknown, Nicholas. Thirty years have I spent in careful restoration of Sir Alexander's glory, ensuring that his name be not forgot. Were it not well now to add mine own glories to the name of Iden?'

There was a long pause.

'If I take your meaning aright,' said Nicholas carefully, 'you seek a life in the world again. Why, this is well; commerce suited you. I shall, if you wish, make inquiries as to companies seeking capital and mercantile argosies. You may buy and trade and so increase your revenues until within them you shall live as liberally as you please. Shall I ride forth, when the roads are clear?'

'Yea. Nay. I would, and yet . . .' Sir Walter's voice grew small.

'Sir, this is excellent good sense.'

'But it fretted my soul to be a merchant,' Sir Walter complained. 'It is no fit work for a gentleman. Sir Alexander won his glory with a sword, in the service of his king.'

'So he did, sir, but men live otherwise now. Any knave with a pistol may drop a knight-at-arms, and the tourneys are all for show. Take heart! Lords win honors by their wits these days, and doubt not that you shall do the same. Be thrifty! Send your neighbors home now, and you shall feast them in greater splendor on another day.'

'But I promised them supper, Nicholas,' said Sir Walter miserably.

A long, long exhaled breath from Nicholas.

'Sir, what shall they eat? There is no more beef slaughtered and dressed. Who hath fowls to sell us, even should we buy? The snows have filled the ways to your farms.'

Another long pause, and then a snuffling sound. Sir Walter was crying.

Creak creak creak. Nicholas pacing furiously.

'We shall make broth,' he said, 'out of the leavings. And put in some unlikely herb, or some color to make it strange. And you shall tell them it is a dish from the Court of the Emperor, that it is the Spanish fashion to sup but lightly after a feast day. Doctor Ruy will not naysay you.'

'I could do that, couldn't I?' said Sir Walter through his tears.

'Aye, and – and – offer that they may, nay, *ought* to be purged and bled by the doctor, which (you shall say) is also the fashion of the Court after a great feast. I warrant they'll get them home in haste then.'

'Thou hast brains, boy, thou hast.' A honk, as Sir Walter blew his nose on the sheet.

'And you shall make them promise of great cheer in some time to come.'

'Oh, good.'

'And so honor is served, with no ruin to your purse thereby.'

'Nicholas, thou hast ever done me good service. 'Tis only a pity —'

Pause. 'Sir?'

'A pity thou art so inclined to Gospelling. It suits not with the time, I fear.'

Dead silence. Then:

'I may cut my coat to follow fashion, sir, but not my conscience.' Nicholas's voice was rigid.

'Well, but thou dost neither. I shall have new livery made for thee, what say you? Not so much black. It puts folk in mind of Lutherans.'

'When you can afford new livery, sir, you may do what you list.'

'I shall, then. Go thou now, and send Jack that I might dress me.'

'Sir.' Nicholas was withdrawing, coming down the hall in a glow of anger. I left the window.

'Sir Walter can't send out for more beef,' I told Joseph abruptly. 'He doesn't have enough money. He and Nicholas were just fighting about it. Can't you do something to help? Prescribe fasting for health reasons, maybe?'

Joseph sighed. 'I can try. He needs to be fine-tuned after all that whoopee last night anyway. All right, I'll pay him a visit.'

'Great!' I ran from the room so I could catch Nicholas halfway down the hall.

'My love! My father fears that immoderate merriment may do Sir Walter harm, and hinder careful physick. He will counsel him to send his neighbors home.'

'My master is already so persuaded, but if thy father's word will strengthen the argument, be it so.' Nicholas leaned against the wall and folded his arms. 'I never heard that wits came with wrinkles, but as he loses the one, it seems he loses the other too.'

'Oh, love.' I put my arms around him, so sorry to see him unhappy, and moodily he held me. As we stood there, a smell came floating up the stairs, a greasy rank smell.

'What reeks so?' I said in distaste.

'Suet pudding from last night. They fry it for breakfast,' he replied. 'We must get these folk out of the house ere we have nothing to feed them.'

'You could make a mess of thin pottage,' I said mischievously. 'Color it with saffron and tell folk it is a rare dish out of Spain.'

It was a stupid slip. No older, experienced operative would have made it. Nicholas glanced down at me with suspicion in his eyes. Only for a moment, but the suspicion was there.

'Why, so I had resolved to do,' he said. 'Dost thou listen at doors, Rose?'

'Nay, love, I have been with my father!' I buried my face against him to conceal my dismay. 'Sweetheart, have courage! All will be well.'

All was well, too, thanks to Joseph. When Sir Walter's guests heard that forthcoming meals were going to consist of leftovers and purges, they found courteous excuses to brave hip-deep snow back to their own homes. Only a few folk lingered, minor gentry so impoverished that even a purge sounded like fun to them so long as it was free. They made a less unreasonable demand on the larder while still allowing Sir Walter to play the host, so everyone was happy. Besides, the more inedible portions of the festal food could be recycled endlessly, if the cook keep grating cinnamon on it to disguise the smell.

So the days of Christmas rolled on cheerily enough. There was no work to do in the garden; there were no guests to shepherd about and explain things to; there were no more frenzied party preparations. Most hours Nicholas and I spent in his little bare room at the top of the house, where the relative chill refreshed us after the stuffiness downstairs.

My love, my love. At night we cuddled together under the blanket and read by the light of his single candle, or talked far into the dark hours. He would never give over his attempts to persuade me that I needed his Christ; and I could not resist the temptation to argue the need to save men's lives rather than their souls. Yet he had some remarkably advanced ideas for a man of his time, he really had.

Mine only love. The household slept below in silence; our

little room seemed cut adrift, the cabin of a ship sailing through the vaster silence of the winter stars. How could anyone think that my lover was a paltry mortal thing? He was an immortal creature like me, and we dwelt in perfect harmony in a tiny world of bare boards and dust, leather and vellum.

You can love like that but once.

I was vaguely aware that terrible and portentous things were happening in the world outside. I heard fragments of news broadcasts coming up from Nef's room, and warning messages were surfacing out of my chronomemory program. It seemed sensible to ignore them, since there was nothing at all I could do about them. One should always avoid unnecessary unhappiness. Especially if one is an immortal. They taught us that in school.

Chapter Nineteen

On the eleventh day of Christmas, January 5, 1555, there was a thaw. There was pouring rain, rushing in gutters, and then it froze again; but the snow had been so reduced that the lanes were open and people could visit one another for Twelfth Night.

Our Christmas parasites used the opportunity to go home at last. Without them the house seemed luxuriously empty, and Nicholas and I got the chance to explore the minstrels' gallery.

It was entered from a third-floor passageway, through a tiny dark door that looked like a cupboard. Nicholas had to bend nearly double to squeeze through, and my hoops gave me no end of trouble, but once we were up there, it was neat. We stood and surveyed the view of the great hall, and Nicholas drew my attention to the fine carved roundels that were practically invisible from down on the dance floor.

'Red roses,' I observed. 'Red roses were the badge of your Lancasters, in your Roses wars, were they not? I did not know the house was so old.'

'It isn't.' Nicholas grinned. 'But Sir Alexander was a Lancastrian partisan, and so we have roses encarnadined in his honor. Not that any Christian soul hath noticed them these thirty years. I must write them in mine abstract of Worthy Sights to Be Pointed Out to Paying Guests.'

I peered over the rail.

'So far up and such a little space. I wonder they got all those hautboys and base viols up here. They must have been sitting in one another's laps, trying to play.'

We looked at each other. I sidled over to him.

'I recall,' I remarked, 'that when we looked up at the musicians, we could see but their heads and the topmost parts of their instruments.'

Nicholas leaned his elbows on the rail and gave me a sidelong gaze.

'What better place than this,' I decided, 'for a lesson on the recorder?'

'Madam, what can you mean?' inquired Nicholas in his suavest voice. I pounced, and we tussled out of sight, up there on the tiny platform.

A door opened below us, and two sets of footsteps sounded in the great hall. We froze except for Friar John, who fainted dead away. I sat up in a panic, and Nicholas grabbed me and pulled me down. Our hearts thundered, surely louder than those footsteps over hollow cellars.

'I had come sooner, but the snow did not permit,' said a voice. Familiar, somehow. 'And, to tell the plain truth, there have been fearful things that captured my thoughts. I have ridden from Rochester, you may know.'

'Aye. Well, the time spent has been favorable to thy case. I too have had much to consider.' That was Sir Walter. 'I'll tell thee, Master Darrell, I have looked at thine offer with new eyes.'

Master Darrell? Offer?

'Have you so?' the other voice sharpened. 'And what say you to it now?'

'It likes me well,' said Sir Walter. 'I were a liar if I said otherwise.'

'This is a change, certes.'

'Well, well; the case is altered.'

'Ah.'

Creak as they sat down together.

'Shall I —? I shall call for sack,' said Sir Walter, and he did, and they sat there saying nothing while a servant brought sack, and they said nothing while he left, and only after the door shut behind him did they speak.

'Tell me, how much —' began Sir Walter, at the same moment that Master Darrell said, 'I am prepared —' They both halted.

'Forgive me, sir,' said Master Darrell.

'Nay, a thousand pardons. Speak, friend.'

'What I offered, I offer still: half the sum in sealed bags now, and the rest when the cherries ripen and apricots go to market, God send us favorable sun and rain. Even failing that, I have wool in the north, and that's sure. And you spake once of certain provisos . . .'

'In sooth. Thou must keep the name.'

'Oh, sir, the name is all. Therein is the value. Who would pay a farthing to see Darrell's Garden?'

Nicholas turned his head, frowning.

'Well! I am satisfied,' said Sir Walter, and there was a silence as they both drank. Sir Walter set down his tankard and said:

'I am no man for this country life. Look at me, Master Darrell, am I old? Am I palsied? Do I falter?'

'Uh . . . nay.'

'Hadst thou met me but today, thou shouldst say I were no more than thirty. The Greek physick hath given me a new life! Shall I dream it away in this quiet place? Or shall I not rather set out anew?'

Bad feelings in the minstrels' gallery.

'What is it you mean to do?'

'Meseems I have not known mine own heart . . . I thought this garden should be my fame, my child, my all. I see now it is not the end I desire. I, I meant to hold a Christmas revel that befitted mine ancient lineage. It was nothing so grand as I envisioned, for I saw that my neighbors are but lowborn country folk, and I find myself but a little country squire pinched shrewdly by his expenses. I was made for greater things, Master Darrell!'

'But what remedy, sir?'

'Thou shalt hear it. I'll get me to London and try for a courtier. There is power, there are the New Men! Through sale of this estate I'll have ready cash in hand, and haply a Spanish wife of noble birth, which cannot but stand me in good stead at Court.'

'You mean to marry, then?'

'If the lady grant my suit, aye. She hath looked well on me thus far, and I may hope, I tell thee. God knows she is not fair, but she's young, and I doubt not of an heir once I bed her —'

He was talking about Nefer. My astonishment at this was

such that I inadvertently broadcast it, and a second later I felt both Joseph and Nef tuning in to the conversation.

'— and thereby my puling nephew shall have no claim.'

'This lady is one of your guests, then,' said Master Darrell.

'Yes. As to that —' Sir Walter sounded uneasy.

What's going on? from Nef.

Shut up! from Joseph.

'There is a thing thou shouldst know,' said Sir Walter. 'This Lady Margaret is a sort of nurse, after the Spanish fashion, of virtues sober, to that girl thou hast seen in my garden. The girl and her father, Doctor Ruy, are my guests here.'

'For that he is your ancient friend. Aye, I remember me.'

'Yea, even so, and yet thou shouldst know . . .'

Hold it hold it HOLD IT! Joseph was exploding out of a chair, and distantly I heard him pelting down a corridor.

'There is a certain arrangement that I have with Doctor Ruy. He must remain here, he and his daughter, as long as they will; and all that they want of the garden, they must have. Seeds or grafts or bushes entire, and thou must on no account hinder them. Nor mayest thou question them concerning anything thou seest, though never so strange.'

'I like this not so well,' ventured Master Darrell.

'I could say more, if I durst.' Sir Walter gulped his wine. 'So thou meddle not in his affairs but let him do as he pleases, it will be well for thee. He hath powerful friends, hath Doctor Ruy —'

'What, is the man a Spanish spy?' blurted Master Darrell. 'God's death, sir, how could you?'

The shock in Nicholas's face is something I wince at even now.

'No, his masters have —'

'God save you, Sir Walter. I have come of express purpose to seek you out. God save you also, sir.' Joseph appearing out of nowhere, not even out of breath.

A silence that sizzled like bacon.

'This is Master Darrell of Colehill,' said Sir Walter with a little cough.

'Ah. Sir, your servant. You are the gentleman who desires to purchase the garden, is it not so?'

A baffled silence. 'I had not told anyone —' began Sir Walter.

'But me. You recall? When we drank so much sack together. We were grievous deep in our cups, I fear. Have you decided to sell?'

'I had thought to.' Sir Walter let his words out one at a time, like frightened mice.

'You have, of course, told him of our arrangement? I trust, sir, you understand?'

'No, sir.' Very grim, very brief the reply.

'Then I must explain. I belong to a fraternity of scholars. We quest after knowledge of divers sorts, to work great good for men. Our brotherhood is wealthy, and not so respectful of priests as it might be, wherefore the Church hath put us under interdict, and so we work secretly —'

'No more, brother! I know whereof you speak.' Master Darrell's voice had lightened up amazingly.

'You do?' said Joseph, after a pause in which I could hear his wheels whirring. He gambled and said, 'Then in the name of the Widow's Son, I need say no more.'

'You have a friend in me, sir.' Master Darrell's voice was jovial, and there was a brief smack of palms as they exchanged lodge signs or something. Everyone, and I mean everyone, relaxed.

'My studies have brought me to Sir Walter's garden for the rare simples that grow therein.' Joseph picked up the ball and ran like a thief. 'As you may see, casting your eyes on Sir Walter, I have been able to reverse the natural decay of the flesh. I ask but that I be allowed to continue my studies here. I shall pay you well for the privilege.'

'Why, is it so? Then all is well. Tell me, can you . . . uh . . . restore that natural growth of hair, the want of which upon the head of a man who is yet young, shall make him appear older than his years?'

'Are you troubled with baldness? I can cure it without fail, my friend. You may consult with me when you will. But I had near forgot the purpose I came here for! I would remind you, Sir Walter, that you are to fast this night. No sack with eggs.'

'If I must,' grumbled Sir Walter.

'Lovers grow lean for love, and so must thou,' said Master Darrell. 'Tell thy lady thou diest for her.'

'Lady?' Polite professional interest from Joseph.

Sir Walter drew a deep breath. 'As you know – Doctor Ruy – I have made suit to the Lady Margaret. Marriage is my intent.'

Oh really? reacted Nef, without as much laughter as I would have thought.

'Truly? Then sir, God speed you in your suit. Her dowery is not base gold but spotless virtue, which you well know is a far greater treasure.'

'No, er, lands or inheritances, then?' said Sir Walter.

'Not nowadays, though I assure you her forefathers (pure Christians all of them) fought valiantly for the Cross, placing faith above base gain.'

'Oh.'

I'd better lay away my thirty-seven pounds, thought Nef.

'Be ruled by me and take the lady for herself, man.' Master Darrell spoke with a certain bitterness. 'I had not told you all my news yet. A Spanish lady will serve you better than six hundred pounds a year, if you would try Court now.'

'What do you mean?'

'There is great news in Rochester, and we must rejoice. For, look you, this Christmastide the Parliament hath done wonders. England hath repented her sins and returned to the bosom of Rome, I say. The late King Henry's Acts are voted down every one, the Mass is restored, whereat we must rejoice.'

In the great hall there was a shocked silence, until at last Sir Walter said: 'Thou knewst all this, and came into my house so lightly to bargain with me?'

'How otherwise, sir? Is this not great news? Were we to go about sadly, we should be suspected for heretics, should we not?'

'So we should.' It was difficult to read Sir Walter's voice. He was silent another long moment, and then he said: 'So we shall have the abbeys and the monasteries back again.'

'Aye, forsooth.'

'And good sisters shall tell their beads so quaintly again, as they did when I was a child, and there shall be great paintings in the church to show the glories of Paradise and the torments of the damned.'

'Aye, forsooth.'

Joseph's voice, sounding embarrassed: 'Now, as I am a Spaniard, and a loyal son of the Church, I trust you gentlemen will not recall that I spoke of any brotherhood of scholars.'

'Oh, nay.'

'Nay, nay, sir. It is well, nowadays, to have a Spaniard for a friend,' said Master Darrell.

'I certainly count myself as such.' Joseph matched his irony note for note.

Mendoza, are you okay? sent Nef.

'How long, think you, before the bishop's men are sent out amongst us?' asked Sir Walter.

'It is expected that the order to conform goes out before the end of the month.'

'Ah. I have some time, then, to put my house in order.'

I will never understand the English. Sir Walter had cried like a child because he could not serve his guests peacock two nights in a row; but at the news that his civil liberties had been taken away, the man was sensible and calm.

'So.' Master Darrell drained his tankard and set it down. 'I would, if I may, sir, see the accounts for your garden, the better to know what income I may expect.'

'My secretary keeps excellent accounts.' Sir Walter got to his feet. 'Let us go find the books, and thou shalt see for thyself.'

'And I shall take my leave of you, señors.' Joseph was bowing. 'I must to my studies, er, prayers. Remember, Sir Walter, you must fast.'

'Aye. Aye.' And they went out of the great hall, all together.

Nicholas and I sat silent in the gallery for a few minutes. He was nodding, slightly, and his lips were moving, but no sound came out. Finally he gave a little choked laugh.

'Why, so is the silly world turned upon its head,' he said.

'How could they do it?' I whispered. 'How could a people be so foolish?'

Nicholas lowered his head to his knees and wept. His sobs

echoed in the great hall, where only a short time before he had played the winter king in his pasteboard armor.

Arrows you may dodge and fever you may antibody for, but mortal grief is a misfortune you cannot escape. That's a translation of something solemn from my school days. It was, as I remember, the first sentence of an essay about the hazards of taking mortal lovers. The author compares this act to having a gangrenous limb grafted onto one's perfect immortal body. He then proceeds to a little parable about the immortal heart as beautiful machine, flawless and balanced, designed by a master with all protection against weakness and damage – until the heart's foolish owner attaches leads from it to the inferior heart of a badly made mortal engine, thus compromising the integrity of the better design and exposing the owner to all the shocks, faults, and stresses of the lesser model.

See, cyborgs have their Thomas Aquinases too. Though I'd been told, practically from the first day I went into the field, that all that was nonsense and it was actually really okay to sleep with mortals. Nothing to it at all.

It's very important to give young operatives the straight dope, you know?

You can imagine that after a miserable interlude Nicholas and I crawled out of the gallery and walked away down the corridor. He turned suddenly to stare at me. His eyes were red-rimmed and swollen with crying. I had expected them to be bewildered too; they weren't. There was a clear, cold place in them, a country of ice I'd seen at a distance before. No distance now. 'In this life,' he said, 'we must be on our guard.'

'Yes,' I replied uncertainly.

Terrible music was beginning to play, an anthem for that frozen land; but a door down the hall opened, and Sir Walter emerged.

'Nicholas!' he said. 'We must speak, now.'

'Right gladly.' Nicholas turned on his heel and advanced on Sir Walter so rapidly, and drawing himself up so tall and ominous, that Sir Walter shrank back a little. He retreated through the doorway, and Nicholas followed him in.

I had no urge to go and listen to them. For the first time in a long while, I badly needed the company of my own kind.

This sentiment lasted until I got to Nef's room. Opening the door, I beheld Joseph bounding up and down in place like a rubber imp on a string.

'The son of a bitch! The ungrateful, dressed-up chimpanzee! The rotten little two-timing descendant of Saxon drag queens!'

'Ignore him.' Stonily Nefer turned a page of her magazine.

'Ignore me?' Joseph screamed. 'IGNORE ME? YOU GO RIGHT AHEAD AND IGNORE ME, MISS TUTAN-KHAMEN! I'M ONLY GETTING A LITTLE AGGRA-VATION OUT OF MY SYSTEM!'

I put my hands over my ears. The unicorn buried its head in Nef's skirts.

'Ah! Ah! Ah!' Joseph went right on bounding with the precision of a jackhammer. 'I'll kill him! I'll give him cavities and postnasal drip! I'll rig his autonomic nervous system so he does something painfully embarrassing every time he sneezes!' He stopped, staggering slightly as an idea hit him. 'Where's the black hellebore? Where's the nux vomica? Is *he* ever going to get a bedtime cocktail tonight!'

'You're upset about the mission with everything else that's just happened?' I wept. 'The Parliament selling out to Cardinal Pole? The Church getting all those awful powers again?'

'Yes, I'm upset about the mission, and so should you be!' Joseph rounded on me. 'It's in jeopardy thanks to Little Sir Walt, and after months of cleaning out his lousy arteries, this is the thanks I get? Now I have to completely renegotiate the contract with the new owner, which is going to cost the Company money, which is going to reflect badly on me, although you still get to collect your Furbish's lousewort or whatever so what do you care? I guess it's just too much to hope that you might be providing your poor facilitator and group leader with sympathy, understanding, and commiseration. Hell, not you! You're in shock because the monkeys are throwing coconuts at each other! We told you mortals did stuff like this, didn't we? What did you learn at school, anyway? How can you have come out of the dungeons of the Inquisition and still be surprised by anything they do?'

'You were surprised by Sir Walter,' remarked Nef.

'Jesus H. Christ, was I ever.' Joseph collapsed on a settle. 'The nerve. The consummate nerve of the guy. We had a deal! So now he's going to sell the property and go into politics at Court, is he? Well, he'll be sorry he crossed me. I wouldn't accept that marriage proposal if I were you, baby.'

'Oh, I don't know.' Nef laid down her magazine and looked at him. 'I don't particularly want to go to Court. Maybe I can talk him out of it. Maybe I can make him buy a cattle ranch.'

'They don't have ranches in England,' I said. She shrugged.

'Well, you'd have to watch him around the clock,' said Joseph bitterly. 'The guy has no loyalty to anything. Can you beat it? After he gave me his knightly word of honor, too. How could he do this to me? I mean, his garden was his whole life!'

'My God, can't you see why?' I cried. 'You pumped hormones and who knows what else into him, you gave him his youth back, and now it's not just his old clothes that don't fit, it's his old life! That's why he wants a change. Blame yourself!'

'Hey! I only met his price for what we wanted.' Joseph glared at me. 'And his price was youth, which shows he was restless already.'

'I thought the Indian maize was his price.'

'That was the official price.' Joseph examined his fingernails.

'What?'

'Bureaucratic levels of reality,' said Nef. 'Don't worry about it.' I looked from one to the other.

'Are we . . . are we really good for mankind?' I wondered for the first time.

'Sure we are, honey.'

'But everything that little man valued in life we turned to dust for him. Before we came, he didn't mind about getting old. Did we really have any right to step in and change him?'

'Wait, wait, wait. Hold it right there. We didn't just step in and change him without his permission. The dissatisfaction with life was already there in his tiny mind. We only give people what they want, and usually what's good for them. I did what any doctor would do.'

'If a sixteenth-century doctor had the technology,' put in Nef.

'But you can't make a values call on whether or not I should have let him stay a sick old man,' continued Joseph. 'Even if the guy could see it objectively the way we can, do you think for a second he wouldn't have made the same choice? There isn't a mortal born that won't try to cheat Father Time.'

'But he made the wrong choice.'

'Did he? Are you going to make his choices for him? That's a violation of his natural rights, kiddo. Don't forget that mortals have free will. They traded their Paradise for it, and they can jump into manure up to their necks, if they choose to. We don't care. We're not here to make them happy, we're not here to make them prosperous, we're not here to help them on the road to self-realization. We're here to do business for the Company.

'Sir Walters and Nicholases are out there everywhere. But your *Ilex tormentosum* is so rare, it's only growing in one place in the whole world. If it wasn't for the work you've been doing, it would become extinct, when we know it has properties that can save a billion mortal lives. Isn't that, morally, worth the happiness of one old man?'

'But . . .' Unpleasant light had begun to dawn on me. 'Because of what we did for Sir Walter, he's sold the garden to Master Darrell. What if Master Darrell decides to cut down the ilex and replace it with something he thinks is more exotic, after we've gone? Then the ilex will be extinct, except for what the Company has. But Sir Walter would never have sold the garden if we hadn't come and messed with him. What are we doing to cause and effect, here? Does the Company really know what it's doing?'

'Of course it does,' said Joseph instantly. 'And if you worry about this, you'll drive yourself nuts. Really.'

'Just take it on faith, I always say,' Nef told me. 'I mean, everything works out in the end anyway, doesn't it? We know the ilex becomes extinct, because there isn't any in the future except what the Company has. So you must have saved it. So why ask questions?'

'Believe me, Mendoza, there are better minds than yours grappling with this.'

'All the time, honey. Do yourself a favor, don't get metaphysical.'

'Really.'

So I backed away from the void, which was a very deep and very dark void indeed, doubtless chock full of unhappiness for anyone unwisely peering into it for too long. And what is worse, for an immortal being, than unhappiness?

Joseph got to his feet. 'Once again, poor little Joseph finds himself having to hand out sage advice and counsel to younger operatives when he'd rather be crying into his pillow. Does anyone care? Fat chance. I'm going to have myself a glass of sherry and access all the information I have on A) Freemasons and B) hair restoration, and then I'm going to review the microsurgery I was planning to do on the little shit tonight. I hope, I just fervently hope and pray, that I can keep an open and forgiving mind. It sure would be terrible if I connected some of his nasty organic pipes wrong. Or, better yet, planted some exotic disease cultures in timed-release capsules in his gluteal muscle sheath. Boy, now *there's* an idea . . .' He went into his room and slammed the door.

'He's so dramatic.' Nef picked up her magazine again.

'Are you really planning to marry Sir Walter?' I wanted to know.

'Oh, gee, no,' she said. 'He's kind of cute – now – but I don't think the Company would okay it.'

'You'd have to ask the Company first?'

'Of course, Mendoza. So they could see if his proposal was advantageous to them, so they could analyze whether my tour of duty would be compatible with a life with him, so they could evaluate granting him higher security clearance. Frankly, though, after what he just did, I don't think there's a chance in Hell he'd be approved. Doctor Zeus doesn't like double-dealers.'

'You don't mean Joseph is really going to poison him!' I was aghast.

'No, no, of course not. That almost never happens.' She became fascinated by her magazine. 'Hey, can you beat this? The whole Bogart canon is coming out as a set on Ring compatible! We're getting it for thirteen point seven. Isn't that fabulous?'

'Real neat,' I said wearily.

But I was young then and had yet to appreciate the wisdom of Bogart, particularly as regards the problems of three little people not amounting to a hill of beans in this or any other crazy world.

Chapter Twenty

Nothing was the same anymore.

Sir Walter called his entire household together and gave them the news about the sale first. That their religion had just been changed was nothing to them compared with the shock of losing their jobs; they had never been a particularly devout household anyway. There was a private chapel at Iden Hall, dusty and disused, but it had furnished Sir Walter and his people with an excuse for not going to church every Sabbath.

No longer. Almost at once the order went out: Mass was to be celebrated in every church in every village in England, with one hundred percent attendance expected. In each parish a ledger was to be kept with the names of the persons who did not attend, and that ledger was to be turned over to the agents of the bishops, agents sent to each church to ensure the conformity of its flock. Whoever did not attend Mass would be flogged or given other suitable chastisement and returned to the care of the village priest. Those persons found to be resolute heretics would be burned, after a trial proved guilt.

Simple? Straightforward? See how easy it is to restore the true faith to a country? You just have to be firm. There weren't even any Jews to hunt for.

Well, it certainly would have worked in Spain. Doubtless in many parts of France too. But this was England, practically the home of civil disobedience. It has always seemed bizarre to me that the race that invented the tea cozy should also so resolutely refuse ever ever to be slaves.

So the English refused, at first, though of course they surrendered in the end. In one village a man realized that he could settle an old score with a neighbor by reporting him to the bishops' men for heretical opinions. Somewhere else, a man terrified of being betrayed sought to save himself by confessing, and in doing so implicated most of his family and friends.

The old story, at least to a Spaniard. All the same, it took the English a little longer than most to light their fires.

It was decided that the household would be kept together for some months, while all the legal details of the transaction were arranged. During that time everyone was to go to Mass on Sundays, on pain of being discharged immediately.

Nicholas flatly refused. There was a terrible scene in Sir Walter's private chamber, and I don't know what they said, because I turned up the volume on the radio to drown them out; but they emerged with the agreement that Nicholas would remain at Iden Hall for as long as it took to prepare the inventory and financial records for the sale.

'I am not to speak with more folk than is needful, nor am I to arrange anymore with the butcher or greengrocer. Master Ffrawney shall see to that. Neither shall I conduct the penny-paying guests on the Walks Historical, Botanical, or Zoological.' Nicholas paused and squinted at the sky. 'Not that I expect any penny-paying guests for months, if this weather hold.'

We were walking in the garden. It was raw and ugly as only January in England can be; but it smelled better outdoors than in the house.

He had changed, my Nicholas; he had grown pale. The early-morning bloodlessness was with him all the time now.

'What shall we do?' I sighed.

'Why, what you shall do I know not. Truth to tell, I know not mine own course neither.' He wrapped his hands in his frayed sleeves for warmth. 'I must trust in God.'

'You could do that in Frankfurt,' I suggested. He fixed me with a cold look, askance down his high cheekbones, that made my heart beat fast. For days I had been trying to talk him into fleeing to safety.

'Setting aside the risk I should run of arrest,' he said, 'there remains the question of expense.'

'That could be arranged,' I hinted. His look of scorn deepened.

This is the time to rehearse the wise and careful speeches about parting, those slick ways to begin the end. This is when you need to tell yourself, and then tell him, how natural it is to grow in different directions, and that it doesn't mean failure, it doesn't mean love is any less. All that beautifully phrased bullshit, over nerves screaming for release. But God help you if no such speech comes into your head, and you cling to the sullen rock of his shoulder in the night ocean.

'Your father must be dismayed by the sale of the house.' Nicholas looked away again.

'He is.' I did not take my eyes from his face. 'And the new laws make him afeared. We shall not stay in this place much longer.'

'Shall you not? Where shall you go?'

'If we went to Frankfurt, would you come?'

'Your father has no need of a secretary, I think.'

We walked on in that winter pattern of hedges and lanes without another word.

And now the news. And it's grim, we regret to say: today England's first official victim of the Counter-Reformation was burnt at Smithfield. John Rogers, Canon of Saint Paul's, long-time Reformation agitator and translator of the Matthew Bible, died in the presence of his wife and children in a ceremony lasting twenty-five minutes. Your news team had an operative on the scene and, Diotima, can you tell us about it?

Well, Reg, you know I've been in the field a long time, and I've been there for most of the big events of the Tudor regime, but let me say right now this hits a new low. This is on a par with the day the old Countess of Salisbury was executed —

You were there that day, weren't you?

Yes, Reg, and frankly I thought that was pretty bad, I mean, the old woman was running around on the scaffold trying to escape and they had to physically drag her to the block —

And it's, uh, interesting that the countess was Cardinal Pole's mother. Wouldn't you say that incident is the motivation for much of his policies now? Could you say he's settling scores with the Reformation in a deeply personal way?

Undoubtedly, Reg. Anyway, I was there today, and let me tell you operatives listening in: these people are animals. There is not a doubt in my mind. Sick animals.

And now we had to go to Mass again, after happy months of neglect. Once again miserable journeys through Sunday rain, to file into a dear quaint village church of local stone and arctic atmosphere. Lots of bare whitewashed walls, and a priest very nervous and imperfect in his Latin. Nonetheless, it was standing room only, and the wretched faithful, packed in like sardines, were only too glad to be seen there. On prominent display by the pulpit was a great big book, and you can bet it had nothing to do with Common Prayer. Nearby sat an alert gentleman in nondescript clothes, who conferred often with the priest. After these conferences, the priest mixed up his tenses and endings even more, and the gentleman made many notes in a smaller book he kept in his doublet.

For once, I was not bored at Mass. The mortal population for miles around was crammed into that quaint little church, and you could have floated an armada on the high waves of emotion there. Our arrival occasioned a particularly heady gust, of course, as the Evil Spaniards, particularly when Sir Walter accompanied us with every single member of his household but one.

'Why, Sir Walter, you are well met,' said one of our Christmas visitors as we sidled in.

'Aye, forsooth, friends, I hope I am as pious and conformable a man as any in England,' answered Sir Walter, loud and firm.

'I do not see your tall fellow,' remarked someone else.

'No, alack.' Sir Walter looked straight ahead and made a passable sign of the Cross. 'The poor man is grievous sick.'

'Alack, indeed. And is he expected to live?'

'Sir, I scarcely know.'

Everyone turned and looked knowingly at everyone else; then everyone turned cold gazes back to the Spanish visitors, as though it were *our* fault.

*   *   *

The unfortunate Canon Rogers was followed to the stake by Bishop John Hooper. There was a live broadcast from Gloucester, and I had to run out of the room before it was over. His executioners botched the job: they used wet wood, and green wood, and at the last the poor old bastard left off his prayers and screamed for more fire, because only his legs were burning.

As the days went by, a butcher was burned alive, then a barber, then a weaver, and more common folk followed them to the fire. The prisons began to fill with the condemned from all ranks, all classes. It was true that some died political deaths, old scores from the previous reign settled at last. But most people were dying for things like being seen reading their Bibles, or even for only listening to the Bible being read.

The Spanish were bewildered. In Spain the Holy Inquisition was a gloomy duty, propelled along by the riches it brought the Holy Office from the confiscated property of the condemned. That was easy to understand: who wasn't motivated by profit? But how to explain the brutal zest with which these country constables dragged penniless apprentices to martyrdom? What to make of reverend old bishops fighting like Punch and Judy, squalling curses at each other from their respective sides of the flames? It was all so *personal*.

Even our prince decided that he'd had enough of this crazy country, and gave the order that all his remaining countrymen were to get themselves home to Spain.

No escape for us synthetic Spaniards, though. Too much to do. There was another thaw and more rain; all manner of splash and trickle ran everywhere, and blind green shoots found their way up to the sun. My work began again. I was mostly alone in the garden now, Nicholas being kept indoors. Sometimes the old gardener appeared, tramping about with sacking and a shovel, but he would neither speak nor look at me. That suited me fine. My loathing for mortals was growing like the garden.

I took blossom and cutting of an apple men would not taste again for centuries, until it was – will be – rediscovered in Humboldt Province. I took wildflowers, tiny ephemera cf the hedgerows: soon men would know them only through images in tapestries, their names would be forgotten, and there would come a day when even hedgerows themselves would be plowed under by an England that no longer remembered what it was. But when the industries have come and gone, the little flowers will seed and bloom again. Men will not even notice they've returned; but the land will know. This is the purpose of my life.

Men burned; flowers were rescued.

It was all drawing to a close. Nicholas spent his days with the documents for the sale, long hours drawing up inventories of goods. All the furnishings were to be sold; all the plate was to be sold. The cabinets of curiosities and the tapestries were to be sold. All the careful gathering of a lifetime was to go for ready cash. If Sir Walter had been dead, it would have been very sad, but since he was selling his own dreams, nobody felt anything. Nicholas woke me muttering in his sleep: '*Item*, one salver of Italian plate. *Item*, one pair of bronze candlesticks, representing satyrs . . .'

One day, when he was at work, someone went into his room and took all his books away. I saw white smoke billowing from the kitchen chimney, smelled burning paper, never guessing that his translations of Saint Paul were cooking dinner. He never guessed either, until we opened his door that evening.

What a surprise. What petty devastation: flakes of wax, chips and flattened beads of candle wax, scattered all over the bare table. Moth wings. Great square vacancies in the dust of the tabletop, and a broken candle lying on the floor, wrenched from its drippy socket between two volumes. But no volumes. All that crazy-tumbled pyramid of thought and argument was gone.

We just stood and stared by the light of the new candle we had brought. When it sank in that practically everything he owned was so much ruffled ash in the kitchen grate, I was the one who broke down and cried, and wanted to go accuse somebody. Nicholas was too stunned to hear my tempest. He wandered over to the table and stood looking down at the place where his books had been. There was a long stream of wax lying there, a solid river broken off at its source. He picked it up and turned it in the light, examining it intently.

Finally he said, 'Wherefore art thou angered?'

I stared through my tears. 'Thy books are burnt!' Get red in the face, Nicholas, please, storm downstairs and grab Master Ffrawney by the throat.

He shook his head.

'It is a sign. One more test. The Word of God is not so much paper and calfskin. These gross forms have been destroyed. Perhaps this is to signify that I loved them too much. Perhaps I sinned in pride, having so many books.'

This kind of talk terrified me. I went across the room to him, physically to close the gulf I could feel opening between us. There was something glinting on the bit of wax he held; I looked at it closely and saw it was a moth. Its charred body was trapped in the frozen flow of tallow, legs clumped all askew, and the powdery wings that stuck out were shredded and broken.

How cold that room was.

You must understand that I would not sit there and watch. Mortals can make a poetry of death; they have to. What is too horrible to look in the face must have a mask. Still, mortals have the urge to pull away that mask, as the stupid girl does in the film, and the angry specter jumps out roaring.

We are not like that. No romantic Death for us. Like cockroaches or mold, he must be driven out: spray for him, scour him away, put him out in the sunlight. Unclean.

I made a plan.

'Joseph.' I opened his door. He looked up at me unfocused: he had a ring holo made like a pair of spectacles on his nose and was relaxing with a film. 'We have to talk.'

'We do, huh?' He sighed and switched off the holo. Folding it up, he put it in his doublet and pulled out a stick of Theobromos. 'Mood elevant?' He offered it to me.

'No, thanks.'

He shrugged and commenced peeling the silver paper off one end.

'How soon before we leave here, Joseph?'

'That's up to you, isn't it? Sit down. How long before you've taken as much as is worth taking out of the garden?'

'Only a few weeks. I'll have a complete growing cycle on the ilex by then, and enough samples on everything else for full in-lab reconstruction.'

'Say a month, then.' He leaned back and put the end of the stick in his mouth. 'Sooner, if you can manage it, because in case you haven't been listening to the news, the rest of the Spaniards are ditching the joint. It would be nice if you and I could do likewise. Save us the cost of paying off Master Darrell, too.'

'What about Nef?'

'She's going to HQ, and they're finally sending her north with a new cover.'

'Oh.' I got up and paced. 'Well, look; I need you to do something for me.'

'Oh really?' He raised his eyebrows. 'What?'

'Save Nicholas.'

'He'll die, Mendoza,' Joseph said. 'Eventually. They all do. You know that.'

'But he doesn't have to die now. Not while he's a young man. He has no idea how dangerous it is here now, he won't listen to reason, and I've talked to him until I'm going crazy trying to get him to flee to Zurich or somewhere safe. He won't listen to me. This is why you have to help me.'

'I have persuasive charms, baby, but I'm not that good.'

'Like hell you're not. I know what you are. You can sell anything.'

'Mendoza, people have to want to be saved. Did you want to die in Santiago? No. Did Sir Walter want to get old and sick? No. Do you understand what I'm trying to tell you? What can I offer this guy? Big healthy buck in the prime of life like him. He doesn't like me, he doesn't trust me, and if a nubile little thing like you can't make him catch a fast boat to the Continent for his own good, I've got a feeling that I too shall argue in vain.'

'I'm not asking you to argue with him. Look, I have it all worked out. Give me a drug that will make him look dead.'

'You mean like in *Romeo and Juliet*?' Joseph was incredulous.

'Just like that. Slip him the drug just before we're ready to leave, do the coffin trick, and smuggle him out with us when we go. Keep him on life support until we get to Europe, leave him in an inn in Zurich, where he can wake up with a headache and no memory of how he got there. But he'll have a purse of Swiss gold. And I'll never see him again, Joseph, I promise.'

'Mendoza, did you ever see the movie? The poison bit didn't work out so well. All kinds of stuff could go wrong with your plan. I might miscalculate the dosage.'

'You wouldn't.'

'This is a plan dreamed up by a desperate person.'

'Is there any reason it positively wouldn't work? Huh?'

'Where do you think I'm going to get a drug like that? I don't exactly keep a box of them under my bed. Oh, a Juliet special? Yes, I just whipped up a batch.'

'You *can* make a batch. You must know a formula. Give me a list of what you need, and I'll get everything.'

'Mendoza ... I'll try. Okay? I can't guarantee anything, and I wish you wouldn't get your hopes up about this —'

'You can do it.' I thumped him on the shoulder. His stick of Theobromos broke, and he looked at me reproachfully, but I was already exiting on a wave of confidence.

So that was my plan.

Actually, that was only one of my plans, but they all began: *As soon as I get Nicholas out of here ...*

Chapter Twenty One

The days went by as I clipped and dug and collected. Sir Walter proposed to Nef and was refused with a great deal of tact and charm. She told him she was too old for him (certainly true), too poor, and anyway had been betrothed since childhood to a hidalgo of Castile who had sailed away to the New World. Though the hidalgo had never returned, doubtless slain by savages somewhere, honor compelled her to wait for him. This news was received with great dismay by Sir Walter, but his tears were in vain. He became resigned; he let her keep the unicorn as a symbol of their lost love. It was pretty obviously a goat now anyway, both little horns poking out bravely; and thus Sir Walter could be gallant and rid himself of an embarrassment at the same time. Within a day he had convinced himself that there were plenty of wealthy noblewomen in England who'd fall for him.

One day it rained. And the next day it rained, and the next. Then it rained again. Venturing into the garden meant sinking ankle-deep in wet leaf mold (a substance found only in the British Isles, thank God), so I opted to stay indoors and watch Nicholas take inventory.

Rain pattered down, and light came gray and watery through the windows of the great hall. I sat on the staircase hoping to avoid the drafts, my skirts all tucked up around my ankles, and helped Nicholas with the inventory list. Chin on fist, I watched as he crawled up and down the stepladder before an enormous curio case. How bleak and unforgiving the light, picking out every threadbare place in his black robe. No new livery for him now: Sir Walter wasn't going to waste the money.

'*Item*, one head of a Scots king,' he announced.

'Thou liest!' I lowered my quill to stare.

'There.' He pointed to the topmost shelf, and I looked up to meet the blind stare of very former majesty. The man had died young: had very good teeth and a lot of red hair and beard, still bushy.

'What is he doing here?' I looked away and jotted the entry.

'Little enough nowadays, I warrant you. *Item*, one head of a queen.' He reached to the back of the shelf and pulled it out for me to see. 'Supposed to be Queen Guenevere.'

'Who supposes so?' I jeered. 'That's a man's skull with a yellow wig glued on't!' A Roman man, to be exact, about fifty years of age and dead of – plumbism? No. I scanned deeper and found the flint projectile point. Poor old centurion. I hoped my tour of duty in Britain turned out better than his had.

'This was a man? So these are not the locks caressed by Arthur? Well, farewell Sir Walter's two pound tenpence. He ought to have known it were no true queen's head at that price. Though mind you' – he put it back and moved down another shelf – 'there was a time when queens' heads went for less in this land.

'Now, Rose, make a new heading of Popish Impostures —' He halted. 'Nay, I see I am too slow. Someone hath been and changed the sign in this case. Rather write, Holy Relics Miraculously Preserved from the Late Heretics. *Item*, fifteen pieces of the true Cross. *Item*, six crystal vials of the blood of Christ, with lead stoppers. *Item*, seven glass vials of the same. *Item*, a finger of Saint Winifred. *Item*, a finger of Saint Ethelbert. *Item*, a toe of Saint Cuthbert, with an otter's tooth affixed therein. *Item*, a tooth of Saint Ascanius.'

He climbed down and came to sit beside me, shaking from an urge to laugh or cry. 'A trove the Pope himself must envy. Yet I tell you, Sir Walter bought them cheaply when the monasteries were broken up. For a long while there was a card whereon was writ large how these were counterfeits made by greedy monks to rob honest Englishmen.'

'One of those fingers is a chicken bone.' I put my arm around him. A couple of the little bones actually did show a faint spectrum of Crome's radiation, though, so maybe they were the true toes of saints after all.

But there were footsteps. A door opened, and people came

into the great hall. Sir Walter, Joseph, and Master Darrell. Joseph was saying:

'Now, having compounded this, you must rub it well into your scalp —' They noticed us sitting there. Joseph gave me a tiny apologetic shrug, and Master Darrell doffed his hat to me, courteous fellow. But Sir Walter strode forward and said:

'How now, Nicholas, not finished yet? I would have this abstract done afore next Christmas, boy.'

He had been such a charming little old man. What a bastard he was, young.

'You bid me be exact, sir, and there is much to account for.' Nicholas bowed slightly.

'Well, thou must be precise. Look you, Master Darrell, here are wonders indeed. Where is the sword of Charlemagne, Nicholas?'

'Sword of Charlemagne?' Nicholas frowned.

'What, art turned parrot? Tell me where it is, boy. Ha! I see it there. Look up, Master Darrell, it is the French Caesar's very blade.' He pointed to a sword mounted on the wall high above the case. Nicholas consulted his list. Sir Walter went on: 'This same blade, sir, was presented to our late King Henry Fifth, when he did conquer France. It came into this country, I am told, when —'

'That's the sword of Roland, sir.' Nicholas looked up.

'When – what?'

'It is Roland's sword. Not Charlemagne's.'

Sir Walter's eyes quite popped with annoyance. 'I think I know mine own goods, boy. That is the sword of Charlemagne. Roland had a horn, Charlemagne had a sword.'

'With respect, sir, the horn of Roland is in the second cabinet in the east gallery, and this is Roland's sword. You bought them both from a peddler in Wapping. Charlemagne's —'

'God's blood, must I prove it to thee? I see I must.' With a great show of impatience, Sir Walter seized the stepladder and bounded up to the top. The sword was still well out of his reach, though, so he got up on top of the cabinet and stood cautiously.

'Sweet Jesu, sir, have a care!' cried Master Darrell.

'Aye, aye.' Sir Walter turned unsteadily and looked out

at us all: couldn't resist the urge to see what the view was like from up there, I guess. I wondered briefly if he could see into the minstrels' gallery.

He remembered why he was there and grabbed for the sword. 'Here! Now thou shalt see —' But it was only hanging between two sixpenny nails and came loose sooner than he expected and plummeted downward. He jumped back, nearly fell, as with a hiss the sword dropped behind the cabinet and thunked into the baseboard. Nicholas looked disdainful. I had to hide my face in my hands to keep from snickering, and it was well I did, for little Sir Walter grew as furious as a cat up there on his hands and knees.

'Why was that not hung more securer?' he cried. 'I might have been killed, thou fool! And now we must move the cabinet to have the sword back again!'

'Peace, sir, another time,' soothed Master Darrell. 'I am certain it was Charlemagne's sword, none other.'

'It must be got out!'

'We shall have some of the household move the cabinet later, my friend.' Joseph came and steadied the ladder. 'But descend now, I pray you, lest you fall.'

'We shall have it moved *now*, and I shall prove to thee . . .' Reckless in his anger, Sir Walter scrambled to his feet again. Bad move. He overbalanced and tottered. To avoid falling, he threw himself backward against the wall. His feet pushed at the top of the cabinet, and it toppled slowly outward. I screamed, and the men shouted, for Joseph was standing underneath.

Now, a scene in slow motion:

Joseph's eyes met mine. It wasn't that he couldn't get out of the way in time: we had both been alerted when the center of gravity began to shift. He could have been safe on the stair beside me in that first fraction of a second after the cabinet started falling. But there were two mortals staring fixedly at him, who would have seen him blink out.

My God, what are you going to do?

Make it look good. Cross your fingers.

As artifacts and pieces of saints began to rain down on him, Joseph found the exact place of least momentum, lightest impact; positioned himself there, threw up his arms, and waited. Crraassh, it came. A mortal man would have been broken like a matchstick. Joseph, though, took the weight and folded with it, telescoped and bent like a spring but did not crush. Nothing can shatter our cyborg skulls. BOOM. Dust settling.

Normal time again. Sir Walter sprawled amid cobwebs, fractured in a few places, but nobody was paying him any heed because I was screeching fit to wake the dead, frantically clawing at the cabinet. Nicholas and Master Darrell were beside me at once, and some of the servants ran in, and by combined effort we hoisted the cabinet up about two feet. I let go at once and flung myself underneath, ruining my hoops.

'Rose!'

Joseph looked like a cubist painting. He unfolded as I slithered to him.

Damage?

Pull me out.

I got him by the shoulders and pulled, and he swore, but I backed out rapidly with him. When we emerged, he feigned unconsciousness. Kneeling beside him, I wrung my hands and lamented in Spanish, while the following subvocal conversation was going on:

Damage?

Soft tissue injuries, multiple, minor. Right ankle sprained. Right wrist sprained. Left shoulder sprained, separated, massive hematoma —

Here comes Nef.

Have you got —

Yes. What dosage?

Six point three.

Beside me Nef joined in the hysterics, seizing Joseph's face in her hands and neatly pressing the drug patch into place behind his ear.

Better. Thanks.

'Oh, Jesu, is he slain?' Sir Walter staggered up, looking ghastly pale. I could hear Nicholas shouting for someone to fetch a surgeon. Joseph turned his head and moaned feebly. Nef shrieked her joy that he was alive and began to pray. I cried out that it was a miracle, blessed be the

Holy Virgin and Saint James, et cetera. Nicholas crouched down beside me.

'Sir, can you hear me? We have sent for a surgeon. All will be well.'

'A surgeon?' Joseph's eyes flew open.

'He speaks!' Master Darrell bent close. 'Master Doctor, it is God's mercy you yet live. We thought you smashed like an apple.'

'No, God be thanked,' Joseph murmured. 'But let me have no surgeons – I pray you!'

'But sir, your hurts must be seen to,' protested Nicholas.

'My daughter shall tend to me. Have I not taught her physick?' Joseph tried to sit up and gave a cry of real pain.

'Peace, Father, all shall be as you wish,' I reassured him. Nicholas stared at me, and I gave him my most beseeching look. So he helped make a litter out of a tapestry and a pair of boar spears and carried Joseph up to our rooms. Once Joseph was set down, Nef chased everyone else out of the room so we could get most of his clothes off him.

What a mess. He looked like a peach that hadn't been packed in excelsior before it was shipped, and was subsequently dropped and stepped on. Pulpy devastation. A veritable field of blossoming purple. Even as we watched, though, he was healing. Bruises roiled beneath his skin, spread, changed color, faded like clouds across the sky at sunset.

'Kind of pretty, isn't it?' Nef surveyed him.

'Shut up,' he groaned.

'Oh, you're doing fine. The sprains are binding back up, aren't they? I think the swelling's even going down. That shoulder's going to give you trouble, though. I had one once like that and it took most of a week to heal.'

'Is that all.' Joseph writhed.

'We'll put a fake splint on the arm.' Nef turned to me. 'He can wear a sling to immobilize that side. If we were at HQ, they could go in and staple him up right now, but out here – gee. These things can be awfully tedious when they happen in the field.' Her unicorn wandered in and tried to jump up on the bed.

'Keep that thing out of here!' railed Joseph. 'And that goes double for their damned surgeon. Leeches biting me, that's all I need.'

'Fuss, fuss, fuss.'

'I'm in pain, dammit!'

'Not like you'd be if you were a mortal,' Nef pointed out.

'If I were a mortal, I wouldn't be feeling anything because I'd be dead now,' Joseph snapped.

'There art thou happy,' Nef told him cheerily.

By the time we got the splint on him, the bruises had all but disappeared. I left him in bed watching a holo and went out to see if I could help clean up the wreckage downstairs. I found Nicholas waiting just outside the door.

'Shall he live?'

'Aye, Saint James be praised for a miracle.'

He came close to me. 'Yet thou hast no belief in Saint James, nor in miracles neither. If there had been no miracle and thy father had been killed, what then? Hast thou any family but him? Any friends?'

'None,' I replied. 'If my father were slain, I should be alone in this foreign land. I have no husband, nor am I like to.'

He leaned down and kissed me. What a long, lovely, lose-your-balance kiss. We hadn't kissed like that in weeks. *Say you'll come away with me!* But though he held tighter, he didn't say it.

'What of the case of relics?' I gasped, when we came up for breath. 'There was fearful disarray there. Ought we not to sweep it up?'

'Let Sir Walter go picking in the dust for his trash,' he growled. 'I have done with him.'

I threw my arms around his neck and hugged tight. He made a harsh sound and we fled away, up to his room.

I was certain I'd won. People who struggle with their consciences and triumph over them get a certain look on their faces, disappointment mingled with relief. They don't say much. I thought Nicholas's silence was a sure sign that he'd decided to do something wrong by his standards.

But he never did say he'd come away with me.

We spent the rest of the day in his room, being what used to be called wanton. I was thrilled, I was intoxicated.

Everything would be all right. If only he would say something, though . . .

The rain stopped some time before twilight. A north wind came up, sharp and cold as crystal, and shredded away the clouds. It drove their rags far out to sea, so that a red sunset flared in through the windows, and later piercingly bright stars.

'Sweetheart, we should rise,' I whispered at last. ' 'Tis past the hour of six, surely. Folk will wonder where we are.'

'We may burn in Hell for all they care,' he said out loud. I jumped a little, it had been so quiet in that room.

'Maybe,' I said. 'But I must see how my father fares.'

He nodded at that but made no move to get up with me as I rose and dressed. I left him there in drafty starlight and went down into the depths of the house.

Smoky and too warm: they had built up the fires. Supper cooking. I was so ravenous, I could have eaten the Christmas pie. There might well have been some left, bubbling away and evolving into a strange life-form on a forgotten shelf in the pantry.

It was quiet outside Nef's room: no radio on. I looked in on Joseph and found him wide awake in darkness. 'Where's Nef?' I lit a candle.

'Down having supper,' he replied. 'Say, you wouldn't mind pouring me some sherry, would you? About three bottles?'

I looked around for a decanter and filled a glass. He took it in his good hand and tossed the drink back in one gulp.

'Are you still hurting that bad?' I looked at the empty glass in awe. He held it out for a refill, and I obliged.

'Wait'll you do this to yourself some day, little cyborg. Healing hurts. Pain and I are becoming old friends. It invites me over to watch football matches in holo, and we've loaned each other money. Old friends. Heck, yes, I sure do hurt.' He chugged his drink again.

'Should you drink so much with the patch on?'

'Won't affect it. It's the shoulder that's giving me hell. Everything else healed right up. But the Pectoralises Major and Minor and a host of their neighbors have parted company with Mr. Clavicle. They need a mediator in a big way.'

'I'm really sorry.' I poked up the fire. 'Can I get you anything?'

'Just another shot of amontillado. Listen, this is kind of going to put a crimp in my abilities to, uh, make secret knockout potions and so on . . .'

I grinned, pouring out his refill. 'Don't worry about that. It may not be necessary. I think that issue's going to resolve itself real soon.'

'No kidding?' He looked at me searchingly. 'Somebody's listening to reason? Well, glad to hear it. Just the same, with my arm like this, I wouldn't want us to have to pack our bags and run for anywhere for at least a week. Keep that in mind, won't you? In case any of your plans involve dramatic departures.'

'Hey, baby, trust me.' I smiled and exited on that line.

Down the dark staircase into firelight. It occurred to me that in a month's time I might be in a different city, away from the rain and smoke and dark corridors of England. This cheered my heart so much, I danced a saltarello all the way to the bottom of the stairs and ran breathless into the great hall.

Same old tableau there, a few people more or less. Francis Ffrawney standing all self-important in new livery. Being a groveling toady had paid off in a big way. Sir Walter looking very stiff and uncomfortable and somehow suddenly older; nevertheless his beard wagged on implacably about something to Nef, who was nodding in boredom as she poked her spoon around in a dish of baked beans. She was a great listener, that woman.

As I came skipping in, they all turned to stare at me with varying degrees of the same expression of disapproval.

'God give you good evening, gentles.' I curtseyed. 'I am come lately from my father, who hath slept and waked with a rare appetite. Which portends (as Avicenna saith) a speedy recovery, God be thanked. Wherefore I would take him some new loaves of bread, some hot broth, perhaps a joint of beef or a chicken, and some strong ale . . . ?' Nef raised eyebrows at me, but Sir Walter waved his hand at Master Ffrawney.

'See to it, Francis. How now, Lady Rose, doth thy father so

well? I am glad. I would not for the world have him miscarry in my house.'

I felt a storm of giggling coming on. 'Trust me, sir, his miraculous preservation was due to none other thing but the great abundance of holy relics of the saints that fell in profusion about him. Yea, surely, the very finger of Saint Ethelbert stood upright to ward off the terrible blow.'

Mendoza, you brat, watch your mouth.

'Say you so? It may be.' Sir Walter nodded solemnly. 'I myself was shrewdly bruised, I fear, and want your father's physick much. But sit, child, and thou shalt hear how I have won a sharp bargain with Master Darrell . . .'

Yawn yawn yawn. The little weasel had got a clause put in the sale contract for a room to be set aside for his use, if he should ever come back to visit Iden Hall: the idea being that as a kind of celebrity exhibit himself, he deserved free bed and board. I could see how he had cleaned up in the wool trade all those years ago. He seemed ready to go on about the clause for hours, so when Master Ffrawney returned with a huge tray, I jumped up and took it from him.

'Señor, you are too kind. I shall away to my poor, dear father with this bounty at once. Yet though it be excellent wholesome, I believe it shall do him less good than your prayers.'

'Why, so we shall pray for him,' Sir Walter called after me as I sped off. I paused long enough to curtsey again, didn't spill a drop of ale, and hurried on. I took the stairs two at a time. Fresh-baked bread, oh boy. Capon broth and a roasted capon too. Joseph blinked at me foggily as I set the can of broth beside him.

'Have some chicken soup,' I said, snatching up his candle. 'Trade you.'

'Room service?' he called, but I was already gone.

So at last back to Nicholas, who had put on his shirt and breeches and was sitting on the bed looking out at the little square of night sky. I set down the tray on the table where his books used to be; the candle danced and flared in the draft.

'Supper,' I announced. He turned in the candlelight, and my heart lurched painfully. It was very strange, because this surge of love swept away all my merriment and left me feeling the need to hold him and cry. I rushed to him, blinking back tears.

'What, Rose, is thy father worse?' He put his arms around me.

'No.' I hid my face against him. 'But I am sick with love.'

He was silent a moment at that, stroking my hair.

'So am I,' he said at last. 'Who shall heal us?'

'We haven't got the fever by the book.' I wiped at my eyes. 'All this heat, all this sorrow should have come at the beginning. By now we should have been cool to each other and free of pain.'

'Would to God we were,' he said. 'And yet that's blasphemy, to rail at love. No more of this talk.'

We had our little supper, crowded together at the table, while the draft ruffled the candle. We could hear the wild air prowling round and round outside, buffeting for a way in through the window. We didn't talk much. I watched him eat. Half dressed and unshaven as he was, he looked dissolute. Hard. I wondered what he'd have been like that way. There are plenty of gentlemen adventurers around, bastards by birth and inclination both. I'd have loved him anyway: better for him to have been a rogue like Tom than a righteous martyr. At least we wouldn't be sitting in this chilly room now, amid the ghosts of his books, in a fearful country.

Well, who knew? Maybe in a month's time we'd be in some other drafty little garret somewhere, sharing our bread by some other candle or by no candle at all. But we'd be free. Running together.

To the end of his tether.

That popped into my head so sudden and discordant, I scanned for Joseph, but he wasn't there. What a nasty thought. I'd have to learn to keep all such nasty thoughts well to the back of my mind in the future. We'd have forty years at least, and everything would be wonderful, wonderful. Love on the run through Renaissance Europe. Grand romance, as in the films. High adventure, and it was only just beginning.

At last Nicholas leaned back from the table and sat with his arms crossed, looking at me.

'Thy father,' he said. 'How long shall he lie abed until he heal?'

'Why, some days, surely,' I said uncomfortably. Why did he want to talk about Joseph, now of all times? 'He is hurt sore.'

'Yet he would have no surgeon to tend him, but only thee,' Nicholas mused. I knit my brows.

'Doctors have but poor opinion of each other. He trusts no physick but his own.'

'But must he have thee by him the whole time he mends?'

Aha. 'Nay, love, or I should have been by his side this whole while.'

He nodded thoughtfully. 'Couldst thou leave him?'

My soul leapt right up like the candle flame. I looked him straight in the eyes without smiling and said, 'Aye.'

We were going to elope after all. And what an opportunity: Joseph disabled and Nef absorbed in her radio and magazines. When might such a chance come again? Though I hadn't finished my work . . .

Nicholas got up and went to the window to peer out. The wind was higher; black branches whipped against the stars. 'Well,' he said, 'it is no night for faring abroad. It is bitter cold, and all the lanes will be foul with mud.'

'I fear no cold,' I said at once. He looked over at me and smiled wryly.

'Nor I,' he said. 'But we should leave tracks in mud, and be followed.'

Oh, right. Of course.

'Too wet to fare abroad.' He came and leaned forward, taking both my hands. 'But if this wind continues, it will dry out the roads soon. In some two days or three, one horse might bear two riders to the sea, leaving no mark of their passing.'

Yes, a horse. How foolish I'd been to think of running out now just as we were. How clever he was at planning. Clearly this was going to work out well.

'Art thou fearful?' He leaned closer.

'I? Nay!' Was my face doing something I wasn't aware of? His eyes were a little sad.

'My Rose is scarlet sometimes, and other times white pale. Come to bed, sweetheart. Thou to rest, and I to think. It is a long way yet until morning.'

A long way until morning.

I must finish this. I began it as a kind of therapy, and, like pulling one's own tooth, it becomes unbearable as the inevitable conclusion nears. But I find myself back in that room again, seeing that sad candle, that girl expecting a miracle. So let's finish it.

Joseph lay awake in pain, in darkness. The amontillado had long since been metabolized down to sugar and water, leaving him mercilessly sober. The capon broth was busy providing him with protein and hydrating vital tissues; but even its most enthusiastic proponents cannot claim that chicken soup is a narcotic.

'Screw this,' he told himself at last. Groping one-handed, he pushed back the sheet and crawled out of bed. From beneath the bed he drew a slim wooden box, awkwardly thumbed the combination, and removed a small leather case. This he unrolled, and spread its contents out upon the counterpane.

Steel rods, the size of pencils. They had peculiar grips and buttons and tiny winking lights. He studied them for a long moment and hummed a little song to himself. It was a very old song. He had learned it as a child, and it evidently held some soothing association with a pleasant memory, for he had found that humming it helped him self-induce a light trance state.

After about five minutes of contemplation he got up and wandered around the room, slightly glassy-eyed. His little song was doing its trick. He found five wax tapers in a drawer and carried them to the hearth, where he crouched down and held the tips into the coals until they ignited. Light bloomed. He stood up and arranged the surface of his writing desk, sticking the tapers upright in a tankard, fanning them out. He found a mirror in his travel bag and propped it up in the candlelight. When he was satisfied with the arrangement, he took off his sling.

The humming had become a chanting now. With his good

hand he collected the instruments and moved forward to regard himself in the mirror.

Pulse, slow. Heartbeat, slow. Respiration, very slow and deep. His right arm was warm and had good color, but the rest of his skin now was pale, especially over the left side of his chest. He depressed a button on an instrument, and there was a hiss, followed by a strong smell of cloves. He put down the instrument, took up another, and applied it to his shoulder. No blade was visible, but his skin parted in a long red line. He extended the line down in a semicircle, back and forth. His skin peeled back in a sheet, gradually exposing the musculature underneath.

There was no bleeding. As he worked, there were pinpoint flashes of green light. The chanting resolved into words, in a language long forgotten, about some boys with new spears who go down by the river to hunt bison but catch ducks instead, and take them back to their girlfriends who live under the cliffs, who are not impressed and won't dig garlic for them anymore . . .

It was dark where I was, except for the hole the fire shone through and the red red coals, and they gleamed in the priest's eyes but not in Joseph's where he watched in a corner. My eyes hurt. And I couldn't breathe. I tried to get out of the chair, but my hands were pinned straight through by the spines of holly leaves. Merry Christmas. Jesus Christ, said Joseph, they'll bury you alive.

'Rose!' The terrifying darkness faded into Nicholas's staring face. He had me by the wrists. 'Rose, in God's name!' Only his room. Only England outside, with her buffeting wind and her stars wheeling late through the night. Only the candle, burned low through the hours so its big flame staggered like a drunkard.

'Los Inquisidores,' I stated. I lay back down, and it began again at once, the fire, the darkness, the suffocation, and with a scream (silent, I had no breath) I fought my way back upright. Without another word Nicholas swung me out of bed and stood me on the cold floor.

'Walk with me.' Three times around the room, and I was wide awake, shivering in my shift. It was clammy with sweat.

'I couldn't wake up,' I explained. He helped me back to bed and sat beside me. My heart was hammering still, so loud he must have been able to hear it. Carefully he arranged the blanket and smoothed my hair back. He was shaking too, his face twisted by pity and revulsion.

'Thou hast dreamt of Spain.'

'I did. I was there again. I was where they – they —'

He was not looking at me but at the shadows on the wall. 'They killed thy mother.'

'She wasn't!' I cried in panic.

'Ssh! 'Tis well, 'tis well. See, love, that was long ago. Thou art safe –' and he halted, because he couldn't really tell me that truly, could he? Not in this England. He got up to put on his breeches and shoes. I only watched him, too exhausted and confused to move. He went to the door, and I protested and stretched out a hand.

'Wait, love. I will fetch thee a posset,' he promised.

Joseph, deep in his trance, became aware that someone was outside his door. His exterior consciousness began to return. Circled by the blaze of light from five waxen tapers, he turned around as the door opened.

I sat bolt upright. I hadn't screamed, I wasn't having a nightmare. But somebody was.

There was a horrendous crashing. The door flew open, and a figure hurled itself at me. That was too much for my nerves. I winked out.

I was across the room watching Nicholas fall on the bed. He got up slowly, staring at me, shocked forever. There was no color in his face at all. His eyes were like glass. He came at me. Again, I winked out.

I was on the other side of the room. He spun around and caught at me again.

I was standing on the bed. He came after me.

I was perched on the windowsill. He leaped.

I was on the ceiling, wedged into the angle of the beam where no human woman could ever have held on.

The chase ended there. He regarded me, panting. I regarded him, neither breathing nor moving. He took a step backward and collapsed. 'Nicholas,' I said in a tiny voice.

He sat up at once, fixing his gaze on me. Dragging himself backward until he reached the chest at the foot of his bed, he threw it open and fumbled inside. He pulled out a sword. So his books hadn't been his only possessions.

Gasping, he set his back against the wall and took the sword out of its sheath. He held it in both hands, the pommel resting on his drawn-up knees, the point directed at me. Neither of us moved for some few minutes, while the sound of his breathing grew quieter. How the wind roared and threatened to get into the room with us.

'What art thou?' he said at last.

To answer such a question, in such a position.

'Come, tell me, for I must know.' His voice grew stronger.

I drew a deep breath. 'I am not mortal.'

'So much I'd guessed.' He actually laughed, a low cold laugh. While I was fleeing him, his face had been like an animal's, almost unrecognizable. I thought he had gone mad. But he hadn't: his eyes were clear now and very, very hard. I moved an arm, and the sword point jerked up at me. 'Nay, do not come down,' he said sternly. 'Whilst thou art up there, I cannot be persuaded this is a dream. Nor would I kill thee. Can I kill thee?'

'No,' I informed him.

'No, not with a sword, if thou art a spirit.' Looking at me steadily, he reversed the sword so that the cross-shaped hilt was toward me. When I did not flinch, he spun it back. 'Ha! That's a fable. Thou hast worn crucifixes and read Scripture with me. So much for the devil in the old play. But I charge thee, Spirit, to tell what thou art.'

'A spirit whose heart breaks,' I said faintly. 'A spirit who can bleed.'

He glanced at the door, nervous. 'True enough. Thy flesh is palpable, I know that well. Oh, God help me, that I suspected what thou wert and still loved thee. Thou wouldst scarce eat of our mortal bread. Thou hadst never seen snow nor frost. A hundred things betrayed what thou wert, and still I loved thee.'

'I am still what I was,' I pleaded.

'But the *world* has changed. What I have learned in this one hour —' His eyes widened. 'To think I sought to save thy soul! And thou wert ever seeking after mine. Lord God, why hast thou shown me this fearful thing?'

'Nicholas, let me come down.'

But he did not answer me, staring slack-jawed as revelation came to him. 'Once,' he said, 'I betrayed the faith for the sake of my sinful flesh. The way to atonement has lain before me all this while, but I did not take it, for love of thee. I would have run away with thee and saved myself again. My flesh hath ever been mine enemy. And how sweet, how reasonable were thine arguments that led me to damnation! Nor could I have ever seen the trap, unless God made it plain. Which He hath done!'

He struggled to his feet, looking up at me. His face was shining, shining with fire.

'My love – for truly I may call thee so, since thy failure hath been my salvation – my love, thou hast lost. Return whence thou camest, and tempt me no more.'

I think he expected me to vanish then, but I was in danger of falling on him, so racked with gripping were my arms and legs. 'I can't go like that,' I wept. 'I have to climb down.'

'Then I shall leave thee.' He backed toward the door. 'If I can. If I can get out of this house alive, I shall. And then the way lies clear and straight. Farewell, Spirit!'

He turned and bolted. I heard him thundering down the stairs, and then the screaming began: deep, full-throated screams of alarm in purest Castilian Spanish. I fell at last and scrambled to the doorway.

There was Nef down on the landing, immovable as rock in front of Joseph's door. She was in her shift, and her hair was down around her shoulders. She brandished a lighted candelabra at Nicholas, who was edging warily past her, holding out his sword.

'Murderer!' she howled. 'Seducer! Lucifer incarnate!'

And I realized that doors were opening and people were running from all parts of the house to stare. Nicholas realized it too. He made a break and got past her, and, running to the edge of the great staircase, vaulted into space from the top step. Like a star he dropped out of the light, and I was sure the fall would kill him.

'Nicholas!' I ran shrieking.

He hit the floor below with a crash that shook the house. I sped after him, but Nef reached out and took my wrist in a grip of iron.

'Stop,' she said quietly. And even as I sagged to the floor crying, I heard him get to his feet and run on, and there was a boom as the doors of the great hall were flung open. The wind was let into the house at last. Rejoicing, it swept up through that dusty place, bringing in the smell of a cold spring morning.

Chapter Twenty Two

The story told itself. Everyone had seen it happen. The duenna, steadfast and formidable; the wretched daughter in tears; the father pale as his sheet, a terrible wound in his shoulder, begging – for the honor of his family name – that no more should be said about this lamentable occurrence.

Several of the household offered to ride out and find Nicholas, that he might be hanged; though there were others who shrugged and spat, and whispered to one another that something terrible had been bound to happen sooner or later, with Spaniards in the house. Sir Walter told me I was an evil daughter and ought to be beaten soundly. He would gladly beat me himself if Doctor Ruy so wished. Doctor Ruy thanked him graciously but declined.

My own plan was to lie in the corridor where I had fallen and cry until the world ended. I was prevented from doing this by Nef, who dragged me into her room and shut the door after us. She then directed a shrill volley of Castilian abuse at me, which greatly edified the listeners outside. Joseph explained, and explained, and explained. When it began to grow light outside, everyone gave it up and went back to bed.

'It was just the worst luck in the world,' Nef told me. 'And I've seen some bad luck in my day. But, honey, the relationship couldn't have gone on anyway. We were leaving soon. He was about to be fired. This way there was a hell of a scandal, but at least our cover wasn't blown.'

I listened without comment. Failing my plan to lie on the floor, I was perfectly content to lie in bed and cry until the world ended.

'Now, I know nothing I say helps,' Nef went on. 'You may not believe this now, but you're not the only person this has ever happened to, you know.'

Great.

'And it could have been worse. What if I hadn't come out? What if he'd gone back in there and attacked Joseph? We'd have had to kill him then, and what a mess that would have been to cover up. Even if he talks about what he saw, wherever he is now, who's going to believe him? Half the servants are convinced they saw the whole thing just the way Joseph says it happened. So we're safe. Your reputation's a little soiled, but what the heck. You'll be out of here in another month.'

I couldn't live that long.

'Hey, baby, what can I say?' Joseph shrugged, not easy with his arm in a sling. 'I should have locked the door. My one mistake. Well, okay, I shouldn't have been doing self-repair in the field. But have you ever had a shoulder separation? You try living with a thing like that for a whole week. Really painful. Nothing like the pain I'd feel if I ever, ever thought you had some crazy idea about ditching the Company and running off with a mortal. Not that you *could*, of course; they built all sorts of subprograms into you to make you betray yourself if you ever tried dereliction of duty after all the money they spent on you. But you're a good little operative, I know you'd never do a thing like that. Say, did the guy happen to mention why he felt it was necessary to run back down with his sword to try and kill me?'

I didn't respond.

'I guess he thought I was kind of, like, the Devil or something, huh?'

I closed my eyes.

Joan entered the room as silently as a mortal can, and I lay with closed eyes pretending to be asleep. Do Not Disturb. But I didn't hear her pulling out dirty linen or pouring wash water, so after a moment I squinted through my lashes to see what she was doing.

She had an amulet of some kind and was waving it over our things: the baggage, the credenza, even the dirty linen. Her lips were moving in some kind of chant. She turned to look at me, and I saw her extend her hand in the old, old sign against evil, fingers pointed like a devil's horns. Then she crept out.

Well, I knew now conclusively: I could never have walked away and left Nicholas anywhere. It would have killed me. It was killing me now.

I slept and dreamed he had come back. It had all been a misunderstanding: everything was all right now. Somehow he had accepted the truth about me and didn't mind. We kept packing our belongings to go to Europe, but when I'd get to the door, he wouldn't be with me, and I'd have to go back and look for him.

I couldn't get warm. Nothing would warm the bed. I couldn't figure out what to do with my arms and legs while I slept, either.

'Hi there,' said Joseph pleasantly, backing into the room. His arms were full of cut green twigs. 'Beat it, goat.' The unicorn skittered away from him and then came bleating back, looking for a handout.

'Whew. Now that the weather's warming up, maybe we can persuade Nef to keep Fluffy here outside.' He dropped the twigs on my credenza. 'So. You're probably wondering what I'm doing with all this shrubby stuff. Well, I knew you weren't feeling like doing any work or anything, but the garden's just greening away and I thought: Say, I'll bet I could take some of those specimens myself. All it involves is cutting off leaves and branches, right? Something like that. And what a good idea to speed things up when it's getting more dangerous to stay in this country every day. Not that I want to put any pressure on Mendoza, I told myself. So I just found a pair of clippers and hacked off a bunch of stuff I thought looked interesting.'

I looked at what he had brought. Hacked was too mild a word. I shuddered to think what the plant must look like now.

'Yeah, I grabbed up a little of everything. Of course, I'm not a botanist, so I can't really tell what's important and what isn't, but I figured if I just kept slashing away, I'd get something we need. Now, let's see. How do you turn this thing on?'

He twisted a few knobs, and the console lit up with a warning beep.

'Gee, this must not be right. It's asking me if I want to override. Well, let's let it warm up a few minutes. I can just take the time to look through what I bagged and see if I got anything useful. Here's some of that ilex stuff, for instance.'

What a ruin he'd made of the stem. Had he used his teeth, for God's sake?

'Yes, sir, this is pretty interesting. Really funky leaves and, uh, I guess this is a flower or something —'

'Let me see that.' I put out my hand. He brought the twig. Florets like pale green wax, arranged alternately at the bases of the leaves. 'Were they all like this?' I demanded.

'Could have been. I didn't notice; I'm not a botanist, you know that.'

I swore softly.

'Is it important? Is it, like, the final all-important step in the growth cycle you've been holding us up here so you could get? Boy, wouldn't that be swell? But don't worry. Don't bother to get up. I'll process it for you, if I can get the credenza working.'

I got out of bed.

The official word to the residents of Iden Hall was that I was doing penance for my wicked behavior. I must travel all through the garden on my knees, saying rosaries every hour on the hour, with my grim-visaged duenna by my side. The weather was not sufficiently damp and cold to satisfy those who felt I should be flayed alive, but they had to live with their disappointment.

As for me, I was out in the garden before it was light, working until my breath smoked in the evening gloom. Nef, who would much rather have been in her warm room listening to the radio, was grim-visaged indeed. She had to play her part, though, as I had to play mine.

Work shut my heart in another room and locked the door, so I was free of the wailing thing all day. Only at night was it able to get at me. Nights were hell.

I cleaned out Joseph's entire stash of Theobromos. He

sighed and endured, because I was doing a month's work in a matter of days. *Ilex tormentosum* was caught in its full cycle, absolutely optimum for the Company banks, forever and forever a benefit to mankind. Little herbs of the field, sweet grasses fell to my knife to rise eternal in electronic alchemy. Some nights, the best nights, I never went to bed at all; the blue light of the ultravey kept me safely out of that horrible terrain while Nef lay grumbling, holding up a pillow to block the light.

I had always thought we were made perfect: but if they could make us sleepless, and heartless, what a lot of good work we could get done.

Bright weather and steadily warmer. The smell of the land changed: that dead black coldness was blowing away. The north wind blows, and you look upward, at chimney pots and leafless branches, but the south wind blows, and you look down, where all wakeful things stretch green in the light of the young sun.

I was doing the very last work on the roses. They weren't as important as the ilex; *Rosa pellucida* would produce no miracle cures, but in a hundred years its distinctive flowers would open in no mortal garden. It would be rediscovered in the twenty-first century, in the abandoned garden of an old house in Oregon. What long chain of engineered circumstance would stretch back to me, here in the sunlight of a spring day in 1555?

'My favorite broadcast is on in six minutes,' Nef informed me in a martyred tone. I looked up, startled.

'Oh?'

'It's on Red Shropshires,' she explained. God only knew what Red Shropshires were, but I decided to be accommodating.

'Nobody's likely to bother me here. I've got my rosary handy. Why don't you go tune in?'

'Thanks.' She was away like a shot. For such a big woman, she could move pretty quickly when she needed to. But, then, we all could, couldn't we? I went on clipping and scanning, because I had work to do.

I sensed a mortal coming into the garden. Who? . . .

Straining, I perceived Master Ffrawney. In a panic I pulled out my rosary.

There I knelt, the image of pious repentance, but he came nowhere near me. I tracked his approach to a spot about three meters away, blocked from me by a dense hedge. There he stopped and settled, and I heard him sigh. What on earth was he doing? But perhaps even crawling sycophants liked to take in a little sunshine now and then. I tucked my rosary away.

No sooner had I resumed work than another of the little monsters arrived. This time I scanned to follow his or her progress. His, definitely. Male, about thirty-five, five feet six inches tall, weight one-forty, chemical profile . . . Master Darrell.

He was advancing steadily along the main avenue to the house, and would miss me completely. I relaxed. As he approached the intersection of his path and the one Master Ffrawney was seated in, I heard Master Ffrawney rise.

'Good day to you, Master Darrell.'

'Ah.' The other altered his course and proceeded at right angles. 'Good day to you, sir. Most rare weather for March, is it not?'

'Even as the true faith bloometh, so doth England,' responded Master Ffrawney. 'Er . . . have you come a-purpose to see Sir Walter?'

'Aye, forsooth.'

'Alack, sir, he is indisposed.' A wave of embarrassment from Master Ffrawney, and some covert sexual excitement too. Sir Walter must be with the laundress again.

'Oh.' A creak as Master Darrell sat down. 'Well, well . . . perhaps *you* would know. I have been studying the household account books and would have some speech thereupon with some responsible person. Having heard of Master Harpole's disgrace – and I trust no evil came to Sir Walter thereby? – I say, having heard of it, I wondered who hath been appointed to keep accounts now?'

'I have that task, sir, until a new secretary be found. And may I say, sir, that Sir Walter haply had resolved to rid himself of that vile heretic already —'

'Good. Good. So you keep accounts now? Tell me, have you been long in this household?'

'Twelve years, sir.'

'And you know well, then, how much money hath been spent to maintain the garden?'

'Why . . . yea, yea, I do. Better, I may say, than that foul heretic who, when he was not lusting after wenches, was polluting his heart with Lutheran books.'

'Aye, forsooth, but let him alone for now. You shall remain in the household, shall you, when it is given over?'

'No, sir, I am Sir Walter's man.' Pride swelled in him like a pimple. 'He desires me to go to Court with him. You see I wear new livery, special for the purpose.'

'A great honor.' Masked annoyance in Master Darrell's congratulation. 'Yet I could wish – I will be frank with you, Master Ffrawney, and do you the office of a friend. I could wish you less honored and more fortunate.'

'I do not understand your meaning, sir.'

'Master Ffrawney, I am often in London. Sir Walter hath not been there this many a year. He doth not know how the ground lies outside of Kent. It is not so easy to make one's fortune at Court as at a wool mercer's. I have seen many a noble knight unable to pay his tailor. Need I say that where the master goes hungry, his man starveth? You face no safe or comfortable prospect, Master Ffrawney.'

'Oh, sir.' Master Ffrawney sounded thoroughly alarmed. 'Surely Sir Walter is so liberal and excellent in his person, and so faithful a son of the Church, that he must win wealthy friends in London. Yet an he doth not, what remedy for me?'

'Fear not, Master Ffrawney, for here I stand like a loving cousin to counsel you. Whatever wage Sir Walter promised you, I'll double it. You shall be my secretary here, supplying the place of that Harpole who is gone, and shall remain safe in this noble hall. And (to tell you in your ear) you shall fare better thereby than Sir Walter, ere long.'

It was at that precise moment that Master Ffrawney switched allegiances, if the chemical composition of his sweat was any indication. He wanted to be wooed, all the same.

'Sir, shall I desert him I have served so faithfully and so long? I'll tell you plain, he payeth me handsomely indeed.'

This outright lie was a mistake, for Master Darrell had been reading the household accounts, after all.

'Handsomely, say you?' smirked Master Darrell. 'If you think you are well paid now, you shall think me as liberal as Croesus. I mark how Sir Walter hath paid out divers sums this long while for certain curiosities. the verity of which I do doubt. Sure I have seen his unicorn: if the man had no better judgment than to buy a plain goat for twenty pounds eightpence, it is a miracle he hath kept himself out of debt as long as he hath. Thrift shall be the new order of the day, I tell you, and there shall be no more cockatrices nor sea dragons bought from peddlers. And why should not some of these grounds be planted out in bright stuff, less rare but easier to maintain, that maketh a better show? And why should folk pay but a penny at the gate, when they might just as well pay twopence?'

I nodded. As I'd thought: the end of the garden as I'd known it.

'This is excellent sense, sir,' Master Ffrawney agreed. 'I oft did think, in days past, that Sir Walter spent his substance unwisely. But in this he was much misled by his man Nicholas, you must know. Well, of him we shall speak no more. He shall be brought to justice some day, and God will deal with him then.'

A wave of puzzlement from Master Darrell. 'Shall be? But he *hath* been.'

Now wonder and excitement from Master Ffrawney. 'Hath he been taken? I thought all had been kept quiet, lest shame come to the Spanish doctor. And is he hanged indeed?'

'Hanged!' Master Darrell was frowning. 'Nay, he is condemned to burn.'

My heart wasn't beating. I couldn't hear it beat.

'Burn? Go to!'

'Aye, in Rochester. Jesu, what hath happened here? Didst thou not hear how he was taken preaching in the marketplace at Sevenoaks? They say he ranted heresies like a bedlam man, and not in the way of a plain Lutheran neither, but the old heresies – thou knowest whereof I speak. Hath he done some offense here too?'

Master Ffrawney's joy was incandescent. It fairly shone

through the hedge. I could almost see the little green leaves shrivel and curl with its intensity. He proceeded to tell the whole juicy story, but I didn't stay to listen. I had been carefully packing up my tools. I set them in my basket, got to my feet, and walked away.

I walked right out of that garden. Out through the fantastical gate with its gilded whirligigs and pennants, out into the lane beyond, where long meadows sloped down to a river and pollarded willows grew. No, that was south. I mustn't go that way. Rochester was due north. I had to find a road that would take me north.

I kept walking.

When I had gone some eight kilometers, it occurred to me that they might be burning him even now. Sobbing, I began to run.

Chapter Twenty Three

It was a long way, fifty kilometers or more. I had to wade rivers. I saw the osiers and weirs and other uniquely English features of the landscape. I walked through orchards just leafing out in green mist, no blossoms yet. I crossed chalky downs, with stands of beech trees. Sometimes I ran, and sometimes I walked. Sometimes I followed a road, and sometimes I cut across broad expanses where sheep grazed. I saw examples of *Dianthus carolphyllus albans* and *Cerastium holosteoides* and *Polygala caeruleis*.

I saw thieves, possibly murderers. Near dark I passed through the outskirts of a little town and saw some men standing around a well. I remember their hard stares in their bearded faces. Probably they didn't often see a young lady in Spanish dress out alone at sunset. Not in Cosenton, or wherever it was.

One of them followed me. About a mile onward, I picked up his signal, coming swiftly after: his pulse was racing, he was excited. Rape, probably, or robbery. I tucked my crucifix inside my bodice and looked around for a place to hide. There were trees nearby, very dense and dark, darker now with night falling. I left the road and went in among them. Nothing there but birds, settling in for the night. I climbed into a good old oak, tearing my dress but who cared now, and sat primly on a branch with my hands folded, waiting.

Presently he came along, and I could see him by infrared, his blood glaring out hot through his clothes. He slunk at a quick trot, as a dog on bad business does, with his excitement hanging around him like a bad smell. I sent a blast of loathing at him. He must have been a psychic dog: he faltered and turned about in the road and actually came a few paces near my tree. I sent images into his mind of violent assault, murder, bloodshed. It must have excited him, because he nosed even closer. In desperation I conjured up the supernatural: white clammy specters coming at him out of the trees, arms wide to embrace him. That did the trick. He took to his heels and ran back the way he'd come. I sat trembling in the oak branches for a while, hating the mortal race.

Except Nicholas, of course.

There was a waxing moon for a few hours, and by its light I found my way on through cold England, across green hills. Somewhere off north was the sea, and away to my left was a river that snaked down to it, growing wider with each curve. The Medway, it must have been. Yes, Rochester was on the Medway. The smell of the river and the turning stars guided me after the moon went down.

Sometimes, a long way off, I could see candlelit windows. There were mortals in the warmth behind those windows, up late: sitting up with sick ones or reading solitary or having late-night suppers of toast and mulled wine. I would have liked some toast and mulled wine. Any other time, I would have thought sentimentally about the people in the candlelit rooms, living out all the poignant details of their little mortal lives. Not tonight. I passed on through the dark with the knowledge that if I knocked on one of those doors, was welcomed into one of those warm bright rooms, they would be bright for only a moment: then, as at Christmas, all the lights would go out, and I would be alone in the dark with time and its dead. Better to walk the night.

Morning took a long time coming. The first thing I noticed by its gray light was that I had wrecked my clothes: there were rips and trails of lace everywhere, and mud, and wet dead leaves. Too bad. The second thing I noticed was a castle sticking up on a mound by a big gray curve of river. There were pointy parts of building below it – a cathedral.

I accessed all my store of maps and literature. Yes, that must be Rochester. Smoke curled upward from it. Oh, let it be chimney smoke, harmless chimney smoke. Or a hundred men with pipes? No, not pipes. A few years yet before tobacco became a habit among civilized men. What would it be like to live, as some future generations would, in perpetual clouds of herbal smoke? It must be a sweet kind of smell. Perhaps it would be like incense. A shame about the carcinogens, of course, but with all the medical advances of that era, the mortality rate would probably balance out even with now.

So I babbled to myself, on the road to the city, and the sun climbed higher in the sky. It did not dry me out much. I was encountering mortals on the road now. They did stare at me as we passed each other. Either my clothes were in a worse state than I thought, or they didn't often see señoritas here.

An old woman was puffing along slowly toward me with a basket under her arm. She was as much a wreck as sixty mortal years could make her, but my goodness what pink skin she had. That's the English for you.

'Good morrow, good mother.'

'Eh?' She looked up (she was only about four feet tall) and noticed me for the first time. Her blue eyes widened in a stare.

'Art thou come from yonder town, good mother?'

'Eh? Aye.' She couldn't make up her mind to curtsey to me, not being entirely sure what I was, so she wobbled a bit and flapped her apron to be on the safe side. I reached up to smooth my hair and found a long oak twig sticking straight up like an antenna. Wonderful.

'Thou wilt pardon me for my wild appearance, good woman, as I was set upon by thieves.'

'Truly?' Instant rush of interest, and not sympathy, exactly, but a certain enthusiasm. She came closer.

'I must know, goodwife, whether there hath lately been a man burned at Rochester?' I held my breath and waited.

'Nay, lady, but there is to be.'

Whoosh. 'I pray you, tell me when?'

'Why, on the morrow, lady.' Her eyes assessed me. 'Spanish, are you?'

Must be the cut of my gown. 'Why, so I am,' I answered cautiously.

'Then you've lost none of your sport. The man burneth tomorrow betimes.' She shrugged her basket closer to her and walked on. I walked on my way too, light-headed as all hell. Nearly a whole day before? Surely I could come up with some kind of plan.

Rochester was a very old place. It smelled old. Moldy, too. The air of decay probably came from the ruin that about a third of the town was fast becoming. It had been a monastic town, so the Reformation had smashed it pretty well. There seemed to be one main street that dove straight through without taking the traveler anywhere much. To either side of it the town was self-enclosed and secretive, blind as a maze. Only, looming over all, was this big cathedral that looked like it might fall on you at any time. I didn't like the cathedral. But I wasn't there to like it, was I?

So many mortals now, along the main street, and all staring at me. I saw a man coming out of a house. He seemed to be important; his surcoat had fur trimming on it.

'Reverend sir.' I curtseyed deep before him as he regarded me in astonishment. 'Can you tell me where the man is, that was brought here from Sevenoaks?'

He took forever to answer. Really, had he never seen a Spanish ghost before?

'If you mean the foul heretic, lady, he is held fast at the bishop's house.'

Ah. I was getting somewhere. I pulled my crucifix out of my bosom. He goggled at one or the other. 'I pray you, sir, is he a great tall fellow, without a beard?'

'Aye, fair maid, he is. Wherefore would you know?'

'Oh, sir!' All right, he was looking at my bosom. I made it heave and brought it closer to him. 'I have sought the recreant this many a mile, through wild country as you may plainly see, all that I might dispute with him concerning the true faith, to lead him out of error into salvation.' I found my rosary and waved that at him too. He blinked and replied:

'That were a great pity, lady, for the man hath remained constant in his heresy and is to die for it.'

I swooned. Not really; but it put the ball in his court, and my feet were killing me anyway. There was an outcry all around me, and I was lifted up and carried into the house, with much covert squeezing of my behind and even more covert tugging at my gold crucifix. Both remained attached, however. I was revived with a shot of aqua vitae and came to with suitably faint requests for data concerning my location. Many staring English faces assured me I was in the Lord Mayor's house and need not fear, for they were all honest folk here.

I checked my cross and rosary, then sought the face of the

man I'd first spoken to. He must be El Alcalde de Rochester. I played my scene to him and played it well, too: wept for the man Harpole, explained that I had striven to save his soul but he had fled me, adamant in his heresy, though because there had been some tender feeling between us that had nothing to do with theology I thought I might still manage to reconcile him to the Church. Might I not be given this chance?

But the Lord Mayor was shaking his head.

'Child, he is condemned. You may save his immortal part, aye; but the knave hath argued so coldly, and so shrewdly, and hath such a wicked reputation beside, that you will never see him pardoned. Be content; there is no remedy.'

'But I must see him!'

'Well, that may be done,' said a lady, clearly the mayor's wife. 'But who are you, child? Are you not Spanish?' *Hola*.

'I am the daughter of Doctor Ruy Anzolabejar,' I said, as proud as though it were true. 'And what honorable love there hath been between myself and this poor man I will not say; but I charge you to think whether you would deny a soul one last persuasion that might be its salvation, and break a maiden's heart into the bargain.'

The Lord Mayor and his wife exchanged glances. She got up and encouraged her neighbors to leave. When she came back, the Lord Mayor said delicately:

'Lady, your intent is praiseworthy, but I must tell you that though this is a godly place wherein most folk do love our queen, our prince, and his holiness the Pope, as well they ought, yet there are certain vile persons here who have acclaimed the man Harpole as a martyr. This has hardened him to his villainous intent. These ill-wishers may do you some harm if you attempt to dissuade him.'

'Let them,' I said. 'I care not, so his precious soul is saved.' So there. The Lord Mayor cleared his throat.

'Why, then – then you may take some buttered eggs with us, and rest you from your wearisome journey, and perhaps after dark I may take you to where he is kept.'

'I must go to him now,' I insisted. 'What, shall I lose one instant of the brief time I have left to convert him?'

'Fie for shame, husband!' cried the wife. 'Put a cloak about

her and take her round about by the old way. There's none
will see her in the vineyard.'

'So shall I do.' He looked at her indignantly. 'And was
about to so propose, ere thou prated at me.'

In the end we both went covered up in cloaks, through
a mass of ruined walls and green garden, all around under
that big cathedral. We went into the back garden of a
big house, and the Lord Mayor courteously explained my
purpose to several persons of importance, including Bishop
Griffin himself. As in take after take of a comic film, I played
my scene out some three or four times. Finally everyone agreed
I should have my shot at the condemned man. So after an
agony of wasted time, I found myself in front of a little low
door, with a mail-clad soldier turning a key in the lock.

The key was ornate. The lock clanked. These physical
details claimed my attention, I found them absolutely fascinating, and of course the reason was that I had no idea
why I had come to see Nicholas or what I was going to say
to him. But I went in, and there he was.

He was sitting quiet and composed on a narrow cot, the
single piece of furniture in the room. His eyes widened as
I came in with the Lord Mayor, but he did not react
otherwise.

The Lord Mayor lectured Nicholas sternly about his fate,
and told him how he didn't deserve this virtuous lady coming
to reason with him, but since she was here, the Lord Mayor
would see if youth and virtue might succeed where reverend
wisdom had failed to shake Nicholas's sinful heart. I was
assured that if any violence was attempted on my person,
I had but to cry out and I should be rescued instantly, and
this bad fellow would be the worse for it. Having said his
say, the Lord Mayor took his leave of us. The door closed
after him. We were alone.

We looked at each other in silence. Nicholas was muddy
and torn too, and bruised besides; pale, thin, and unshaven.
His face had changed.

'Welcome, Spirit,' he said at last. His voice had changed,
too.

'May I sit down?' I requested. Then I realized there was
only the bed to sit on. He got up and gestured for me to sit.

My legs were trembling, so I sat and pulled off my shoes, which hurt my feet very much. He leaned against the wall with his arms folded, watching me.

'How should a spirit have such muddy toes?' he wondered.

'Didst thou think I flew here?' I looked at him. 'Think again. I have walked the whole way from Iden Hall.'

'Ah.' He looked at me steadily.

'See?' I stretched out my feet. 'No hooves.'

A smile came and went, chilly, strange.

'To tell truth, I am glad thou hast come,' he said. 'This mortal air was getting a sweetness to it that made my heart cold to my duty. It made me wonder whether I had only dreamed – what thou knowest of. I was growing weak in my resolve. Now thou art here to test me, like a good friend, and I see it was no dream and am strong again.'

I couldn't think what to say at all. My eyes filled with tears.

'Aye.' He nodded. 'Weep, Spirit. I will not falter.'

'Oh, this is stupid!'

'I may tell thee, thou hast done me great good. Before mine eyes were opened, I believed as any weak and sensible man doth: that God exists, because we have been taught so, but there are no miracles and our only duty is earthly charity. More, I believed there were no devils nor spirits but only wickedness in men. For who has ever seen a serpent that spake with a voice, to tempt men from God?' What a strange look for me as he said that last. Almost kindly. 'But, having known thee, I learned the truth of what thou art, and mine eyes are opened.'

I had certainly shown him there were more things in heaven and earth than were dreamt of in his philosophy, hadn't I? He eased himself down into a sitting position on the floor.

'Regard what thou hast done. In every respect where I doubted, thou hast made me believe.' He leaned forward. 'Were it not for thine ever witching me away from my duty, I could think thou wert a spirit of a different kind entirely.'

'I am,' I said, without much hope.

'It may be so,' he admitted. 'But what thou art I cannot guess.' There was another long silence. 'Where is thine argument?' he said at last. 'Where is thy subtle persuasion? Wilt thou not beg me to lie, and recant, and get mercy from the bishop?'

'Thou wilt not,' I said. I was so tired. 'They will kill thee, and I have no power to help —' My voice broke. By reflex he got up and came to me with a gesture of comfort, then froze.

'Ah,' he said. 'This is temptation too.'

I let my head fall backward, for exasperation and weariness. He sat down again. After a moment he ventured:

'Wert thou mortal once?'

I nodded.

'And art thou damned eternally?'

'No.' I laughed. 'Yes! Oh, I must be.'

He frowned. 'What wert thou, being mortal?'

'I told thee what I was.' I looked down at him. 'A child of Spain. And by chance, and by lies, I came into the dungeons of the Inquisition there.' He looked uncomfortable then. 'Oh, yes, señor. Didst thou think I was only a mask of Satan, with no real heart to be broken? What thou lovedst was real enough. Suffering and all. Muddy feet and all.'

He jumped up and went to the window, and stood there staring out.

'Hast thou never heard,' I tried to put it a way he might understand, 'of spirits who partake neither of Heaven nor of Hell?'

'The heathen and the dead children,' he whispered, 'who are neither damned nor saved.'

'Just so.'

He turned around and looked at me with such dread in his eyes, I grew angry. Was he superstitious? This man? I clenched my fists. 'Now hearing you'd been arrested for yelling in the street, I came weeping all the way here and never slept, and was followed by a murderer, and had neither rest nor food, and God knows why I troubled myself, for I knew you'd only say I was Satan come to tempt you. I wanted to save your life! But I'm too late! You have your martyr's crown, your horrible death! Oh, I could have gone away with you – I would have run away from my duty and lived with you in any street in Europe, I'd have read your awful Scripture and listened to your awful sermons and worshiped your awful God —'

'Stop!' He seized me by the shoulders. 'Stop! Stop!'

'Don't you tell me to stop!' I screamed at him. '*You* talked and talked —'

'But if I could have *saved* thee —'

The door flew open. We both turned, expecting the guard. It wasn't the guard, though. It was Joseph.

'Excuse me.' He marched right up to us, looking determined, and threw a punch at Nicholas. He had to jump a little to connect with Nicholas's jaw, but he connected, and Nicholas crashed backward into the wall.

'Mendoza, out. Now.' Joseph turned to me.

This was too much. This was grossly unfair. I collapsed sobbing on the bed. Joseph exhaled angrily and went to the door, where the Lord Mayor was peering in with a rather frightened face.

'I must have some private speech with my child, it seems. Pray pardon me.' And he swung the door shut, bang. Turning back, he said:

'Okay, Mendoza, get up. I've just ridden thirty miles on an extremely unpleasant horse and I don't feel like having an argument. You are in a lot of trouble.'

'No!' I cried. 'You can't make me leave now!'

'Now? Not leave now? What do you want to do, stay here until they torch the guy?'

Nicholas was struggling to his feet, staring from one to the other of us in bewilderment. Cinema Standard was enough like Tudor English for him to be able to understand about one word in three of what we were saying.

'I don't know! God, God, help me, I can't save him!'

'What language are you speaking?' inquired Nicholas in Latin.

'Shut up, creep. Oh, and by the way,' Joseph continued in Latin, turning to him, 'would you tell me why you were trying to get into my room with a sword? It takes something more to kill me, as you no doubt have guessed.'

'I never went to your room to kill you,' said Nicholas. 'I was trying to get out of the house without being killed. I went to your room only for medicine, to calm your daughter. You know what I saw when I opened your door.'

'I know. You ought to have knocked. But do you understand you are a dead man?'

'Truly I know it,' said Nicholas, with a little of his former sneer. 'But I die in a just cause. And I will testify to the truth until I have no voice.'

'You mean to denounce us to the world, then?' Soberly, Joseph put his hand on his pouch, where he kept his little glass vials. I opened my mouth, but no scream came out.

'By no means. Who would believe me? The ranting of a madman is not regarded. I mean to put my last breath to better use.'

'Very wise of you, I'm sure.' But Joseph's fingers were still working at the fastening. Nicholas saw the fear in my eyes.

'Thou art not her father!' he blurted out in English. 'Though I'll lay odds thou art the same demon who stole the child and made her what she is.'

Dead silence. Joseph surveyed him.

'Boy, you're good at figuring things out. Isn't he? Except that if anybody's the devil in this room it's *you*, buster.' An extraordinary bitterness came into his face. 'I've seen you before. I know you, all right, preacher man. Age after age, you come back. You always lead the crusades. You're so damned golden-tongued, other people just flock to die for your causes. You die with them, it's true, because you're stupid enough to believe your own great lies; but you always come back again somehow. Oh, I know *you*.'

No hair-tearing, no jumping up and down. Only his voice dropping to an unexpected bass with Nicholas staring at him, unable to comprehend.

'You think I'm not her father?' Joseph thundered. 'I took her out of the grave and gave her eternal life, which is more than your lousy God would have done! You're the one who seduced her into believing that your miserable little cult matters a damn, when she knows nothing matters less. You're the one who's made her hate what she is. How's she supposed to live, now, after what you've done to her heart?'

Not understanding him, Nicholas had stopped listening and was watching me where I cowered on the bed.

'So thou canst disobey him,' he said softly. 'So thou hast a free will and may choose.'

'Mendoza, get up. I'm taking you out of here.'

Nicholas held my gaze, and I could not look away. 'Stay with me until I have suffered tomorrow. Be with me at the end. I cannot rest otherwise, nor wilt thou rest. This thou knowest, love.'

Joseph seized me and pulled me to my feet. 'Mendoza, we're getting on two fine horses I paid ready cash for and we're riding south. We are not going to watch an auto-da-fé. Come on.'

My heart felt like a balloon.

'You can't make me leave if I don't want to. Can you?' I said to Joseph. 'I'm already in trouble. I'm staying until it's over tomorrow. When it's over, I'll go back with you, and the Company can do whatever it wants to.'

Joseph let go of me. 'It might teach you a lesson, at that,' he said. 'All right.' He looked at Nicholas. 'Young man. Do you know how many burnings at the stake I've had to sit through? Seven hundred and nine. Yours may be the first one I've ever enjoyed. In anticipation of that, I thank you.'

He swung the door open and pulled me out with him.

I went obediently enough. I let Joseph lead me back to the Lord Mayor's house with the Lord Mayor practically bowing and scraping beside us the whole way and telling us about his cousin who had married one of Katherine of Aragon's grooms. Apparently he offered to put us up for the night, too, but I missed what he and Joseph said to each other in that regard, because I was in a fog.

Something had happened in that cell that made it all right between us again. My own Nicholas had been looking at me at the last, and not that cold godly stranger.

At the Lord Mayor's house we were shown to an upstairs room, quite nicely furnished. Food and hot wine were brought for us; soap and water in a basin for me. I watched as Joseph talked to people. He explained, he apologized, he made arrangements, and at last he closed the door on the last mayoral wish for our pleasant stay in Rochester.

Turning around, he leaned against the door and stared at me.

'You shouldn't have said all those awful things about

Nicholas,' I said thickly. 'Not true at all. Petty of you.
Coming back age after age?'

He put his palms to his temples and pressed, as though he
were trying to keep his brains from exploding.

'I mean, what, you believe in reincarnation or something?'
I went on.

'You're how old now, Mendoza?' he inquired, with tremendous self-control.

'Nineteen. Maybe.'

'Nineteen, huh?' He took his hands down and began to
pace. 'Jesus. This must be what it's like to have a real
daughter. What are they teaching you kids back there? As
for reincarnation, it's realer than you think, smart-ass. There
are only so many personality types among mortals. They just
use the same ones over and over. Zealots like your Nicholas
keep turning up, and every time they do, they make trouble
for everybody. He's screwed *you* up, the son of a bitch. When
this guy burns tomorrow —'

'Oh, he won't burn,' I said dreamily. 'He's going to recant.
That's why he wants me to be there. He'll save himself, and
then what will you do? He knows all about us. And he
understands – isn't that incredible? A mortal capable of
understanding the truth about us? See, you won't have any
choice. You'll have to recruit him for us now. Give him
tribrantine. And you know he'll be the best mortal worker
we've ever had, once we explain the whole truth to him.
Imagine all that intellect and all that zeal working for us!'

But he moved away from me and took hold of the bed rail
with both hands.

'Mendoza,' he said, 'you can sleep in the saddle. We'll go
slow. I'll lead your horse. Just come away with me right now,
and I swear I'll fix everything with the Company about your
going AWOL. May be I can even get you out to the New
World. There are people who owe me favors out there. Please,
Mendoza. For your old pal who got you out of Santiago?
Don't stay here.'

'Didn't you hear a word I just said?' I demanded. His
shoulders sagged.

'You'd better get some sleep,' he said.

*   *   *

It was still dark when I opened my eyes, but I was wide awake at once. Joseph sat motionless in a chair by the window.

Rochester. Today. Nicholas.

'It's April first,' I said. 'Fool's Day.' Joseph nodded.

'Five A.M., as a matter of fact. Want to go back to sleep for a few hours?'

'Don't be stupid. I have to see him.' I jumped out of bed and got dressed. I felt very light, very unreal, and my heart was pounding.

I had thought we could just leave the house quietly, but when we went downstairs, the Lord Mayor's household was awake and bustling. So we were offered breakfast (I was too nervous to eat) and given cushions by the fire while the Lord Mayor got into his mayoral robes, because of course he had to attend the public event, and we, being his guests, had to wait for him. It took him forever to get dressed. His wife fussed around him and adjusted his chain of office and his big flat cap with its curling plume. The plume was an ostrich feather. It must have come from Africa by way of Spain. Wasn't the world a small place nowadays?

It was gray when we left the house. A light wind had risen in the night and blown away the fog. The Medway sparkled dully, waiting for the sunlight. The stars were going to bed, faint in a sky pale as blue chalk. Everything green was turned to the east, where it was bright and growing brighter.

The people, though, were drawn to the precinct of the cathedral. There, right by the bishop's palace, they had set up the stake. I saw it from a distance before I knew what it was. What drew my attention to it was the stream of mortals: from every door and lane they emerged to hurry toward it, like rats after the Pied Piper. Some mortals only glanced at us as they came out. Some bowed and slowed, and made to trail behind us as though they were members of our party. Some mortals spat at us and ran. They all looked alike, though.

But the stake. How could anyone pay attention to anything else? It was black with pitch and stood straight up out of a platform of logs. There were tidy bundles of brushwood stacked close by and a perimeter of bleachers, yes, actual spectator seating. Why, they'd thought of everything. We might have been in Spain.

Joseph had taken my hand in his and was squeezing tight. Was he worried? We were shown to seats. Seats of honor in the front row, no less, though some people in the crowd muttered against us. Then came out the bishop and the other ranking clergymen of the area, in solemn procession. Everybody stood. Respectfully, after the religious had been seated, the rest of us sat down again. Just like at Mass.

We waited. The sky grew lighter. What a sweet wind had sprung up, all fresh the way it is in the early morning.

In the midst of a prayer led by the bishop, they brought out Nicholas. You could see him from a long way off too, like the stake. He towered above his guards.

Oh. He was stripped to his shirt and hose. Indecent, somehow. Didn't they give the condemned in this country sanbenitos to wear? Wondering that was a mistake, because it called to my mind a long-buried memory of shuffling figures all chained together, the tall points of their hats bobbing like antennae. I had screamed when I saw them. Where had I seen them? When? Was I sweating cold then, as I was now?

Then as now, people stooped to pick up stones and flung them.

Like men braving heavy rain, Nicholas and his guards put their heads down and slogged on. Stones clattered on the metal pot hats of the guards. They swore at the crowd and swung their pikes before them. Nicholas could have run away then, but he didn't. He didn't even look up until a flint struck and gashed his scalp. Blood ran down the side of his face. As he stood staring, his eyes met mine. The guards grabbed him, and he walked on. He came to the stake.

Suddenly he moved, he struck into the crowd and caught me up close to him. Only for a second, a split second, and then his guards were pulling him back and he was shouting hoarsely:

'Ego te baptismo! In nomine Patris, et Filii, et Spiritus Sancti! Amen!'

I was shocked numb. I put up my hand to my face. His blood was smeared on my face, in my hair. He had a look of desperate triumph in his eyes, though the guards were beating him with their pike staves. Stumbling, he let them back him in among the logs. He fell against the stake.

What was happening?

He let them clamber up beside him and chain him there. A big loop around his chest, another about his legs. Three little kegs of gunpowder were brought and fastened up with him. Then the guards jumped down and began to lift the brushwood bundles into place with their pikes.

Weren't they going to give him a chance to recant?

The bishop stood up and began solemnly to tell him off, but Nicholas didn't listen; his gaze was fixed on me with a kind of black delight, and I felt so stupid, sitting there, because I was only just beginning to understand.

'. . . to the everlasting shame of them that bore thee, and clothed thee, and taught thee, and sheltered thee! Wilt thou not so far amend thy life, man, as to renounce thine error? Speak, for thine hour is at hand,' commanded the bishop.

It was what Nicholas had been waiting for. He swung his head from side to side, taking in his audience. 'Yea, the hour is at hand!' he shouted. 'Not mine hour alone but all England's hour, when it shall be tried in the sight of God! Gentlemen, my sin was very great. Ye know it well, all of ye, for it is your sin too and its name is Silence! O England, we knew the truth! We had the stone wherewith to build the New Jerusalem! And we neither spoke that truth nor built that city, being prudent, fearful men, and see what woe hath overtaken us now! The Lord hath sent a plague of Romish cardinals to drink our blood —'

'Fie! Wilt thou slander, thou?' cried the bishop.

'Do I slander? I humbly cry you mercy. I do but confess my sin. We have all sinned, we righteous men who kept silent when you crept back into England. Now you have returned in your power to forbid us the very Word of God! And who shall we blame but ourselves, who have let you return? O England, men will wear no chains but what they bind on with their own hands!'

His voice was beautiful. God, how beautiful. People were listening with their mouths open and greedy satisfaction in their eyes. Even the bishop, though his face was growing steadily more purple; he didn't want to miss a word, not a single damning word.

'Well, I will wear no more chains, gentlemen! I never will be silent again! Yea, you smile and say I am chained now, and soon will be silent enough. Yet I wear no such coils as all of ye. How will it go with ye when ye stand in shame before Almighty God, wearing such a weight of silence? England, is your flesh so dear to you as that? Is the flame so terrible?'

'Thou shalt know!' the bishop told him and, turning, gave the order. A soldier brought a torch and thrust it in among the piled brushwood. I lunged forward, and yet I could not leave the spot where I stood: there was an audible crack as muscle strove against bone. Joseph muttered an exclamation beside me and put his hand on my shoulder.

'Go, set the fire to blaze, for I will not peril my soul to keep out of it any longer!' Nicholas's voice came back like a great bell, drawing the crowd's attention from the first little curls of smoke. 'I will escape the prison of earthly flesh that confineth ye all!'

And he turned and found me with his eyes, and his look went through me like a sword.

'I call on thee to break down the prison wall! What, wilt thou live on for endless years in this dark place and never come to Paradise? Thou art a spirit, and wilt thou not come back to the love of God? *Thou mayest choose!* Look, I stand in this door of flame and I tell thee it is but a little way through. Wilt thou not rise and walk with me?'

And he held out his hand, through the fire. But he was wrong: I couldn't choose. I was rooted where I stood. I could no more have walked into those flames than lifted that stone cathedral on my back. I had no free will.

Fire shot up and danced through his outstretched fingers, caught at his wide sleeve. He closed his eyes for a moment in pain. The contact was broken, and I looked away wildly. I was closed in by a circle of eager faces, rapt faces, Catholic and Protestant alike. He could be a heretic or a holy martyr to them, so long as they got to watch him die. This quaint people, pink-faced Lord Mayors and goodwives and honest tradesmen, were leaning close to see the intellect of an angel reduced to so much greasy ash. This people, whose wicker holocausts had shocked even the Romans; they had become Christians, but they hadn't changed. I met Joseph's sad black stare.

Nicholas made an agonized sound, and I looked back at him. The flames were high now. 'Spirit, I charge thee, follow me into Paradise!' he choked, and then his voice rose clearer and louder than before. 'I am thine only husband and thou art my bride! *I am the same that waked thee among the apple trees where thy mother bore- thee, where thy mother brought thee into the world!* Come, and I will stay for thee! Oh, Jesu have mercy – oh – OH, JESU HAVE MERCY —'

Never say God doesn't answer prayers. The powder blew then and killed him. He became a column of fire and light as the sun rose over England.

While the crowd made appreciative noises, Joseph was finally able to pull me away from there; and we left that place.

Chapter Twenty Four

I t some later point, not connected by memory to anything preceding or following it, I was riding along a lane with Joseph. All the trees were in bloom: white blossoms and sweet scent everywhere. Apple trees. Every kind of flowering tree.

Joseph was talking to me as we rode along.

'You aren't feeling anything much right now,' he was saying, 'because you're in shock. It's a protective reflex. It'll last for a while. Eventually you'll feel again, and when you do, you'll be hurting pretty badly. But your work will help, Mendoza. Only your work will take the pain away. You'll need it like food and water and air.

'I'll see to it they don't take your work away. This wasn't your fault, this was a hell of a thing to happen to you your first time out in the field.'

He was correct, it was. I looked at all the details of his clothing as we rode, fascinated by the patterns in the cloth. He watched the road for a while, and then he said:

'Yes, I can cover everything up, I know what I can do. Don't worry. And think of the relief, Mendoza, this whole nasty business is over. It ended badly, but it's over. Nothing to be afraid of now, nothing to break your heart hoping for. The mission was a success, too, and we're out of here. New location, nothing to remind you of unhappiness.'

Oh, yes, I had to get out of England. He peered at me.

'Maybe I can get you posted to the New World. Hey, there's a great base where you could do research work, lots of peace and quiet there, maybe I can fix it so you won't get another assignment right away. What do you say, Mendoza?'

Yes, that sounded like what I needed.

He leaned toward me from his horse. 'Okay, Mendoza?'

I blinked in surprise. Wasn't I agreeing with him? He took the reins from my hand and shook his head.

We got back to Iden Hall, I remember that very clearly. I thought it would hurt, but it didn't hurt, because it wasn't the same place. Nothing at all looked familiar.

Only my work area met me like an old friend. I went straight to it and got busy wrapping up my projects for travel. I worked steadily there until we left, however many days that may have been. One day, when I was in the middle of an entry, Joseph and Nef told me that I had to dismantle the unit for packing. So I logged out, and they told me to pack my other things too.

Joan came in while we were closing up our trunks, no doubt to discreetly inventory the linen to be sure we didn't make off with anything at check-out time. Nef attempted to press a shilling on her by way of tip, but Joan drew her hand back as from a snake.

'Thank you, mistress, but I will none,' she snapped.

'How now?' Nef stared at her. 'Wherefore art thou displeased with us? Have we not ever treated thee well?'

'Ay, mistress, it *seems*; but God knows this is not the house it was when ye came into it, and a many strangenesses have happened, and whose doing were they?' She turned a killing look on me. 'And there was a holy martyr lately burned for his faith at Rochester, they say, but *I* say he had been living still, had not some here meddled with him.'

Nef stepped swiftly to my side and put an arm around me, but I had taken the blow without blinking. Why blanch at the truth?

'We need no reproaches from the likes of thee.' Nef glared at her. 'Leave us!'

'With a right good will,' retorted Joan, and flounced out of the room.

When the servant came to help us carry our bags down, it wasn't a servant I knew. I saw no one as we descended the staircase for the last time, went through the great hall for the last time, went out and climbed into our saddles and rode out through the garden the way we'd come. Not a sign of Sir Walter or Francis Ffrawney. Had they gone away to

London? But that had been a lifetime ago. I didn't look back as we rode, knowing that the house had already faded to transparency and would vanish altogether if I turned.

So through the whirligig gate, Joseph, Nef, and I. Just beyond it a farmer was pulling up in his cart, and he gave us a bright expectant look as we came abreast of him.

'Be ye folk come from the great house yonder?'

'Aye, good man,' replied Joseph.

'Then I have a marvel for ye, gentles. Grant a look, sir, only a look —' And he jumped down and pulled a cover of sacking from the back of the cart. There, lying in the straw, was the complete skull of an ichthyosaur half embedded in a rock.

'Sir, you see? The very dragon's head of the dragon Saint George slew. It came out of a rock nigh to my house. What say you, sir, is it not worth an angel at least?'

'Without doubt.' Joseph stroked his beard. 'But I fear thou hast come a long way for naught, man. Iden Hall hath been sold. There is no market here anymore for such things as dragon's heads.'

The man's mouth fell open. He gave such a howl of dismay that the unicorn struggled and bleated in Nef's arms. 'Say not so! I have carried it clean from Lyme, sir!'

'Sad but sooth, my good man. Though I'll tell thee, there's an inn on the road to Southampton, the Jove-His-Levin-Bolt, where they might pay thee for a look at this skull,' Joseph offered.

'Nay, out upon Southampton! If I've come on a fool's errand, I'll no further with the damned thing!' the farmer yelled, and he hauled off and kicked the wheel of his cart. His horse reared, the traces flew up, and the cart dipped backward, tipping the skull out into the road. It rolled ponderously, wobbling end over end, to the edge where the embankment dropped away, poised there a thudding second, and then went over, picking up speed as it went, bumping away down the long sloping meadows of Kent. The last we saw, it struck a log and bounded into space, completely clearing a hedge and crashing out of sight below. For all I know it is rolling still.

'You'll be sorry you did that, in the morning,' Joseph called to the farmer, who had gone storming off.

'When will they ever regret what they do?' Nef brooded.

'Oh, some morning or other,' said Joseph lightly. And we rode on.

Not that morning, though, nor for many others.

Poor Queen Mary never had her baby, because of course it was only a tumor. She went right on burning her subjects, though, in the hope that God would somehow produce a baby from somewhere if she did His will resolutely enough.

She never birthed her Counter-Reformation, either. In November 1558 she died, quietly in her pointless bed, and Elizabeth got the throne. That was it for the Catholic Church in England. The burnings stopped abruptly. The Protestants were reinstated. England did an about-face into a Golden Age.

But you missed it, Nicholas. You should have listened to me.

I missed it, too, because six months after leaving England I was stepping out of an air transport at New World One, and I was fine, just fine. I'd had therapy, I'd had drugs, I had lots of new clothes, and the AAE recommendation had mysteriously vanished from my personnel file. Happy me. Best of all, I was in New Spain.

I was discovering that a transport terminal was a pretty good indicator of the status of the outpost. New World One glittered: fabulous Mayan murals, gold leaf everywhere, inlaid floors. I wandered around the lounge, staring. A transport hostess with a spectacular feathered headdress. Jade cups in the coffee bar. Art objects, for God's sake, mounted on brackets above the announcement speakers. A little cross-legged god vibrated slightly as I was asked to report to the arrivals office.

The arrivals office looked like a hothouse. Thick bluegreen glass, terra-cotta, flowers crowding the walls. A smiling woman in tropical whites came to the window. I had on tropical whites, too. With our hoop skirts we looked like a pair of wedding cakes.

Wedding cakes. Grooms and brides. A thought like a loose plank in a bridge, to be stepped around.

'Hi there.' A musical voice. 'Botanist Mendoza? Did you have a good flight?'

'Reporting. Yes. Where do I sign in?'

She dimpled about something. 'Well, your personnel coordinator is waiting right through those doors. You'll want your arrival packet first, of course.' She drew out a handsomely embossed portfolio and pushed it across the desk to me. 'You might want to remove the complimentary Theobromos right away. It melts out in the sun.'

'Hot here, huh?'

'This is a tropical paradise,' she informed me.

'Nice. Thank you,' I said, took the portfolio, and headed for the exit.

Neat doors. A bas-relief sculpture of two jaguars rampant, battling with each other. When I got close enough, the jaguars disengaged as the doors slid apart, vanishing into silhouettes. A blaze of white light struck through the doorway. I stepped out. I faced heat. Light. Complex smells and sounds. A horizon of towering green as far as the eye could see, a mild and tolerable green, out to the edges of a blue sky transparent with the intensity of sunlight. Off to the west, a city of red and white pyramids: New World One. And here, right before me, four mortals and a man of my own kind. The mortals, all four, dropped on their faces.

'Hail, child of gods!' they cried.

I stared at them, dumfounded, and then up at the Old One. He looked amused. He was a vision in white: white doublet and white trunk hose, white skin, white canvas conquistador's helmet. His hair and pointed beard were flaming red. He was lounging in an open sedan chair. 'Welcome to New Spain,' he said.

'Who the hell are you supposed to be?' I inquired.

'Quetzalcoatl,' he replied. 'As it were.' The mortals got to their feet, and they too were a sight to behold, each one clothed like a Mayan prince in gold and feathers. Their faces were sad and noble; they had big high cheekbones, curved noses, and sullen mouths. I swallowed hard. I looked past them at the guy in the sedan chair.

'Botanist Mendoza reporting in,' I said. My voice didn't shake at all.

'Personnel Coordinator Victor, at your service.' He made room for me on the seat beside him. 'Hop in, and we'll take you to your suite. Boys, collect the lady's luggage.'

As we were jogged along, he said:

'A protégée of Joseph's, eh?'

'Yes.'

'And you've just spent two years in the field? In the Old World? How grueling.'

'Yes, it was.'

'My word.' He leaned back. We went sailing by mahogany trees like standing gods. 'Well, life is just a little more gracious in these parts. You'll like it. Joseph pushed quite a few buttons to get you in here, you know. Any questions I can answer for you?'

'Do you have flush toilets and hot showers?'

He smirked. 'And four restaurants. And an eighteen-hole golf course. And cocktails served in the main courtyard every afternoon at four.' He glanced at his chronophase. 'We'll be in plenty of time. We're mostly scholars here, and we enjoy our little rituals.'

Wow.

'What about the —' I gestured at our mortal bearers, their plumed hats waving as they ran. 'Isn't this kind of exploitive?'

'No, no, it's prestigious for them. They're all intercepted sacrifices. This way they get to be Servants of the Gods without dying. We acquire most of our mortal staff that way. They're the most devoted fellows you could imagine.'

'No kidding?' A red stucco wall rose before us, and we were carried in through the gate. Victor gave me a tour around: acres of plush lawn, fountains, courtyards, flowers, water-lily pools, parrots. The chaos of the jungle outside, but within the perimeter of that high wall, absolute manicured control.

'Boys, Botany Residential Pyramid.' Victor waved an arm. He leaned back beside me as they took us down a boulevard toward a white palace. 'The red building over there is the botany lab, and the gardens are on the other side. The residential suites are really first-rate. There's a PX on the first floor and laundry facilities, though I'm afraid we've had some complaints because Botany Residential has to share its pool and gymnasium with Support Tech Residential. Yes, a few ruffled feathers over that. I hope you won't feel slighted.'

I looked at him sidelong. 'I'll manage,' I told him.

We pulled up in front of Botany Residential, and Victor took me into the concierge's office, where we registered my retinal pattern, and so up to my suite. Four rooms, all for me. The walls were smooth bare plaster, and there any resemblance to a cell stopped.

'Complete entertainment center here.' Proudly Victor swung open the doors of a vast console. 'It's tied in to our library. Over forty million entries to choose from, and here's the receiver for Radio Maya. Liquor cabinet over there, sauna over there. You're scheduled to meet with your departmental director at 1830 hours for your briefing.'

'Great.' Business at last. 'Where's the director's office?'

'Oh, he's reserved a booth at El Galleon.' At my blank stare Victor added, 'Our premier restaurant. Formal dress, of course. If you call the porter service from the lobby desk, a pair of the boys can take you there in ten minutes, though I should tell you —' he lowered his voice a little – 'it's considered correct to attend cocktail service at half past four precisely and remain until six, and then arrive early for dinner.'

'Oh.'

'Etiquette,' he explained. 'It's very important here.'

'I see.'

'I'm sure you'll fit in quite well. I'll just toddle on now and leave you to your own devices; daresay you'd like privacy while you unpack. If you have any other questions, the answers are most probably in your arrival packet. I'd suggest you read it through before your briefing.'

'I will, thank you.'

He bowed, and I curtseyed, and I was alone again.

By the time I had showered, dressed, tested the bed and the holo reception, it was hours later. I decided to walk to the main courtyard on my own legs. I wasn't really up to being a goddess in a chariot yet. Besides, I found the Mayan profile disconcerting.

So of course the cocktail waiters were all Mayans.

'What would the Daughter of Heaven prefer?' mine inquired politely, putting down a napkin at my elbow. I was unnerved but stared hard at him: no resemblance at all, really. Not straight on.

'What have you got there?' I nodded at his tray.

'Dry vodka martini. Tequila on the rocks, rum and soda, rum and tonic, margarita. Might this slave suggest the margarita?'

'Sure. Thanks.'

He set it down and glided off. I settled back and picked up my arrival packet. There was a round spreading oil stain on the cover: whoops. My Theobromos had melted. I opened the front and peeled my complimentary stick off the first page of the brochure in order to read all about New World One and its calendar of social events for the coming year.

After a while, though, my attention wandered. The breeze through the white arches of the court was very pleasant, and the splashing of the central fountain was pleasant too, as was the chattering of the little green parrots in among the flowering vines. How soothing it all was. I could sit here, just like this, for years and years. I probably would, wouldn't I?

I only became aware that my eyes had filled with tears when I noticed some commotion in the treetops, far off outside the perimeter wall. I blinked and looked again. There were monkeys out there fighting, screaming and pelting one another with rotten fruit.

Shuddering, I reached for my drink.